RAGS

TY DRAGO

NEOPARADOXA™
Pennsville, NJ

PUBLISHED BY
NeoParadoxa
A division of eSpec Books
PO Box 242
Pennsville, NJ 08070
www.especbooks.com

Copyright ©2022 Ty Drago

ISBN: 978-1-949691-85-6
ISBN (eBook): 978-1-949691-84-9

Copyediting: Greg Schauer, John L. French
Interior Design: Danielle McPhail
Cover Art and Design: Lynne Hansen, LynneHansenArt.com
Cover Processing: Mike McPhail
Interior Art: Jason Whitley

FOR THE REAL NICK AND KELLEY NELSON, WITH LOVE.

FOREWORD

On December 10, 1982, the famous Steel Pier in Atlantic City, New Jersey was destroyed by fire. The pier, with its music hall, exhibitions, world-class entertainment—and, yes, a diving horse—had been a tourist staple and the crown jewel of the Atlantic City Boardwalk for almost a century before the first casino was built.

To this day, the actual circumstances behind the fire remain a mystery...

December 7, 1982
ATLANTIC CITY, NJ

CHAPTER 1

THE FIRST ONE TO GO DOWN

—IS THE PIMPLY-FACED GANGBANGER IN THE LEATHER JACKET. ONE second, he's laughing with his crew, getting off on how scared I look, and how Corinne's just gone and passed out at my feet. The next, he gets grabbed from behind and yanked into the shadow of one of the big steel pilings, the move so sudden and swift that it almost seems like a magic trick.

A moment later, Pimples screams.

A moment after that, his body gets tossed out from behind the piling as if he were a rag doll instead of 160 pounds of wiry muscle. He flips end over end and lands with a loud *thump* in the sand. There he writhes, groaning and clutching his face with both hands. Despite the patchwork of shadows beneath the pier, there's no mistaking the blood.

His face has been slashed.

Wait. Did I say "slashed?" Well, that's wrong.

His face has been all but peeled away, like an apple skin.

And the whole thing took maybe five seconds.

For several more seconds, nobody moves. Not me. Certainly not poor out-of-it Corinne. And not the three other bangers encircling us, either.

They're all in their late teens or early twenties, stoned out and itching to hurt somebody. A teenage girl like me coming out here was foolish, plenty foolish. But bringing my nine-year-old foster sister along cranked "plenty foolish" up to "outright stupid." While being under Steel Pier at midnight wasn't exactly safe at the best of times, running into *these* dudes was the kind of boatload full of bad luck that could rachet "outright stupid" all the way up to "stone dead."

Except, suddenly, that boatload of bad luck had turned on the tide.

"What happened to you, man?" one of the bangers yells. He stares at his homeboy, who's still wailing piteously. Then, realizing that Pimples has got nothing to say just now, he looks fearfully around. He's still clutching an open butterfly knife, the one he planned to use to cut away my coat and clothes to "get a peek at the candy."

Another of the gang yells out a stream of cusses that would have had Aunt Kell grounding me for sure. Then this third dude draws a gun—a snub-nosed .38 revolver—from inside his coat. He starts waving it around, scanning the gloom for a target.

A figure emerges from behind the pillar.

He's still bathed in shadow, but I get the impression of old clothes, mismatched and well-worn—a mixed bag of dumpster pickings from behind a thrift store. Most of it looks tattered, little more than rags. He's not a particularly big dude, and his shoulders are pretty slim. But, for all that, there's something about him—a "presence"—that's hard to overlook. It seems to run through the air like electricity.

Oh, and he's holding an enormous bloody knife.

"Who the hell are you?" Butterfly demands.

"Who cares?" Thirty-Eight adds. Then with another imaginative cuss, he fires. The muzzle flash is blinding and the noise deafening, bouncing off the concrete underside of the pier and momentarily drowning out the surf's constant rumble.

But when the noise and flash subside, the figure's gone. Not dead. Not shot. Just *gone*.

Only now, something sticks out the front of Thirty-Eight's chest, jutting through his coat. It takes me a moment to get what it is—the point of a knife. *His* knife. Rag's knife. It's got a long blade of black metal that gives back none of the lamplight leaking under the pier from the nearby Boardwalk. The blade's darkness is so complete—so perfectly *empty*—that it almost looks like a triangular bit of Thirty-Eight's chest has been somehow erased.

But the truth is way simpler.

The banger's been impaled from behind.

I try to scream, but I can't seem to make a sound.

Thirty-eight's eyes roll up inside his head. He topples over, revealing Rags, who leans down and smoothly pulls his knife out of the banger's back.

My mind reeling, I take in the raggedy man's moth-riddled wool coat and the heavy hood he's wearing that completely conceals his face. I can't tell anything about him. I can't even say for sure it's a "him."

Two gangbangers remain. One is Butterfly, who's taken to bobbing and weaving in a way that I guess is supposed to look badass. The knife he's waving is hilariously small compared to the one Rags wields. Nevertheless, the dude does his best to compensate.

"Back off, man!" he screams. "I'll cut you! I'll cut you wide open!"

Rags doesn't reply.

The last banger, the youngest of them, who hasn't said a thing so far—and who didn't seem all that psyched about joining in his homeboys' rape/murder party in the first place—just stares.

Then he turns and runs face-first into a steel piling.

Sounds dumb, I know, but it's easier to do in the dark than you'd think. He staggers back from it, moaning and cupping his palms over what's got to be a broken nose. Then he drops to his knees in the sand.

Butterfly apparently sees this as an opening and charges forward, yelling like an Apache in one of those old John Wayne movies Uncle Nick likes to watch. His knife is raised, his eyes wild from dope, desperation, and a double-sized portion of fear.

Rags kicks him—hard.

He does it like it's nothing, just lifts his foot, wrapped in an army boot that looks about fifty years old, and drives it straight into Butterfly's sternum. The gangbanger's Apache cries downshift into an agonized wheeze as he doubles over and then goes flying. Three feet. Six feet. Nine.

Jesus, how strong is this dude?

Butterfly's body slams into a piling—the same one that Pimples' was pulled behind—with terrific force. Despite the surf and the sound of Broken Nose's nasal sobs, I hear the dude's ribs crack. He manages a kind of broken wheeze before he drops to the sand, either out cold or close enough for it not to matter.

I try to scream again. Nothing. I try to move. Can't. I *want* to throw myself over Corinne's body. She's still unconscious, though how the girl—this sweet, precious little girl—can stay fainted through all this noisy carnage is beyond me. I'm not even sure what good I'd be doing, shielding her like that. I mean, this dude's knife is more like a machete, easily long enough to pin us both to the dunes.

But she's my foster sister, and I have to do something!

Except I can't freakin' move!

Fortunately, the raggedy man isn't interested in us. Instead, his attention turns toward the only remaining banger.

Despite his whimpers and obvious pain, Broken Nose is doing his best to crawl away.

"Abby?"

It's Corinne. When I glance down at her, her eyes have opened. She sounds groggy, disoriented.

"Shhh!" I hiss.

"Abby? Where are you?"

I start to reply. But before I can get the words out, I hear footsteps in the sand behind me — light, almost silent — and my heart freezes up. I glance over my shoulder. I don't want to. It's more reflex than conscious thought. After all, if Rags has decided it's my turn, there's probably not much I can do about it, and something tells me I'd rather not see it coming.

But it's *not* coming, at least not yet.

Instead, the raggedy man walks past us, slow and with an eerie grace, almost close enough to touch. He doesn't even glance at Corinne or me but instead approaches Broken Nose. The last banger is still crawling, but when he sees what's coming after him, he manages to scramble to his feet and stumble desperately forward, making for the open beach beyond the pier.

He doesn't get there.

Rags explodes into motion, a patchwork blur that tears up the sand, dodging one piling after another. Then, leaping up and vaulting smoothly sideways off a third, he pivots in mid-air and lands less than a foot in front of Broken Nose.

Dude's a freakin' acrobat!

Broken Nose shrieks and tries to backpedal, but he's nowhere near fast enough. A grimy fist snaps out, cobra-quick, catching the banger's coat and pulling him up and off his feet like he weighs nothing.

Broken Nose starts wailing.

"Please…" he stammers. "Please don't … I didn't hurt nobody! I don't even know those guys!" He covers his bloodied face with trembling hands and sobs.

I don't blame him a bit.

For several *long* seconds, Rags just studies the dude. Then, as I watch, he slowly raises his knife.

And before I even realize I'm going to, I yell, "No!"

To my surprise — scratch that, astonishment — Rags stops. He tilts his head past the banger he's so easily holding up and looks at me from under his cowl.

My mouth goes dry.

Even so, I steel myself and say, "Please. Enough."

He seems to consider a little longer. Then he drops Broken Nose, who lands hard in the sand, blood spraying across his already messed-up face. But, for all his terror, he's no fool, and he's up and running a moment later. Okay, maybe "staggering" is a better word, but at least he's getting away—abandoning his homies, sure. But getting away.

And Rags is letting him.

The whole fight, start to finish, lasted maybe forty-five seconds. Now, around us, one dude's dead, one's broken and unconscious, and one's sobbing and trying to keep his face attached.

My breath catches as Rags comes toward us. My first instinct is to run. But it's like my legs are rooted in the sand. The best I can do is try to twist my body and put myself between him and Corinne. I'm only partway successful.

"Abby?" Corinne asks again.

"Shut up," I murmur. Shouting doesn't seem like the smart move right now.

Rags stops about four feet away, looking at me with eyes I can't see. Under his hood, his features are a complete void, the shadows so deep that there might as well be nothing there at all.

I swallow, looking at the blade. Rags clutches it tightly in his right fist, which is mostly buried inside the long, wide sleeve of his ratty wool coat. I can't even tell the color of his skin.

For the first time, the smell of him hits me. Coffee grounds, urine, mildew, and rotting food. It's almost like he's *made* of trash!

Then he speaks.

It's the first time he does, and his voice sends the mother-of-all-chills down my spine. It's raspy, like fingernails on a blackboard, and hard to listen to. It seems *wrong*, not quite human, and just the sound of it sets my teeth on edge. It doesn't help that his words are bullshit.

"*Vanyan sòlda.*"

I almost reply, "What?" But then I catch myself. The last thing I want to do is strike up a conversation with this head-case.

He raises his hand, not the knife hand, but the other one, his left hand. When he points, I get a quick glimpse of his skin. Except I don't. What I see is totally caked with grime, oil, and sand. I still can't tell what color he is. But it's not a big hand. That much I'm sure about.

With one finger, he points up the beach, the way we came, toward the same set of stairs that Corinne and I used to get here.

He's letting us go.

With a ton of effort, I gulp down what little spit I've still got. Then, glancing around one last time at the carnage, I whisper, "Thanks."

For a long moment, Rags doesn't respond. Then his head nods ever so slightly.

And he's gone.

I don't mean he leaves. I don't mean he runs off, cat-quick like I've seen him do. I mean, he just kind of vanishes. Like a ghost.

Seeing it turns me cold in a way the December midnight air can't explain.

My heart's going wild, and I'm sweating.

Can you be freezing and sweating at the same time?

Seems you can.

"Abby?" Corinne says. She pulls herself weakly up to a sitting position. "Where'd you go?"

"I'm right here," I tell her, a little irritably. *Is she blind?* I think, immediately feeling bad about it. Corinne's not brave. She never has been. Fainting was like her go-to response when the bangers surprised us—not much of a defense mechanism, but the only one she's got. Besides, maybe she hit her head when she dropped. There are all kinds of things in the sand beneath the pier: rocks, discarded chunks of concrete, broken beer bottles, and worse stuff.

I'll have to check her for cuts or bumps — once we find some light.

"It's cool," I tell her. Then, finally, I get moving. "Keep your eyes closed," I say, reaching down and taking her hands. "Don't look around. You hear me, pumpkin?"

Corinne doesn't argue. She just lets me pull her up. Then she hugs me, hard and desperate. I hug back. Nearby, the Atlantic Ocean roars and crashes.

Moving in slow, halting steps, I lead my foster sister away from the bodies and toward the somewhat safer Boardwalk, our little midnight adventure cut short.

I *could* say that's how the whole thing started.

I could, but I'd be lying.

That's just where I've decided to start *telling it.*

CHAPTER 2

My Parents Named Me Abigail

— Abigail Lowell. Of course, why they named me that — if Abigail was my grandmother, some favorite aunt, or just a nice name they got out of a baby book — is something I'll probably never know.

At the age of four, I was found wandering through the crowds on the Atlantic City Boardwalk. It was a bright summer afternoon, and I had on shorts and a dirty t-shirt. I was skinny like I hadn't eaten in days.

And I was crying.

A cop found me and took me to "Family Services," two words that, to me, will always mean blank grey walls and overworked, underpaid suits who try to be nice but can't quite pull it off. There I got questioned but couldn't tell anybody where my folks might be or how I ended up alone on the boards.

I knew my name and how old I was, but almost nothing else. Over the next several hours, my photo got passed around in the shops all up and down the boardwalk. They even checked with the local elementary schools, though they were closed for the season. But, in the end, they found zip. Nothing at all. Finally, yet another official stranger who was "there to help" showed up and whisked me off to a foster home — the first of many.

I remember none of this.

My earliest memory is of getting spanked. I don't recall where I was at the time or even why I was getting hit. But I know it was by someone named Judith who didn't like me, probably one of the hundred foster mothers I burned through during the early years. Okay, maybe it was closer to a dozen. But when you're a little kid, it seems like more — an endless parade of cramped, shared bedrooms, cheap food, and the learned habit of carrying everything you own from place to place in a green trash bag.

At least, that was how it was until I came to the Nelsons.

Nick and Kelley. For years they ran a state-funded orphanage out of a former hotel they owned half a block from the Boardwalk. Since 1962, when the State of New Jersey abolished orphanages in favor of the "kinder and better" foster care system, Aunt Kell and Uncle Nick went from being "caretakers" to "foster parents," and the average of a dozen kids under their roof went from being "orphans" to "children of the state."

I was eight when I got delivered to the lobby of what the neon sign atop the roof announced to be "THE CALM SEA ARMS." By then, I'd been in the System for four years, and the constant upheavals—a new foster home every few months—had left me, well, broken.

I stole stuff, usually from stores but sometimes from my fosters, which was probably the main reason I got moved around so much. I also hoarded food, having learned that eating regularly could be a luxury in a house crammed with foster kids who were just as messed up as I was. My foster parents would rail at me whenever they found moldy bread or half-empty cereal boxes under my bed. They'd tell me I was "selfish." They'd tell me I was "bad."

After a while, I guess I believed it.

Eventually, you get yourself a rep in the System. I was a "problem kid"—so the social workers kind of got used to moving me around. It became a routine. I'd hit a house, get into trouble, get into more trouble, and finally get moved.

Over and over again.

If it sounds like a pretty shitty childhood, well, you're right.

But everything changed when I found the Nelsons.

They were old, older than any fosters I'd ever had, and the moment I met them, they scared me. Truth is, they were only in their mid-fifties, but to me, that was ancient. Besides, old people always scared me back then. I still don't know why. I remember standing in that lobby—with its shabby-but-clean furniture. There were, as I've said, something like a dozen kids already living in the place, and the lobby was a common area where everyone pretty much did whatever they felt like doing: board games, Lincoln Logs, even hopscotch. The hotel's only working television was in there as well.

You get the idea—noisy and busy.

A girl my age waved at me and smiled. I stared back at her, clutching my trash bag a little tighter.

Uncle Nick talked to the social workers. He's a big dude, Nick Nelson, tall and broad-shouldered. Not scary exactly, but *imposing*, hair shaved close and skin even darker than mine.

He seemed — solid to me.

Then, while I watched him, Aunt Kell came up and took me aside. She was kind of short and, not fat, exactly. Just *round*, with a big bosom that, at that age, I found weirdly comforting. Her hair was long and white, tied up and held with a ribbon. Her skin, lighter than her husband's, looked like old rawhide, but there was something about her smile that almost cracked the walls I'd built around myself — and that's saying something.

I remember she handed me a small tin box. It had a picture of Princess Leah from STAR WARS on it. "Abby," she said in a kind, soft voice. "This is yours. You can put anything you want in it. If you want to put food in it, you can… as much as will fit. And you can keep that food for as long as you want. But you'll need to be careful because keeping the wrong kind of food too long can make you sick."

I knew that from bitter experience. I expected her to lecture me on why I didn't have to hoard anymore, or even tell me what kind of foods were safer to store than others. But she didn't. She just handed me the box and then pulled a wristwatch out of her apron.

The watch wasn't a cheap digital, but had actual hands and a leather band. "This is yours, too," she said. "All my children get one. You can wear it or not. That's up to you. Personally, I think it's good to always know what time it is. But, Abby, it's a wind-up. No battery. So, you'll want to remember to keep it wound every few days."

Then she turned the watch over and let me see the back. My initials were there — scratched in, not engraved. But to me, it looked like a miracle.

I felt my eyes light up. I couldn't help it.

That's how it began at the Calm Sea Arms. I ended up staying there longer than six months, longer even than six years. This old hotel's become the only home I've ever known, and Uncle Nick and Aunt Kell are the only parents I remember.

I don't tell them I love them, though I do.

I don't call them '''Dad' and ''Mom,' though I want to.

I have eleven foster brothers and sisters. Some I like. Some I don't.

A couple I even love.

And Corinne is one of those.

In fact, loving her is kind of what got us into trouble under the pier tonight in the first place.

The craziest thing is: we somehow get away with it.

Corrine and I make it back to the hotel, climb atop the dumpster in the alley to the fire escape ladder, and then in through that "special" second-floor window without anybody knowing a thing.

She clings to me almost the whole way back, neither of us saying much. I let her do the climbing ahead of me and, once we're safe in the hallway, I see her to her bedroom as quietly as I can. She and I are both in the "Girl's Dorm," which is really just the hotel's second floor. The boys have the third. The idea is to keep us nice and separated. Uncle Nick and Aunt Kell sleep on the lobby floor, and the boards creak something fierce, especially when the hotel's quiet. So, each of us learns pretty quick how to shuffle our feet when we walk at night and to keep to the threadbare carpet when we can.

Both dorms have eight bedrooms, which means there's enough to let each foster kid have one of our own. It's pretty amazing. Most of us have never had a private room in our lives, something that the Nelsons know perfectly well. Honestly, it'd be so much simpler for them to cram us in, three or four to a room. That would surely make cleaning and upkeep easier.

But they don't do that. They never have.

It also means I'm able to get Corinne into her bed without worrying about waking anyone else. She slips under the covers without complaint, most of her tears and shakes having stopped. I wonder how much of what happened tonight she'll remember in the morning. Hopefully, not much at all. Corinne might be nine, but, like a lot of fosters, she's younger between her ears. "Emotionally stunted," they call it, which is as freaking stupid a term as there ever was. Corinne's become what she needs to be to survive in the System, what works for her. As far as I'm concerned, it doesn't need a label.

Just like Corinne doesn't need more bad memories to fill her dreams.

"Abby?" she whispers when I kiss her forehead.

"Yeah, pumpkin?"

"I'm sorry."

"For what?"

"For getting us in trouble."

"It's okay."

"You're not mad?"

"Nope. Now, goodnight. We've got school in the morning."

She nods. Then, as I straighten and turn toward the door, she says again, "Abby?"

"What?"

"Are you gonna tell Aunt Kell?"

I feel my heart sink. "About what?"

"About you going out with me to look at the moon on the water?"

That was the start of it. Corinne loves the moon. Some nights, when a few of us sneak up to the hotel's roof after lights out to smoke, drink, or whatever, she follows us. To be honest, it used to bug me. But then I found out that she's not interested in us at all. Instead, she just sits under the big neon Calm Sea Arms sign that's mounted up there in letters ten feet tall and stares at the moon.

Tonight, after lights out, she snuck into my room and begged me to take her out to the beach so she could see the moon on the water. "Tomorrow's my birthday," she announced, though I know for a fact that, like me, she doesn't *know* her birthday. "So, *please,* Abby?"

I knew it was a bad idea when I agreed.

I just didn't realize *how* bad.

"Do you want me to?" I ask her cautiously, standing halfway between her bed and the door. "Talk to Aunt Kell, I mean."

"No. She'll be mad. I don't want her mad at me on my birthday."

"Then I won't say nothing."

She smiles sleepily. "Thanks, Abby."

"Sure thing, pumpkin. Good night."

"G'night."

I slip out of her bedroom and down the hall to my own. Around me, the second floor is graveyard quiet.

This may sound weird, but it's not until I'm safe in my room and pull off my clothes, until I look down and see blood—*honest-to-God human blood!*—on my black sneakers, that I start seriously freaking out.

How did I even *get* blood on me? I wasn't anywhere near Pimples when Rags dragged him behind that pillar. Thirty-Eight had to have been something like a dozen feet away when he got stabbed from behind. And Butterfly, unlike his homies, got broken instead of cut.

Then I remember Rags standing in front of me, still holding his knife. His bloody knife.

Was he really that close?

I didn't think so at the time, but—

Feeling suddenly nauseous, I take off my shoes and run down the hall to the toilet.

I don't throw up, though I want to. Instead, I end up splashing cold water on my face and then my shoes, rubbing them with paper towels until there's not a trace of red. Then, feeling a lot less better than I'd like, I go back to my room, pull on my cotton jams, and climb under the blanket.

That's when I lose it.

Not completely, mind. I mean, I cry, but I don't sob. I don't make noise. I don't wake anybody.

It's a thing you learn when you grow up in the System.

You cry alone.

The terror I felt when those drugged-up bangers closed around us on the beach, corralling us under the pier like dogs trapping a pair of rats, runs through me like ice. Weirdly, it isn't almost losing my own life that freaks me out the most. It's Corinne. The idea that she might have ended up just another dead orphan was almost enough to send me down to the bathroom again for another round of "Will She or Won't She?"

Yet, if Rags hadn't shown up, that's *exactly* what would have happened.

Rags.

That dude frightens me, no lie. But not because he threatened me. Instead, it's what he did to protect me, to protect my little foster sister, that scared me, and not a little bit because some part of me, and I get how this sounds, *appreciated* his brutality. But no. "Brutality" isn't the right word. Savagery. What he did to those dudes under the pier was savage but not brutal. Until tonight, I didn't know there was a difference.

But there *is.*

The tears flow for a while. Finally, as my heart rate slowly slips back to normal and what Tyrone calls my "scare buzz" drains off, I sit up, wipe my face, and spend just a minute looking out through my window at the night.

Only to scream—almost—when I see *him* staring back at me. My hands shoot to my mouth, my eyes going wide. I feel my stomach clench and, all of a sudden, the scare buzz is back with interest.

Rags.

Rags is right there.

Except… no, he's not.

I blink, shuddering. Then I stand on wobbly legs and step closer to the window. By the light of the moon, which hangs waning in the late fall sky, I can see that the fire escape's empty. But he *was* there. I spotted his shape, crouching in the gloom, his heavy hood hiding his face, his long, black-bladed knife in his hand. He was there! I know it!

It takes me a while to fall asleep after that, but eventually, I manage. And, strange as it sounds, I don't dream about Rags or bangers or blood and carnage. Instead, I dream of the sight of the massive pier, as we saw it from the beach—big and blocky, mysterious and amazing. It always looks to me like an enormous treasure chest, full of history and secrets rather than gold. And, in the dream, like when I'm awake, I'm drawn to it.

See? Strange.

But there's a lot about the pier I haven't told you yet, a lot you need to know. For now, though, let's just say that I love that place, as rundown and derelict as it's become. The truth is that when Corinne came to my bedroom after lights out and begged me to take her to the late-night beach, I did it partly for her and partly for me.

You see, Corinne went for the moonlight.

But I went for the pier.

CHAPTER 3

ATLANTIC CITY'S HEART

— HAS ALWAYS BEEN ITS BOARDWALK AND, UNTIL PRETTY RECENTLY, THE HEART OF THE BOARDWALK WAS STEEL PIER.

Opened on June 18, 1898, Steel Pier *used* to jut a half-mile out from the Boardwalk and over the Atlantic Ocean and was nothing like the piers they have today. Back then, before Disneyworld in Florida or even Disneyland in California — two places I've never visited, Steel Pier drew folks from all over. Sometimes called "The Playground of the World" in its day, it was part carnival, part theater, and part circus. The biggest names in music gave shows there, folks I've only ever seen in pictures and old movies. The Temptations, the Supremes, and the Ink Spots all played there in one of the two music halls. Back then, they had dancing, boxing, clowns, acrobats, and even a high-diving horse.

For decades, it rolled along, building its rep and, when necessary, changing with the times. It switched owners more than once, with each new rich white dude putting his own spin on the place. Over the years, it got hit by storms and hurricanes, damaged by fires and floods. But always, it got rebuilt, renovated, and reopened with music and fanfare.

Until something came along just a few years ago. Something even Steel Pier couldn't survive.

The casinos.

The first was Resorts. It sits more or less right across the Boardwalk from the now grim and quiet front facade of the pier. Resorts is flashy and bright, filled with slot machines, craps tables, and Roulette wheels. It was the first casino to hit the city but not the last, not by a long shot, and not even the fanciest of them. Resorts, at least, looks like what it is: a big, glittery hotel. The next one, Caesar's, built a year later on two blocks of freshly demolished history, looks more like a palace than a place to eat, sleep, and gamble. "Spectacle" is the word Uncle Nick uses. Legalized gambling, he says, is a "license to go over the top."

And I've seen pictures of Las Vegas that prove it.

Before long, the Boardwalk I used to know, the Boardwalk I've always known, was gone, replaced by a line of futuristic adult theme parks, all facing out to sea. And Steel Pier? It closed up back in '78, the same year Resorts opened. In fact, in what's got to be the best example of "adding insult to injury" I ever heard of, Resorts went ahead and bought it.

She's been derelict ever since. After years of neglect, Steel Pier, once the Queen of the Boardwalk, is pretty much forgotten.

Except by me.

I dream about the place—a lot. In these dreams, Steel Pier's at the top of her game, with folks all dressed for summer in swimsuits, shorts, and sunglasses. Back then, the pier was *alive*, with thousands of tourists riding its rides, seeing its shows, and playing its games. I love those dreams. They're so vivid, so real, that in the morning I can almost believe they actually happened, almost believe I was really there.

But recently, my Steel Pier dreams have been getting *darker*.

More on that later.

Yeah, I know it's weird—a sixteen-year-old girl kind of obsessed with what's basically an old abandoned amusement park. But we all got our "things," right? Corinne likes the moon. Tyrone, the "Top Boy" here at the hotel, he's got football. Jeff's heavy into motorcycles, even though as far as I know, he's never come within ten feet of one, much less ridden any. Darlene, the "Top Girl," is all about make-up. Tish, another of my foster sisters, digs jazz music. Aunt Kell loves to cook and is all about Jesus. And Uncle Nick? Well, his thing is, and always has been, family. Us. I've never met anybody more steady, more comfortable with himself and his life than my foster father. Or so I've always thought.

More on that later, too.

The only alarm clock in The Calm Sea Arms is Aunt Kell, who knocks on every door between 6:40 and 6:45 am. Then she makes the same announcement. "Breakfast at seven!" It's a sound I've been hearing for so long now that I'm not just used to it, I kind of count on it. It's funny how you can take pleasure in the small stuff.

And this morning's no different.

Around me, in the hotel's other rooms, the Nelsons' foster kids begin to stir.

I hear Tyrone first. He isn't the oldest of us. But he's the *biggest*, a high school varsity linebacker whose broad shoulders seem to fill every room he walks into. Right now, he's laughing at something, the sound so loud that it booms through the ceiling from the Boys' Dorm like thunder. He's probably joking with Jeff, the freshman whose room is right beside his.

Tyrone's been a Nelson Kid, as we sometimes call ourselves, since his mom died seven years ago. Jeff's newer than that. He got taken away from his alcoholic dad when he was six, and he's been in the System ever since, getting bounced around plenty before ending up here last summer, just in time for the start of the school year. Unlike his bull of a neighbor, Jeff doesn't say much. He's short and stocky and seems nervous most of the time.

We see a lot of that.

"Shut up, Tyrone!" another voice bellows. This one's closer, just a few doors down from me here in the Girl's Dorm. "It's too early for your shit!"

That'll be Darlene. She *is* the oldest of us, turning eighteen in just four months. Over the years, a bunch of kids have hit that mark under the Nelsons' care—enough of them that, when Darlene's turn comes, I know exactly what to expect. There'll be a party. A big one. Bigger than Christmas. Then my "adult" foster sister will meet with Family Services and check herself out of the System.

After that, she'll have to move out to make room for others. It's what happens when a kid grows up in foster care. At eighteen, they cut you loose. No college fund. No parental advice.

Good luck, kid.

My turn'll come in just under two years. It's something I try hard not to fret over.

But I don't want you all thinking the Nelsons abandon us once we age out. They don't—not like the State of New Jersey does, anyway. Lots of former fosters keep in touch. A few even visit pretty regularly. Most stay local, as getting out of Atlantic City isn't easy without money. Besides, with the casinos and all, jobs *can* be had around here. Uncle Nick helps them with that. He still has connections from when he used to gamble.

Footsteps fill the corridor. Our rooms haven't got individual baths. The hotel—back when it *was* a hotel—was too old and cheap for that. Instead, each floor shares just two johns, with a "shower monitor" assigned to make sure everyone gets washed according to their rotation. At the Calm Sea Arms, you only get to shower every other day. Today's the boys' day. It's a way to conserve hot water.

Twelve kids.

Someone pounds on my door. "Come on, Abby!" Darlene calls. " Get your lazy ass out of bed!"

I sigh. We used to get along okay, Darlene and me. But lately, she's turned into one of those girls who likes to pull you down and stand on you to make herself feel taller. I don't know if it's hormones that turned her into such a bitch, or something else. God knows there's plenty of stuff that can mess with you in this life.

Either way, I don't like her much anymore.

I wonder if Corinne's still asleep. One thing about my "little sister": once she's out, she's *out*. The building could come down and she wouldn't wake up. The thought makes me smile a little.

Then, like a wave crashing down, I remember—really remember— what happened last night.

I pray to God Corinne didn't dream about it, that she was so out of it when it all went down that somehow it didn't fully register. She can be like that sometimes. It's another defense mechanism that a lot of the younger kids cling to.

It's not real. None of it's real. Just close your eyes, and the world will go away.

As for my own dream last night, it's already fuzzy. It was a bad one, I know that much, and one I've had at least once before. Something about the pier, Steel Pier, but inside it not under it. And Rags. He was there this time, I think. But that's about all I can dredge up.

"Abby! You in there?" Darlene yells. The doorknob jiggles, but she doesn't open it. We don't lock our doors in this hotel. It's a house rule. But another rule says that you don't open a sib's door unless invited.

Darlene's a bitch, but at least she's not *that* far gone.

"I'm up!" I croak, my voice sounding strained and thick.

"Well, get downstairs!"

Then I hear her stalk off, and I breathe a sigh of relief.

But I still don't move. Just now, I can't.

Jesus, Corinne and I came close last night, *real* close. To buying it, I mean. Both our names almost ended up featured in a one-column article in the Atlantic City News: TWO LOCAL ORPHANS FOUND RAPED AND MURDERED BENEATH STEEL PIER. And they'd have done it too, those drugged-up psychos. I've got no doubt about that.

Pimples and Butterfly and Thirty-Eight. Maybe Broken Nose, too. All of them were wasted, probably on smack — which can make you seriously mean.

Yeah, things could've gone real south if Rags hadn't shown up.

But just who the hell *is* he?

He looked like a bum, one of thousands I see around the city every day. At night they roam the streets and Boardwalk like ghosts, begging or stealing their way through each passing year. Most fry their brains on dope or booze. Some can barely talk, and many stagger and stumble around like they're trying to make it through a funhouse barrel.

But not Rags. I've never seen anybody move with that kind of — "grace" is the only word I can think of. Not like a dancer's grace. More like a panther's grace, fast and silent and dear God, deadly. I shudder. Not that I'm sad about those bangers he killed or trashed while defending us. Nope, not a bit. But the *easy* way he did it — it had this mesmerizing quality to it, a terrible, scary beauty.

There's another knock on my door, softer this time. Something about it sounds — secret.

With some effort, I climb off my bed and pad barefoot to the door. Against the back of the door is an old, full-length mirror. All the rooms have had them ever since this place really was a hotel. In it, I catch my reflection. I look tired, *real* tired. In truth, I'm not too happy about my looks on the best of days. My forehead's too high, my lips are too full, and my hair — well, don't get me started on my hair. Add to that not much in the way of boobs or hips, and I'm sure as hell no Tyra.

But today, I look even worse than usual.

I just hope nobody… important's on the other side of the door.

When I open it, Jimmy's standing there.

Shit…

"Hi," he says.

I try to say "Hi" back. It comes out as a dry-throated croak.

Jimmy's tall, the *right* kind of tall. True, he's not as big or larger-than-life as Tyrone — and not so quick with a joke. Also, he doesn't swagger around in Tyrone's "I can do anything" jock kind of way.

But he *is* beautiful.

"You okay?" he asks. He's also sixteen, though a couple of months younger than me. Even so, he's got this deep baritone voice that I never get tired of listening to.

My heart jumps into my throat. It's a tight fit, but I manage to squeeze a word past it. "Sure."

"It ain't like you to hang back like this. You're gonna miss breakfast." He says this all in a rush like it's something he practiced. A little voice in the back of my mind wonders if Jimmy was looking for an excuse to knock on my door. But, no. He's into Sarah, isn't he? Haven't I seen them up on the roof, all cozy with each other, most lately when Tyrone took me up there to do some making out?

Oh, yeah. Tyrone.

That was last Halloween, and we only did it that one time. Thing is, Tyrone makes out where and when he can, and he's not too choosy about who with. With him, you don't expect anything to come of it. Every Nelson girl learns that lesson, some the hard way. A lot of them fall for him heavy.

But not me. The kissing was nice and all. But Tyrone's just a little too much—Tyrone. Not that I've got a ton of experience, mind. But, if our time together up on the roof taught me anything, it's that I like my men, well, quieter.

Like Jimmy.

"Have… you seen Corinne?" I ask.

"Corinne? Not sure. Aunt Kell sent me up to fetch you."

"Oh." I feel a stab of disappointment. Was this just an errand to him? But then I remember that Aunt Kell doesn't usually send boys to fetch girls or vice versa, especially not the older ones. She's determined to keep things "proper" under her roof.

If she only knew what sometimes goes down *over* her roof.

So then why would she have sent Jimmy to drag me out of bed when any of the girls would have done it?

It's a question I don't ask.

He clears his throat. "So… um. Okay. Come on down. Don't want to be late for school."

Right. School. Sure.

I almost died last night, but I've got geometry to learn.

Jimmy turns and heads down the hall toward the main stairs. I look after him for a few seconds. Then I sigh, close the door, and get dressed, moving in a kind of fog, my mind churning. Most of it's bad churn, like chum in the water, all blood and darkness and fear. But the rest feels nicer, more immediate.

Jimmy smelled good.

I don't think I ever noticed before, but God, the scent wafting off him was — well — *masculine*. Of course, today *is* the boys' day to shower, so he's probably clean, right? I mean, I think his hair was a little wet. That was probably why he smelled so great.

I suddenly wonder what *I* smell like to *him*?

I don't even want to consider it. The very idea makes my skin crawl.

Despite all my — I'll call it what it is, *angst* — when I finally make my way down the big staircase to the lobby, I'm actually feeling pretty good. After all, as horrific as last night was, and it was freakin' horrific, it looks like I'm in the clear. If I know Corinne, she won't remember most of what went down. And since nobody else knows we snuck out and didn't see us coming back in —

Let's just say the idea of sitting at the big table in the hotel's kitchen eating whatever Aunt Kell's cooked up feels about as comfortable and appealing as snuggling under a favorite blanket.

But then, when I'm halfway down the stairs, I spot Uncle Nick. He's standing in the middle of the lobby with his hands on his hips and wearing a look that any Nelson Kid would know in a heartbeat. He's pissed. Major pissed. But, for once, the thing he's pissed about isn't one of us, but instead a dude who standing in front of him — holding a briefcase.

Uh oh.

CHAPTER 4

TROUBLE COMES

—THE WAY IT OFTEN DOES IN MY LIFE: WEARING A SUIT.

The stranger's got on this fancy three-piece, pin-striped number. His hair's slick with product, with a touch of gray at the temples that's just *so-perfect* I figure he must dye the rest of it. Between all that and the little leather briefcase he carries, he might as well have stamped "lawyer" on his forehead.

He and Uncle Nick and Aunt Kell are huddled together in the middle of the lobby, all standing. Evidently, Lawyer Man hasn't been offered a chair, much less a trip to Uncle Nick's office, which is a bad sign.

My foster father's glaring at the dude while, beside him, his wife's fiddling with the little silver cross that she wears on a chain around her neck. She only does that when something totally stresses her out.

"How many times do I have to say no to you people?" Uncle Nick demands.

"It's a generous offer, Mr. Nelson," the lawyer says. He's got a rich man's voice, full of education and superiority. Dude couldn't be whiter if he was Casper the Friendly Ghost.

Uncle Nick's expression darkens further, but Aunt Kell puts a hand on his arm. Then, to the lawyer, she says in her most patient "Mom" tone, "It would be, Mr. Shanks, if we were interested in selling."

Nick Nelson's from Jamaica and got sent to Atlantic City by his mom when he was a boy. There's a story there, but it's not one he ever talks about. He's about as dark as dark gets, though he doesn't have that Bob Marley "mon" accent that you hear so much on TV.

Kelley Nelson, on the other hand, is pure local.

"Mrs. Nelson, let me assure you," Lawyer Man says, his tone oh-so-professional and oh-so-patient. He sounds smugly confident, more than a little condescending, and way overpaid. "I understand how you feel. After all, you've owned this building for a long time—"

"It's been in my wife's family for close to eighty years," Uncle Nick interrupts. He looks impatient the way a volcano that's about to erupt looks impatient.

"My mother and father ran it as a hotel," Aunt Kell adds. As always, her head's cooler than her hubby's, but I can see she's getting riled, too. "I was raised here. It's my home."

The lawyer nods, and I get the feeling he knew all that ahead of time, that — whatever he's doing here — he came forearmed with knowledge of all things Nelson.

What is *this?*

I open my mouth to ask.

But a hand grabs mine, and, startled, I look over to see Darlene standing beside me wearing her most judgmental scowl. She puts a finger to her lips and whispers, "Come on."

I start to protest, but the tug she gives me goes past her usual bossiness and makes me think that maybe, this time, I ought to listen to her. So, begrudgingly, I let her pull me along the wall, as far from the lobby's drama as we can get. Then, as she pushes open the swinging kitchen door and yanks me through, I glance back once more at the Nelsons and Lawyer Man.

They're openly arguing now. Though they've taken to speaking so low that I can't hear them anymore, I can tell that nobody in their little circle's anything like happy.

Next to the lobby, the kitchen is the biggest room in the hotel. The Calm Sea Arms never had a dining hall or even a cafeteria. But the kitchen's big enough to have once provided room service to all thirty-two "guest suites," which means it's got three stoves, two big sinks, two fridges, and a freezer. All of these are old but functional, and Aunt Kell keeps them so spotless that they shine like new.

There's also about fifty feet of stainless-steel counter space that runs along the walls and a butcher block kitchen table in the middle that's big enough to land a plane on. It's around this big table that we take most every meal. And, right now, it's here that the Nelson Kids are gathered, eating breakfast.

Well, almost all of us.

Corinne's nowhere in sight.

Meanwhile, Darlene's doing her "Darlene Thing," which means barking orders.

"Ten minutes, everyone!" she exclaims, pointing at the big wall clock that hangs over the nearest sink. "Finish up!"

A few grumble. Most just keep shoveling pancakes in their mouth.

To me, Darlene says, "Get something to eat. And make it quick."

"What's going down out there?" I ask.

"Not your business."

But Tyrone says, "It's everybody's business. That dude wants to buy us out."

I blink. "Buy the hotel?"

"Yeah."

Then Tish, who's sitting across from Tyrone, adds, "I think he's from one of the casinos." Tish is fifteen, and she and I are tight.

"Sit and eat," Darlene says. "Eight minutes."

I make myself sit, not because I'm especially hungry. I'm not. But because I know that if I miss breakfast, I'll *get* hungry later, and lunch'll be a long way off. While I'm cutting up a couple of pancakes, I ask Tish, "You mean like Caesars or Resorts?"

"Sure," she replies.

"Naw." This comes from Jeff. He's that freshman I told you about. "Not them. This guy's from a smaller outfit."

"How do you know?" Darlene asks, interested despite herself.

"Heard him say the name of his bosses as I went by. Some French name. Definitely not one of the big casinos."

"French?" Sarah asks. She's seventeen, and the oldest girl outside of Darlene. A high school junior, like me.

"Eat," Darlene says. "Six minutes."

Jeff replies, "Yeah." Then he goes back to eating.

"They won't sell." This comes from Jimmy. He's sitting down at the far side of the table, near the middle schoolers and the tods. The middle schoolers don't say much. They're usually new to the hotel and still too unsure, if not outright scared, to feel a part of things yet. "Tods" is short for toddlers, kind of a nickname for the elementary school kids in the hotel, the youngest of us. Jimmy likes taking the young ones under his wing, often playing games with them when the rest of us are too "cool" to be bothered. Hide-and-seek up on the empty floors or one of the old board games that the Nelsons keep in the toy closet behind the front desk.

I quietly like him for doing that. But some of the others don't. They say he's brown-nosing, making them look bad. There was even a "hearing" about it. But more on hearings later.

"Of course, they won't," Darlene says. "Four minutes. Finish up."

"Maybe they won't get a choice," Tyrone says.

"What's that supposed to mean?" I ask, a little more sharply than I meant to.

He shrugs his huge shoulders. "Some of the folks coming into Atlantic City these days don't exactly take 'no' for an answer."

Jeff and Sarah both cuss at that, which earns them some giggles from the middle-schoolers. "Language, children," Darlene scolds. This does nothing but get her a tableful of eye rolls. Frowning, she adds, "Look, everything's cool, okay? Aunt Kell and Uncle Nick'll handle it. Now, time's up!"

As kids get up and pile their dishes on the counter beside the sink, I start actively wolfing the rest of my food down. Darlene watches us all with her most critical eye. I've known a few Top Girls since I started living here and, of them, Darlene takes the job the most seriously. By a country mile.

"Where's Corinne?" I ask her.

"Sick. Don't talk with your mouth full."

Annoyed, I open my mouth and give her a good look at the mush of pancake and syrup I've got going on in there.

"Ugh!" she exclaims, looking away. "Ever try the mature thing, Abigail?"

"Yeah," I say, despite my mouthful. "It sucked."

Somebody laughs. I glance over and see that it's Jimmy. Instantly, my face gets hot.

Corinne's sick.

The thought stops me cold. She was fine last night out on the beach. Not so much as a sniffle. I feel a stab of alarm. Swallowing, I ask Darlene, "What's wrong with her?"

"Who?"

"Corinne."

"I don't know. Aunt Kell just said she's sick. Now get your ass up. It's time to go."

"Language, child," I admonish sweetly.

That pisses her off. *Score!*

Turning away from me, she announces, "Everybody, grab your bags and head out the back." Then she points at the line of packed lunches that Aunt Kell prepared this morning. Our foster mom knows all of our dietary needs, all of our allergies, and all of our tastes. And she gets up at the crack of dawn every weekday morning to make our individual lunches and prepare our group breakfast.

A special lady.

"What she gimme for lunch today?" Lita, one of the middles, asks.

"Don't know," Darlene replies. "Let's go."

"Hope it ain't tuna," Gabe, another middle says, peering into his lunch bag.

"Isn't," Darlene tells him.

His face brightens. "It ain't tuna?"

"No. Yes. I don't know. But you should say 'isn't' instead of 'ain't.'"

Gabe's face tells her exactly how he feels about her grammar lesson.

Then we all split, filing out the kitchen door and into the alley. Currently, the Nelson Kids go to a total of three schools: Indiana Avenue Elementary, Central Junior High, and A.C. High. All three are within a few blocks, and the kids heading to each one walk together in a tight group. This gets drilled into us early on. You stay together. You don't talk to anyone, not even each other. You don't stop for anything.

And it's a rule we all follow, more or less. Of course, that doesn't mean we high schoolers have to share the sidewalk with the little kids. Instead, we almost always turn toward the north end of the alley instead of the south. This sends us a block out of our way, but at least it means we don't have to feel like babysitters.

There are no goodbyes, no "have a nice days."

There are just too many of us for that. We're not the Waltons.

Going our own way also happens to take me and the other highschoolers out onto Virginia Avenue, which fronts the Calm Sea Arms. It's a cold morning, and the only folks about are the ones who have to be, so we've got the sidewalk pretty much to ourselves.

Except for the limo.

"Check it out," Jimmy says. And we do.

It's one of those stretch jobs, at least twenty feet long and gleaming silver. The windows in the back are tinted, though we can see the driver well enough. He's a big dude in a uniform, cap, and sunglasses, his face so expressionless that it might be painted on.

Limos are rare enough, but what really makes this one stick out is the open passenger door — and the old woman standing outside of it.

She's major freaky.

First, I say "old," but that's more like an impression. I wouldn't be able to tell you how old she is if you stuck a gun to my head. Fifty? Sixty? Eighty? Her face isn't all that lined, but I can still see there are years on it, maybe a lot of years. A century or more, for all I know.

And that's not all.

At maybe five feet tall and ninety pounds, there's not much of her. But what is there catches the eye. Her skin's dark as mine, maybe darker, and her hair's long and dreaded and has what looks like small animal bones sewn into the locks. She's wearing a long coat of what, to my ignorant eyes, looks like mink — or something like it, and big laced-up shoes that might be even older than she is. Her hands are small and bony, with gold rings on some of the fingers, and she's smoking a long-stemmed pipe of some kind, her eyes fixed on the hotel's front doors.

"Who the hell's that?" Tyrone asks.

"Keep walking," Darlene says.

"Think she's with the lawyer man?" I ask.

"Maybe," Jeff says.

"She must be rich," Sarah remarks, pretty much unnecessarily.

"You figure?" Tish asks her snidely.

"Keep walking," Darlene says.

We keep walking.

The woman pays us no mind as we stroll right past her, just a knot of teenage kids on their way to school on a chilly Wednesday morning. Her eyes never leave the hotel's frontage, and she's motionless, I mean still as any statue, like she's concentrating on something, or maybe listening — though there's nothing to hear. The hotel's revolving doors have rubber seals that keep the cold out and sound in.

Then, abruptly, her eyes lock on mine.

It happens fast, and it happens *hard*. I stop in my tracks, feeling Tish bump into me from behind. She offers up an annoyed cuss, or at least I *think* she does. Right now, I barely know she's there.

The woman's eyes *have* me.

It's like falling down a deep well, getting swallowed up. I suddenly feel small and naked before a spotlight, everything seen, everything exposed.

I try to say something, but nothing comes out. I try to move, but my legs feel nailed to the concrete.

The woman takes the pipe from between her black lips and blows out a plume of smoke. Then she says, her tone thoughtful, her words delivered slow and deliberate, "You got the blood in you, child."

I almost ask her what that means, except a part of me's afraid to know.

Then I feel Darlene take my arm. "Come on, Abby," she says. She doesn't sound bossy right now. Quite the opposite. She sounds like a worried big sister trying to ease me away from a cliff or something.

I stagger with her a couple of steps, and suddenly, like a door slamming shut, the strangeness ends. By the time full awareness comes flooding back into me, I realize that we're twenty feet down the block from the limo, and everyone's looking at me like I've grown horns.

"You cool?" This comes from Jimmy.

"What?"

"That was weird," Sarah remarks.

"Shut up," Darlene tells her.

Jeff asks me, "Did she say something to you?"

"Who?" The word comes out sounding hollow and distant.

"The old lady!" he exclaims with a nervous laugh.

"You just *froze*," Jimmy says, coming forward with concern on his face. Usually, him paying me attention like that would make me squirm. But not this time. Instead, I look over my shoulder and back up the block. I'm just in time to see Lawyer Man stalk out through the hotel entrance and, with a nod toward the old woman, slip in through the limo's open door. After a few moments, the woman turns her pipe over, taps it out, and climbs in after him.

As we all watch, the big car pulls away from the curb.

"Come on," Darlene says, blowing out a sigh. "We'll be late for school."

"Who *was* that?" Sarah wonders aloud.

"What did she say to you?" Jimmy asks me.

She said I've got the blood in me, whatever that means.

Out loud, however, I lie. I'm not sure why, but I do.

"I… don't know," I tell them.

CHAPTER 5

SCHOOL IS SCHOOL

—SO I WON'T BURDEN YOU WITH ALL THAT BORINGNESS. LET'S JUST SAY I get through the day without a single pop quiz, which is good. Because, messed up as I am right now, I'd have probably flunked it hard. Fortunately, as things turn out, all I've got to do is get through the usual six-and-a-half hours.

And I do, though, by the time the 3pm bell rings, it feels like at least a week's gone by.

But then, *finally*, I'm moving, spilling out with hundreds of other kids into the late fall sunshine. I see Tish first, just the flash of her face in the mass of people. As I head that way, I find her with Sarah and Jimmy. Jimmy offers up a smile when he sees me, and I try to pretend it doesn't make my insides—do stuff.

"Abbs!" he says.

"We're going up to the arcade," Tish tells me. "Wanna come?"

"What about Tyrone and Jeff?"

"Tyrone's got football practice," Sarah says. "I don't know about Jeff."

"Machine shop," Jimmy says.

"How about Darlene?"

"She's meeting us there. You coming or not?" Sarah asks, and, from the tone of her voice, it's pretty clear she's hoping for a 'not.' I don't have any real beef with her, but I know she's tight with Darlene. And, since the Top Girl's down on me, she is too. That's how the world works.

Which means that, on any other day, I'd have gone with them up to the Boardwalk, if only to piss her and Darlene off.

But not today.

"I'm headed home," I tell them. "I want to check on Corinne."

"What for?" Tish asks. "She's fine. Come on, Abbs. Come with us!" Tish's a whole lot cooler than Sarah.

"Yeah," Jimmy adds. "She's probably faking it to get a day off. Shit, *I've* done it."

"Me, too," Tish agrees.

Sarah says nothing.

I manage a laugh. "Me, too," I admit. "But I'm still worried. I'll see y'all later."

"Suit yourself," Sarah declares and, with that, she turns and stalks off in the direction of the ocean. Tish watches her go for a second, shrugs at me, and then follows.

"You sure?" Jimmy asks, lagging behind. Does he seem genuinely disappointed, or am I just hoping he does?

I work up a smile. "It's cool. Go on. I'll catch you at dinner."

"Okay."

And, just like that, I'm left to take the same walk I took this morning, only this time alone.

The Nelsons give their high school fosters two hours of free time every school day. Uncle Nick encourages us to use it for homework, but—big surprise—it usually gets spent on other stuff. Football. Machine Shop. Other extracurricular activities. Or, maybe more often, just hanging out, either up on the boards or at one of the stores on Ventnor or Atlantic Avenues. My thing usually involves a trip up to the Boardwalk to check out Steel Pier. But not today. Today, I need to find out if Corinne's really sick—or if there's something else going on.

Yeah, that's right. I'm afraid of getting into trouble.

I mean, who isn't?

Anyway, as I make the five-block walk back to the hotel, I'm nervous about more than just Corinne. I keep flashing on the freaky old lady and what she said to me. Just one line, but it's bouncing around in my head like an earworm. What did she mean that I have the "blood" in me? Whose blood? What kind of blood? And how could she possibly get all that from me just walking past her?

A lot of questions.

At least everything looks normal as I round the corner onto Virginia Avenue. The front of the hotel's quiet. No limos. No lawyers. No old ladies. The booster shot of normalcy loosens up the knot in my stomach.

And that's when I spot him.

Rags.

He's no dream this time, no "trick of the eye" through a dark bedroom window. This time, it's broad daylight under a sunlit blue sky, and he's one hundred percent real.

He's standing on the hotel's rooftop sign, the big one that says "Calm Sea Arms" — or would, if all the neon worked. These days, when Uncle Nick bothers to light it up at all, it just says "Cal S Arm," which has inspired some of my lamer sibs to nickname the hotel "Mr. Arm's Place."

Trust me. The joke gets old.

There are plenty of people on the street, but none of them seem to notice him. If I'm honest, I might not have noticed him myself, except something made me look up at just the right time. Call it a funny itch, or maybe the way you automatically look when you imagine that someone's called your name from a distance.

I won't say our eyes meet, since I can't see his. Just like last night, his whole face is swallowed up by a grubby hood that looks like it's made of either old leather or oiled burlap. But, while I stare up at him, I know on some level that he's staring right back at me. It's an impression that gets hammered home when he raises one arm and points. Except he doesn't use his finger.

No, he points with his knife.

A chill rolls right down my spine.

I look where he's pointing. The Boardwalk is ahead, just half-a-block past the hotel.

He wants me to go up to the boards?

I shake my head no. No way.

But he keeps pointing.

Not a chance. I ain't going anyplace on this dude's say so!

But he keeps pointing.

Nope. I gotta see Corinne. I gotta know if she's really sick… or if she remembers something that might get me grounded for a month, if I'm lucky. I don't have time for this!

He keeps pointing.

Finally, and as close to against my will as things can get without it really and truly being outside my control, I nod. It's a brief nod, barely there at all, but it seems to satisfy him. He lowers his arm —

— and moves.

In a blur, he's gone from the sign and atop the roof of the building next door, having cleared the alley in a single bound. It's hard to explain what it's like to watch him do this. He's fast, *impossibly* fast, and that's wild enough. But there's also this feral, predatory quality to it, like last night. It kind of reminds me of a jungle cat, maybe. Or a wolf.

Seeing him this way, mystery in motion, the knife in his hand and his every movement so precise and deliberate—it's both terrifying and, well, exciting.

I follow.

I don't exactly run. But I move fast, weaving in and out as I cut through the folks in my way. If I draw any stares from them, I don't notice. My whole attention is fixed on the dude above me, the weird, scary figure that's leading me on, *beckoning* me on, toward—what?

I take the stairs up to the boards two at a time, my breath coming in ragged gasps. For a minute, I scan the Boardwalk in both directions, but there's no sign of Rags, just sunlight and people and the rush of the ocean as I turn south.

The Boardwalk follows the shoreline for five miles end to end, a century-old walkway of tightly interconnected planks of pressurized wood fastened atop a concrete foundation and elevated six feet over the sand and twelve feet above sea level. At its widest, this walkway is maybe sixty feet across, with the beach on one side and a line of stores, pizzerias, and, lately, casinos on the other. In the summer, it's thick with tourists, tens of thousands of them, hitting the beach during the day and the restaurants and slot machines at night. But now, in the middle of the afternoon on a pre-winter's workday, only maybe two dozen folks are in sight, all of them bundled against the cold ocean breeze.

Given the time of year, most of the pizza joints and souvenir shops on my right are closed and will be until May. The same is true of almost all the small businesses that line the landward side of the boards. Everything shuts down from Labor Day to Memorial Day.

Except the casinos. The casinos are always open. And that's where everybody's going.

Everybody, that is, but me.

I keep looking for Rags, but the rooftops are empty. I suppose he could be mixed in with the people on the boards, but something tells me if he was, I'd know it. He's the kind of dude who'd draw some attention.

So, where is he?

Almost without planning to, I start walking. I'm cold, but the boards feel good beneath my sneakers as I navigate the thin crowd. Nobody says anything. Nobody even makes eye contact. Uncle Nick says it wasn't always like this. Back in "the day," people smiled when they strolled past the piers, tipping hats and nodding to their fellow tourists.

But most of these folks aren't tourists. They're gamblers.

As I keep moving, listening to the roar of the surf, I can see the piers lined up before me on my left, looking shiny and almost alive in the afternoon sunshine.

There's more than one of them. Since all I've been doing is talking about Steel Pier, I get why you might think otherwise. Going from north to south, they're named Garden, Steel, Steeplechase, Central, and Million Dollar. Most are closed for good, but in the distance, I can just make out construction being done way down at Million Dollar. One of the new casinos bought it and is turning it into something. I'm not sure what. Another casino, maybe.

As I get closer to Steel Pier, I spot Resorts. The hotel-turned-casino stands tall on the Boardwalk's landward side, across and maybe half-a-block down from the shorter, blockier, quieter, and, in my mind anyhow, way more interesting pier. Unlike some of the newer casinos, which are all glass and metal, Resorts used to be a regular hotel, and from the outside, you can almost convince yourself it still is. The frontage is all bricks and windows, with a line of revolving doors that seem to be forever spinning.

I've gone inside once, just once. It was a few years ago, right after it first opened. There was a lobby, just like at the Calm Sea Arms, but *much* bigger. And there was this archway that let you onto the gambling floor. I remember the noise coming out of there. Laughing and yelling, the clink of coins and the sound of bells. A whirlwind of color and lights. And people, hundreds of people.

Winners and losers — mostly losers.

But the energy of it was — enticing, so much so that I found myself heading that way.

Of course, I didn't get far before some security dude stopped me and ushered me right back out.

Kids and casinos don't mix.

My glimpse was quick, and I didn't catch too many details before getting the bum's rush. But one thing stuck out. There were no windows. Oh, the hotel's got windows on its upper floors, like I said, but not in the casino. Not one.

Later, when I asked Uncle Nick about it, he told me it was the casino's way of encouraging people to forget about time. "Without windows or clocks, they're hoping you'll lose track of everything: the hour, your money, yourself. That way, you spend more."

"Sounds like a trap," I told him at the time.

And I remember him getting this odd look on his face, part wistful, part fearful. Then he replied in kind of a haunted voice, "It is."

I move my gaze away from the huge casino. Any interest I had in it is long gone. These days, if I feel anything at all for the place, it's dislike. Where everything else on the Boardwalk keeps slowly dying, Resorts and its ilk thrive. The casinos were supposed to turn Atlantic City around. But most folks figure it's done the opposite. I know Uncle Nick does. So does Aunt Kell.

So, do I.

They may look pretty. But under all the lights and noise, they're like an insult, like a stain.

So, I dismiss them and turn my attention toward the ocean—and Steel Pier.

From the front, Steel Pier doesn't look like the other piers on the Boardwalk, and probably not like what you think of when you hear the word "pier." Yes, it sticks out over the ocean, lifted up above the sand and water by dozens of steel and concrete pilings. But, where most piers are just fancy carnivals, often with a big gate as its way in, Steel Pier's front door is a lot grander.

The entrance is an enormous, two-story building that used to be called the "Casino," even though no gambling, at least not the legal kind, ever went on inside. Instead, it was more about a variety of tourist attractions on the first floor and a fancy music hall on the second. These days, if anybody talks about it at all, they just call the derelict old structure the "Theater." I've heard Uncle Nick use that term a couple of times, so I guess I'll stick with it.

Besides the music hall, inside are the remains of an arcade, an aquarium, and even a Hall of Mirrors. There used to be a radio station in there, too—though that disappeared along with the crowds who used to pour through the place in its heyday.

In fact, other than Resorts employees coming in once in a while to store boxes and other stuff, no one's really been in there in years.

Except me, that is.

And apparently, Rags.

He's standing atop the Theater's roof in full sunshine. Even so, it seems like he's somehow bathed in shadow. It's tough to describe. I mean, he's *there*, clear as day. But at the same time, there's this unreality to him. Not ghostly. But more as if he's a reflection of some sort, though of what and on what I can't begin to guess.

For most of a minute, we just look at each other.

Then he gestures to me.

Come.

I find myself moving, though the sensible part of my brain is once again screaming at me not to.

As I watch, he vanishes the way he did last night. No panther-like movement this time. Just there and gone, like a magic trick. And, while I certainly never saw him do it, on some level, I know — *know* – that he's gone inside the pier.

Just like I know — *know* – that I'm going in after him.

There are still some people around, but they're ignoring me completely. Most of their attention's focused on Resorts, making it easy for me to slip over to the oceanside of the boards and then down a short gangway that runs along the north edge of the pier. There's a gate there. It's padlocked, but I found out long ago that one of the links in the chain is broken. If you twist it just right, the whole thing lifts off.

I do this with easy familiarity. Then I slip through the gate and reverse the procedure. It wouldn't do for anyone to see the open gate and come poking around.

There are often cops on the Boardwalk.

Past the gate is a narrow service walkway that follows the pier's northern edge and leads to a single unmarked door. The door's always locked too, but there's one pane in its glass frontage that's been broken for years. I know because I broke it. I keep expecting them to fix it, but they never do. I guess even that tiny repair is more than the new owners want to spend.

I reach my hand through the broken pane and unlock the door from inside. Then I turn the knob. The hinges groan, but the sound's lost in the constant crash of the surf below my feet.

Inside is a wonderful silence. I'm in a corridor on the Theater's first floor that only the employees used, back when there *were* employees, back when this place was alive with music and people. It runs between what used to be Martin's Aquarium on my right and what used to be the Alfie the Sea Lion Show on my left. At the end is an old "Staff Only" door that I slip quietly through, making my way into the Lobby.

It's not like a hotel lobby. It used to be this big open area where folks got dressed up and had drinks before taking in a show at the music hall upstairs. But a decade ago, the then-owners decided that was a waste of space. So, they cut it down, adding an arcade, lots more food concessions, and even a picnic table area. All of it indoors. Weird for a pier.

In the center of the Lobby, however, is something that hasn't changed. It's a wide staircase leading up to the second floor. Uncle Nick once told me that the stairs used to be carpeted. These days, they're just steel and wood, but sturdy enough.

I've explored this pier from top to bottom and end to end a dozen times, always alone. The Nelsons don't know I come here and would freak out if they did. Even Tish and Corinne, the sibs I'm closest to, aren't clued in.

I mentioned it to Tyrone once, that night he took me up to the roof to swap spit. Lost in the moment, I spilled the whole thing, how I come here, most often at night, and sometimes spend hours wandering the old, empty rooms, corridors, and open, lonely spaces where there was once so much action, so much life. I even tried to explain how it makes me feel. It's not scary. It's—"magical" was the stupid word I used at the time—like looking into the past.

He seemed to think about it for a bit. Then he remarked, "You're a creeper."

I felt my face flush. "I'm a what?"

"A creeper."

"A creep? Are you calling me a creep?"

He laughed. Tyrone has a deep laugh. "No, girl. A creeper's somebody who likes to explore old, abandoned places, not to steal stuff but to just… I dunno… get the vibe."

"Oh."

"It's cool. Like being an adventurer."

Well, I decided. *That's just fine.*

Then we went back to kissing.

But I never forgot the word. *Creeper*.

And now, a little over a month later, I remember it again and decide I really am cool with it, being a creeper, at least where Steel Pier is concerned.

So much happened here for so long, and often I swear the memories hang on the walls like old photographs. Sometimes I think I hear voices—laughter, singing. I suppose the place could be haunted. But, somehow, I don't think it's anything as easy, as simple as that.

Partly, I think it's just what Tyrone said.

Vibe.

But more than that, there's a weird familiarity, too.

I sometimes wonder if maybe I was born on Steel Pier.

This time, though, as I make my way through the cold dark maze of halls, I find myself asking — well, myself — *why?* I mean, today isn't about exploration, is it? Today, I'm looking for somebody.

Do I really *want* to see Rags again? And, if I don't, what the hell am I doing here?

The Theater is a big place, with plenty of nooks and crannies. But Rags brought me here for a reason. And, crazy as it is that I've accepted the invite, it only makes sense that if I keep wandering, he'll find me.

And since I last saw him on the roof, I head upstairs.

The big staircase leads up to a kind of waiting area with doors that open into what used to be the music hall. This is where all the head-liners did their shows, dudes from the twenties, thirties, forties, and fifties. Back then, most of the top names in the entertainment world played the pier, and folks came from all over the state, all over the region, to see them.

But that too is long gone.

More recently, the music hall's been replaced with a boxing ring. It sits along the northern wall, with rows and rows of empty seats extending up the aisles southward, away from it — but only on one side, very different from in the Rocky movies. Not a whole lot of boxing actually happened here. It was a kind of last-ditch effort to keep the pier going, another brilliant idea that didn't pan out.

Right now, though, seeing it, the question that pops into my head is an odd one.

Why do they call it a "ring" when it's a big square?

I should ask Tyrone. He'll know.

Or… maybe I'll ask Jimmy instead.

But then I see something that knocks the idea right out of my brain.

Rags is standing in the middle of the ring —

— looking at me.

CHAPTER 6

A PILE OF TRASH THAT MOVES

—THAT'S WHAT HE LOOKS LIKE. LIKE I'VE SAID BEFORE, THE DUDE'S NOT all that tall. He's sure as hell no Tyrone, or even a Jimmy. But there's a presence to him—a power—that's hard to pin down but impossible to deny. He's just standing there, still as a statue and, while I can't see his eyes, I can somehow tell that those eyes are fixed on me.

I know I should be scared. *Really* scared. Except, I'm not.

I just look back at him, my surprise wearing off.

Then, stupidly, I wave.

He doesn't wave back.

No lights are on in here, but it's daytime outside, and there *are* windows set up high against one wall. The sunlight pouring in at an angle throws shadows everywhere, making a patchwork of the surrounding rows of seats and even the ring itself, so that Rags stands half-in and half-out of the gloom.

It suits him.

I should get the hell out of here. Just turn and run.

But I don't. Instead, my feet carry me down the aisle, in hesitant but relentless steps, right up to the base of the ring.

Rags still hasn't budged an inch.

I clear my throat. It sounds like a duck quack. "Um…" A shitty beginning. I try a do-over. "Thanks again. For last night, I mean."

He doesn't move or speak, but I can feel his gaze on me. I'm not cold anymore. Instead, my skin's hot, as if this dude is cooking me with his eyes.

I keep glancing down at the frayed cuffs at the end of his moth-eaten, woolen coat sleeves, half-expecting to see that black blade of his slide into view like something out of a slasher movie. Why'd he bring me here? Because that's what happened. If I didn't know it before, I know it now.

I got summoned.

Could it have been to take out a witness to what he did last night? I guess it's possible.

So… tell me again why I'm not running.

Then he speaks. "*Vanyan sòlda.*"

I almost jump out of my skin. His voice is scratchy, barely human. "Wh… what?" I gasp. My heart starts hammering.

He raises his hand toward me. I gasp as I look at it. But at least it's empty. No knife. Not *yet*, anyway.

I don't move.

His hand stays there, steady as a rock. The fingers are filthy, caked with all kinds of stinking crap. But I think — I *think* — the skin's black.

Does he want me to — hold it? Is this some kind of psycho come-on? At least, he's too far away to reach me. And, if he so much as steps in my direction, I'm freaking gone!

Sweat stings my forehead. "Look," I say. "I don't know what you want."

He steps in my direction.

No, not steps. The dude almost seems to teleport. He's so fast that it takes me a second to really grasp what's happening. One instant, he's smack dab in the middle of the ring, motionless. The next, he's barely three feet away.

Here's the weird thing. As sudden as it all happens, I don't get any feeling of danger from him. Well, no, that's not true. Danger *drips* off this dude. I don't think he could brush his teeth without it being scary as hell. But it's a danger that seems tucked away at the moment, kind of how the freaky clown is "tucked away" inside a jack-in-the-box.

I should run, but I don't. Instead, I hold my ground, barely. My eyes never leave the dark hole where his face should be, and I'm trembling something awful.

He stops at the ropes, the three horizontal lines of padding that completely surround the boxing ring. From there, he continues to study me, once again statue still.

Then he says, "*Aksepte mwen.*"

I blink. The words, if they even *were* words, mean nothing to me.

Okay. Enough.

"Look," I say. "I need to get back. I got homework." Just saying it sounds lame.

Rags doesn't move.

But then another voice floats down from the southern side of the arena, beyond the public entrance I came through just now. It's a dude's voice, calm and competent. And he's not speaking to *us*. "Watch where you're walking, gentlemen. Jesus, it doesn't look like anyone's cleaned this place in months!"

Startled, I glance toward the source of the voice. Then, alarmed, I look back at Rags.

He's already in motion, vaulting over the ropes like a gazelle. He lands in front of me, and I just have time to notice that his landing didn't make any sound at all — before he wraps one arm around my waist and claps a hand over my mouth. Then, before I can react, I'm yanked off my feet and carried up a side aisle toward the back of the arena.

Up there, a row of faded red draperies, purely for decoration, hang along the wall from floor to ceiling. Behind it is just enough space for someone to stand — someone small. Rags pulls me back there and deposits me on the floor, his arm still around me, and his hand still pressed over my mouth.

My heart's slamming against my rib cage. His hand smells like garbage, nearly gagging me.

Slowly, tentatively, he removes it.

I take a deep, shuddering breath. I still can't move. He's holding me too tight. But I can peek out through a gap in the curtain, no wider than an eyeball.

Just as I do, I see three dudes enter from the far side of the boxing ring. Two of them are strangers. *Freaky weird* strangers. Obviously related, brothers, maybe. Both are big, Tyrone-big or bigger, and they swagger around like they know it. One's got dreads so long they'd make Bob Marley jealous. He's got a broad chest and arms like Board-walk pilings. Six-four, at least, and maybe two hundred and twenty pounds.

The other's smaller, but not by much. A little leaner. A little wirier. No dreads on him. No hair at all, not even eyebrows. It's a weird look that makes me wonder if his whole body's hairless and, if so, did he do it to himself for some reason, or is it a medical thing?

Both have got on these mirrored shades, which seems stupid given the bad light in here. All macho affectation. Both are dressed in match-ing suits. Jet black. Red power ties. Shiny leather shoes. They probably think they're as cool as all get out, but to my eyes they look more like posers. The suits belong on bankers, not an oversize Marley look-alike and a black Uncle Fester.

The third dude, however, is no stranger.

He's Shanks, the lawyer who visited the Calm Sea Arms this morning.

"Well," Shanks says to the other two, offering a shrug. "Here it is."

Baldy's eyes scan the dimly lit arena. "I think I remember this place," he says to the big dude. He's got what Uncle Nick calls an "islander" accent. I wonder if he's also from Jamaica. "Grann brought us here once, didn't she? Last time we were in the States."

"Yeah," Dreads replies. He's got a really deep voice, and hearing him use it is like listening to thunder form sentences.

Baldy says, "Gotta be, what? Twenty years ago? When we were maybe twelve. Saw Joey Bishop. Grann thought he was funny as hell, but I was just bored."

"Yeah," Dreads adds. Obviously, a dude of few words.

"I didn't realize you'd been here before, Mr. Bernard," Shanks remarks, looking a little put-out.

Baldy grins. He's got bad teeth. "Not upstairs, not lately. But Steel Pier and my family go back aways. Isn't that right, Bap?"

Dreads nods.

"Anyhow, this place, in particular, has changed plenty," Baldy says, looking around with his hands on his hips. "For one thing: the stage's gone."

"No stage," Dreads agrees.

Shanks nods. "As I said, Resorts bought the entire pier a few years ago with an eye toward annexing it. They converted the former theater into a boxing arena. But, when the venture didn't make money, they closed it down."

Baldy smirks. "Of course, it didn't make money. It's a dumb-ass idea if I ever heard one. Don't even look like a proper boxing ring. The problem is that this pier wasn't built for that kind of entertainment. It was meant to offer class and variety."

"Class and variety," the other echoes.

"'Except this town ain't about class and variety… not anymore."

"I'm sure you're right, Mr. Bernard," Shanks says. He's got on the same pin-striped suit as this morning, though I've got to admit it looks better — "righter" — on him than on the Bernard Bros, whoever *they* are. "In any event, as I told you… told you both… Resorts has no interest in selling or leasing Steel Pier. In fact, trespassing is strictly forbidden as parts of the pier are considered unsafe. Insurance issues. It was only by pulling a few strings that I was able to get the keys and 'unofficial' permission to show it to you."

"Thanks, man," Baldy replies with a broad grin. He's got a gold tooth that sparkles in the uneven light. Cliché, I know. But he's got one. "Except my brother and I aren't looking to buy the place."

Shanks seems confused. "No? I assumed —"

Baldy shakes his head. "Nope. See, there's an old saying back home. When you have to get your shoes muddy, best to wipe them on somebody else's porch."

"I don't understand."

"Sit tight. You will. Bap?"

Dreads nods and walks back up the aisle to the arena entrance, gesturing with one massive hand. A moment later, two more men appear. Both dudes are white. They're both wearing jeans, turtlenecks, and black leather jackets. And, from what I can tell, both fit firmly into the "thug" category. Between them, they're half-leading and half-dragging a skinny dude in street clothes and wearing an apron. He's maybe forty, with thinning hair and a wild, half-frantic look on his face.

I get a lump in my stomach at the sight of him.

This guy is scared.

Scratch that. Terrified.

When he sees these three, especially the one in the middle, Shanks goes pale.

"There he is!" Baldy declares. He claps the lawyer on the back and steps around him, meeting the bookends and their prisoner as they near the edge of the boxing ring. "You remember Ira Kaplan, don't you, Shanks? He works at Virginia Drycleaning. In fact, his brother owns it. Isn't that right, Ira?"

I feel myself shudder. Virginia Drycleaning. I know the place. It's right next door to the Calm Sea Arms, though I've never once had any reason to go inside. There's not much that needs drycleaning in an orphan's life.

Kaplan looks back at Baldy with rummy eyes. His lower lip trembles. He might even be drooling a little in his terror. "Please…"

"Shhh," Baldy tells him, as if addressing a child who's spoken out of turn. He even puts a snide finger to the dry cleaner's lips, drool or no drool. To the lawyer, he says, "You *ought* to remember Ira. He's the one who bounced you out on your ass last week, after you delivered our latest offer to his brother, Dave. Guess that makes him the 'bouncer' at that particular establishment." Then he laughs, as if this is a great joke, which it isn't.

Dreads laughs too. Suddenly, there's *menace* in the arena, as thick and real as morning fog on the beach.

And I think I know where this is going.

No…

"Mr. Bernard," Shanks says, and by the edge in his voice, I figure he must feel it too. "I've already taken steps to have Kaplan's shop closed for fire code violations. It's only a matter of time before he's forced to sell."

Dreads utters a Darlene-style snort.

Baldy replies, "Yeah, we know. Here's the thing. We're tired of waiting. We've already got the plans. After tonight, we'll have the money. The only thing still missing is the city block of Virginia Avenue real estate we need."

"Mr. Bernard," Shanks protests. "Eighty percent of the block owners have already agreed—"

"Eighty isn't one hundred, is it? As it is, we're stuck with *two* hold-outs. The orphan hotel and Kaplan's drycleaning place."

"You'll get them," the lawyer insists. His eyes are wide, and he's licking his lips.

"Damn straight, we will. Right, brother?"

"Yeah," Dreads growls.

Then he nods toward the boxing ring.

The bookends lift Kaplan off his feet and literally carry the struggling, screaming man to one side of the ring, to almost the exact spot where I had stood when I was talking to Rags. Once there, they toss him over the ropes with no more effort than throwing a bag of trash into a dumpster.

Kaplan lands hard, groaning, the wind knocked out of him. For half a minute, he just lays there, grunting and gasping, while the Bernard Bros and the rest all watch him expressionlessly.

Then, as the little dude recovers, Dreads climbs over the ropes and joins him in the ring. Looming over the dry cleaner, the bigger Bernard carefully takes off his suit jacket and drapes it over the nearest ropes. Then he does the same with the crisp white shirt underneath. What's left is the broadest chest I've ever laid my eyes on. The dude's ripped like

Schwarzenegger. I don't think I've ever seen anyone built like him before, at least not in person.

Dreads starts circling the groaning dude, flexing his enormous hands.

Kaplan looks up at him, his face pale with terror, his eyes wild. "No!" he wails. "Wait! Please! What is it you want?"

"From you?" Baldy replies from outside the ring. He's leaning over the ropes, looking like the trainer in that *Rocky* movie. "Nothing. You ain't the owner of the drycleaners. That's your brother. What we want is *his* signature on a little piece of paper saying he's sold it to us." As he says this, he's got a look on his face that makes me shudder, even trapped as I am in Rag's strong grip.

He's into this.

"What I do want is to send the right message," Baldy goes on. "And not just to your brother. I want to send it to his neighbors too. One message, two recipients. Get it?"

Kaplan stares at him as if he's speaking a foreign language. Then he glances up at Dreads, who looms over him like a cresting wave. A big, mean cresting wave.

The bookends remain expressionless.

Shanks looks like he wants to heave. I know exactly how he feels.

"Mr. Bernard, wait," the lawyer says, fairly choking out the words. "This… this isn't necessary. I'm close to a deal, especially with Mr. Kaplan's establishment."

"Not close enough," Baldy replies, never taking his eyes off the terrified man in the ring. "We've been back in town for two months now, and nothing's moved. We're ready. Ready to build. What is it you like to say? Time is money? Well, we took that advice to heart. But your way of getting things done isn't working for us anymore. Too slow. So, my brother and I talked it over with our Grann, and we've decided to move things along our way, the *old* way."

"But…" Shanks stammers. "You can't just…"

At this, Baldy spares him a quick, amused glance. It's the kind of glance Uncle Nick and Aunt Kell sometimes give one of the little kids when they say something adorable.

Then, turning back to his brother, Baldy nods.

Dreads rumbles, "The *old* way."

It's the longest sentence I've so far heard him utter.

He reaches down and grabs the dry cleaner by his shirt, and yanks him to his feet so hard that Kaplan nearly flies out of his shoes. Then, without so much as taking a second breath, Dreads punches the dude in the face.

Teeth go flying.

Kaplan doesn't cry out. He just goes down—hard.

I almost run out there. I can't help it. But Rags is still holding me around the waist, his arm like a vice. I look at him, what little I can see of him. "Stop this," I whisper.

He shakes his head.

"Why not?" I demand, louder than I should but not as loud as I want. I'm not looking to get caught here. In fact, I'm scared shitless of getting caught here. But this can't just—happen!

Rags doesn't reply.

Down in the ring, Kaplan seems to have shaken off the worst of the shock. He's on his hands and knees, scrambling away and drizzling blood on the ring's rotting canvas floor as he nears the ropes on the far side. But when he looks blearily up, he sees that the bookends have easily beat him there, cutting off any escape.

Dreads follows, his every step slow and precise.

Shanks begs, "Please… don't do this. I'll get you the properties! I swear it!"

Baldy shrugs. "Maybe yes. Maybe no. We figure: why chance it? We *know* this works."

Kaplan claws at the ropes, sobbing. He's trying to speak, but his voice sounds thick and nasal. His nose is broken.

I try again to squirm free of Rags and do—what?

I don't know. Something!

But it's no good. He's way too strong for me. I can't move, not an inch.

Dreads pulls the dry cleaner to his feet and hammers him again, this time keeping him upright with one hand on his throat while his other does the damage.

And it does a lot of damage.

Each blow is wet and horrible and makes my stomach clench tighter. I squeeze my eyes shut as the beating goes on and on until I lose count and think I'm about to go crazy from the horror of it.

Then it stops.

Hesitantly, reluctantly, I open my eyes.

Down in the ring, Dreads still holds Kaplan upright. The dude's face is an awful mess, and he's clearly out of it. Seeing this, the giant looks over at his brother, who nods.

Then Dreads' huge hands clamp down on either side of Kaplan's head and give it a firm twist.

I hear a loud *crunch*. It's a sound I know I'll never stop hearing.

Never.

The drycleaner's lifeless body drops to the mat.

Shanks heaves, whirling away and staining his fancy shoes with whatever he had for lunch.

"Where?" Dreads asks. He's sweating, and his hands and fore-arms are covered — and I mean *covered*, like paint — in poor Kaplan's blood.

Baldy replies, his smile gone, all business now, "Let's send the hands to his brother. Keep the rings on 'em, just so there won't be any confusion. But the head, *that* goes to the hotel."

Dreads nods.

The hotel.

They're going to send that dude's head *to Uncle Nick and Aunt Kell!*

That's more than I can take. Without meaning to, I let out a sound. Just a gasp or squeak or something. Not much at all.

But, at the same time, *too* much.

Both Baldy and Dreads look up. So do the bookends.

Suddenly, the atmosphere in the arena changes completely. Where, a second ago, it was menace and violence, with the coppery scent of blood filling the cold still air — now it abruptly switches to something even darker. Something predatory.

The afternoon's "entertainment" has just turned into a hunt.

"Check it out," Baldy says, and one of the bookends immediately nods and moves to obey. Wordlessly, the big dude heads up the side aisle toward the drapes where Rags and I are hiding. His eyes scan left and right, missing nothing.

I realize two things at the same time.

First, while our hiding place seemed like a good one, I now see it as a trap. There's no place to go except out into the open arena, in full view of everyone.

Second, I'm alone. Rags is gone.

The bookend approaches, looking scarier with each advancing step. One hand is at his side, while his other pulls a black pistol out of a shoulder holster under his leather jacket. His pale face is set in a look of blank professionalism.

He'll find me and kill me… and not lose a minute's sleep.

Then something moves past the dude, like a shadow. There and gone.

In the next second, he starts screaming.

The pistol falls as both his hands shoot up to his face. Even in the bad light, I can see blood pouring out from between his fingers.

"What?" Baldy yells at him. "What just happened?"

Still screaming, the bookend turns in a circle, lowering his hands.

His eyes are gone.

Both of them have been gouged out, lids and all.

This time I clamp my own hand over my mouth.

"Jesus!" the other bookend exclaims. Then he pulls his own gun.

As the blind man staggers back down the aisle, his screams turn into pleas of "Help me! Help me!" that would probably be accompanied by tears if he still had tear ducts. After several steps, he loses his balance and crashes down onto one of the rows of seats. He must land badly, hurting himself, because he immediately starts screaming again.

Baldy stares up at the guy, his mouth open. Then he looks back at Dreads, who's still in the ring and still covered with Kaplan's blood. Dreads comes to the ropes, not swaggering anymore, but smooth and cat-quick. He jumps over them, lands beside his brother, and goes up to the fallen dude, yanking him to his feet. The blind bookend now has a bloody lip from his fall to add to the empty eye sockets, and he teeters as Dreads holds him up.

"What happened?" Dreads growls in his deep, deep voice.

The dude tries to speak, drools some, and then tries again. "Don't… know…" he finally says, his voice hoarse from yelling. Then, in a high, panicked pitch, he adds, "I can't see nothing!"

"Worthless," Dreads mutters.

Then he throws the bookend back into the seats, and not gently. The dude hits hard and just lies there, moaning.

Down by the ring, Baldy pulls out a radio and puts it to his lips. "Get in here. Both of you. Now!"

Then, as his eyes scan the arena again, I duck quickly back from the tiny break in the drapes through which I've been watching.

He didn't spot me. I'm sure of it.

At least, I think I'm sure of it.

"What *was* that?" Shanks asks. He's still standing on the other side of the ring, as far from the action as possible. There's vomit on his lower lip. "What just happened?"

"How the hell should I know," Baldy replies. He glances at the other bookend, who looks ready to charge up the aisle after whoever—or whatever—just mutilated his homeboy. "Stay put," Baldy tells him. "Wait for the others."

"I didn't even see the guy," the bookend says.

Baldy points to an archway that's up in one corner of the arena, about ten feet from where I'm hiding. From my perspective, it might as well be ten miles. He looks back at Shanks. "Do you know where that goes?"

The lawyer, pale and trembling, makes a visible effort to think. "Uh… just a hallway. With changing rooms for the boxers."

Wrong.

There *is* a corridor back there, and it *does* lead to the changing rooms, but that's not the only place it goes.

It goes to the old Hall of Mirrors.

Nobody's been through it in years—except, of course, *me*, during my solo visits—but the old glass maze is still there. It's a sweet little labyrinth of mirrors that's better designed than any of the carnival ones that the Nelsons occasionally treat us to. These days, of course, it's pretty dusty from disuse, and some of the glass is cracked, probably from years of cold and neglect.

The maze has only one way in or out, and it's much, much harder than it looks to navigate.

A hand touches my shoulder.

For an instant, it's all I can do not to scream.

Rags is right beside me, tucked behind the drapes. I have no idea how he got back again without either me or the bad dudes spotting him—but then I can't imagine how he left our hidey-hole unseen in the first place.

Another of his vanishing tricks.

Two more dudes have arrived. They look pretty much like the bookends. Just another matched set of guns and muscles. Baldy meets them halfway up the opposite aisle, and he's talking to them animatedly while Shanks, Dreads, and the other bookend watch.

A minute later, they all come looking.

Looking for us.

It seems like a big search party for such a small place. No way are they going to miss me. True, I'm not the one who blinded their home-boy, but something tells me that distinction won't buy me much in the way of "Go home, girl. No harm done."

Rags motions for me to follow him.

I shake my head and mouth, "They'll see us!"

Once again, his arm snakes around my waist. He stinks to high heaven, and he's scaring the crap out of me. Even so, I'm weirdly glad he's here.

But then he pushes the drapes aside, and we move.

My heart jumps into my throat. Any second, I expect to hear shouts and then gunshots.

I'm going to die on this pier!

And, oddly, I'm not surprised.

Except none of that happens. No shouts. No shots.

Because, while we are running, it's no kind of running I've ever done. I barely feel the worn carpet beneath my feet as we race along the arena's back wall toward the archway I mentioned before, crossing the aisle that the thugs are already heading up. The bookends—there are three of them now—all have guns drawn. Baldy and Dreads follow be-hind. Dreads' shirt is still off. Shanks brings up the rear, looking sweaty and nervous and not at all happy to be here.

They're all right there! They're gonna see us!

But then I notice how slow they seem to be moving.

It's not quite like they're standing still, but it's close. Their legs slog as though through deep snow, or maybe mud, as if each step is an effort. Except none of that effort shows on their faces, almost the way the sloths move down at the Cape May Zoo. Deliberately and ridiculously slow.

For a few heartbeats—mine, not theirs—I watch them. They're pissed off and, to varying degrees, scared. And who could blame them? They just saw one of their own get blinded without catching so much of a glimpse of who did the blinding.

But they're not seeing us.

That's because Rags moves fast. And, right now, he's making me move that fast, too.

How is he doing this?

Then that question turns to dust when, all of a sudden, he stops doing it.

For a second or two, no more, he freezes at the corner of the arena, right in front of the archway that leads to the locker rooms and, beyond that, the Hall of Mirrors. He doesn't warn me or anything. In fact, he doesn't say a word. He just stops.

In plain sight.

"Whoa!" Baldy exclaims.

Beside him, his brother stiffens but doesn't make a sound — while the three bookends all gasp in confused surprise and, after a moment's hesitation, raise their guns.

"Who is that?" Shanks asks nervously from behind them all.

"We got him," Baldy replies. Then, to his thugs, "Take him out."

What are you doing? I scream inside my head. But before I can turn the thought to words, which I probably won't have time to do anyway since the bookends are about to ice us both, Rags moves us again.

To the hunters, it must look as if we appeared out of nowhere for a split second, just long enough for them to spot us, and then vanished again. To *my* eyes, it's like the world around us has once more braked to a crawl.

I see the bookends slowly — so slowly — raise their pistols. I see the very beginning of fresh shock register on Baldy's face. I see Dreads' muscles tense up. I see Shanks go even paler.

Then Rags pulls me through the archway and into the narrow corridor beyond. Behind us, still in the arena, I can hear the approach of the dudes with the guns.

"You let them see you!" I whisper to Rags.

Really, Abbs? You've bought into his magical powers so fast that already you're going to dis him for not using them?

Rags doesn't reply, and he doesn't look back. He just carries me deeper along the hallway, past unmarked doors that I know lead to the old boxers' locker rooms, around a tight corner, and into the Hall of Mirrors.

That's when it hits me.

He let *them see us… to lead them here, into the maze.*

Uncle Nick once told me that there are two ways that folks deal with danger. Either fight or flight. I've always considered myself a flight kind of girl.

But not Rags.

Rags is all about the *fight*.

And Steel Pier's abandoned Hall of Mirrors is his chosen battle-ground.

CHAPTER 7

THE SMELL OF BLOOD

Behind us, I hear them coming. Baldy, Dreads, and their thugs are *trying* to be quiet, but together they probably weigh more than a half-a-ton, and I'd have to be deaf not to know where they are.

I think I can even hear Lawyer Man's frightened panting.

A sharp stench wafts up along the hallway. It mixes with the blood and the ever-present sour odor that Rags puts off like cologne. At first, I wonder if it's coming from the boxers' changing rooms, maybe left over from the last undersold bout. But that was years ago, and even the worst man-stink doesn't last forever.

No, what I'm smelling is *fear*.

Shanks is scared. And the bookends, after what happened to their homeboy, have got to be scared too. Even Baldy's probably feeling some of it. But not Dreads. No, something tells me *that* dude wouldn't know fear if it bit him on the ass.

He's just really pissed off—and out for payback.

Rags pulls me around a corner and through a fire door that kicks up a cloud of dust as it opens. Inside, we find a room that, like many on the pier, is longer than it is wide, stretching out in the direction of the beach and breakers. Maybe twenty feet across and almost a hundred deep, it's got a high ceiling that, like the floor, is made of staggered wooden planks, a lot of which have rotted out over time.

Ahead, filling most of the available space, is a labyrinth of standing glass panels.

The Hall of Mirrors.

I've been in here before, of course. But always alone. I've wandered the cold darkness of the maze with only a flashlight to guide me, and, more than once, I've spooked myself with my own reflection. It's a creepy place at the best of times. But now, with one killer holding my hand and others in hot pursuit, creepy's turned into terrifying.

The front entrance to the Hall of Mirrors is on the public promenade, beyond the wall to my right. But that was boarded up ages ago. These days, the only way in is through a secret back door, originally put there for emergencies or easy maintenance. It's disguised as just another standing glass panel but has hidden hinges.

Is this Rags plan? Get us both in there and hunker down, hoping that Baldy and Dreads will lose us and just give up?

Not a chance.

But I don't dare tell him that as he pulls me toward the correct mirror in the back outside row of the maze. His fingers deftly search for, and find, the little hole that serves as a latch. He turns it, swinging the mirror out in front of us.

Then we're inside.

Seems this dude knows the pier at least as well as I do.

As Rags closes the door again, I spare a moment to look around.

The glass panels, each one seven feet tall and three feet wide, are all yellowed. Some have silver paint on the back of them, making them mirrors. Some are more or less clear. A few are concave or convex so that the reflections they give back are weirdly twisted.

Overall, the years have been pretty kind. A number of the panels are cracked, and a couple have shattered completely since the last time I was here. But the rest still stand.

I slip behind one of the mirrored panels, concealing myself. Rags joins me, moving in close, as he did behind the drapery, his body reeking of refuse.

Nearby, just on the other side of the back row of panels, I hear incoming footsteps. My heart, which hasn't stopped hammering since I spotted Rags in the boxing arena, now leaps up into my throat.

"They'll find us," I whisper.

Rags says nothing.

Someone else speaks. I think it's one of the bookends. "Where'd he go?"

I hear Baldy Bernard reply, "In there." Unlike me, these dudes don't seem to be whispering. I guess they don't care if we can hear them.

"In the maze?" the bookend asks.

"Ain't no place else," Dreads says in his deep, rumbling voice.

Then I hear Shanks. He sounds nearly as scared as I am, and that's saying something. On some level, his fear pisses me off. *He's* not the one these maniacs are hunting!

Then again, neither am I.

"Mr. Bernard," the lawyer says plaintively. "I realize how upset you must be about your man back there. But following this... lunatic into that old maze is..." His words trail off.

Suicide?

"You want to go home, Shanks?" Baldy asks him.

"Uh... no, sir."

"Glad to hear it. James, you and the guys go on in and hunt this guy down."

For a couple of heartbeats, no one responds to the order, and it occurs to me that the bookends don't like the idea of the maze any more than Shanks does.

Dreads growls, "Problem?"

A nervous silence drags for a few moments. But then fear of the Bernard Bros trumps fear of Rags, and all of the bookends hastily accept.

"But... how do we get in?" one asks.

"Must be a door," Baldy replies.

I risk a peek. The panel beside the mirrored one behind which I'm hiding is clear if a little foggy with age. By leaning over just a little, I can peer past the tight seam between the two panels and see the knot of men standing near the fire exit.

The moment I do, Baldy pulls a gun and fires.

For a single, heart-attack-moment, I *know* I've been spotted.

Why'd I look? What the hell's the matter with me? Now I'll die here, and they'll probably never find my body. The Bernard Bros'll see to that. Aunt Kell and Uncle Nick won't ever know what happened. I'll just have disappeared, vanished off the face of the Earth.

Just like my parents.

I'm sorry...

But then a panel further along the row shatters. So does the one behind it, raining broken glass and mirrored shards down on the wooden floor.

"There," I hear Baldy say. "A door."

And my heart starts beating again.

"We gotta move," I whisper, turning toward Rags.

But he's gone.

Oh my God.

The thugs approach, their footsteps reluctant and wary.

And I realize that *I* need to be gone, too.

Behind me, the back row of the maze ends with an inward turn, the first of many. Of the six panels between here and there, three are glass, and three are mirrored. I stay low and move as fast as I dare, hoping—praying—it's gloomy enough in here that none of the dudes will spot the movement.

Ten steps later and I'm there, unshot and, as far as I can tell, unseen.

Around the corner's a short row of mirrors. Cold and empty. No sign of Rags.

Behind me, I hear the crunch of glass.

Again, I move, ducking down and following the corridor deeper into the maze, making first a right and then a left. I'm mindful of every step, as I know some of the floorboards have rotted out. At the same time, I wrack my memory for the maze's complicated floorplan. There's no way out that I'm aware of, other than the way I came in—plus, of course, Baldy Bernard's new "door." But there *are* little nooks and crannies. If I'm careful and quiet, I may be able to stay hidden long enough for them to give up the search.

Where. Is. Rags?

But I know the answer. Or think I do.

He's on the hunt.

Please, God. No more blood. I don't want to see more blood!

I make another turn, moving from mirror to mirror as quickly as I can. Out of the corner of my eye, through the milky panels of clear glass that I can't help passing, I spot dark shapes. The dudes are hunting for me.

If I can see them, surely they can see me and, at any instant, I expect to hear a shout or a gunshot.

I don't.

We're deep in the maze now, where the shadows are heaviest. I've nestled myself in a corner created by the meeting of two mirrored panels, and I begin to think that, maybe, I might just get out of this alive.

Then, without warning, one of the bookends rounds a bend and steps out in front of me, no more than six feet away. In one hand, he's holding a big flashlight that he sweeps in both directions. As I watch, frozen in place, the light washes over me and stops.

Then, wincing in the glare, I see the dude's other hand come up, the one with the big black pistol in it.

"No," I hear myself beg. "Wait."

He shoots.

I figure that's it. I'm dead. End of story. Roll credits. No way could he miss me at this range, not pinned in his flashlight beam. I'm so sure of this, in fact, that it takes a moment for me to realize that, somehow, he *did* miss as the mirror behind me shatters. So does the one behind that and the one behind *that*.

Then, a split second later, a dark blur hurtles past me, throwing itself at the bookend like a pouncing lion. He leaps on the dude, his black knife slamming into the bookend's chest with hammer force.

The dude's breath explodes out of him in a wheezing spray of blood. Then he goes down—and stays down.

And, just like that, Rags is gone again, and I'm looking at a bloody corpse.

Sweet Jesus…

Footsteps come running. They're slowed down by the labyrinth, of course, and that gives me time to drag my eyes away from the body and go even deeper into the maze. I want to lose myself, *need* to lose myself, and not just to escape the remaining two thugs.

I've seen two people die, and three others get slashed or crippled, all in the last twenty-four hours. And it's too much. Way too much. I can almost feel my brain shutting down like an over-heated engine.

Keep moving. Just get out of here.

I'm racing through the maze now, taking every turn I come across and quickly losing my bearings. Within a minute, I realize that I'm completely lost. That stops me, forcing me to catch my breath and *think*. That's when I notice that the panels on each side of me are "fun" mirrors, which twist my reflection into fat-short on my left and tall-thin on my right. But I don't look at them. My mind's screwed up enough as it is.

But knowing they're there actually *helps*.

Like I said before, I've explored this maze *a lot*, and those facing fun mirrors make a handy landmark. I'm near the back, close to what used to be the public entrance before it was boarded up. Not good. I've been running myself into a corner like a panicked mouse. Time to be smarter. Time to use the only advantage I've got.

I know this maze. They don't.

Doing my best to keep my heart from climbing out of my mouth, I start moving again, as quickly as quiet will allow. This time, though, I double back, trying to follow the mental map in my head.

Some distance away, I can see the remaining two thugs, sort of. They're like lumbering dark shapes, just visible now and again as they pass by panels of foggy glass. Each of them has the same kind of flashlight as the first dude and, since they're the only source of light in this place, the glow they cast is crazy and uneven, throwing shadows everywhere.

As far as I can tell, the thugs have split up, probably at one of the maze's early forks, either to cover more ground or to prevent me from doing what I'm doing now —

— slipping behind them.

I stay low and use the shadows.

As I do, I find that I can hear them talking to each other. Their voices are very low — I get the feeling they're using the same kind of radio that Baldy was — but I can still hear them clearly enough.

"See anybody?"

"Nobody! You?"

"No… wait. Damn it! James got iced! I just found him!"

"Where you at? I'll come to you."

"Don't! Keep looking. The son of a bitch's in here someplace!"

I turn left, pass two rights, and then turn left again. Now that I'm letting myself think, the maze's pattern is coming back to me. I'm pretty sure I can do this, make it back to the broken panel Rags and I first came through. Of course, Baldy, Dreads, and Shanks might still be there.

But one thing at a time.

Then Rags steps out in front of me.

I have to bite my tongue to keep from screaming.

He doesn't say a word, just looks down at me from the darkness of his hood. Once again, I can't see his eyes, but I can *feel* them on me. It makes my skin crawl.

"Let's get out of here," I say in a barely audible whisper, so low that I'm not at all sure he'll even hear it.

He shakes his head and raises one arm, pointing with his knife deeper into the maze, toward where the thugs are still searching away from us.

"No," I mouth, loudly as I dare. "No more killing."

He doesn't respond.

"Please," I say, just like I did last night under the pier. "Please, don't."

Slowly, maybe a bit reluctantly, he nods.

Then he *jumps.*

I gasp, unable to contain it. Instantly, the flashlights freeze in place.

"Behind us," I hear one of the others say.

Shit.

The flashlights turn around. As they do, I look up.

Rags is on the ceiling.

The freaking ceiling.

My poor brain can't immediately compute what my eyes tell me. A figure draped in ratty old clothes and a heavy hood is clinging to the wooden boards overhead like a spider. Then, as I watch, the figure swings down and then up again, driving his knife into the planks, and using it to keep him aloft.

It's crazy. Impossible. But then so is moving almost too quick for the eye to see.

Then I realize where he's going. He's headed toward the flashlights, toward Baldy's last two thugs.

Suddenly, my fear goes into overdrive, and I can't move, not an inch. All I can do is stand there, maybe three rows from the maze's exit, and watch him, whatever the hell *he* is, play leapfrog with his knife across the ceiling.

The bookends don't see him. It's too dark in here, and their attention is focused on what's ahead, not above. At one point, the pair of them appear to meet up, though it's hard to be sure through the cockeyed rows of glass and mirrors. But their flashlights definitely seem to converge.

Then one goes out, turned off.

And I hear a thug say, *"I'll light the way. You keep going."*

"Yeah."

Glancing up, I spot Rags. He's come up to them, at least I think he has. Maybe he's even passed right over their heads. His knife makes a faint *thunk thunk thunk* each time it jabs into the ceiling joists. But if the thugs notice, they give no sign.

Then he drops.

For a second or two, I lose him in the confusion of light and glass.

But then he's there, right in front of Baldy's thugs, his knife at his side.

"Jesus!" one of them yells.

Then they both raise their guns and fire.

Glass shatters loudly, panel after panel, sending shards flying in every direction. I crouch down and cover my ears. It goes on for what seems like a long time but is probably more like ten seconds. Then it stops — and slowly, *so* slowly, I rise to my feet to look.

A good quarter of the maze is gone. What's left of it, scattered bits of glass and broken mirror, covers much of the floor like a carpet. The two thugs are staring at the spot where Rags had been, their guns smoking. Where I am, the panels are still mostly standing. But even so, I feel horribly exposed. At any moment, I expect one of them to see me, adjust their aim, and swat me like a bug.

But then I see what they don't.

Rags used a mirror.

He was *never* in front of them. He was *behind* them.

And he still is.

One of the thugs must sense something because he whirls around, a warning on his lips.

But, before he can get the words out, Rags kicks him.

Remember the kick he gave to that banger under the pier last night? Well, this is that times five. His booted foot catches the big dude right in the breadbasket, knocking him off his feet and straight into the second dude, sending them both flying.

I expect them to go maybe three or four feet, but it's more like a dozen. They clear the ocean of broken glass completely and hit the nearest wall of still-standing panels like twin freight trains.

More of the maze shatters, this time brought down by two stunned thugs instead of bullets. One row. Two. Three. That's how far that kick sends them before they both hit the floor, bleeding and groaning.

But alive.

A psycho of his word, I think.

Rags' hooded head turns toward me.

I don't move.

He waits.

I still don't move.

He keeps on waiting.

And I realize, with a weird kind of certainty, that this isn't finished. It can't be. Not until I go over and join him.

There's no sense to the idea, but the feeling's strong.

So, moving as if in a dream, I walk on shaky legs across the floor of crunching, broken glass.

Rags doesn't move as I approach.

Blood drips from his knife.

Our exit from the maze is clear now, ploughed first by guns and then by flying bad guys. From here, I can even see the fire door. There's no sign of Shanks or the Bernard Bros. Evidently, they bailed, probably when all those bullets started flying.

Between here and there are the thugs. Both look to be in a bad way. I try to feel sorry for them but can't quite manage it. I don't know how badly they've been hurt, but something tells me they're not going to be coming after me anymore. Not tonight.

I look at Rags.

"Thanks," I say.

I don't expect him to reply. But he does. "*Aksepte mwen.*"

It's the same thing he said back in the boxing ring. Of course, I *still* don't know what it means.

I try to form a reply, but nothing comes.

He waits.

I struggle to find my tongue but can't. So, I just sort of shake my head, which he seems to consider an answer. With an odd little tremble, he turns and, in that crazy way he has, vanishes.

Just like that, I'm alone in the middle of a broken maze with one dead body and two mangled killers. So, I do the only thing I can think of, the only thing that makes sense.

I go home.

CHAPTER 8

I'M BROKEN

—WHEN I GET HOME. COMPLETELY BROKEN. I DON'T REALLY REMEMBER leaving the ruined maze, much less Steel Pier. I don't remember the Boardwalk or the faces of the gamblers and other folks I must have passed. But I can imagine their expressions. I can imagine what they must have seen in my eyes.

The first real thing I know is the front entrance of the Calm Sea Arms. It looks like an island in the middle of a raging ocean. Safe, comforting.

I'm shaking badly by the time I push my way through the revolving door and enter the lobby. For one horrible second, I think it's empty. None of the other high-schoolers are home yet. Everybody takes their two free hours seriously, and everybody squeezes every last minute out of them. Even the middles aren't around.

Except Corinne.

She's sitting on one of the big old threadbare couches that, together, form what Aunt Kell calls the "hearth," even though it's got no fireplace. It's here that family meetings go down, everything from birthday parties to the "Big Good-Byes," which happen whenever a Nelson Kid is either adopted or, way more likely, turns eighteen and ages out of the System. There's room enough there for all of us, which means that Corinne looks very small as she sits there alone.

At the sight of me, she cups her mouth as if to shut off a scream.

"Hi, pumpkin," I say, trying to smile and totally failing.

She stands and looks at me, her eyes as big as saucers. "Abby? Wh—at happened?"

I almost tell her I'm fine, but I'm not. I almost ask if she's still sick, but right now, that doesn't seem as important as it did. Instead, I stumble down the two carpeted steps between the revolving door and the lobby proper. A part of me wants to go and hug my foster sister, wants it bad. But another part feels—I don't know—*unclean*, I guess, and doesn't want to get that on her. Not her.

"I—" I start to say.

"Oh, dear Lord!"

This comes from the direction of the kitchen. I glance that way and see Aunt Kell emerge through the swinging doors, carrying a small plastic serving tray. Tea and cookies, no doubt for Corinne. It's her go-to whenever there's a child in need of comfort.

But when she sees me, she drops all of it.

An instant later, probably reacting to the noise, Uncle Nick barrels out of his office behind the front desk. He takes in his wife, the fallen snacks, Corinne, and finally me. His face goes ashen.

"Abby!" he exclaims. "What the hell?"

Then the two of them come rushing up to me.

That's when I start crying.

Remember when I said System kids cry alone?

Yeah, well, shit changes.

"Where are you hurt, baby?" Aunt Kell asks. She starts probing my face and neck while Uncle Nick all but yanks the winter coat off me. Corinne stands nearby, her hand still over her mouth.

"What?" I ask.

Aunt Kell's fingers come away sticky and red. "You're bleeding!"

"I... am?"

Uncle Nick says, "It's all over you. My God, Abby! Where does it hurt?"

"It don't," I reply, confused. Then, I suddenly remember the book-end who stumbled across me in the maze. I remember Rags running past me and pouncing on the dude. I remember the spray of—

"It... ain't my blood," I hear myself say.

That stops them both cold. They stare at me, then look at each other, and then start staring at me again. Aunt Kell takes my hands. "Then whose blood is it?"

Before I can answer, Corinne blurts out, "It was *him*, wasn't it?"

I feel my stomach drop. I'm surprised it doesn't hit the floor.

"Who?" Uncle Nick demands.

Corinne looks horrorstruck, but there's no missing the guilty expression she's suddenly wearing.

Aunt Kell steps back, her hands on her hips. She's giving us both the "eye" now. "Start talking," she says in that voice she uses when she wants to make absolutely sure she gets what she's after.

"I—" I start to say.

But, again, Corinne beats me to it. "Last night, I asked Abby to take me down to the beach after light's out." She's hanging her head, her eyes glued to her shoes. "I wanted to see the moon on the water."

Uncle Nick's face darkens immediately. Aunt Kell shakes her head, a look of disappointment that any Nelson Kid would recognize in a heartbeat. "Abigail, what were you thinking?"

"I don't know," I say, though I do.

So does Nick. "She was thinking about that damned pier."

His knowing that surprises me, though maybe it shouldn't. I don't exactly hide my love of that place.

I swallow but don't reply.

"We should talk about it later," Aunt Kell tells me in her "firm but fair" tone. "Right now, let's get you cleaned up."

"Not yet," Uncle Nick says, holding up a hand. He's got these long-fingered hands, like a piano player. "Early this morning, a man was found dead on the beach. Under Steel Pier, in fact. Two more were badly hurt. Very badly. They're in the hospital right now."

Again, I swallow but don't reply.

Aunt Kell looks at me in horror. "Abigail! Please tell me you and Corinne don't know anything about—"

Corinne starts crying.

Great, I think.

At that moment, Darlene comes through the revolving door. At the sight of her, all of us go quiet, except Aunt Kell, who calls out, "Hello, dear!" But Darlene, I notice, has got her Walkman on her head, and she's strutting along like she's listening to music. Michael Jackson, probably. She doesn't look at me or anyone else but instead heads right past the hearth and goes straight up the stairs.

I breathe out a sigh of relief. The *last* thing I need is for my sibs to see me looking like this.

"Let's go into my office," Uncle Nick says. "Kelley, bring Corinne. Abby, try not to touch anything. I'll get you a washcloth for your face. Go."

We go.

The Bell Captain's office is small and cramped, even with only four of us in here. I'm on a folding chair in the corner. Aunt Kell doesn't want me sitting on the couch, and I don't blame her. While my coat, which took most of the blood, is already in the wash, my jeans and sneakers aren't exactly untouched.

She and Corinne take the old sofa while Uncle Nick settles himself behind his desk like a king on his throne, or maybe a judge at his bench.

"Now," he says, steepling his fingers in that way he has. He looks at Corinne, who's huddled up against Aunt Kell, still crying. Then he turns to me and, with a sigh, commands, "All of it."

So, I tell him all of it.

As I do, Corinne cries harder, and both my foster parents look at me with mounting shock. When I get done explaining about the stuff that happened under the pier, Aunt Kell asks in a horrified whisper, "Why didn't you *tell* us?"

"We didn't want to get into trouble," I reply.

"Trouble? Baby, you could have been killed! Both of you!" She holds Corinne more tightly against her bosom, something my little sister clearly loves.

"Besides that," Uncle Nick says. "There's a maniac on the loose. You had a responsibility to report what you saw."

I feel my face flush. I lower my eyes.

He asks, "Did you ever see this man's face?"

"No," I reply.

"And he didn't threaten you, either of you?"

"He saved us," Corinne says, still buried against Aunt Kell.

I look up and meet his eyes. "Straight up, Uncle Nick. He saved our lives."

"And killed a man to do it!" Aunt Kell exclaims.

I can't deny it, so I don't reply at all.

"We'll have to call the police," Uncle Nick says thoughtfully. "They'll want statements from both of you."

Corinne and I both nod miserably.

But it's not over.

Uncle Nick says, "Now, what about the blood? *That* didn't happen last night."

"No…"

And I tell them about this afternoon, about the pier.

About Rags.

I don't leave out a thing. It's hard, but I don't.

After I'm finished, Aunt Kell kisses her silver cross and says a prayer.

At the same time, Uncle Nick's hand slaps the desktop, making us all jump. He rarely loses his temper, but when he does, he can be damned scary, like a force of nature. "Abby Lowell!" he exclaims. "What in God's name possessed you? Why would you follow that... lunatic into an abandoned pier? You're smarter than that, or at least I thought you were!"

"I don't know!" I wail. I get that I sound like a child. But it's the truth. I really *don't* know what made me chase after Rags.

I just—did it.

Now, and to my own horror, Aunt Kell starts to cry. It's not something she does often, and even Corinne looks shocked. For most of a minute, no one says anything.

Finally, and in a low voice, Uncle Nick asks, "You were right beside this person. You let him lead you around in that place. Do I have that right?"

I nod, feeling sick. I didn't notice the blood during my whole walk back here, but now I can smell it. It fills my nostrils, sharp and metallic. "Yeah."

"And you still can't tell me what he looks like?"

I shake my head.

"Black or white?"

"Black, I think. I'm pretty sure his hand was black."

"Are you sure it was a 'he?'"

That gives me pause. "I... think so."

"You think so?"

"I dunno. An impression."

"But it could have been a woman?"

Aunt Kell, who's wiping her face with a tissue from the box beside the couch, says, "How could a woman move the way you say he does? How could anybody?"

I shrug.

"I don't know what to make of that part of it," Uncle Nick replies. "Frankly, if it wasn't for the blood that's all over you, Abby, I'd think you imagined it."

For some reason, that pisses me off. "I didn't imagine it! It happened!"

Nick's on his feet in an instant, leaning across the desk. "Don't take that tone with me! I'm not the one in the wrong here, and you goddamn well know it!"

I flinch and look away.

"Nicholas," Aunt Kell admonishes. "Language."

"Sorry," Uncle Nick mutters, sitting back down. "Kelley, you checked her head, right? No cuts? No lumps? Nothing to show she fell or got hit."

"I don't think so," his wife replies. "But let me get her in the shower and clean her properly."

"I can shower by myself," I say

Aunt Kell gives me a pointed look. "Can you?"

"I'm not a child," I tell her irritably. I probably have zero right to be irritable, but there it is.

"Oh, you're not?! Given the way you've been behaving lately, I'm sure you can see my mistake!"

It's a fair point, a *sharp* point, and she stuck it to me good. For a woman who never had children of her own, she's a mom down to her toes. I try to think of something to say back, but nothing comes. So, for a few seconds, the two of us simply glare at each other.

"Abby," Uncle Nick says in that commanding tone of his. When I look at him, my feathers still ruffled, he sits back and steeples his fingers again. "Okay, let's say it all happened pretty much the way you told it. This 'Rags' guy is scary enough, but let's put a pin in him for a minute. You say the lawyer was there? Mr. Shanks."

I nod.

"And you're sure it was the same man who came by this morning."

"It was him."

"Did he see you?"

"Don't think so."

"But you're not certain."

I think back. Think hard. "He didn't see me," I say with more conviction.

"Did any of them?"

"No," I say. Then, shaking my head, I add, "I'm not sure."

"Okay. Now, you mentioned something about a… souvenir… that these brothers are going to be sending us."

Inwardly, I shudder. I kind of glossed over the bit where Baldy ordered Kaplan's hands to be sent to his brother and his head to the hotel — not because I don't think the Nelsons should know. They absolutely should.

But Corinne's already shook up enough.

Now, though —

I say, "It's going to be bad, Uncle Nick."

He looks levelly at me. "How bad?"

I glance back at Aunt Kell. She sees something in my face and pulls Corinne close, covering the girl's ears.

To Uncle Nick, I say quietly, "Mr. Kaplan's head."

His face goes ashen again. Aunt Kell bites her lip.

For something like a half-minute, nobody says anything.

Finally, clearing his throat, Uncle Nick breaks the silence. "All right. I'm going to call the police. Kelley, why don't you take the kids upstairs. Abby does need to get cleaned up. But then bring them back down. I'm sure the cops will want to talk to them both."

"Are we going to jail?" Corinne asks, once more on the edge of tears. Honestly, sometimes that girl's too much.

But it's a good question. Corinne's blameless, of course. And so am I, at least for last night. But this afternoon involved what some folks would likely call "breaking and entering." That's bad enough. But did what happened with Rags also kind of fit "aiding and abetting?"

The idea makes my insides twist.

"Nobody's going to jail, baby," Aunt Kell tells her.

Uncle Nick says nothing.

At that moment, somebody knocks on the door. All of us jump about a foot. Corinne makes a noise that's more than a gasp but less than a scream.

"Who is it?" Aunt Kell asks.

"It's Darlene. Jimmy just came in carrying a package. He says somebody left it out front. It's addressed to Uncle Nick."

I look at my foster father. He looks back at me. We're both thinking the same thing.

Facing the door, Uncle Nick says, "Just leave it there, Darlene. Thanks." Then he turns back to us. "Upstairs. All three of you."

Aunt Kell is off the couch in a moment. She's all business, her arm around Corinne's thin shoulders. "Come along, Abby."

As Aunt Kell opens the office door, we both spot the package Darlene left. It's big and square, heavy cardboard. The address is scrawled across it in black marker. There's no postage. This was a drop-off, not a mailing. Some things, I guess, shouldn't be put through the post.

"What's that?" Corinne asks. She knows something's being kept from her. I can tell by the look on her face.

"Nothing important, baby," Aunt Kell says, leading her by the hand.

I look over my shoulder at Uncle Nick, who's come out from behind his desk. "Go on," he tells me. "I'll take care of it."

So, I do.

The lobby's empty. Looks like Darlene headed back up to the Girl's Dorm. Aunt Kell marches Corinne and me up to our rooms. At my door, she says, "Go in and get yourself some clean clothes. I'll get Corinne here settled and then heat up your shower. "

I nod miserably.

As the two of them head down the hallway, I open my bedroom door.

On the floor is a sheet of paper. It's torn, lined loose-leaf, clearly ripped out of somebody's marble composition book.

On it is a single number.

11.

Apparently, Darlene wasn't as buried in her Walkman as I thought. She's called a hearing—for eleven o'clock tonight.

Crap. That's just great.

CHAPTER 9

COPS ARE SCARY

—AND ALWAYS HAVE BEEN, AT LEAST AS FAR AS I'M CONCERNED. MY foster parents are all about "the law" and "what's right." But I learned way back that those two are definitely *not* the same thing, at least not in Atlantic City. In this town, there's a long history of the police running their own games. Pretty much every kid under this roof, each of us a vet of the System, knows it.

The only folks who don't are Uncle Nick and Aunt Kell.

Corinne and me get questioned by two of them, a man in uniform and a woman in plainclothes. The woman, who introduces herself as Detective Rauch, is clearly in charge and does most of the talking. Her manner's easy, conversational, and she puts out a pretty decent vibe. She smiles with what looks like real sympathy when we tell our story yet again.

The dude, a patrolman named Carfanno, is something else altogether. He's a smirker. I get the feeling he doesn't much like Rauch and likes having to take orders from her even less. Throughout most of our retelling, he just stands in the background, leaning against the wall with his arms crossed and one foot braced up like he's just waiting for a reason to come at us.

We're in the pantry, a big storage room right next to the kitchen. It's where Aunt Kell keeps the dry goods, and there are boxes everywhere. Dozens of them. That's what Corinne and I are sitting on instead of chairs. It's comfortable enough. Coming in here was Uncle Nick's idea. The pantry's got more room than his office, and it offers more privacy.

For her part, Aunt Kell stays out in the lobby, welcoming the other kids as they come home—and making sure they all stay out of the kitchen. While she's promised not to tell my sibs what's going down, there's sure-as-shit no missing the cop car out front. Between that and what Darlene saw in the lobby—well, they all know something's up and that it's not good.

I'm going to get an earful about it tonight at the hearing.

The cops ask loads of questions, sometimes the same questions asked a different way. Corinne gets tired fast, and I try my best to fill in the blanks for her. For most of it, Uncle Nick stays with us

But then, as the questions wear thin, Carfanno makes a suggestion. He convinces his boss to split Corinne and me up. Uncle Nick doesn't like the idea, but cops are cops, so he goes along. They decide that he, Rauch, and Corinne will head into the Bell Captain's office while I stay here with Officer Smirk.

"You okay with that, Abby?" Uncle Nick asks me.

I'm *not* okay with it, not one bit. But I get that Corinne's only nine and needs him more than I do. I don't like the dude he's leaving me alone with, but I can handle him. So, I tell him it's cool.

Yeah. How stupid am I?

Once they're gone, Carfanno has me go over it again, the "it" being Rags. He's a tall thin white dude with a pointed nose and deep-set eyes that seem to drill into me. Within a minute or two, he's come in real close, looming over where I'm sitting. I pretend it doesn't intimidate me. I tell myself it's fine. I can hear Aunt Kell out in the kitchen, cleaning up. I can yell for her if I need to.

Even so, I feel very alone right now.

"So, little lady," the cop says, throwing up something that's supposed to be a smile behind his laser-beam eyes. "Tell me again how you met this guy. What's his name? Rags?"

"That's just what I call him," I reply. "I don't know his name."

"You don't?" He acts surprised. "I thought you two were friends."

Friends? I don't get exactly what the deal is with me and Rags, but I sure wouldn't call it "friends." "I first saw him last night and then again today after school. I don't think he's said more than five words to me. How's that make us friends?"

"Well, seems to me that both times you got yourself in trouble, and he showed up to bail you out. Sounds like a friend to me."

Put like that, it kinda does. But I still don't trust your smiling ass.

I don't reply.

He looms a little closer. I do my best not to squirm. "So, from what you're saying," he tells me. "Your friend Rags has killed at least two men. Does that sound about right?"

"I guess."

"And assaulted how many others? Five? Six? Hurt them pretty bad from what you've been saying."

"I guess.

He smiles dangerously. "Now, Abigail, why don't you tell me who he is."

"I don't know."

He leans in really close and whispers in my ear, "I don't believe you."

This dude's wrong—just *wrong*. I've known more than a few cops over the years. Every kid growing up a ward of the state does. Most of them at least make an effort to be nice, though it usually comes off as a little phony. But this one's in a different league. He's *trying* to scare me.

Shit, he *is* scaring me.

Once again, I think about yelling. If I do, Aunt Kell will come running. And, if I know her, she'll do it with a skillet in one hand.

But then Officer Smirk straightens up and says, "Easy, girl. You and me, we're just having a quiet chat. You make a fuss, and I'll have to tell your fosters that you went for my gun. If that happens… well, you're liable to find your pretty self in Juvie… or at the very least yanked out of here and reassigned to another home. You want that?"

I don't. The very idea terrifies me.

The Calm Sea Arms is the only home I've ever had.

I swallow and shake my head.

"Good. Now, then. I want you to tell me your friend's name."

"If I knew it, I would," I say. I'm trembling. I hate it, but I am. Even so, it's a lie. Whoever it is under all that grime and garbage, the mystery dude who can vanish like smoke, move like a spider, and kill like swatting flies, Smirk's right about this much: he has been there for me.

No way in hell am I ratting him out.

Officer Smirk stands there for a moment, considering. Then he turns and picks a plastic container up off the floor. It kind of looks like a cooler, with soft sides and a long canvas handle. It's zippered shut, and the word "EVIDENCE" is printed all over it in big block letters.

I stare at it for a long moment, not understanding.

Then suddenly I *do*, and my whole body goes cold.

When the cops first showed up, they went into the Bell Captain's Office with Uncle Nick, just the three of them, while Corrine and I waited out in the lobby with Aunt Kell. When they finally returned, that was when we were ushered through the kitchen and into the pantry. I'm pretty sure Carfanno was carrying this cooler at the time, but I was too nervous to really think about it.

Cops collect evidence. And today, at the Calm Sea Arms, "evidence" means a box delivered to our front door, a box with no return address and no postage.

"You know what's in here, don't you, little girl?" Smirk asks, still grinning his scary-ass grin.

Again, I don't reply—though, of course, I *do* know. It's a fact that must show on my face because Officer Smirk's smirk grows even smirkier.

"Want to see it?" he asks. He says this kind of on the sly like he's sharing a secret with me, like he's doing me a frigging favor.

"No," I say.

"Oh, come on. Take a look."

As he unzips the cooler, I feel my stomach clench up. But I don't say anything, not a word, even when he tilts it so that I can see what's inside. And all the while, I keep thinking, *This has got to be illegal, right? I mean, that's evidence, isn't it? He shouldn't be showing it to nobody, least of all a teenage witness.*

But that's exactly what he's doing.

And I look. I can't help myself.

Officer Smirk warns, "Don't scream now, little lady. If you do, you know what'll happen…"

Before last night, I'd never seen a dead body, much less a severed head. Since then, violence seems to be dogging my every step. But this is different.

This is right in my face.

Right in my freaking face!

Kaplan's eyes are open and milked over. His skin is gray and hangs loose on his skull. His hair is thickly matted with blood. But his neck is the worst. Whatever decapitated him looks like it must have been dull, or at least serrated, a saw rather than a knife. The stump of the neck is jagged and ripped in places, the skin shredded, reminding me of grated cheese.

Scream? It's all I can do to keep from vomiting!

"Ain't pretty, huh?" Officer Smirk says, sounding almost sympathetic. He gives me a few more seconds—during which, try as I might, I can't seem to pull my eyes away from that dead face. But then, blessedly, he straightens up, zips the cooler closed, and puts it back exactly where it was when he picked it up.

Then he turns to me. "Now, as things are, Mr. Bernard plans on putting somebody *else's* head in a box like that one. This time, it'll be your foster dad… a message to his widow to sell and sell fast. That's how he and his brother do business." When he sees the look of horror on my face, he almost laughs. "Yeah, it's pretty rough, I know. You don't see that kind of thing in this town anymore. But I'll say this, the Bernards pay well, and they know how to get things done. You have to respect that."

Again, I want to scream, but his warning about getting me relocated keeps ringing in my ears. Maybe he can make good, and maybe he can't. But no way am I risking it.

"Here's the good news, little girl," he tells me. "There might just be a way for you, you, in particular, to save him. Mr. Bernard's plans for Mr. Nelson are strictly business. But he's got a *personal* beef with your friend, Rags. What happened with his guys on the pier today has really pissed him off, and I think I can get him to cut your foster folks some slack… give them time to see the sense in just selling and walking away with their skins and some money in their pocket." He leans close. "And all you have to do is give me Rags' name. If you really don't know it, then you need to *find it out*. You hear me, girl?"

I don't—can't—answer.

Fortunately, he doesn't seem to need one. "I'll give you twenty-four hours. That's until this time tomorrow. You call me with that name, and I'll take care of it, easy peasy. But, if you don't, then you can bet on seeing your foster dad's head in the next box. We clear?"

I nod, too horrified to do anything else.

"And you won't tell anybody about this deal, right? You'll keep it between us. Because if you do anything else…" He lets the rest hang in the air.

The air that smells coppery.

"I won't tell," I reply. The words come out thick like they got stuck in my throat.

"Good. That's good." He hands me a slip of paper with a phone number on it. "Call me with the name. Don't be late. I haven't known Mr. Bernard long, but I can already tell you that he doesn't like to be kept waiting. You put that away, now. It wouldn't do for anyone to see it."

I pocket the paper. As I do, footsteps sound out in the kitchen. Timing's everything, I guess.

Officer Smirk does his smirk again as he straightens and steps back from me. Moments later, the door opens, and Uncle Nick comes in with Detective Rauch. Corinne isn't with them.

"We all good here?" Rauch asks Carfanno.

"All good. Abby and me had a nice chat, but I don't think anything new came out of it. She's a good girl. I believe her when she says she's told us all of it."

"You, okay?" Uncle Nick asks me. Apparently, he's seen something in my face.

I manage a smile. It sucks as smiles go, but it's the best I've got just now. "Everything's cool."

He nods as though he accepts my answer, maybe without entirely believing it.

Rauch says, "Well, we have what we need for now."

"Do I gotta sign something?" I ask.

"No, sweetie. You're a minor, so your foster father signed for you. Same with your sister. We're good."

And just like that, they leave, taking the box with them.

Uncle Nick and I walk them out to the lobby and see them off. Then he turns to me, "You sure you're okay?"

"I'm fine."

"Then go get ready for supper. After that, I want you in your room for the night. Homework and bed. You can figure on that being your life for the next two weeks. School and your room. You got that?"

"Yes, sir."

"You'll respect it? You'll respect the grounding?"

"I will, Uncle Nick."

His manner softens, and he pulls me into a gentle hug. I welcome it, *need* it, and it's all I can do not to cry.

"You scared me," he whispers as he holds me. "You scared us both. Promise you won't do it again."

And so, I promise. Just like I promised to "respect my grounding." But both are lies.

Because I've got less than a day to save this man's precious life.

And, later tonight, I've got the hearing.

CHAPTER 10

It's Cold, Dusty, and Creepy

—UP ON THE FOURTH FLOOR, WHICH OF COURSE, IS WHY WE USE IT FOR OUR HEARINGS.

These go back to way before I became a Nelson Kid.

Nobody knows how they started. At least, nobody still in the System and still under this roof. In a way, the fact that they exist at all is kind of a compliment to Aunt Kell and Uncle Nick. Foster kids have this problem with control: we don't have any, so we're always looking for ways to get some. Usually, this control search turns into some kind of rebellion. Petty stealing. Food hoarding. I've talked about it before.

Hearings are like that, but not.

Hearings are the Nelson Kids' way of keeping the peace, of quietly taking care of some of the shit that goes down in the hotel without "bothering" our foster parents. We get that keeping twelve kids healthy and fed is a full-time job, one that runs both of our folks ragged every day, seven days a week. So, when one of us steps out of line—and I mean *way* out of line—more often than not, it's the Nelson Kids who find out about it first. And, again, more often than not, it's the Nelson Kids who deal with it.

Tonight, the one who's stepped out of line is me.

Not anybody can call a hearing. It has to be either the Top Girl or Top Boy. Right now, that's Darlene or Tyrone. This time around, it's Darlene, which kind of sucks. Like I've said before, I'm not exactly her favorite sib.

Hearings get held after lights out. The Nelsons are early-birds and are almost always in bed by ten-thirty. So, hearings usually start after that. Everyone gets a note under their door notifying them of the chosen start time, and the subject of the hearing's usually expected to show up last.

So, it's no surprise that, when I climb the two flights to the fourth floor and head down to Room 420, the furthest room from the Nelsons' side of the hotel, everybody's already there. Since the tods aren't usually invited — they can't keep their mouths shut — there are only eight of them, all sitting Indian-style on the moldy old carpet in a half-circle, with a big lit candle in front of them. All have their coats on because it's cold up here, their breath showing as white vapor in front of their faces. When I step in from the hallway, no one says anything. Knowing what's expected, I cross to the far side of the circle and take my place on the floor, rubbing my hands together for warmth and waiting expectantly.

Nobody bangs a gavel. Nobody rings a bell. This isn't a sorority initiation. Instead, Darlene says, "When I came home from school, Abby was covered in blood, and Corinne was crying."

I glance over at Corinne. Of all the kids, she's the only one not looking at me.

Darlene continues, "I put my stuff in my room and went back downstairs in time to see the four of them, Uncle Nick, Aunt Kell, Abby, and Corinne, go around the front desk to the office and shut the door. So, I went over and listened from outside."

Figures. Should've expected that.

"What'd you hear?" Tyrone asks. He looks huge beside Darlene, who's maybe a hundred pounds soaking wet.

"Abby's friends with a killer," Darlene replies, and the accusation's made all the worse by her matter-of-fact delivery.

The other kids gasp and murmur. Jimmy gapes at me in shock, and I feel myself die a little inside. Jeff scowls. The middle-schoolers look scared.

Sarah says to Darlene, "That ain't what you told me!"

"Yeah, it is!" Top Girl shoots back. "Last night, Abby dragged Corinne out to the beach to see her precious pier, and they both got cornered by a bunch of drugged-out gangbangers. This psycho showed up, killed one of them, and put two in the hospital. Abby told nobody."

"That true?" Jimmy asks. His eyes are wide.

Before I can answer, Corinne does. "Abby didn't drag me," she says in a small voice. "I wanted to see the moon."

Darlene barks out a laugh as if that's the stupidest thing she's ever heard. Beside her, Sarah does the same. Sarah's thing, by the way, is hairstyle mags. Did I tell you that? She buys them every chance she gets and, sometimes, even dumpster dives behind salons or steals them from newsstands. Like she could ever afford to do herself up like the women in those pages. But it makes her a natural ally for Darlene, the Make-Up Queen.

"It's true," I say.

"And then *today*," Darlene goes on. "Abby spots this guy again and follows him into freaking Steel Pier! This time, she runs into that lawyer from this morning and the dudes he works for. They end up hunting her, and, once again, her homeboy kills at least one of them."

"Jesus," Sarah whispers.

"This is crazy," Jeff mutters.

Can't argue with that.

"Abby… what's going on?" Jimmy asks. He's looking directly at me, and something in his face drives away any desire I might have to lie.

"She's batshit crazy!" Darlene exclaims. "That's what's going on!"

"Shut up, Darlene." This comes from Tyrone, his tone firm but surprisingly patient. "Let her talk."

I start to speak, kind of trip over my words, then steady myself and try again. "I don't know what's going on. This dude's scary. There's no doubt about it. But he's also saved me twice. And Corinne, too, last night. It was stupid for us to go out. I know that. And Darlene's right. Corinne went for the moon, but I went with her for the pier."

Darlene points at me as if I've just admitted I'm a witch. "See? What did I say?"

"We've all snuck out," Jimmy says. "This is bigger than that."

"Yeah." This comes from Tish, who hasn't said a thing so far, despite being my closest friend in the house. "We have. You too, Darlene. Don't think we ain't noticed."

Darlene glowers but says nothing.

"Go on, Abbs," Tyrone says. In the candlelight, he kind of looks like a big, friendly bear.

So, I take a deep, shuddering breath and say, "I call him Rags. I don't know his real name. He looks like the street-est street person you'll ever see, smells like a dumpster. But I ain't never seen nobody move the way he does."

"Kung-fu," one of the middles says. His name is Gabe. He's in sixth grade and is all about karate movies.

"More than that," I say. "He's fast… crazy fast."

"And he kills people," Darlene says.

"Yeah. He does that, too."

"Who's he killed?" Jeff asks.

"I told you!" Darlene snaps. "He attacked some bangers last night and killed at least one of them. It was in the newspaper!"

Jeff faces her. He doesn't say much most of the time, but he doesn't intimidate so easy either. And he knows how to handle the Top Girl. "Bangers. So, they had stuff on them? Knives, right?"

"And a gun," I say. "One of them shot at Rags."

"Did they hit him?" Corinne asks, sounding concerned. So, while she witnessed more than I thought last night, more than I would have wanted, at least she didn't see everything.

"No," I tell her, tell them all. "He was too… fast."

"Ain't nobody faster than a bullet," Tyrone remarks.

I don't say anything, mainly because I'm not sure I agree anymore.

"The point," Jeff says. "Is that the guys last night were dangerous on their own. What about the pier today?" He turns to me. "How many did he get?"

A funny choice of words.

"One," I reply. "Though he messed up three others pretty bad."

"Did they have weapons?"

I nod. "Guns. And they used them."

"But he was too fast," Tyrone says. "Right?"

Again, I nod.

"Jesus," whispers Sarah for the second time.

"Seven people!" Darlene points out needlessly. "Seven people either dead or in the hospital because of this lunatic."

"Seven *bad* people," Tish points out.

Sitting between Corinne and Gabe, Lita starts crying. She's the youngest of the middles, especially between the ears, even younger than Corinne. Gabe, her older brother, rubs her back. It's a sweet gesture.

"But not the lawyer," Tyrone says. "Not the dude from this morning. This 'Rags' didn't get him."

"No," I reply. "He was there, but he stayed back."

"Smart," Jeff says.

"Chicken shit," Jimmy says.

"Abby's brought some bad stuff into *our* house!" Darlene points out. "I don't care how 'nasty' these people were. It's because of her that we have to deal with them. Now, what are we gonna do about it?"

"What exactly do you *want* to do about it, Top Girl?" This comes from Tyrone, the Top Boy.

Darlene looks like she'd breathe fire on him if she could, but the fact is he's got a point, and everyone here knows it. The only "punishment" hearings can ever dole out is to tell the Nelsons about whatever the kid's particular transgression is. Well, in my case, they already know. So, from that perspective, this whole late nighttime tribunal thing is pretty — what's the legal word?

"Moot," Jimmy says. "It's all moot. Uncle Nick and Aunt Kell already know."

"I'm grounded for two weeks," I mutter.

Darlene's a bitch, but she's nobody's fool. She knew that full well when she called this hearing. No, her goal here isn't to rat me out, but instead to "freeze" me out, to turn the others against me and make me an outcast in my own home.

What I don't know, not really, is *why*. Sure, we've had our beefs, but this feels a lot bigger than the usual sister-versus-sister rivalry shit.

Then Tyrone says, "Well, it seems to me like maybe this Rags man can help us."

"What?" Sarah asks, looking horrified.

Darlene actually hits him, slapping his shoulder hard. But Tyrone, being something like three times her size, doesn't even notice.

"He's right," Jimmy says. Then, when the angry and horrified looks all turn his way, he adds, "Look, we all know what's going on, even if we don't want to talk about it. The whole Boardwalk is turning into casinos. It's been happening for years now. There are only a few holdouts this close to the ocean, and the Calm Sea Arms is one of them. This isn't the first time somebody's tried to buy the Nelsons out."

"Those were letters," Tish argues. "Not a lawyer at the door."

"That's kinda my point," Jimmy tells her. "This dude —"

"Shanks," I say. "His name's Shanks."

Jimmy offers me a nod. "—Shanks is working for *somebody*, somebody who ain't Resorts or Caesars or the Golden Nugget."

"Who else is there?" Sarah asks.

"Trump?" Jeff suggests. "I hear he wants into Atlantic City."

Jimmy shakes his head. "Nobody that big. We're in a good location here. But it ain't the Boardwalk proper. Valuable real estate, sure, but not prime enough to draw that kind of attention."

Following his thinking, I say, "This could be worse than that."

"Worse?" Darlene asks with a sneer. This whole thing has gotten away from her, and she knows it.

"Yeah," Jimmy agrees. "The big casinos got the green and the political clout, but they also gotta play by the rules. From the get-go in Atlantic City, the Casino Control Commission has shut down the Vegas mobs from getting onto the Boardwalk. But other gangs, smaller ones, are sneaking in… setting up casinos of their own off the boards. I've seen more than a few of 'em around town lately."

"Me, too," Tyrone says.

"Me, too," Tish says.

"Me, too," I say. "Shanks is working for somebody named Bernard. I heard them talking today. They're after this whole block, and they're pushing every business on it out." Then, after bracing myself, I add, "I watched them beat this dude to death, right in front of me. This was in the boxing ring in Steel Pier. Kaplan. His brother owns the drycleaners next door."

"Oh my God…" Darlene whispers. For the first time, she's put away her bitchiness. "I know him. Aunt Kell sends some of her clothes there."

"Not anymore," Jeff mutters.

Jimmy frowns, thinking. Then he meets my eyes and asks, "That box that Uncle Nick got today…" His words trail off.

So, Tyrone finishes for him. "What was in it?"

"You don't wanna know," I reply.

"Jesus," Sarah says for the third time. Aunt Kell would be scolding her if she heard.

"Maybe we should call the cops or something," Gabe says. Beside him, both Lita and Corinne nod enthusiastically. I quietly marvel at them. They're all just young enough to think that's a good idea.

Tyrone, who's had more bad experiences with the A.C. police than most, looks about to reply, but I beat him to the punch. "They sent two cops to talk to Corinne and me today. A man and a woman. At one point, they split us up into separate rooms. The dude stayed with me, alone in the pantry. In there, he told me he's working for Bernard and that 'Mr. Bernard' wants Rags' name, his real name."

"But you don't know it," Jimmy points out.

"No, but he figures I can get it. And if I don't, this Bernard's gonna… do something bad."

"So, Bernard… what? Owns the cops? Bribes them or something?" Tish asks, looking sick to her stomach.

"Maybe just a few," Tyrone says.

"The lady cop was really nice," Corinne remarks.

"Even so, we can't risk it," Jeff says.

"No, we can't," Darlene mutters.

Jimmy turns to me, "Abbs, do you think you can find Rags again?"

"I… don't know. It ain't like we exchanged addresses. Today, it was more like *he* found *me*. But, if I go back to the pier, then maybe."

"But you're grounded, ain'tcha?" This comes from Gabe.

It's adorable. Really.

Everyone ignores him. Darlene turns to Jimmy, "So you want to rat him out to Bernard?"

Jimmy shakes his head. "No."

"Then what?" I ask.

"I think Tyrone's got a point," Jimmy replies. "I think we should ask this dude to help us."

Darlene looks shocked—check that, *scandalized*.

"You're as crazy as *she* is!" And we all know which "she" Darlene is referring to.

"The enemy of my enemy is my friend," Tyrone says.

"Get that out of a fortune cookie?" Darlene demands bitterly.

"He's right," Jimmy says. "Unless you got a better idea… Top Girl."

Darlene opens her mouth and then shuts it again.

Jimmy turns to me. "So, we find him and talk to him and ask him to help us fight Bernard and Shanks."

"Bernards," I correct. "There's two of them. Brothers. A big one and a not-so-big one. I think the not-so-big one is the boss."

"Whatever," Tyrone says. "One thing at a time. You in, Abbs? You up for this?"

"Yeah," I say without much thought. "I'm in. But… it can't wait for tomorrow afternoon."

Sarah asks, "So, you're gonna what? Cut school?"

I shake my head. "I'm going tonight."

"Crazy," Darlene says.

"No, it ain't," Tyrone tells her. "And you'll keep your mouth shut about it to Uncle Nick and Aunt Kell. Right, girl?"

Darlene, for all her faults, doesn't want to be an outcast any more than I do. "Yes. Fine. Right."

"I'll go with you, Abbs," Jimmy says, and, just like that, there are butterflies in my stomach. The very idea of going on some half-baked adventure alone with him is enough to drive back some of the shadows that have been closing around me lately.

But then Tyrone says, "Me, too."
And Tish adds, "And me."
They both smile.
Well, shit.

CHAPTER 11

UP ON THE BOARDWALK

— A COLD WIND BLOWS OFF THE OCEAN, CHILLING ALL FOUR OF US TO THE bone, despite our coats. Seaside winters are like that. Then, to *really* jazz things up, a light rain starts falling the minute we hit the boards.

"Great," Jimmy mutters.

Tish adds, "I'm regretting this already."

Tyrone says nothing.

It's just past midnight. There's not too many folks around. Well, not out on the boards anyway. In the summer, "casino hopping" happens a lot, with tourists moving back and forth between the Nugget, Caesar's, Resorts, and the Trop all night long. But this time of year, with the wind and the cold and the rain, even the hardest of the hardcore slot jockeys are opting to stay put.

We hunker down under our coats as best we can and try to stick together for warmth as we slog along. All the while, I scan the rooftops, looking for some sign of Rags. I know this whole thing was my idea, but now that I'm out here, exhaustion feels like a yoke around my neck.

Just how many times am I gonna put myself in hot water during one twenty-four-hour period, anyhow?

"See anything?" Jimmy asks.

"No," I reply.

"Keep going," Tyrone says.

This time, Tish says nothing.

Steel Pier looms ahead of us, blocky and dark and reaching like a huge arm out across the gray water. The moon's behind the clouds and the casinos cast so much glare that the whole of the pier is bathed in deep shadow.

Even so, I watch for movement anywhere along its silhouette. But either Rags isn't here, or he's choosing not to be seen.

"What do we do if we don't find him?" Tish asks. "I mean, maybe it's raining too hard, and he… I dunno… stayed home or something."

"Don't sound like a 'safe-and-dry-at-home' kinda dude to me," Tyrone tells her. "Right, Abbs?"

I start to reply and then stop, motioning for the others to do the same.

"What?" Jimmy asks. At least he has the good sense to whisper.

I point toward the pier, though not at its roof but instead at the Boardwalk in front of it, where the shadows look deepest.

Tyrone says, "Is that a car?"

"It's that limo," Tish announces. "The one from this morning!"

"Keep it down!" I tell her in a harsh whisper. "Sound carries up here."

"Not in this rain," Jimmy says. And he's probably right.

"Since when can you park a limo on the boards?" Tish asks, actually sounding a little put out.

Tyrone replies, "I seen it before. Back before they opened the gambling places, investors and such would sometimes do it. I think you need a special permit, or at least the right palms greased."

"Maybe it's a high roller," Jimmy suggests. "And Resorts is giving him special treatment." It's possible, I suppose, given that the entrance to Resorts is close by.

Then, as the four of us watch, standing there huddled together in the cold rain, a dude in a chauffeur's cap climbs out from behind the limo's wheel. Wordlessly, he opens the rear door, standing aside to let two men exit.

The first is Baldy Bernard, and, by the lights shining from inside the car, I can see he's dressed in another fancy suit. Straightening, he says something to the limo driver, who nods respectfully.

Next comes Dreads. Except, he doesn't so much exit the limo as kind of *unfold* himself out of it. His legs are long and thick as tree trunks, and his shoulders are broad enough to belong to *two* dudes. He's even bigger than I remember him. I swear the roof of the limo looks like it barely reaches his waist.

Beside me, Tyrone whispers. "Holy Jeez. That's a big one."

"I know," I say. "Those are the two brothers from today in the boxing ring."

Jimmy asks, "The ones who beat the dry cleaner dead?"

"Yeah. The giant with the dreads did that. His brother watched."

Tish says, "Let's get the hell out of here."

"They can't see us," Tyrone assures her. "It's too dark, and there's too much glare from the open car—"

The car door closes, and everything goes black.

A moment later, one of the three men produces a flashlight.

"Okay…" Jimmy says. "*Now*, let's split."

"You all go ahead," I tell him. "I need to see what's happening."

Tish grabs my hand. "Abbs, no way!" She says this louder than I would have liked.

Twenty yards ahead, the dudes suddenly stop moving.

The flashlight beam swings in our direction.

"Come on," Tyrone whispers. He starts to lead us back the way we came. The problem is that the Boardwalk doesn't offer a lot of what anybody would call cover. The shops to our right are all closed and shuttered. To our left are the stairs to the ocean.

Behind us is nothing but wide-open boards.

"No," I say. "This way." As I'm still holding Tish's hand, I pull her along with me, hoping with all my heart that the guys follow.

They do.

I lead them a dozen feet to the beach stairs.

Meanwhile, alerted by our footfalls, the flashlight cuts through the curtain of rain. But, as I hoped, the dude holding it points it first at the shops and only then slowly sweeps it our way. By the time its glow, speckled weirdly by the shadows of countless raindrops, finds our stairs, we've already hit the sand and are crouched safely out of sight.

Words reach me. They're distant but clear enough, almost like a radio signal. *"Who was it?"* A deep voice with an island drawl. Baldy.

"Not sure. Maybe nothing." I don't know this voice. The driver, maybe?

"I'll check it." That one's definitely Dreads. I'd know it anywhere. It's the deepest voice I've ever heard. Just hearing it now makes my stomach knot.

"No, brother. Let's get inside. We're already late." A pause. *"You stay here. Right here. And keep that light on. If you see something suspicious, report it to one of our guys inside. If you see something more-than-suspicious, put it down. Got me?"*

"Yeah," the driver says.

Faint footsteps reach my ears, followed by the sound of a door opening on old hinges.

"They've gone inside the pier," I remark.

"What?" Tyrone asks. "How do you know?"

I blink and look over at him. In the rainy gloom, he's nothing but a big dark shape. No features. "I could hear it. Couldn't you?"

"I didn't hear a thing," he says.

"Me, neither," Jimmy adds.

Tish squeezes my hand. "Can we *please* go home?"

"Go," I tell them. "But I'm here to find Rags."

"Rags ain't here, Abby," says Jimmy.

"No, but he will be."

"How do you know?" This from Tyrone.

"Both times I've seen him, it's been in and around the pier. I think maybe this is where he lives."

"Abbs, this is nuts," Tish says.

"You sound like Darlene," Jimmy remarks.

"Well, maybe she's right!"

"Keep it down," I tell them. "Look, I'm doing this. But there's no reason why you gotta do it with me. Go home. I'll see y'all in the morning."

"I'm going with," Jimmy says.

"Me, too," Tyrone says.

Beside him, I hear Tish sigh one of her sighs. Long and exaggerated. It almost sounds forced, even theatrical, except that she means it. It's just how she sighs. "Look, even if we do go in, we ain't gonna get past whoever they got watching the front door."

I grin. I know that sounds crazy, given the risk we're all about to take. But, somehow, I'm less afraid than—kind of exhilarated. "Who said anything about the front door?"

There's a lot of ogling as I lead them across the sand and to a flight of steps that I'm familiar with. There's a gate that's supposed to block them off from the public, but the padlock's been busted for at least a year. I only have to twist the shackle to slip it free. Then, once I'm through, I put it back the way I found it. Folks, as a rule, don't question what they see, and, at least as far as I know, this little trick's gone unnoticed.

"You do this a lot?" Tyrone asks.

"More than she should," Tish replies for me.

"It's cool." This comes from Jimmy, and I have to turn away to hide my smile.

The stairs are rickety and nothing like quiet, but the surf is close enough to drown out the sound as we climb two flights to the northside walkway and the locked door that, like the gate, isn't so locked. This part's the same route I took this afternoon after school.

A minute later, we're in that staff corridor that leads to the Lobby. I'm more than a little nervous about heading that way, though. Baldy and Dreads walked in through the pier's front entrance, which could very possibly put them right in our path. So, I figure we'll start our search right here and hopefully give the Bernard Bros a wide berth.

Tyrone says, "Shouldn't there be... I dunno... police tape or something? Ain't this a crime scene?"

It was a fair point. I told Rauch and Carfanno all about what happened in here, how two guys ended up dead, one because of Dreads and the other because of Rags. You'd think a ton of cops would be here, taking pictures and drawing chalk outlines.

But they're not. The Theater's quiet, like a tomb.

"I don't know," I say.

"This place is freaking me out," Tish complains.

"Where to, Abbs?" Jimmy asks.

I don't know that either. On the way over here, I figured we might check out the boxing arena upstairs. After all, it's where I stumbled across Rags the last time. But that takes us close to the Hall of Mirrors.

And I don't think I ever want to go there again. I mean *ever*.

But then Tyrone asks in a whisper, "So... where are the bodies?"

"What?"

"The bodies!" he says, still whispering but with an edge I don't much like. "That dry cleaner the Bernards iced, and that dude Rags knifed."

"Gross..." Tish whispers.

Tyrone ignores her, "Where are the bodies at?"

"Gone, probably," I say.

"Let's check."

I swallow dryly. "Um... all that happened upstairs. Let's stay down here, for now, cool?"

But Tyrone says fiercely, "I wanna see them."

"What for?"

"I dunno. I just want to."

"I don't," Tish says.

Jimmy adds, "Me, neither."

"That makes three of us," I say.

I keep my eyes on Tyrone, who regards us all as if we're wearing chicken suits. "Whatever, you wusses. So just tell me where they are. I'll go alone."

"No," I say.

"Why the hell not?"

Jimmy starts to answer, but I beat him to it. "For starters, there are at least two limo-riding psycho killers in here with us, so maybe you don't want to go wandering around by yourself. You're Top Boy, bro. How's about acting like it!"

Tyrone glowers at me, looking more like a pissed-off toddler than a high-school football player. "Okay. Fine. Whatever."

Satisfied, I put a finger to my lips and motion for the rest to follow me.

We start our search in what used to be the aquarium. Of course, the fish and their tanks are long gone. What's left looks like a sad theme room in a bowling alley, just brightly painted walls with sharks and manta rays swimming on them and a tile floor the color of coral. And boxes. Lots of boxes.

There's no sign that *anyone's* been here lately, let alone Rags.

"Doesn't this place have an arcade?" Jimmy whispers at one point.

"That's on the south side of the pier, across the Lobby," I tell him.

"Any games left?"

"Nope. Sold off long ago. It looks like this now, just storage for Resorts."

"Where do you think those two dudes went?" Tish asks.

"I don't know."

"This is stupid, Abbs."

I don't say so, but she might be right.

"Let's look upstairs," Tyrone suggests.

I sigh. He's like a dog with a bone. "Might as well, but we'll skip the Lobby stairs. I know another way."

There's a staff staircase that leads up to the boxing arena, coming out in what used to be the backstage when that place was still a music hall. I lead us that way, wincing each time the old wooden steps creak loudly under somebody's foot. Halfway up, I have them all stop and listen. But the pier's silent.

I'm beginning to think that whatever the Bernards were "late" for isn't happening in the Theater, but someplace else on Steel Pier.

The boxing arena, when we get there, seems to support that idea. It's completely empty. No thugs. No Rags.

"Is that blood?" Tish asks, pointing to the spot up one of the aisles where Rags blinded the first of the bookends.

"Yeah," I say.

Jimmy pulls out a flashlight that he borrowed from the kitchen before we snuck out. Up until now, we haven't needed it. But, with a nod from me, he switches it on, running the light around the big arena. "Over there," he says. "There's more blood in the ring."

He's right. Whatever's left of poor Mr. Kaplan looks like a dark stain on the old canvas boxing floor.

"Damn," Tyrone whispers.

I sigh. "Listen, y'all. The next place to look is the Hall of Mirrors. I was really hoping we'd find him before now. But, since we haven't, you need to get that it might be bad back there, worse than in here. So, if you want me to check it alone, I will."

Tyrone actually laughs. "Not a chance."

Jimmy's less enthused. "Right behind you, Abbs."

Tish looks like she might vomit. It reminds me of Shanks. "Yeah. All for one and that shit."

"Okay," I say. "Let's take it slow."

As we move up the aisle, skirting the blood, I keep listening for the slightest noise. Rags won't make any. But the Bernard Bros will, especially Dreads. But I hear zilch, which convinces me all the more that the Theater's empty.

Except for us, that is.

"Jesus, Mary, and Joseph," Tish gasps as we turn the last corner and step into the big, long room where the mirror maze *used* to be.

"Whoa," Jimmy says.

Tyrone, for his part, utters a low whistle. Then he pushes past me.

"Watch it!" I tell him in a harsh whisper. "There's broken glass everywhere."

"Yeah. Sure."

There's nobody here. Not alive and not dead. Whatever happened after Rags and I split this place this afternoon, somebody clearly came back and cleaned up. The blind dude and the other two who got their asses literally kicked by Rags are probably in the hospital. As for the corpses? Kaplan got carried off by the Bernard Bros to get cut up for delivery. And the bookend? Was he in the morgue, taken by the cops? Or was he in a shallow grave someplace, buried by Baldy and Dreads where he won't get found? A loose end tied off. A covered track.

"More blood," Jimmy says. He's wandered a little way from us and is now standing just inside what's left of the ruined maze.

Wordlessly, the three of us go over there.

It's a lot of blood, a pool of it at least six feet across, *way* more than what was in the boxing ring.

"Jesus," Tish whispers.

"Your dude did this?" Tyrone asks, looking at me.

My mouth is dry. "Um… yeah."

He nods, all somber now. Then he straightens up and says, "Sorry, I had to be sure."

"What?"

Tyrone makes a sour face. "I kinda needed to see if you were telling the truth."

I feel my pissed-off switch getting flipped. "You thought I was *bullshitting* you all?"

"*I* didn't," Jimmy says. When I look at him, I see that Tish is clinging to his arm. It bugs me in a way that I'm not ready to admit to right now.

Tish says, "A part of me hoped…" Her words trail off.

"That I made it all up?" I ask her. "That I'm nuts or something?"

She shrugs. "Just a part of me."

I blow out a sigh. "It's cool. I get it." And I do. We all grew up orphans in Atlantic City. We know how hard the streets can be. People get offed. It happens.

But not like *this*, though. This is next level. Psycho level.

Rags' level.

So maybe I don't blame them for doubting me.

"Ain't nobody here," I tell them all. "We need to keep looking."

"Where?" Jimmy asks. "I mean, we *saw* those dudes come in here. They had to have gone someplace."

"Maybe they already split," Tish suggests hopefully.

I shake my head. "No, didn't you hear? They were late for some kind of meeting. They're definitely on the pier, somewhere."

"I didn't catch that part," Tyrone says.

"Me, neither," Jimmy says.

"Well, I did," I tell them. "Listen, I know this is messed up. All *kinds* of messed up. So, if y'all wanna split, I won't blame you. But I need to find Rags. Time's short. And every bone in my body's telling me that where the Bernards are, Rags'll be."

"Maybe so," Tyrone says. "But if there ain't nobody here, where we gonna look? Those dudes weren't dressed for this weather. Is there another place on this pier where an indoor meeting could happen?"

I think. It doesn't take long. "Just one," I tell them all. "The Golden Dome."

CHAPTER 12

THE GOLDEN DOME

— IS ONE OF THE SADDEST PLACES ON A PIER THAT IS ALREADY PRETTY SAD.

It's a fairly new addition, having been built just twelve years ago, taking the place of a fancy ballroom that stood in the spot forever. By then, Steel Pier was already sinking, financially, I mean, with fewer and fewer people willing to pay the then $3 fare to leave the Boardwalk and check it out.

For a while, the dome was a concert hall, mostly for white singers. David Cassidy played there, so did the Monkees, dudes I've only ever seen in TV reruns. At the time, it must have looked pretty modern, almost Disney World modern. But now, unused and more or less forgotten, it's just kind of pathetic.

Getting there's easy enough.

We slip down the Lobby stairs and out the rear of the Theater. Behind it, in a huge open-air section of the pier, is what amounts to a giant vacant lot, one that happens to stick out over the beach and ocean. In this spot, once upon a time, there was a kind of water circus with dolphin acts, high-divers, and the like. All that's gone now, and, for some reason, the space has been turned into a parking area for old busses and trolley cars, more than a dozen of them. Whether they were put here for the winter season or they're simply derelict, like so much else on the pier, I don't know. To my eyes, it's just more sadness.

As we move quickly through this big space, the rain starts coming down hard. All of us are soaked and cold. I can actually hear Tish's teeth chattering. Not for the first time tonight, or the last for that matter, I feel a deep stab of guilt. Yeah, I know they all volunteered. And, yeah, I know I've been giving them chance after chance to call it quits.

But, for all that, I'm almost desperately glad they're with me.

And so, like I said, guilt.

Beyond the buses and trolleys, the pier keeps going, running past a long flat building where something called Taber's Tarzan Jungle used to be. There's also a row of boarded-up novelty shops, an abandoned

Haunted Ship ride that's been long since stripped for parts, and the site of the once-famous Diving Bell, now just an old sign. As I lead us past them, I see my sibs eyeing up the ruins, and I wonder if any of them feel what I do. Can they almost hear the music, the laughter, the excitement that used to fill this place? Or is it all, to them, just a pile of trash?

I decide not to ask.

Besides, the Golden Dome's right ahead of us. And, based on what I'm seeing, I can already tell I guessed right.

The Bernard Bros' meeting is here.

About twenty feet from the entrance, I stop us all short. A half-dozen dudes mill about under the awning there, talking and smoking.

There are lights on inside. Steel Pier's still got electricity. Parts of it do, anyway, since Resorts uses it to store stuff. But this is the first time I've seen the dome lit up or anything else this far back. We're almost a quarter-mile out over the Atlantic Ocean now, way past the point anybody besides me ever goes.

At least, most of the time.

"Looks like a meeting to me," Tyrone remarks.

"This is crazy," Tish says. "I'm freezing."

"Abbs, you sure you want to go in there?" Jimmy asks.

"I'm sure," I reply.

"You figure *he's* in there?" Tyrone says hopefully.

"Why should he be?" Tish asks, sounding pretty pissed. Can't say I blame her. "He ain't been anywhere else so far. I'm betting he's home watching David Letterman."

I look over at the Golden Dome. I *need* to be in there — though, if you put a gun to my head, I couldn't tell you exactly why. All I can say is that something's happening on my pier tonight, and I've got to know what it is.

Hold up. Did I just call it my *pier?*

"Listen," I say, feeling like a broken record. "Y'all don't gotta do this. It sucks out here, and this whole thing's crazy and probably dangerous as shit. So, please… I'm saying please… just go back the way we came. I got it from here."

"Come with us!" Tish begs.

I shake my head.

"This still about Rags?" Jimmy asks pointedly.

I almost lie. But he deserves better. They all do. "Honestly, I don't know. But I'm going in."

"Then so am I," Jimmy says.

Both Tyrone and Tish nod their agreement, though Tish is a little slower about it.

"Fine," I tell them, hiding my relief. More guilt. "Then I think I know a way in around back."

"You *think*?" Tyrone asks.

I sigh. "I *know* there's a way in around back. I just don't know if *they* know about it."

Apparently, they don't—since, when we get there, there's no sign of any guards. It's an "employees only" door that leads backstage. Like so much else on the pier, it has a busted lock, though in this case, it's only busted because somebody hit it with a brick about a dozen times.

And by "somebody," I mean me.

The minute I open the door a crack, words come leaking through. Whoever it is sounds pissed.

"I don't give two shits how 'busy' you are, Bernard! I'm not used to being kept waiting, especially on cold rainy nights and in a place like this. What the hell made you pick this rat-infested hole, anyway? You don't even own it! Besides, there's word on the street that some serious shit went down here this afternoon, leaving you with three guys in the hospital and one in the ground."

The next voice I hear is Baldy's. No doubt about it. I'd recognize those smooth island undertones anywhere. *"That was a separate thing, Mr. Spagliano. It doesn't concern you or this meeting."*

"If the cops are going to come pouring in here to investigate your 'separate thing,' then it damn well does *concern me!"*

"That won't happen. Believe me when I tell you that the right people have been... convinced... to look the other way. The Atlantic City Police won't be taking any interest in Steel Pier, at least not until I tell them they can."

A third dude calls out, *"Bullshit! Nobody's got that kind of pull!"*

"Yeah!" yelled another. *"How much money does it take to buy a whole police force?"*

That drew some laughs from the crowd, and not kind laughs. More like the laughs you get when you embarrass yourself in class.

Baldy, however, takes it in stride. *"In my experience, not every problem is best solved by throwing money at it. My brother and I used... other methods. I assure you, we won't be disturbed."*

Yet another dude chimes in, sounding bitter. *"Couldn't help but notice that your limo pulled right up on the boards while we all had to park in Resort's garage and walk through the wind and rain."*

But Baldy's got an answer for that one, too. *"A last-minute decision made because we were running late. I apologize for how it may look, but no disrespect was intended."*

"Fine." This sounds like Spagliano again. *"Let's get this over with."*

"Absolutely. Now, I have a slideshow."

"Oh, Christ!" Bitter Dude says. *"What is this, a board meeting?"*

"Of a sort," Baldy replies smoothly. *"Just relax, gentlemen. This won't take long."*

"We goin' in or not?" Tyrone asks me. "You're just standing there!"

"I'm listening," I tell him.

"To what?"

"Never mind. Come on."

I lead them into a tiny entranceway with a short flight of stairs heading up on the left. They're rickety as hell, and so we climb them one at a time, doing our best to limit the creaks. At the top is a long space with a heavy, moth-eaten curtain instead of a right-hand wall. The light's bad in here, but I know from earlier trips that this is the rearmost stage curtain and that it's been hanging like this for at least a decade. The smell of it—mildew and dry rot—hits my nose hard, harder than usual, so that for a moment, it's all I can do not to retch.

Baldy's still talking, though I'm too focused on moving quietly to pay much mind to what he says. Something about zoning and square footage.

At the end of the curtain is a ladder going up into darkness.

"Not happening," Tyrone whispers as I start to climb.

"It's sturdy," I tell him, keeping my voice as low as I can, barely audible. "Just take it slow."

But he shakes his head and, despite the darkness and cold, I can see that he's sweating. "Uh huh. Sorry, sister. I don't do heights."

"Me, neither," Tish says.

I look at Jimmy. He visibly swallows. "You're *all* afraid of heights?" I ask, maybe a little more harshly than I need to.

Jimmy shakes his head. "No. But, Abbs…"

"But what? If we want to see what's happening, there's an old lighting catwalk up there that'll do it for us. It's safe. I've been up there before."

He meets my eyes, and, all of a sudden, I understand something that I didn't until right now. These kids, my sibs, came out here tonight to support me. Sure, they did it for Uncle Nick and Aunt Kell. Of course, they did. But they also did it on *my* say-so and based on *my* accounting of events. Every step of the way, there was risk, even outright danger, but they came anyhow, no matter how many times I offered them an out.

But now I'm asking them to climb an old ladder in the dark and stand thirty feet over a stage on a rickety catwalk that hasn't been used in years. And, on top of that, I'm acting like it's the most natural thing in the world because, to me, it kind of is.

I'm a Creeper.

But they're not.

"It's okay," I say to Jimmy. "It's cool." Then I turn to the others and add, "This time, I mean it. Y'all get outta here."

Tish says again, pleading now, "Come with us."

"I can't. I gotta know what's going down. That dude in there's coming after us. He's coming after Uncle Nick, and he's gonna… hurt him if we don't…" My words trail off.

"Don't *what*, Abby?" Tyrone asks in a pointed whisper.

"Stop him," I reply weakly.

"How?" Jimmy asks.

"We can't," Tish tells me.

"No," I admit. "But Rags can. Go home."

Then, I turn my back and start climbing again. I don't look down, not because the height bothers me, but because I don't want to see them gone down there. Right now, and for the first time, I don't want to be alone on Steel Pier.

So, I climb.

At the top, the catwalk wobbles more than I remember. I've only risked coming up here once before, after school about two months ago when the air was a lot warmer, and there was a lot more light. Right now, I'm moving along in almost pitch darkness except for the glow from Baldy's slide projector.

Any high school kid in America would recognize the scene going on thirty feet below me.

A theater. An auditorium. Maybe two hundred seats, all old and dusty and no doubt creaky with disuse. In the front rows sit about two dozen people, all men, all in suits. None are smiling. They're all looking hard at the dude on the stage, the dude who's talking and working a carousel slide projector while he does. It's a teacher thing, one I've seen a thousand times. But it's different, too. Because Baldy isn't trying to instruct. He's trying to impress.

And so far, I don't think he is.

Then I notice the current slide. It's a photograph, a shot of the front of a place that I'd know in a heartbeat, which I guess is kind of ironic since seeing it almost stops my heart.

The Calm Sea Arms.

And Baldy's saying, "…a squeaky-clean record, and believe you me we looked. To say this old couple runs a tight ship doesn't do it justice. They've had street kids moving through this old place for twenty years, and not one of them has ever had to get moved someplace else. Not one. There've been no complaints against the Nelsons about anything, not sex stuff, not slave labor stuff, not even some drug stuff. Nothing. All of which means we can't touch them, not legally."

"Bullshit." This comes from a short, bull-necked guy in the front row. I recognize the voice. Spagliano, whoever he is. Based on the nods he receives from some of the other audience members, I get the impression that this dude's either in charge of them or pretty close to it. "Nobody's that clean. This Nelson guy's got a past, don't he?"

"'Course he got a past," says a voice, smooth as silk but at the same time sharp as any knife. I know *that* voice too, and hearing it sends a chill down my back. Leaning over the railing, I peer toward stage left. Standing there, half-buried in shadow, is Dreads. And beside him, almost hilariously dwarfed by his size, is the old woman from the limo.

"You got the blood in you, child."

She looks the same, ancient without seeming exactly old. She's wearing a dark-colored dress and a velvet jacket with buttons that gleam like gold. Bones still litter her tightly braided hair. But that's not all of it. It's not even the worst of it. Her *eyes* — they shine, almost like an animal's in the dark, and I swear it looks if as the shadows aren't just surrounding her but *coming* from her, as though she sweats shadows the way most of us sweat water.

Just seeing her makes my stomach clench.

Without stepping forward, without moving a muscle, she seems to have grabbed the room the way a hand grabs a throat. "Everybody got a past," she says, *almost sings,* in her thick island cadence. "He once liked him the dice too much, ran up some debt. But that there's an old stain, and it's off his soul now, probably for good. What Nicholas Nelson holds in his heart these days is *virtue.*" She adds an edge to the last word as if it's a curse. "A woman's virtue by the smell of it. Kelley Nelson's, his wife's virtue. Oh, yes. She's the one who cast off his demons. I'm sure of it. His love for her is his strength."

"Who the hell is this?" Spagliano demands, rising to his feet. He's not a big man, but he carries himself like he is.

Baldy fixes the dude with a hard stare, all of his earlier calm respect gone. "This is my Grann," he says. "And she's forgotten more about the world than you'll ever know."

Spagliano sneers at this. A few of the others laugh, but I notice the laughter's subdued. You know, like laughter in a church—or at a funeral. "Your sweet little Granny, huh? Well, that's just precious. Thing is, Bernard, I'm an old-fashioned guy. I don't happen to think that women belong at meetings like this. *Business* meetings. Or, if they have to be here, I think they should at least keep their mouths shut."

Dreads starts forward, his ham-sized fists clenched, but Grann puts a hand on his arm. Though she's maybe a third his size, the gesture stops him at once. Then, before Baldy can respond to Spagliano, she does it for him. "My name," she says, drawing herself up to a full height that, while nothing like tall, somehow *looks* tall, "is Adelaide de la Fosse. Madame Adelaide to you, fine sir. And, since my grandson here…" She nods to Baldy. "…has gone to such trouble to educate y'all, it seems only proper for you to listen." Her accent is thick, kind of French, but at the same time not. But, more than that, there's a power in her voice, subtle yet strong. It seems to fill the auditorium. I can almost sense it coursing through the catwalk railing under my hands.

Spagliano laughs uproariously. Maybe he can't feel the energy, though I notice that nobody else in the audience laughs with him. "No, you *listen*, lady!" He says, pointing a beefy finger at her. "*My* name is Tony Spagliano, and I don't take shit from any old—"

Madame Adelaide raises a hand. It's a small gesture, almost casual. At the same time, she says, "*Silans,*" in a whisper that's nevertheless somehow loud enough for everyone to hear. I don't know what the word means, but its effect is clear and immediate.

Spagliano halts mid-sentence, his eyes widening. When his mouth moves again, no sound comes out. Then he clutches his throat like he's just been Darth Vader-ed and falls back into his chair. Immediately, the four men closest to him, his homies, I guess, all start tending to him, asking what's wrong.

"Grann?" Baldy says nervously.

"Don't fret, Simon," the old woman replies. "He's right as rain. He just won't be talking again tonight. And, being a talker, that scares him a little. Why don't you go on with your… what'd you call it, *cher*?"

"My presentation," Simon says.

"*Ah oui.* Go on, now. Misye Spagliano will be keeping his peace."

But Simon looks skeptical, and it's easy enough to see why. Half of the other audience members are on their feet now, staring at Spagliano as if he's caught fire or something. By now, the dude in question seems to have calmed down—at least a little, though his hand, its pinky ring shining in the projector's backwash, stays at his throat. Around him, a couple of his thugs are reaching inside their jackets, but their boss shakes his head, motioning for them to sit.

On the stage, Madame Adelaide and her grandsons haven't moved an inch.

Some of the other dudes in the audience look like they want to bolt. But, when Spagliano's guys settle down, so do they. Gradually, everyone takes their seats again, though this time, the smug smiles and laughs, nervous or otherwise, are gone.

How the hell did she do that?

"*Maji.*"

I almost jump right out of my skin.

Rags is standing beside me, just inches away. How I didn't see him, or *smell* him, for that matter, is a complete mystery. He's leaning over the catwalk railing like I am, our postures almost identical. All his attention's fixed on Madame Adelaide.

That word he just used…

Did he just say… magic?

Maybe yes and maybe no. Another mystery for another time. Right now—well, I'm just glad he's here.

I know. Crazy, right?

Down below, Baldy clears his throat and starts presenting again. But this time, my attention's split. I want to know what the Bernards' got planned for the Nelsons and the hotel, but I also want to talk to Rags. In fact, right now, I don't know which one I want more.

I clear my throat and whisper, "I… I need your help."

His hooded face doesn't turn my way but instead stays locked on the goings-on below us. "*Aksepte mwen.*"

I try not to sound exasperated when I whisper back, "I still don't know what that means!"

He doesn't reply.

Suddenly, I'm pissed off. I want to reach over and throw back that heavy hood of his. But, try as I might, I can't get my hands to leave the railing. A part of me, something that goes deeper than my anger, freezes me rigid.

Do I really want to know who's under there?

What if… what if there's nothing *under there?*

Baldy says, "We've gotten a hold of every other property on the block. All of them, prime off-Boardwalk real estate: a deli, a pawnshop, and a dry cleaner. The dry cleaner was especially tough. The owner just refused to sell. Tragically, his brother turned up dead on the beach a few hours ago, and now he seems downright eager." On the screen, he's showing a drawing of our block of Virginia Avenue. It's hand-sketched but done well, with each of the properties clearly labeled. There's the Calm Sea Arms right in the middle, the biggest of the four boxes. On one side of it, across the alley, is Erlton's Pawn, owned by old Meg Erlton and her family since liquor was illegal, at least according to Aunt Kell. On the other side, the western side, is Kaplan's Dry Cleaning and then the Virginia Avenue Deli.

A murmur moves through the audience. One of them looks about to say something, maybe even protest, but then he glances at Madame Adelaide and thinks better of it.

Baldy smiles, showing a lot of teeth and as much warmth as an arctic blast. "I know what you're all thinking. The Bernard Brothers are playing hardball. That's not how it's done in A.C., not anymore. These days, with gambling legal, there's plenty of opportunity without drawing that kind of… attention."

There are a few nods from the seats, but, again, nobody says a thing. Spagliano is working just fine as an object lesson, which I suppose was the point.

"Weeell," Baldy continues, drawing out the word. "Thing is, my brother Baptiste and I learned a long time ago that, when you want a piece of something, you got to grab it hard. Isn't that right, bro?"

"Yeah," Dreads says.

Their Grann smiles then, and her smile makes Baldy's look like a summer heatwave. "Good boys," she says.

Baldy changes slides. This one's the same as the last. Only now there are "X's" through all of the property boxes except the hotel. "Once we land the orphanage," he says. "We'll be ready for demolition. That'll take us into March of next year. And by late fall, we'll have broken ground on this."

He changes transparencies again. This time, Virginia Avenue is gone. Well, no. That's not quite right. The street's still there. It's just that everything on our side of it is missing, replaced by a single big box, colored a blood red.

"The biggest independent casino/hotel in Atlantic City," Baldy announces proudly. "We plan to call it Bourbon Street. Four floors of games, two theaters, three restaurants, and four hundred and twenty guest rooms, all just steps off the Boardwalk."

He brings up the next slide. This time it's one of those architect's sketches of a broad, blocky building with gleaming windows, a pool on the roof, and Atlantic City's ever-changing skyline behind it. "How will we draw business off the Boardwalk, you ask? Simple. Our liquor will be half-the-price. So will our food and our rooms. But the quality... the quality will be there, but with a touch of class that Caesars, the Tropicana, and any of the others won't match."

This apparently being the end of the show, Baldy switches off the projector and walks forward on the stage until he's lording it over everybody. "It's a money maker, gentlemen. And if you all want a piece of it, we're willing to make that happen. So, questions?"

At first, no one responds. Half of them are looking at Spagliano, whose face mixes scared with seriously pissed off. The other half are eyeing Madame Adelaide with something close to awe. Can't say I blame them.

I mean, she just hexed a dude.

Am I looking at a... witch?

On the stage, Baldy spreads his hands. "Don't be shy, gentlemen," he says with his smarmy smile. "I promise you, my Grann won't give you the same treatment she gave Tony there... so long as you stay respectful. This is a serious opportunity. I thought you were all serious men. Was I wrong?"

So that's what this is: a sales pitch. Now, I don't know much about real estate. Okay, I know nothing about it. But even I can guess that turning that architect's sketch on the screen into a reality is going to take money, a *ton* of money.

Finally, one dude asks a question. Baldy answers it. Another pipes up. Baldy answers him, too. Over the next few minutes, as folks start relaxing, the discussion gets nice and lively. At least, for them it does.

For me, it gets boring as hell. Jeez, even Rags, still standing beside me, seems to slump a bit.

Then, without warning, the whole thing turns interesting, and not in a good way.

"Brother," Dreads calls from somewhere off stage. Until this moment, I didn't even realize he was gone. "Look here."

Then he marches out of the shadows dragging Tyrone by the hair. As big and strong as my football player foster brother may be, his kicking and struggling doesn't slow Baptiste Bernard down even one step as he crosses the stage. At the same time, from the opposite wing, two other dudes appear. Each of them has a gun out and is pushing Jimmy and Tish ahead of them.

Oh, no. Oh, God.

Baldy eyes my sibs, his face all but expressionless. A murmur goes through the audience. Tish is visibly crying. So's Jimmy, but he's doing his best to be more street about it. His back is straight and his jaw's set, even with tears streaming down his cheeks. Meanwhile, Tyrone's cursing like nobody's business, trying uselessly to pry Baptiste's fingers out of his hair.

"Let him up," Simon says to his brother.

With a curt nod, Baptiste reaches down with his free hand, grabs a fistful of Tyrone's coat, and pulls the two-hundred-pound kid to his feet like he's Aunt Kell lifting a toddler. When, still cursing, Tyrone takes a swipe at him, Baptiste sighs and delivers a slap to Tyrone's face that would have knocked him down all over again if the huge dude hadn't kept him upright with his other hand.

Simon looks them over, one at a time. "Don't know them," he finally pronounces.

Then Madame Adelaide says, "I do."

"Grann?"

"These three, and a few others, walked past me this morning on the street outside the hotel."

"You're sure?" Simon asks. Then, when she fixes him with a hard look, quietly adds, "Of course, you are. Sorry, Grann."

Baldy turns back to my sibs. He approaches Tish, who tries to pull back. But the thug behind her prevents it, his body like a wall.

"Little girl," Simon coos. "You from the Calm Sea Arms?"

Tish sobs. Then she nods.

"You two? The same?"

Jimmy says nothing. Tyrone, still reeling from the slap, probably couldn't answer if he tried.

Simon considers. "Well, now. What to do with you…"

"Let us go," Jimmy says. I'm impressed with how steady his voice sounds. He's *got* to be terrified. Shit, these dudes don't even know I'm up here and *I'm* scared out of my mind!

"Yeah?" Simon replies, as if he finds the idea — intriguing. "After what you heard? You figure that would be smart of me, kid?"

Jimmy manages a shrug. "Why not? Nothing illegal's going on here. Even if we tell the cops, they ain't gonna care."

"And if you told Mr. Nelson?"

"It wouldn't be nothing he don't already know."

Simon laughs. "What do you think, Bap? You want to let the little snoops go?"

"Don't care about those two," Dreads replies. "But I want this here one. He thinks he's tough."

It's a lot of talking for the big dude. Too much.

I suddenly feel way colder than the air inside the dome can account for.

"Grann?" Baldy asks.

The old woman regards the kids for a long moment. Then she shakes her head. "Nothing there. Nothing that matters much, anyhow. Do as you will."

Baldy nods. "Okay, bro. You can have your fun with the big one." He turns to Jimmy and Tish. "We'll drop you both out on the boards."

"Wait!" Tish exclaims. "What about Tyrone?"

The Bernard Bros both laugh. Nobody else joins in. "Oh, we'll send him home too, little girl. Except that'll be in pieces. And you can tell the old man as much when you see him. Tell him all his little spies managed to do was get one of them beat to death."

"Don't!" Jimmy screams. He lunges forward, but the thug at his back holds him fast. "Don't you freakin' touch him!"

Baptiste laughs again. "I want that one too."

Simon shrugs and replies, "Who am I to get between a man and his art?"

Oh, sweet Jesus.

This is my fault!

Then, before I even know what's happening, Rags vaults over the railing.

CHAPTER 13

HE FALLS TO THE STAGE

—THIRTY FEET DOWN, IN SOMETHING LIKE SLOW MOTION, HIS ARMS SPREAD and the flaps of his long, ragged coat whipping around him like demon's wings. I expect to see him break against the hard boards of the stage. But, at the same time, I somehow *don't* expect it.

Against all logic, a part of me knows—*knows*—that Rags will land just fine, thank you.

And he does.

His heavy, rotting army boots hit the stage with almost no sound, his appearance in the middle of the action so abrupt that, for several seconds, nobody really notices.

Then, in a blur of motion, the thug holding Tish is grabbed and tossed like a rag doll. Yelling, his arms and legs flailing, the dude sails at least ten feet through the air, right off the stage and out over the audience. The wise guys, if that's what they are, scramble to get out of the way as he hits the seats with an audible crunch of breaking bones.

"What the hell?" Simon Bernard exclaims.

"It's him, boy! It's him!" This comes from Madame Adelaide, and it confuses me since, as far as I know, she's never seen Rags before.

Baptiste drops Tyrone and charges forward, roaring like a bear, but his grandmother's small hand catches his arm. Amazingly, instead of pulling the old woman off her feet, the big dude stops cold, though he strains like an angry dog at the end of its leash.

The audience are all on their feet now. Guns are drawn. A *lot* of guns.

The thug gripping Jimmy pushes him away and turns toward Rags, his pistol coming up. He fires but misses, the shot brushing past Rag's hood and drilling into the curtain behind the projection screen.

Then Rags is on him, the black knife opening the dude up like a pinata. The thug screams, his gun clattering to the floor as he and his killer fall together.

Jimmy stands there, looking dazed. So does Tish. Even Tyrone, always so cocksure, sways on his feet as though drunk.

"Run!" I yell to them. But as high up as I am, I don't know if they can hear me.

"Run!" Rags commands, and he points off-stage with his now bloody, dripping knife.

Tyrone moves first, crossing the stage with his athlete's speed. He comes within arm's reach of Simon, who's drawing his own gun, a shiny nickel-plated revolver that's as big as any I've seen. As my foster brother pushes past him, Baldy points the muzzle at his back.

No!

Rags *blurs*, grabbing hold of Tyrone and yanking him clear just as the pistol fires. The bullet tears into one of the struts that holds up the lighting catwalk. I feel it vibrate through my feet. Meanwhile, Rags puts himself between my sibs and the gun. Tyrone, regaining his balance, takes hold of Jimmy and Tish and starts pulling them backstage toward the way we came in.

Good! I think furiously, desperately. *Get out! Get them out!*

Tish cries, "What about Abby?"

"Don't worry about me!" I call down. "Just go!"

Rags, still facing Simon, says in his raspy voice, "Just go!"

Jimmy stammers, "No… wait…"

"Come on!" Tyrone says, and he all but drags them out of sight.

Seeing this, Simon curses and readies to fire again.

Behind him, Madame Adelaide calls out, "Simon! Don't!" But Baldy ignores her.

Then, just as he's about to pull the trigger, the gun is gone.

In fact, Simon's whole hand is gone.

Rags' black blade arced down and lopped it off as neatly as chopping celery. The cut was so quick that it's a split second before anybody in the auditorium registers it.

Then Baldy screams as blood shoots from the stump.

A lot of blood.

A *ton* of it.

Simon drops to his knees, wailing and clawing at the wound. As he does, Rags moves in on him, raising the knife again.

"*Iwa!*" Madame Adelaide calls. The voice, as before, is thick with command.

Rags pauses. As I watch, his hooded face slowly turns her way. In the audience, about half the dudes have their guns trained on Rags. The other half pour out the door, Spagliano and his homeboys included. Frankly, that's the smarter move for my money.

Baptiste's fists are clenched, and he's visibly trembling. But he's not moving. Not a step. Not so much as a flinch.

Adelaide comes closer. She takes slow steps and keeps her hands in plain sight. Rags follows her every movement, his body poised, making me think of a rattlesnake on the edge of biting.

"*Iwa*," she says again. "*Iwa acheté. Lespri Bondye fè nwa.*"

I've got no idea what language it is, much less what's being said. But Rags seems to get it. At least he isn't attacking her and has apparently lost interest in Simon.

"But who do you belong to?" the old woman asks in English. I notice that her tone is calm, even friendly. "Not those children, surely. You come now to protect them, but you don't belong to any of them. I'd know if you did."

Still, Rags doesn't move.

Simon, with a show of self-control that you kind of have to admire, has pulled off his belt and wound it around the stump. Still on his knees, he's no longer screaming, though his face is twisted in agony, his entire bald head glistening with sweat.

"All of you… get out," Madame Adelaide tells the audience. "Put away your guns. You can't kill it, and if you try, it *will* kill *you* as sure as the sun sets. Mind, it might kill you all anyway. That's what it does. That's what it's *for*. And I ain't sure what's stopped it up until now. But take what blessings you can from it and go while you still got beating hearts. This here meeting's over. If y'all looking to live, get out now."

For a moment, I think it'll work. But then, one of the dudes utters a heavyweight cuss and fires at Rags.

And I think: *Uh oh. Bad idea.*

Rags, who's been standing still on the stage, less than an arm's reach from Simon and with all his attention fixed on Adelaide, blurs yet again. He shoots past Simon and his grandmother and crosses the stage in two lightning-quick bounds. At the footlights, he jumps, clearing an impossible amount of space like a pouncing leopard. The audience dude with the gun keeps firing, his bullets tearing into first the stage's rear curtain and then into the ceiling as he tries, and fails, to follow Rag's flight.

Then the hooded figure lands on him, and the man's throat opens wide.

He drops the pistol. Then he drops himself.

And Rags turns on the others.

Some of them put away their guns and raise their empty hands high. Others *shoot*.

And the ones who do shoot, maybe a dozen of them, all die.

He goes from one to the next, moving too fast to really see. The black blade doesn't flash—you've got to reflect light to "flash." But it cuts, slashing necks and piercing bodies. Men scream. Men fall. Weapons fire, but every shot misses, most of them boring harmlessly into the ceiling as their owners fall dead.

The whole thing takes maybe fifteen seconds.

And, just like that, Rags is on the stage again, covered in blood and not even breathing hard. Behind him are more bodies than I've ever seen, ever wanted to see, ever dreamed of seeing even in my worst nightmare.

Steel Pier's Golden Dome has become a charnel house.

Madame Adelaide, who's been tending to her maimed grandson, now straightens and holds up a steady hand. "Peace, *gadyen*. You're out of enemies here."

Gadyen. Is that… his name?

Rags lowers the knife and just looks at her.

"Do you know me, *iwa acheté*?" the old woman asks carefully. Beside her, Simon has collapsed, either unconscious or close to it. The stump where his right hand used to be is a gory mess, but at least it's no longer bleeding. Did Adelaide do that?

Behind her, Baptiste still stands where she left him, practically trembling with rage as he glares at Rags. "Lemme go, Grann," he says in his rumbling voice. I swear the dude could order ice cream and sound menacing. "I can take him. I can kill him."

His grandmother's head whips around, her eyes flashing dangerously, "Quiet, boy! You know nothing! He'd kill you before you got two steps!"

Dreads' mouth closes, but I can see he doesn't believe her. Still, he hasn't moved, and I suddenly wonder if he even *can* right now, or if Madame Adelaide has somehow frozen him solid, zapping him kind of like the way she zapped Spagliano.

Meanwhile, the old woman faces Rags again, who, like Baptiste, hasn't budged. The knife's still in his hand, the tip of its blade pointed at the floor, dripping red.

"Don't you see before you the one who invited you, *gadyen?*"

Rags speaks. A single word, as dry as any desert. "No."

"No? But I *did*! And no easy task was it, neither. It cost me a piece of my soul to do it, to reach you in the black and pull you to this place. You owe me."

"No," Rags says again.

I expect her to get mad, the way she did with Dreads just now. But instead, she kind of tilts her head, the bones in her hair rattling, and regards him. "So, that's how it be. I may have invited you, but someone else opened the door. Except, they ain't opened it all the way yet. No, you're here but only halfway." She gestures out at the dozen dead men, whose broken bodies litter the first few rows of seats. "Now, halfway is halfway, and it's enough to let you do what you do, be what you are. But it ain't nothing beside what you'll do and be when that door's wide, is it?"

Rags says nothing.

"Leave us, *gadyen*." Madame Adelaide makes a dismissive gesture. "Your work's done for tonight. Whoever your doorkeeper be, they got nothing to fear from us, not now. Go and leave us in peace."

For several long seconds, Rags doesn't move. Then, his shoulders relaxing, he turns and just kind of melts away — vanishing, like he always does.

Suddenly, and for the first time tonight, I'm afraid.

I know that sounds nuts, given everything I've seen, but it's true. Yeah, I was scared earlier, but that was fear for my sibs, not for me. Never once was I worried about my own skin, until now.

As a fresh silence falls over the Golden Dome, I stand very still. The last thing I need is for a creak of the catwalk to betray me.

Slowly, I turn toward the ladder, keeping one eye on the stage below. Down there, Madame Adelaide calls Baptiste to her side, and, together, they gingerly lift Baldy to his feet. Baptiste wants to get him to a hospital, but his grandmother apparently has other ideas. "Find his hand, *cher*. Find it and bring it down with you. I may be able to do something with it."

"But Grann. Who *was* that?"

Impatiently, the old woman replies. "Not a 'who' 'at all, boy! But you know that! You both know just what it was… and yet you and your brother were both still ready to have at him like fools! Now, hurry! We got no time, not if we want to save your brother's hand. Mind me and go find it!"

As Dreads obeys, stomping around in the shadows while he searches, I make my move.

But I only get three steps before I spot a figure standing right at the top of the ladder. For a second, I think it's Rags, and I feel, of all things, a stab of relief. But then Jimmy whispers, "Abbs, where are you?"

"I'm here," I tell him, my voice barely audible. Sound carries in places like this.

He scans the catwalk. Then his eyes settle on me, and he actually jerks a little bit in surprise. "Oh!" he says, his voice is shaky but thankfully not loud enough to be heard down on the stage—I think.

Even so, I put a finger to my lips to shush him.

"I… didn't see you there," Jimmy says, blinking in the bad light.

"Good," I reply. "Means nobody else did neither."

"But it was like you…" His words trail off.

He's scared half crazy. Anyone can see that. But he's also here, and alone. Wherever Tyrone and Tish got to, Jimmy was the one who decided to come back to look for me.

That says something, but it's a something that can wait.

"I was here the whole time," I tell him, smiling despite—well—everything. "Come on, let's split."

Jimmy nods vigorously. "I hear that."

He goes down first, and I follow. Fortunately, while the catwalk might be creaky, the ladder's solid as a rock, and we make no real noise. Outside, there's a bit of chaos, what with the men who split the dome trying to figure out what to do next. Fortunately, it's raining harder than ever, and that's enough of a curtain to hide us as we head back the way we came. Together, Jimmy and me slip through the Theater to the staff doorway and the rickety old stairs that take us down, first to the sand and then back up to the Boardwalk.

Tyrone and Tish are waiting for us in the rain, standing under the light of a lamppost.

At the sight of me, Tish comes rushing forward with her arms spread.

Then she stops and *stares*.

And, Jimmy, seeing me for the first time in good light since we left the catwalk, gasps, and staggers away a step. I look at them both.

"It's okay," I tell them. "I'm fine."

Tyrone comes forward. The smile I saw on him when we stepped back out onto the boards just now is gone. "Abby," he says. "What happened in there?"

"Rags saved you," I reply.

"Yeah, I dig that. But what happened to *you?*"

"Nothing. I was on the catwalk."

"Were you?" Jimmy asks. I hate how wary he looks.

"What the hell's the matter with you all?"

Tish swallows and says, "Abby, you're covered in blood!"

I look down at myself and see, to my horror, that she's right. For the second time that day, I'm Carrie after the bucket fell. Except, this afternoon, I was able to tell myself it was because I was nearby when Rags spilled it.

This time, I was thirty feet up.

"But... I *can't* be," I hear myself say.

Jimmy reaches out tentatively, so tentatively, and takes my hand. I look down at his, realizing with a sick detachment that he'll need to wash it now. Because my own hands are red. Sticky red. Just like my coat and pants. Just like my hair and face. I can *feel* it now. Warm and tacky, like rubber cement.

"Let's get you home," he says. "Let's get you cleaned up."

"Might not need to," Tyrone suggests. "All this rain'll probably rinse you clean before we get back."

"If you don't freeze," Tish says.

"Did you... you know... talk to him?" Tyrone asks carefully.

I swallow. "I started to... but then y'all..." I shake my head. "It went down too fast."

The three of them nod, looking miserable.

"Come on," Jimmy says, giving my hand a squeeze. It suddenly hits me that this is the first time a guy's held my hand. Funny. It felt so natural when he took it that I didn't notice.

I follow my sibs. Wearily, gratefully, I give up the leader thing and let them take me home.

As we go, Madame Adelaide's words keep ringing in my ears.

Gadyen.

Iwa acheté.

Invitations from the "black" and half-open doors.

Yeah, I know. You all probably have it figured out by now, at least partway, right?

Well, what can I say? I don't. Not yet.

Not even close.

CHAPTER 14

WE GO STRAIGHT TO OUR PARENTS

—WAKING THEM EVEN THOUGH IT'S NOW ALMOST TWO IN THE MORNING. We do this together and without even talking about it. After what we saw, what we *lived through*, it seems the most natural thing in the world. All the street cred there is don't make you brave in the face of the likes of Simon and Baptiste Bernard.

Or Rags.

The rain helps with the blood, but not as much as you'd think. By the time we get up to the second floor and back to the Girl's Dorm, I'm no longer covered, exactly. But there's no hiding it. Tish wonders if maybe I should take a shower before—you know—confessing. But I shake my head. We're past hiding what's going on. Uncle Nick and Aunt Kell deserve to know all of it, every bit. More than that, they *need* to know.

Because Uncle Nick's still in the crosshairs.

So, together, we all head down the main staircase, cross the dark lobby, and slip through the door behind the front desk. Beside the Bell Captain's Office, there's also a staff breakroom that our foster folks turned into their bed-chamber. It's got his-and-hers employee bathrooms right outside and even lockers and a shower. Or so Aunt Kell says. For as long as I've been a Nelson Kid, it's been my foster parents' private space. Nobody goes back here without permission.

When Uncle Nick opens the door, bleary from sleep, he looks pissed. Then he takes in our expressions and pissed turns into concerned. Then he gets a good look at *me* and concerned turns into frightened.

"Come on in," he says.

Aunt Kell's already wrapping a robe around her nightgown. It's rare for us to see the Nelsons in anything other than day clothes. Usually, both of them are up, showered, and dressed before any of their fosters have even opened their eyes. The only exception is Christmas, when they dress like Dickens characters. Uncle Nick even has a pointy felt hat with a tassel on the end that he twirls around to make the younger kids laugh.

Okay, sometimes I laugh, too.

At the sight of us, and without asking a single question, Aunt Kell fetches blankets from a handy closet. I can tell by the way she's fidgeting with her cross that we've shaken her badly. My belly feels like there are rocks in it.

"Sit," Uncle Nick commands.

There's only one chair in the room, and Aunt Kell takes that. Nick settles himself on the edge of their queen bed. The rest of us pull up some floor. We don't mind. We're still shivering, but the blankets help — though, as I wrap mine around my shoulders as tight as I can, I can't help thinking of a shroud.

Uncle Nick says, "Now, talk."

So, we do. It's just like in the Bell Captain's office this morning, except there's more of us, and nobody's crying, not even Tish, who cries pretty easy.

We tell them everything, absolutely everything. Even the crazy stuff.

When we're done, Aunt Kell says, "It's awful! Unthinkable!"

Uncle Nick nods. "But, Abby, you haven't explained about the blood."

"That's 'cause I *can't*. I was nowhere near what went down on the stage. Tish, Jimmy, and Tyrone were actually closer. Way closer. In the maze this afternoon, it kind of made sense. But *this*... this don't."

"Okay," he says, more to himself, I think, than me. "Okay."

"We've got to call the police again," his wife announces.

I expect Uncle Nick to agree, but he doesn't. "Not this time."

Aunt Kell looks shocked.

He turns to me, "How sure are you that this policeman I left you alone with is bent?"

"Totally," I tell him. "And he's probably not the only one."

"Probably not. We can't risk the authorities."

"Then what do we do?" Aunt Kell asks him.

"I don't know."

The words are out before I can stop them. "Rags'll help us."

Aunt Kell gasps. "Abigail, you can't be serious!"

"Like Uncle Nicks says," I tell her. "We can't go to the cops. The Bernards have already shown us what they'll do to get what they want.

I saw what was in that box. I *saw* it! Rags is our only shot at fighting them."

"She's right," Jimmy says. "I seen the way that dude moves. It's like nothing I ever… well, he took down the two who had Tish and me without blinking an eye."

"This is horrible!" Aunt Kell whispers. "There's got to be another way, Nick. We could get a lawyer."

When he replies, Uncle Nick's looking right at me. "We can't afford a lawyer. You know that. And, even if we could pay for a Shanks all our own, what makes you think that would stop these people?"

Aunt Kell juts her jaw out. "Then we should just give them what they want. Sell."

This time, Uncle Nick *does* look at her. "You don't mean that."

"I don't *want* to. Of course, I don't. This place, this hotel, this *home*, is my whole life. But Nick, if it's that or more violence, more death…" Her words trail off as a tear slides down one of her cheeks. Impatiently, she wipes it away.

"What would happen to us?" Tish asks. "If you sold, I mean."

"Most of you would get reassigned," Uncle Nick replies. "The only reason the state lets us care for as many kids as we do is because we've got the room, and we've been doing it for twenty years. We're grand-father past a lot of new regulations that would have limited us in all kinds of ways."

"Not just that," his wife adds. "Uncle Nick and I have proven to the city and the state just how good we are. You kids know we were never able to have children of our own. So, instead, we've dedicated our lives to helping as many others as we can. It's a calling."

"A proud one," he says. "And one we'll lose if we have to relocate."

"But what choice is there?" Aunt Kell pleads. "Already, this situation's threatening our family. Even if this Rags person, this *murderer*, is willing to help us, how much more blood does there have to be before we realize it just isn't worth it?"

"I don't want to get reassigned," Jimmy says in a low voice. I glance over and find him looking right at me.

"Me, neither," Tish says.

"None of us do," Tyrone agrees. "But we ain't gonna get much choice."

"I'm not going!" Jimmy says with surprising determination.

Tyrone offers him a pitying glare. "Let's hear you say that when the cops come and get you!"

Aunt Kell's crying openly now, covering her face with her hands. Still on the bed, Uncle Nick looks ten years older. And it suddenly hits me that the closing down of this place will hurt them at least as bad as us. Over the past couple of decades, they've watched tons of kids come in, grow up, and leave. For us, the Calm Sea Arms is a stop on our way out of the System. A good stop, sure. The best. But still just a stop.

But for the Nelsons, this old hotel is *everything.*

"What's a *gadyen*?" I ask.

Everyone goes suddenly quiet. Even Aunt Kell lowers her hands and looks at me.

Finally, it's Nick who answers. "What's that, Abby?"

"*Gadyen.* It's what Madame Adelaide kept calling Rags. You're from Jamaica. Do you know what it means?"

He nods. "It's Creole for 'guardian.'"

"Guardian of what?" Jimmy asks.

I ignore him. "What about..." I have to wrack my memory for a few seconds. "*Iwa?* Or maybe *Iwa acheté?*"

Nick's face turns ashen. "She said *that,* too?"

I nod.

The Nelsons swap a look, one of *those* looks. Aunt Kell says, "It's late. You kids have school tomorrow, though I think I'll write you notes so you can sleep in a couple of extra hours."

"Sleep?" Tyrone says. "Who can sleep?"

"Yeah!" Tish adds. "What are we going to do about all this?"

"Aunt Kelley and I are going to talk it over," Uncle Nick tells her. "And tomorrow, after school, we'll have a house meeting about it."

"I've got football—" Tyrone starts to say. Then his priorities shift, and he adds, "Yeah. Okay."

"Good." Nick rises from the bed. "Upstairs, all of you. And keep quiet about this. No need to worry your siblings."

"It's their asses, too," Jimmy points out.

"I know," Nick replies patiently. "But give Aunt Kell and me a chance to figure things out before everybody starts panicking. Okay?"

"Okay," Jimmy grumbles as we all climb to our feet. I'm bone-tired, more tired than I can remember. But I'm also amped-up. Don't ask me to explain it.

As my sibs file out of the Nelsons' bedroom, I hang back. Then, with Aunt Kell about to shoo me out, I turn and face Uncle Nick. "You know something about this Rags dude, don't you?" I ask.

Nick folds his arms. It's his way of putting up a wall. "Abby, what you and the others did tonight was brave but insanely foolish. You could all have been killed! It's time for you to leave it alone and let us handle it."

Normally, I'd back right down. Foster kids learn early on to avoid battles because battles get you assigned to a new house. And that's the last thing any of us want, especially here at the Calm Sea Arms.

But this time...

"No," I say.

"What was that?" Aunt Kell asks.

"No, I won't let it go."

Uncle Nick takes a step closer. "Abigail," he says, a warning in his voice.

But I raise my chin and face him head-on. "No, listen to me. Rags and me have a... connection. It started last night on the beach, and it's only gotten stronger since. Maybe that's what the blood's about. I don't know. But what I do know is that you two *can't* handle it. I've seen these Bernard dudes up close, and, believe me, you can't. They'll kill you. Then maybe they'll kill all of us. The cops can't help. Lawyers can't help. Family Services won't do nothing but reassign every kid under this roof. You both *know* that!"

"I don't want any more violence!" Aunt Kell says firmly.

"Hold on," Nick tells her. Then he steps around me and shuts the door. By now, Jimmy, Tyrone, and Tish are probably out in the lobby, wondering why I haven't followed on their heels. It's entirely possible one of them might sneak back and listen at the door, the way Darlene did this afternoon.

My foster father turns and faces me.

But, before he can start lecturing—and, believe you me, the man can lecture!—I run up and wrap my arms around his waist. He's startled for a moment, just a moment, and then he gives as good as he's getting, holding me, hugging me, clinging to me.

"I love you," I hear myself say.

It's not something that foster kids say a lot, or hear a lot for that matter, and the Nelsons get that. In the System, you learn to guard your heart because, if you don't, it's likely to get broke—a lot. In the System, "love" is as dangerous a word as "security" or "forever." For this reason, while the Nelsons *show* love to the kids in their charge, they rarely, if ever, actually *say* it.

Because they know, probably from bitter experience, that most of us wouldn't trust them if they did.

Uncle Nick whispers, "I love you, too."

And a part of my heart that's been frozen for — well, for as long as I can remember — thaws.

"We both do, child," Aunt Kell says in her gentlest tone, the one usually reserved for the new kids. "That's why we have to keep you safe… even if it means you leave us, all of you."

I pull back from Uncle Nick, impatiently wiping at tears I didn't realize were there. "That's what I'm saying. You *can't* keep us safe, not from these people. You already got a head-in-a-box delivered here. And that cop told me that if I didn't get him Rags' name, they'll do the same to Uncle Nick… and maybe you, too, Aunt Kell."

I've told them both this already. But repeating it seems to shake Aunt Kell badly all over again. "Sweet Jesus…" she whispers. Then she kisses her silver cross and holds it up as far as its thin chain will let her. This is her way of "kissing it all up to God." It's something she does.

"We'll figure it out," Nick says. "I promise you."

"Without Rags' help," I reply. "That ain't a promise you can keep."

"Abigail…" he begins.

"Maybe if you pack everybody up right now," I tell him. "Maybe if you call Family Services and give us all up before morning, and then split this place, leave everything behind, and disappear, the Bernard Bros might let you go. *Might.* I don't know. But, Uncle Nick, these are dudes who like killing. They like it a lot. You've turned them down. Kaplan, the dry cleaner, turned them down, and his brother got beat to death in front of me. What do you figure'll happen to you and Aunt Kell?"

"So, we… what, young lady?" Aunt Kell asks, sounding both scared and exasperated. "Just let this maniac friend of yours spill more blood trying to defend us?"

"It's what he does," Uncle Nick says. The words surprise me. So does the odd, faraway look in his eyes.

"Uncle Nick," I say carefully, holding his gaze. "Tell me what you know. Please."

"Don't," his wife begs, coming up and touching her husband's arm. "It's dangerous."

"Might already be too late to worry about that, sweetheart." He looks at me then, and I can tell he's thinking, deciding. Uncle Nick's not much of a storyteller. He rarely talks about his past and *never* about his childhood. So, if he's going to do it now, then whatever it is must be important, even crucial.

Finally, resignedly, he says, "Sit back down, Abby."

Without a word, I do, taking the same spot on the area rug.

Then, alone with my parents in their bedroom, my father — maybe the first time I've really thought of him that way — tells me his story.

CHAPTER 15

SOME THINGS ARE BEST FORGOTTEN

—UNCLE NICK TELLS ME. "SOME MEMORIES BRING NOTHING BUT PAIN. I've believed that my whole life, ever since I arrived in this country, ever since I lied about where I come from."

"Jamaica," I say.

He shakes his head. "Haiti."

"Oh."

"I grew up in Thomassique. That's a commune in the mountains of Cerca-la-Source Arrondissement."

"I don't know what any of that means," I say.

He smiles, though there isn't much humor in it. "It's how Haiti and some other countries organize their population. Instead of states, they have departments. Instead of counties, they have arrondissements, and instead of cities or towns, they have communes. They're just words."

I nod.

"The thing to understand is that Thomassique is in the hills on the eastern edge of the country, close to the Dominican border. I remember it being a beautiful, busy place. Rivers where we bathed and the women washed clothes, farming fields, lots of animals, lots of bugs. And churches. Every Sunday, we attended Catholic mass. My mother, my father, my sisters, and me. Every Sunday, from the time I was still in my *kouchèts*."

"What's a *kouchèt*?" I ask.

This time the smile's a little warmer. "Sorry. It's Creole for diapers. I might do more of that as we go along, Abby. The thing is: I remember it all in Creole."

"Okay."

"Okay. But, in Haiti, parts of it anyway, church is church and religion is… religion. Yes, we were Christian. But we were also Vodouist."

"Vodouist?"

"You've probably heard it called 'Voodoo.'"

"Jesus," I whisper.

"Abigail," Aunt Kell remarks, almost absently. "Language."

"Sorry."

Uncle Nick says, "But the real name for it, the *proper* name, is *Vodou*. And it isn't what you see in the movies, Abby. It's a complex religion with a long history. But it's also a quiet faith. There are no cathedrals. Its temples tend to be small and tucked away, hard to find unless you know where to look. But, for all it hides, *Vodou* is everywhere. There's an old adage that Haiti is ninety percent Catholic, ten percent Protestant, and one hundred percent *Vodou*.

"If you wander most any Haitian cemetery, you'll find it. Little traces of homage paid to the *iwa*: discarded rum bottles, burned candles, or food left at a gravesite of someone who recently died. These gifts feed the soul of the departed, so they have the strength in death to return to Ginen, the land of our ancestors."

I ask, "What *is* an… *iwa*?"

"A spirit. Kind of like a saint or maybe an angel. They're the servants of Bondyé, the god of the universe."

I glance over at Aunt Kell, who's sitting in the chair, her hands in her lap. She's a hardcore Baptist and can't be loving this talk about other gods. But she isn't protesting either, and believe me, she would… if she thought she should. I get the feeling that not only does she already know the story Uncle Nick is telling me, but she also knows what it's costing him to tell it.

So, she's keeping her peace.

Uncle Nick goes on, that faraway look still in his eyes. "As a boy, my mother and aunts used to paint the walls of our home with images of *iwa*, taking the faces of Catholic saints to depict them. The Virgin Mother, St. Peter, St. Patrick, and others. I used to fall asleep in my bed looking at them. It was… comforting. *Vodou*, overall, is very comforting. At its heart, it's a gentle religion, a religion of celebration. There were lots of dances and music when I was growing up, and lots of people were taken by the spirits."

I blink. "Taken by spirits?"

He laughed a little. "Oh, yes. *Iwa* love to get inside you and talk and walk around. It renews them, strengthens them. I once saw my aunt taken by the '*crise de iwa*.' That's a kind of trance. Once the *iwa* gets inside you, it pushes your consciousness down, out of the way. Then it enjoys the way the people around it celebrate and worship it. Sometimes it joins in the singing and dancing. The whole thing can last for hours or even days. But then the *iwa* departs, and the person returns, usually exhausted and not remembering the experience at all. That's how it was with my aunt."

Okay. Can I just say it? This is freaking *unreal*. I mean, this is Uncle Nick, the most straight-thinking, level-headed dude I know, talking about spooks getting in your head and going all Exorcist on your ass. I find myself swallowing a dry lump in my throat, not because I don't believe what he's saying.

But because I *do*.

"Were you..." I start to say. Then I swallow again. "Did you ever get... taken?"

He shakes his head. "No. The *iwa* don't possess children. It's too dangerous for them. You need to be an adult. Otherwise..." His words trail off.

"Otherwise, what?" I ask.

Aunt Kell says, "Nick, are you sure?"

"I'm sure," he replies without hesitation. Then he looks at me, hard at me, all the smiling and laughing done. "Abigail, everything I've said has been about the 'good' side of *Vodou*. Now, I need to tell you about the *other* side."

"The bad side?" I ask.

He nods. "They're called *bòkò*, men and women who deal with the dark spirits, *iwa* who've been cast out by the others for being unworthy."

Aunt Kell chimes in, "Like Satan was cast out of Heaven, child."

I guess that's supposed to give me some context.

But all it does is freak me out a little more.

Then Nick says, "Those are called *iwa acheté*."

"Oh," I say with a small shudder.

We're all quiet for a few ticks.

Then, clearing my throat, I ask, "So, those are like... demons?"

"Yes," Aunt Kell replies.

"And no," Nick adds. Glancing at his wife, he explains, "It's a little harder to label some things as 'good' or 'evil' in *Vodou*, Abby. *Iwa acheté* actually means "broken *iwa*," in that they've lost their connection to Bondyé. This leaves them... open to the will of the *bòkò*, who *are* evil. *Iwa acheté* can be anything from pranksters to weapons of bloody revenge. It depends on which of them is being summoned. But, in any case, they're dangerous, *very* dangerous."

"This is insane!" Aunt Kelly exclaims. "Impossible!"

I almost tell her she's wrong. I almost tell her that, in the last twenty-four hours, I've seen Rags move *so* fast that time around him seemed to slow down and that just an hour ago, I watched him drop thirty feet from a catwalk to a stage and land without making a sound. My "impossible bar" is getting pretty high.

"Sweetheart," Uncle Nick says. "I know how you feel. But I've *seen* things, things I can't explain. And, from what Abby's been telling us, so have our kids."

Aunt Kelley studies her husband for a long moment before sticking out her chin and insisting, "It's pagan."

"That's just a word Christians invented. Would you call Buddhism pagan? Or Hinduism? Or Judaism?"

Aunt Kell's usually calm expression twists with anger. Standing up, she points a finger in Uncle Nick's face. "Don't you lecture me, Nicholas Alan Nelson!"

"Vodou is a religion, Kell!" Uncle Nick snaps back, his expression hard. "The one I grew up with. It's no more 'pagan' than yours."

"How dare you even say such a thing?" his wife exclaims.

I've heard them argue before, of course. Every Nelson Kid has. Usually, Uncle Nick holds his own. But this time, all he looks is stricken. In a small voice that doesn't match his big body, he replies, "When I was twelve, a *bòkò* killed my father."

Aunt Kell stops in her tracks, gaping at him. "What did you say?"

Uncle Nick hides his face behind his hands. He's got such large, long-fingered hands, the skin on the back crisscrossed with scars he never talks about. Seeing him now, I don't get the idea that he's crying. I've never seen him cry. Instead, it's more like he's hiding—though not from us, not from Aunt Kell or me, but from a memory.

Aunt Kell comes forward and puts a gentle hand on his shoulder. "You've never told me this."

"I've never told anybody," he replies from behind his hands. "Ever."

"Abigail," Aunt Kell says to me. Her tone is still gentle, her voice not much more than a whisper. "Why don't you leave us alone now. You should wash up and then get some sleep."

But Uncle Nick lowers his hands and says, "No. She needs to hear this."

"Nicky…" It's the first time I've ever heard her call him that. Always, it's either Nick or Nicholas, or maybe "dear" if she's feeling fuzzy.

"Abby's the *reason* I'm telling this story," Uncle Nick tells her. "I locked it all away a long time ago, sweetheart, long before I met you. I didn't think I'd ever open this door again. But now I have to."

"But… why?"

He meets his wife's eyes and holds them. "Because the same evil that took my father from me is *here*, right now. And Abby, God help us, is right in the middle of it."

Aunt Kell seems to consider, studying her husband as if seeing something there that she's never noticed before. Then, with a nod, she takes his hand and sits down on the bed beside him.

Uncle Nick turns to me, lets out a long shuddering sigh, and begins.

"My father was what was called in my hometown a "modern" man. Though a native Haitian, his mother was born in the States and insisted that her son be educated in America. So, after he graduated school, he went to college at the University of Central Florida, studying political science.

"You see, my father had this dream about… remaking Haiti, bringing her into the twentieth century, as he liked to say. There were others like him, modern men and women who pushed for reform. But they were mostly in the cities. Out in our little town, no one spoke of such things. The national government at the time was still more or less a democracy and open to new ideas. But locally, my father was called a 'troublemaker' and, worse, said to speak *pale mal sou Bondyé*, 'ill of God,' which… over the years… made him his fair share of enemies.

"But the worst of them was Desir. He was a farmer who lived outside of town. Very rich. He used to sweep into the market, buying the best meats and fruits and throwing coin around like it grew out of his pockets. Always smiling. Always well dressed. Everyone kowtowed to him, even the local police. Because, in addition to being rich, he was also rumored to be a *bòkò*. Growing up, my friends told me that most of Desir's farmhands were actually zombies."

I laugh a little. I can't help it. "Zombies? Really?"

But Uncle Nick shakes his head, his expression stone-cold serious. "They're not like you see in that *Night of the Living Dead* movie, Abby. Real zombies don't eat folks or any of that nonsense. They're just people who've been singled out and murdered by a *bòkò* and then… brought back."

Aunt Kell looks about to say something, maybe a repeat of her "impossible" line. But she catches herself and squeezes her husband's hand supportively. In way of reply, he puts his other hand, the one with the wedding ring on it, over hers.

He says, "Almost everybody knew someone working those fields, someone they'd buried and mourned. But no one talked about it. Because if you talked too much, then one night the *bòkò* might send for *you*, you might get sick, die, be put in the ground, and then find yourself in those same fields. So, the whole town just looked the other way.

"Except my father.

"Armed with his American education, he openly denounced Desir. He no longer believed in such a thing as a *bòkò*, he said… and, while he couldn't say who the farmhands were, he knew… *knew*… they weren't zombies.

"My mother and sisters begged him to stop, warned him, again and again. But he wouldn't listen. One day, he went so far as to visit Desir personally and accuse him of… well, I never really found out what the accusation was. Since my father didn't believe in… I guess "necromancy" is probably the closest English word… maybe he said Desir was a fraud or some such thing. All I know for sure is that it made the rich farmer angry. Very angry.

"A few days later, my father, a strapping, healthy man in his mid-forties, fell sick. My mother did all the right things. She called the doctor, who simply said it was a fever, took our money, and left. She sat by his bedside and pressed cool rags to his forehead. She prayed. She fretted. So did my sisters.

"But we all knew what it was.

"He died within a week, withering down to nothing before my eyes. There weren't any last words or bits of wisdom for his only son. By the end, he was delirious. I don't think he even knew who he was. Desir had taken not just his life but his identity, bled it out of him from afar.

"And then, two days after we buried him, the *bòkò* took even more.

"When I found the grave desecrated, crudely and hastily dug up, the loose earth thrown everywhere, I ran home and told my mother. Crying, she told me not to talk about it. She told me to forget my father. Pride had been his sin and what had happened, happened. She begged me not to go looking where we both knew he could be found. And I promised.

"Of course, I was lying.

"I went to the farm the next day. And sure enough, there he was, chopping wood behind one of the sheds, still wearing the clothes we'd buried him in. There was no sign of Desir. No sign of anybody, in fact, at least not anybody living. Just zombies. The place was lousy with them. Tilling. Planting. Carrying to and fro. All simple, repetitive tasks. Absolutely nothing that required thought. And, as I watched my father raise the axe and bring it down, over and over, I knew in my gut that he'd be doing that until his body literally rotted out around him. Only then… only *then*, would that goddamned *bòkò* let him rest.

"Unless I did something.

"Maybe I should have waited at least until dark. The chances were good he'd still be out there. Zombies don't sleep. But I couldn't. I just marched over to where he stood, the man who'd given me life.

"He didn't do a thing as I approached. Even when I called to him, he didn't reply or even look up. He just kept chopping wood. For most of a minute, I stood there, watching him. I don't know if I was screwing up my courage or just trapped by a kind of morbid fascination. But it took all I had to finally reach out and take the axe from him as he lifted it for another swing.

"He gave it up without any protest at all. After I had it, he just stood rooted in his spot, saying nothing, seeing nothing. A shadow, not a man.

"Now, I'd heard that there were a few ways to kill a zombie. Some suggested pouring salt in his mouth and sewing his lips shut. Some suggested touching him with a crucifix or splashing him with holy water.

"But there was only one way that, to my mind, was completely certain.

"With tears in my eyes, I swung the axe at my father's neck. He didn't try to defend himself. He didn't even move. But one cut didn't do it. The axe wasn't very sharp, and I wasn't very strong back then. Besides, such things aren't like in the movies. Not at all.

"With the first blow, the thing that had been my father staggered but didn't fall or make any sound. There wasn't even any blood. After all, his heart didn't beat anymore. Groaning, I pulled back and tried again. And again. Finally, he went down, landing hard in the dirt at my feet, his body jerking as if he was having a fit.

"I remember saying, 'I'm sorry, Papa.'

"Then, raising the axe high, I brought it down a final time, putting all of my anger and grief and horror into it…

"…and cut off my father's head.

"He finally stopped jerking.

"As I dropped the axe and turned to leave, I saw Desir.

"He stood at the door to his house, across the yard. For a moment, our eyes met. He wasn't a big man and of no particular age. If I had to guess, I'd put him at fifty, but he might have been sixty or forty for all I knew. At first glance, there was nothing impressive or memorable about him.

"Nevertheless, I could feel his power. Even from that distance, I could *feel* it.

"Then he smiled and offered me a wave.

"I ran home and confessed to my mother. To this day, I don't know if she was glad, or horrified, or both. She just pulled me close, told me she loved me, and then said that I needed to go to America. She would send me to my grandmother's family in New Jersey.

"I didn't want to go, of course. My family, my friends, my life were in Thomassique. I was flush from what I'd done, which I didn't call murder and still don't. My father had already been dead. I'd simply cut his chains, released him from bondage. And now I thought I could take on the *bòkò*, single-handed if necessary, and finally end his tyranny over our town.

"But my mother wasn't about to lose a son as well as a husband to such foolishness. Before nightfall, I was packed up and driven north to the sea. My whole family went… and, there on the dock, I had to say goodbye to them all, still too shocked to cry. My mother blessed me and told me to be good, and that was it. All of it happened so fast that it didn't seem real, not until the fishing boat she'd paid to take me to Miami left the dock, and I watched her wave to me from the rail and then turn away.

"Desir had taken everything from *me*, too.

"But my mother had been right. You can't fight these people. If I'd stayed, the *bòkò* would have done to me what he did to my father and countless others. What good a twelve-year-old zombie would be on his farm was debatable, but he would've done it if only for the message it would send.

"I never went back to Haiti, and I never saw my mother again."

Uncle Nick falls silent, holding Aunt Kelly's hands like she's life itself. The whole time he was talking, and I mean the *whole* time, tears ran down his face. Tears from the man who never cries.

Without thinking, I get up on my knees and put my own hands over theirs. For a long time, several minutes at least, the three of us stay just like that. It's an intimate, "family" moment, the first I think I've ever had. A part of me hates it because of the pain that caused it. But another part of me loves it, too.

Finally, clearing his throat, Uncle Nick says, "I told you that story, Abby, because I want you to understand what it is you're up against."

I meet his eyes. They're dry now. It seems his crying is done. "Are you saying you think Rags is a... zombie?"

He shakes his head. "Zombies aren't dangerous. In Haiti, no one fears zombies. We pity them. Instead, we fear *becoming* a zombie. No, Abby. I think this Rags of yours is an *iwa acheté*." He pauses for a moment, and I feel him tremble a little. It makes me tremble too. "And I think he's attached himself to you."

"But what does that mean?" Aunt Kell asks nervously.

"I'm no *bòkò*," Uncle Nick replies. "I don't know for sure how it works. But, from what I heard growing up, an *iwa acheté* is summoned to our world by dark magic. But that's only part of it. Once here, it needs to "attach" to a living person. Someone willing, and it can't be just anybody. It needs to be someone of the right '*ly san*,' the right blood."

"What kind of blood?" I ask.

"Haitian, I guess. I can't really say. But it could be more than that. I seem to remember one of my aunts insisting that not everyone can become a *bòkò*. They need to be born with the magic in them. I don't know how true that is."

"But, Uncle Nick," I protest, and I don't much like how desperate my voice sounds. "You said they gotta be willing. Well, I never wanted any of this! I still don't!"

"I know," he says, and this time one of his big rough hands cups my cheek. "But the way he... it... keeps following you, protecting you, I have to assume that, somehow, that attachment happened, whether you knew it or not."

"Is there something we can do?" Aunt Kell asks. "A doctor, maybe? Or could we... I don't know... find someone who knows about this? About how to break it?"

"You're talking about a *prèt Vodou*," he replies. "A *Vodou* priest. But I don't know of any in this country. In fact, the only *Vodou* practitioner I've ever heard of outside Haiti is this Madame Adelaide that Abby's described. And it sounds to me like she's the one who summoned this *iwa* in the first place."

"Maybe we can go to her tomorrow," Aunt Kell says eagerly. "Maybe Abby can just… I don't know… give it back!"

"We'd have to find her. And since she's the grandmother of the ones trying to evict us, I'm not sure how friendly she's likely to be."

"No," I say. "You can't go near her. Simon and Baptiste are bad enough, but something tells me she's worse than either of them. No way is she gonna help us… or help me."

"Then we'll send you away!" Aunt Kell exclaims. "My sister in Delaware, maybe."

I hate the idea, hate it down to my core. And I almost say so, but Uncle Nick beats me to it. "We can't," he says with another headshake. "The state won't let us, and you know it."

"Well, we have to do something!"

"Let me think on it," Uncle Nick says. He sounds tired, so tired, and I begin to get just how much telling that story has cost him. Maybe some things really *are* best left forgotten. "I still have some relatives in Thomassique. Maybe I can try to call them tomorrow, see if they can at least point me at someone or something that might…" His words slip away and, when he looks at me again, there's pain in his eyes. "I'm sorry, Abby. I don't know."

"It's okay," I tell him.

"No, it's not!" Aunt Kell insists. "We have to do something!"

"We got tomorrow," I say. "We'll figure something out." It's bull-shit, and I know it as soon as I say it. But I just can't stand looking at my father like this: broken, scared, regretful.

"All right," Aunt Kell says, sounding a little breathless. "Nick, I'm going to get Abby up to bed. We'll keep her home from school tomorrow. You get some sleep, and I'll be back in a little bit."

Uncle Nick looks from one to the other of us. He's trying not to show how hopeless I know he feels. He told me that terrible story as a warning, but in the end, all he did was remind himself of how powerless he really is.

Finally, in a shadow of his usual voice, he says, "All right."

As Aunt Kell stands up and starts to lead me out of the bedroom, I give Uncle Nick's big hand a final squeeze and ask, "One more question."

"That's enough, Abigail," Aunt Kell tells me, a little sternly.

But her husband replies, "Sure."

"Ever hear of something like… *'vandan solda?'*"

He looks at me, his brow furrowing. "You mean *vanyan sòlda?*"

Do I? I'm not sure.

But, out loud, I reply, "I guess so."

"It's more Creole," he says, still looking confused. "It means valiant soldier. Why?"

Because it's what Rags calls me…

I almost tell him that. After all, I haven't held back much of anything tonight. But right now, I think maybe both of us are too tired to go down yet another rabbit hole. "Forget it," I finally say. "Just something I heard."

Aunt Kell marches me through the lobby and up the staircase. Neither of us says anything. The rest of the Girl's Dorm is dark and quiet when we get there. Everyone's in bed. Well, either that or they're all meeting on the roof or up on the fourth floor again. Things being what they are in the Calm Sea Arms lately, curfew almost seems like a joke. At my bedroom door, Aunt Kell gives me a quick hug. "Get your towel and have another shower. Try to be quiet. Then it's straight to bed."

"Okay," I tell her.

"And say your prayers, child. Ask Jesus for His help. We'll get through this."

But I can tell a part of her, maybe a big part, doesn't believe it. Uncle Nick's story or, more to the point, the *truth* of that story, has shaken her bad.

She doesn't know what to do about this any more than he does.

And I think, for maybe the first time since all this started, that I really am totally screwed.

CHAPTER 16

THAT BAD DREAM

—COMES AGAIN. REMEMBER, I MENTIONED IT A WHILE BACK. WELL, THIS is the third night in a row. Now, I'm not exactly what you'd call a "stranger" to nightmares. System kids get them—a lot. Trust me on that.

But this one's a whole other thing.

In it, I'm doing my creep gig on the pier, alone as always. Everything's still and quiet, and the air has a cold bite to it. But I don't mind. I'm dressed for the chill, and I usually like the quiet. It's comforting.

But tonight, for some reason, the quiet's—different.

Something feels wrong.

I'm deep inside the pier. I couldn't even tell you where. I'm not sure the place I find in my nightmare even exists in the real world. But in the dream, it's all totally vivid. I wander down a forgotten, dusty old staircase, turn a handful of corners, and slip along a narrow hall thick with cobwebs and history. At the end is a door, a red door. As I approach it, something tells me I shouldn't be here, that I should be scared. But I'm not. So, I keep walking, step by step, my footfalls creaking on ancient, salt-soaked wood.

You see, what's past that door is *calling* to me.

My hands find the knob. It's cold, very cold, colder than the air can explain. It's like gripping an ice cube. But still, I turn it and push the door open.

Inside I find a chapel. Or maybe a temple.

A wooden altar stands against the far wall of a six-by-eight room with a low ceiling and no windows. What it used to be back in Steel Pier's heyday is a mystery. But clearly, it's been changed. Recycled. Repurposed.

Twisted.

Because it's clear to me in a flash of utter certainty that *this* is the something wrong that I've been feeling. This place is corrupt, ugly, and sour. It hangs over me like a leering vulture, and I feel its "eyes" on me as I step deeper inside. Atop the altar, which wasn't made to honor any god I ever heard of, stand lighted candles in saucers and what looks like an antique mirror. This mirror's small, only eight or nine inches square, its glass cracked and spotted with age.

It's standing upright, propped up on something.

Then I peek behind it and realize that something is a human skull.

That, by itself, almost makes me run.

Almost.

But I don't. Instead, I straighten and look back at the mirror — into it. But there's no reflection there, not of me and not of the room. It's just black. But that's crazy. When I came in here a second ago, I *know* I caught a glimpse of myself in that glass. I know it!

And *that* almost makes me run.

But I don't. Instead, I look *deeper* into the mirror, into the blackness. Except I can see now that it's not completely black. There's a shadow, a shadow that seems to be moving through that inky nothing, back and forth, like a fish in a tank or a tiger in a cage.

And I suddenly realize, again with a certainty I surely can't explain, that *this* is what's been calling me. *This* is what brought me here.

A voice says in a language I don't recognize, "*Aksepte mwen.*"

And I wake up. Right there. Every time.

So, I guess I can't really blame it on the knocking at my door.

The sun's not even up yet.

I don't have a bedside clock. None of us has. But I *do* have the watch Aunt Kell gave me all those years ago. It's maybe my most prized possession, and, as such, it's almost always around my wrist, even when I'm sleeping.

Blearily, I look at it now.

It's early. Way too early, considering how late I was up last night.

Sleepily, I drag myself out of bed and cross the room. As I do, the knocking comes again, loud and pushy. Inwardly, I give a groan. I know only one person in this hotel who'd knock like that at *this* hour.

Sure enough, when I open the door, Darlene's standing there. Her hands are on her hips, and her face looks like somebody painted "judgment" on it. With her are Jeff, Sarah, and Corinne. Jeff and Sarah look uncomfortable. Corinne looks a little scared.

"What?" I ask them.

"Good morning to *you*, too!" Darlene shoots back.

Jeff adds, "Um… Abby, can we come in?"

I sigh heavily. "Sure." Then I turn away, leaving the door open, and return to my bed. My robe's hanging over the footboard. It's a hand-me-down, threadbare terry cloth number, but it's warmer than my jams, so I put it on.

When I turn around, the four of them fill half my little room, the door now shut at their backs.

Darlene says, accusation dripping from every word, "You almost got Tyrone killed last night!"

And Tish and Jimmy, too, I think guiltily. True, I hadn't asked them to come along. But I hadn't done as much as maybe I could have to talk them out of it, either.

"Well?" Darlene demands.

"Well, what?"

"Are you going to explain yourself?"

"I already did."

They all look at me, confused. And, God help me, I come pretty close to laughing. "Uncle Nick and Aunt Kell," I say. "I told them."

"Well, you didn't tell *us*," Darlene says, pointing an accusing finger, courtroom-style. "You didn't tell *me*. You almost got three of our sibs killed, and you didn't tell me!"

Classic Darlene. She's Top Girl, and she wears it like it's a general's star on her shoulder. She orders everyone around, especially the girls on this floor, like we exist only to obey. Upstairs, Tyrone's Top Boy, and he's *never* like that. Most of the time, it's easy to convince yourself that he's just one of the gang because, when you get right down to it, he *is*. The roles of Top Girl and Top Boy got created to help Aunt Kell manage a hotel full of often messed-up kids. Turning it into a License to Boss is just Darlene's spin.

And, for a second, I almost tell her so. But only for a second. Because then I get, maybe for the first time, *why* it's her spin.

I've got the Pier. Corinne's got the moon. Jeff's got motorcycles. Sarah's got her hair styling. Tyrone's got football. And Jimmy's got—well, I'm not really sure what Jimmy's got. But the point is, as I've said before, each of us has our "thing."

And, for Darlene, her "thing" isn't makeup. It's being Top Girl. It's what gets her up in the morning and lets her live yet another day in the New Jersey foster care system, a System that she'll be aging out of in just a few months. That idea *has* to scare her. I know it scares me, and I still have almost two more years.

Remember when I said System kids crave control?

Well, what's being Top Girl to Darlene, if not control?

So, whatever beef she's had with me lately that's turned her into such a bitch where I'm concerned, I guess maybe I can cut her some slack.

Meeting her eye, I say, "I'm sorry."

She blinks. "You're sorry?" She says it like it's a foreign language or something.

"Yeah." I shrug. "I was beat once Aunt Kell and Uncle Nick were done lecturing me. I went straight to bed. But I shouldn't have. I should've gone to you first. I'm sorry about the trouble we all got into tonight. But I didn't *make* nobody do nothing. You know Tyrone. He jumps in feet first. That's just how he is. And Jimmy and Tish... well, they had my back, and there's no way I can say how grateful I am. I'm just glad we all made it out okay."

For several ticks, they look at me.

Then Darlene straightens and says, "I want you to stay away from Tyrone."

"Say... what?"

"I said, you stay away from him. You hear me, Abigail?" She's keeping her voice low, probably so she doesn't draw any attention. The younger girls on the floor, if they hear shouting, are likely to run right to Aunt Kell with it. But, in Darlene's *eyes*, she *is* shouting at me, maybe screaming.

And all of a sudden, something clicks between my ears.

Being Top Girl isn't Darlene's thing after all. She likes it and no doubt figures she's good at it, but it's not what drives her.

Tyrone is.

The same Tyrone who made out with me on the roof last Halloween.

And Darlene's treated me like a mattress stain ever since.

Jesus.

Sarah says, "Um... Darlene, we gotta get downstairs."

"Yeah," Jeff adds. "She's apologized. What else do you want?"

Darlene doesn't look at them. Her eyes are on me, burning like lasers. I hold my ground, but it's not easy. After all these years in the System, I've learned how to stick a pole up my back and face down anybody. But, right now, I want to turn my head and hide. That's how hard she's coming at me.

"Tyrone's my sib. My *friend*," I tell her in a small voice. "That's it."

She steps closer until we're almost nose to nose. In a whisper that's more like a snarl, she says, "It *better* be."

Then she turns, pushes past the others, and stalks out of the room, leaving the door open in her wake.

Sarah looks after her and then back at me. "I didn't know…" she says, her voice trailing off.

"Me, neither," Jeff adds. He looks insanely uncomfortable. He clears his throat as if about to say something more, but then just kind of sighs and follows the Top Girl out into the hall.

"You, okay?" Sarah asks me.

"Guess so," I say.

She nods. "Come on, Corinne." She turns to leave.

But Corinne says, "I wanna talk to Abby."

"You gotta get to school, little lady," Sarah tells her patiently.

But Corinne stamps one foot in that way she has and repeats defiantly, "I wanna talk to Abby!"

It comes out loud, too loud. Sarah looks at me. I shrug. So, after a moment's thought, she shrugs too and disappears out the door.

Corinne watches her go, then turns to me and says, "Sorry."

"For what?"

"For telling Aunt Kell about what happened under the pier night before last."

Night before last. Was that business with the bangers really less than thirty-six hours ago? It feels like a week or a month.

"I was worried about you," I tell her. "You stayed home sick from school."

Her eyes lower. "I was faking."

"I figured."

"I just… I kept seeing it… when I closed my eyes. You know?"

"I know. It's okay."

"Aunt Kell came in to check on me after lunch, and I just started crying. She told me to come downstairs… that she'd make us a snack and we'd talk before you all came home."

Yeah. That's Aunt Kell's superpower.

Corinne swallows. "But then you walked in with that blood all over you… and I just couldn't—"

"It's okay, pumpkin. Really," I tell my little sister. "Come here and sit beside me."

"I gotta go to school."

"Yeah. But somebody'll come up to fetch you. You know that."

She nods and sits down on the bed. I settle myself beside her and put my arm around her. "I wasn't sure what you remembered," I tell her after a moment.

"A lot. Most of it. I saw the men crowding us. Laughing. I remember throwing myself down onto the sand. I know I shouldn't have. You've told me. So have some of the others. But I can't help it. It's what I do when I'm scared. I just try to be… I don't know… small. I try to hide."

"I get it," I tell her. I almost add, yet again, that running would've been smarter. But this isn't the time.

I say, "I shouldn't have gotten you in trouble like that."

A tear rolls down her cheek. Corinne cries easily, *too* easily for a girl in the System, especially in this town. It's something else I've told her about more than once.

"It wasn't your fault. I wanted to see the moon. I don't know why."

"It's your thing."

She looks sideways at me. Then she smiles — a little. "Yeah. Maybe."

"What do you remember about Rags?" I ask.

She shivers under my arm as she looks up at me. "I saw him… I think. But everything happened so fast. At one point, I reached out for you, but you weren't there."

"What? Of course, I was there! I didn't leave you for a second."

Corinne blinks. "I didn't see you."

"Well, I was there, pumpkin."

"Okay."

"I was!"

"Okay. Anyway, I'm sorry."

"You didn't do nothing wrong."

"Yeah, I did. You don't rat out your sister."

I smile at that. While every girl under this roof is, technically, my sib — there aren't many I would call "sister." Corinne's one. And maybe Tish is another. But the rest, nope.

But, for all that, they *are* my family. A big family, sure. Complicated and screwed up in a lot of ways. We all got baggage, tons of it. And we bump heads, argue, and disobey. Even so, at the end of the day, we're all in this together.

"I love you," I tell her. Like with Uncle Nick, I don't think I've ever said those words to her before, or to any of my sibs, for that matter. But it's true. I love this little girl, love her with all I've got.

She throws her thin arms around me.

For a couple of minutes, we stay like that, sitting up on the bed and wrapped around each other.

Then comes a knock at my door.

"Abby?" Jimmy asks. "You got Corinne in there with you?"

"Sure do!" I call back.

Corinne pulls away from me and wipes her nose on the sleeve of her sweater. "Sorry," she says again.

"Quit apologizing. Now, go to school." I smile and give her a light, playful nose tweak. "Beat it, shorty!"

That earns me a laugh. It's good to hear her laugh. Then I watch as she hops off the bed and, with steps that seem a bit lighter than when she entered, crosses my bedroom and opens the door.

Jimmy's standing there. He's dressed in jeans and a New York Jets sweatshirt. Seems everybody in this hotel's ready for the day but me. "There you are!" he says, grinning broadly at Corinne. "Everybody's waiting downstairs. Split, girl!"

With a final wave in my direction, she ducks under Jimmy's arm and disappears down the hallway. I expect Jimmy to follow her, figuring Aunt Kell sent him up here to find Corinne. But he doesn't. Instead, he stands there and just looks at me. "You, okay?" he asks after a heavy pause.

"No," I reply.

"Me, neither. Didn't sleep much. You?"

"Some. Bad dreams, though. Ain't you going to school?"

"Aunt Kell phoned in that I'll be a couple of hours late. Tyrone and Tish, too. We're supposed to be sleeping, but none of us are. Instead, we spent the morning quietly telling the other kids about what went down last night."

I'd forgotten about the two-hour late thing.

Jimmy goes on, "Uncle Nick wants to talk to us again. But he's waiting until everybody else is off to school."

"Great," I mutter.

He shakes his head as if to clear it. "This. All of this. It's so freaking nuts."

"Tell me about it."

"What did you and the Nelsons talk about after the rest of us got chased upstairs?"

I think for a long moment before answering. "Uncle Nick wanted to warn me, I guess."

"Warn you?"

I nod. "But I can't talk about it."

"More secrets, Abbs?"

"It ain't really a secret," I reply. "It's just… It's not my story to tell. Know what I mean?"

"Yeah, I guess I do. But, Abby, I don't want you hiding anymore stuff, at least not from me. After what went down last night, I'm ready to believe just about anything. Besides, the way you were in there…"

"The way I was?"

"In the dome place. You climbed right up to that catwalk when all the rest of us balked. You did it without any hesitation at all."

"It was stupid."

"No, it was courage. Real courage. Not Tyrone's macho crap or the stuff you see on T.V., but honest-to-God nerve. Is that a new thing, or have you always been like that?"

I don't know how to answer that question, so I ask one of my own. "What about your own courage? You came up the ladder to find me after Tyrone and Tish split."

"I was worried about you."

"More than they were?"

"I guess."

"Why?"

For a long moment, he just looks me up and down. Then, without a word, he steps into the room and shuts the door.

Feeling—something, don't ask me what, I slowly rise to my feet. "What're you doing?"

"We got some time," he says, coming closer.

"For… what?"

Then, without any warning at all, he kisses me.

I'll say it's a good kiss. Though, to be honest, I don't really have the experience to know. The only other kissing I've done was with Tyrone, and this is *totally* different from that. Where Tyrone was full of energy, exciting, and even a little rough, what Jimmy brings is slower, gentler, and somehow more electric. When Tyrone was kissing me, it felt kind of one-sided. He was into it and so figured I was too. And I was, to a point.

But with Jimmy, it's more like he's trying his best to make me feel it from my toes to the top of my head.

And he pulls it off—big time.

It goes on for at least a minute. His hands are cupping my face, his fingers strong and yet tender. My arms snake around his waist, pulling myself as close to him as I can. He feels like solid muscle.

Finally, slowly, he pulls his mouth from mine just an inch or two. Then, as I gaze—and that's what it is, *gazing*—into his eyes, he smiles and whispers, "I been wanting to do that for a long time."

I almost laugh, but it comes out a soft, breathy thing. "What… what kept you?"

"Well, after last Halloween, I kinda thought you were into Tyrone."

"What? No!" I blurt this out, maybe a little heavier than I intended. So, after a pause, I regroup. Then I say, "I mean… yeah, we made out that one time and it was nice and all. But it didn't mean anything. I'm not into him." Then, going for broke, I add, "I'm into *you*."

He grins. It's a great grin, full of teeth and joy.

Then he kisses me again.

Holy shit!

This one goes on even longer until I kind of forget all of it. Rags. The Bernards. Heads in boxes. Everything. To call that kiss great is like calling a hurricane windy. It's… well, I know how this sounds.

But it's *healing*.

When we finally break, both of us are breathless. I see his eyes searching my face and wonder what it is he's looking for. Then those eyes flick over to the bed, and I know.

"We can't," I tell him. "If Aunt Kell catches us—"

"You figure it's possible to get in more trouble than we already are?" he asks with a kind of smile I've never seen him wear before.

My mouth goes dry, and my stomach suddenly turns into butter-flies.

He kisses me a third time, and I feel myself, almost without any conscious thought, leading us back toward the bed.

"I've… I've never done this," I tell him as we lower each other down.

"Makes two of us."

"I mean, I'm not even sure how…"

Jimmy's smile turns brilliant, bright as the sun and twice as warm. "I'm betting we'll figure it out."

And we do.

CHAPTER 17

ALL GOOD THINGS

—COME TO AN END, AND THAT MORNING WITH JIMMY AND ME IS NO different. Once we're finished doing — what we did, I lay in the crook of his arm, my ear pressed against the side of his ribcage, listening to him breathe. His heartbeat's slowly going back down to normal. I suppose it's the same with me.

We just broke *the* cardinal rule of the Calm Sea Arms. I'm talking big-time *wrong*.

So, why does it feel so nice?

Actually, it's way more than just 'nice,' being with him like this. It might just be the best I've ever felt. So easy. So natural.

So *real*.

And, let's face it, there hasn't been too much *real* in my life lately.

We don't say much. We just stay there, wrapped up in each other. At any minute, I half-expect Aunt Kell to come knocking for one reason or another. Jimmy, after all, is expected to go to school in an hour or so.

But she doesn't. The other kids, the ones not in trouble, must already be gone, and the hotel's quiet around us. Maybe Aunt Kell's downstairs cleaning the kitchen after breakfast. Or maybe she and Uncle Nick have their heads together right now, trying to settle on a next move against the Bernards.

Either way, in this moment, I can't quite care.

That is until somebody knocks on my door.

Neither of us says a word. We just throw back the covers and jump, naked, off my bed in sudden, mutual consent, and scramble for our clothes. With a jolt of panic, I realize that I can't find my panties. So, in the next instant, I decide to skip them and just pull on my jeans. Jimmy does the same and, as the knocking comes again and time drains off like water through a sieve, he gives me this lopsided "whatcha gonna do?" smile that makes my knees go a little weak.

A third knock. More insistent this time.

I look at Jimmy. He looks back at me. For a moment, I think about hiding him in the closet, or maybe under the bed. But my life's screwed up enough right now without turning it into a sitcom.

Swallowing, I go to the door and open it. Somehow, I know — I *know* — it's going to be Aunt Kell standing there.

And here I am, feeling like a little kid who's gotten her hand stuck in the motherlode of cookie jars.

But it's Tish.

"Abby, there's —" she begins, only to stop when she sees Jimmy. I watch her take in the whole scene. Then her eyes lower to the panties lying bunched on the floor, almost right at my feet.

How the hell did I miss them?

I paste on a smile that wouldn't fool a blind man. "What's up?"

Jimmy just stands there, frozen and staring, like an animal in traffic.

"Um…" Tish says. Then, as whatever urgency brought her here kicks back in, she holds something out to me. It takes me a second to get that it's a green trash bag, empty.

I feel my stomach drop. A jolt of panic hits me, driving away my embarrassment and making mincemeat out of my "morning afterglow."

Tish says, a sob in her voice, "They're relocating everybody today."

"What?" Jimmy exclaims before I can.

"But…" I stammer. "Ain't they all in school?"

Tish shakes her head. "Family Services showed up with two vans and a cop car right before everybody left. I was still asleep. Tyrone, too. Sarah came and woke us up. She told us they were making everyone sit in the lobby while the social workers talked to Uncle Nick and Aunt Kell back in the Bell Captain's Office. After about an hour, they came out. The social workers handed me and Jeff trash bags… told us to collect the personal stuff for the middles and tods and then give the rest out to the highschoolers. You… you know the deal."

And, of course, I do. All of us do.

"Everybody's in the lobby waiting," Tish says. "I'm supposed to tell you to get dressed, pack up, and come straight down."

Bullshit.

Before I know I'm going to, I push past her and march down the hall toward the stairs. Outside of every door I pass is a trash bag that's full of that sib's belongings and tied shut. While Jimmy and I were doing our thing, Tish was doing this.

I feel sick.

By the time I reach the top of the main staircase, I can already hear yelling and crying coming from the lobby. A second later, Tish and Jimmy run up behind me.

Jimmy tries to take my hand, but I shake him off.

Heading down, I spot Uncle Nick right up in the face of two local cops. One of them is Carfanno, Officer Smirk from yesterday. And he's still earning his name. The other, however, isn't the woman, Detective Rauch. This is a dude, a big one with what looks like a neck tattoo sticking out from under the collar of his uniform, weird for a cop. He's standing at Smirk's shoulder, staring at Uncle Nick the way a hungry dog stares at a plate of meat.

Meanwhile, two women—they've got Family Services written all over them—have lined up my sibs and are taking some kind of roll call. All except Darlene and Tyrone. The Top Girl and Top Boy are with Aunt Kell, who's openly sobbing. Darlene's holding her hand and Tyrone's rubbing her back, their faces more full of despair than I've ever seen.

One of the two women looks up and points at us. "You three! What are your names? Where are your bags?"

Tish replies, "I... guess I left them up in the hall."

"Well, come down. The officers will collect them."

"It's going to be all right, children!" the other says. She's clearly the nicer of the two.

Tish, with a final, miserable look at me, heads down the steps and falls in beside Sarah.

Jimmy and I don't move.

Meanwhile, Officer Smirk tells my Uncle Nick, his tone condescending as hell, "We've been over this, Nelson. There's nothing more to be said. It's all signed and legal. You and the missus there have dropped the ball, and so the State of New Jersey has decided to close you down and reassign these poor troubled youths to other homes. Too many delinquents under one roof, if you ask me."

Never one to be pushed around, Uncle Nick takes a step closer. This makes the other cop, Officer Neck Tattoo, stand more alert. "My 'missus' and I have been caring for children for close to twenty-five years! Some of them have been with us since they were in diapers. And, in all that time, there's never been one complaint, not one accusation of anything, ever!"

Smirk crosses his arms. "Yeah. Yeah. Well, like I said, that's changed. We got several reliable witnesses who put three of your kids on Steel Pier, breaking and entering, then assaulting a bunch of local businessmen. Now, since they're minors, nobody's going to press charges. Be a damned shame to see anyone end up in Juvie Hall. But it seems clear that these kids are out of your control. So, as Mrs. Lejola over there explained, she's got a mandate from a Family Court judge to do something about it. That's all."

Uncle Nick's face is so dark with fury that I worry it might explode. "There's a process for this!" he protests. "A meeting's supposed to happen where we get to tell our side! A hearing!"

Carfanno makes a dismissive gesture. "Red tape. Never been a fan. Come on, kids! Line up! You're going on an adventure!"

But none of the Nelson Kids look very adventurous.

Nearby, Aunt Kell sobs harder while Tyrone, his own face nearly as dark as Uncle Nick's, leaves her side and starts toward Smirk and Neck Tattoo, his fists clenched.

"Tyrone, don't!" This comes from Darlene, who's sticking to Aunt Kell's side. Despite all the shit going down between us, I love her for that.

But Tyrone, no surprise, ignores her.

Neck Tattoo steps forward and puts a snow shovel-sized hand out, like a STOP sign. His other hand is on the butt of his pistol.

"Jesus," I hear Jimmy breathe.

"Wait!" I yell at the top of my voice. Don't ask me why. I have no idea at all what I think I'm going to accomplish. But something really bad's about to go down and, somehow, I need to get in its way.

"You two!" one of the social workers yells again. "I told you to come down!"

So, I throw a cuss her way.

It's a bad one, maybe the worst. I won't say what it is because the page might catch fire. Let's just say it's the one that makes Aunt Kell's head spin around when she hears it.

And, for a second or two, it has the desired effect. Everyone freezes. The social workers look shocked. So do the cops, Uncle Nick, and especially the kids. Even Officer Smirk's face—unsmirks a little. Weirdly, only Aunt Kell seems not to notice. Her eyes are on her husband. Sure, those eyes have gone wide. But something tells me that's not because of what I just blurted out.

"Young lady!" one of the social workers says, all haughty. "That kind of language will not—"

So, I say it again.

"Billy," Officer Smirk says. He looks genuinely pissed now; all of his attention fixed on me. Uncle Nick and Tyrone, for the moment at least, have been forgotten. "Go get them. Let's bring them down and get this done."

Neck Tattoo — Billy, I guess — turns and obediently marches across the lobby, away from Nick and Tyrone, past the social workers and my lined-up sibs, and toward the foot of the stairs.

I watch him as he does. At the same time, I whisper to Jimmy. "Run."

"What?" he asks.

"Give him something to chase."

"You sure about this?"

I shake my head. Like the white dude with the hat and the whip said in that movie a couple of years ago, I'm making this up as I go.

But Jimmy, God love him, does it anyhow.

Offering Neck Tattoo a middle finger before the big cop's even on the third step, he turns and bounds up the staircase to the second floor. With a cuss of his own, the first time he's said anything, Neck Tattoo charges after him. I jump to one side and let him go by. He gives me a hard glance as he does but then dismisses me and goes after Jimmy instead, just like I hoped.

After all, I'm only a girl.

I'm worried about Jimmy, of course, but not *that* worried. He knows this hotel as well as I do. There are a hundred places to hide. He could be up there all day and still not get found.

So, instead, I focus on what's happening down below. Officer Smirk, alone now, looks a lot less cocksure in the face of two big dudes, namely the Top Boy and his foster father. "Look," he says placatingly. "This is getting out of hand. I'm not the bad guy here. I'm just doing what I was told. There's no reason to — "

But, by then, I've come down the stairs at something close to a run. As I go right past the social workers, I hear one of them ask my name, her eyes on her clipboard, before she realizes I'm not getting in line like a good little girl. Instead, I station myself right at Uncle Nick's shoulder. Tyrone's just behind me, looking big and dangerous. It's weirdly comforting to have him there.

"Told by who?" I ask Officer Smirk. "Simon Bernard, maybe?"

The social workers both turn and look our way, their interest suddenly on something besides corralling kids. Apparently, Madame Adelaide's grandson is more well-known than I figured, at least in local city circles.

Smirk fixes me with a hard, warning look. "You don't want to be throwing that name around, little girl."

I smile, "Or what? My head'll end up in a box, like Mr. Kessler's from next door?"

"Abigail!" Uncle Nick exclaims.

But I ignore him. "How much is he paying you, anyway?" I ask, giving the dude a smirk all my own.

Carfanno's eyes keep flicking back and forth between me and the social workers. Both of them face us now, the line of kids at their back forgotten.

The cop's hand moves to the butt of his gun, the way Neck Tattoo's did earlier. But I'm not too worried about that. I'm not some 200-pound football player. I'm a hundred-and-ten-pound unarmed girl. "Listen, you little bitch," he whispers through clenched teeth. "I'm warning you—"

I grin. I still don't know what I'm trying to accomplish with all this lip. I've been in the System too long to think anything I or any other kid says will change a thing. But it feels so *good* to say it! Naked defiance beats the hell out of fear, I can tell you that. "You don't scare me, little man," I tell him. "'Cause I got contacts, too! I got a friend who makes ground chuck outta little creeps who like to run around threatening folks and scaring innocent—"

He slaps me.

It comes out of nowhere, lightning quick.

And it shuts me up and puts me down, hard.

As I hit the floor at Uncle Nick's feet, I hear screams. Kids mostly. The social workers both start protesting, but Smirk yells for them to shut up. Then he yells for his partner, who's probably too deep in the hotel looking for Jimmy to hear him. Uncle Nick stares down at me in stunned horror. He's calling my name, but it seems far away. Shock, probably.

"What the hell's the matter with you?" Uncle Nick demands, whirling on Carfanno.

From where I lay, I see Tyrone step over me, going for the cop.

Smirk pulls his pistol.

Oh shit...

"No!" someone cries, the single word cutting through the chaos like a knife.

For a moment, everyone freezes like they did when I cussed from the staircase, only more so. Officer Smirk's in a shooter's stance. Tyrone's just two feet away from him, fists raised. Uncle Nick's right beside him, one hand on the Top Boy's shoulder, trying to restrain him. His other hand is out in front of the gun in a "don't shoot" gesture that's about as useful as pissing in the wind.

But then I turn my head and look at Aunt Kell—

—who collapses, clutching her chest.

Darlene, still holding one of her hands, goes with her. The Top Girl's already screaming for help.

Both Uncle Nick and Tyrone turn around, the gun forgotten.

Uncle Nick hesitates, but only for a second. Then he runs like hell to his wife's side.

My cheek's numb where the bastard hit me, but that's about as hurt as I am. Frantically, I manage to sit up and tug on Tyrone's jeans.

He's still staring at Aunt Kell, who's sprawled out on the lobby floor with Darlene and Nick kneeling beside her. Behind him, Smirk's gun is still out, but at least he's lowered it, and I get the feeling that the temperature in the room's gone down to a more manageable level.

"Somebody call an ambulance!" Uncle Nick yells.

One of the social workers rushes over, the clipboard falling from her hands. "I'm a nurse," she says, her tone quick but calm. Pushing Darlene aside, her hand touches Aunt Kell's wrist, then her neck. Swiveling her head, she says to Smirk, "Get an ambulance, now!"

Smirk licks his lips, his beady eyes taking in the whole scene. As I sit on the floor watching him, with Tyrone reaching down to finally help me up, I can almost read the cop's thoughts. This whole thing looks bad, and he knows it. And right now, his slimy lizard brain is trying to figure the best way to come out of it in one piece.

After a few seconds, he apparently decides that "coming out of it in one piece" involves not letting my foster mother die.

Holstering his gun, he gets on his radio, calling for an ambulance.

Meanwhile, the nurse/social worker starts doing CPR on Aunt Kell.

With a sick, stomach-churning certainty, I understand that the woman who raised me, the only mom I've ever had, might be dying.

And I can't help wondering how much of it is my fault.

CHAPTER 18

THE SYSTEM MOVES FAST

—FOR A CHANGE.

An ambulance arrives inside of like ten minutes, and paramedics rush through the doors and go to work immediately. The social worker doing the CPR, whose name it turns out is Miss Reynolds, never leaves Aunt Kell's side the whole time, even after announcing that my foster mother was breathing again. In fact, it's not until the paramedics take over for her that she straightens up and finds her fallen clipboard.

In the meantime, almost nobody moves.

Smirk does. With his gun back where it belongs, he marches straight over to the front desk and picks up the phone there. Then, with nobody paying any attention to him—except me—he dials a number, waits impatiently for an answer, and whispers down the line for maybe a minute before hanging up.

Around that time, Neck Tattoo reappears, looking frustrated and a bit confused at all the commotion in the lobby. He and Smirk trade looks. Neck Tattoo shrugs, seeming a little embarrassed.

He ain't found Jimmy.

Smirk waves this away and motions for him to come down.

Now, Miss Reynolds and the other social worker—the Mrs. Lajola that Carfanno mentioned earlier—are back in business, making sure my sibs are lined up. Even Tyrone and Darlene are there, both of them looking too worried about Aunt Kell to offer much in the way of protest. Frankly, I would've figured Lajola to have ushered us kids outside while Mrs. Reynolds was still doing her CPR thing—so we wouldn't, you know, get "scarred" by what was happening. But she didn't. Maybe she was worried about the cold. Or maybe she's just bad at her job.

Some of them are.

For my own part, I haven't moved much since Tyrone helped me to my feet. I'm still standing by the revolving doors, watching everything, my heart in my throat. Then Lajola comes marching over to me and grabs my upper arm. "Time to get in line." Her tone's hard, not the "hard kind of gentle" that every System kid gets to know well, but just plain hard.

Definitely one of the mean ones.

Not knowing what else to do, I get in line, putting myself beside Darlene.

"Do we even know where we're going?" I ask her.

"Do we ever?" she replies without looking at me.

The paramedics place my foster mother — *our* foster mother — on a rolling stretcher. One of them is talking to Uncle Nick, but I can't hear what they're saying.

Suddenly, and for no reason at all, I wonder where Rags is.

"Now, children," Miss Reynolds says. She looks a little shaken but more or less put together, wearing the System like a suit of armor. "I know all of this is very sudden, and I'm sure some of you are frightened. But I promise you'll have a warm meal and a safe place to sleep tonight. Now, there are two vans outside. Some of you will be assigned to one and the rest to the other. Mrs. Lajola here will be driving the first, and I'll be driving the second."

"I know some of you have been under the Nelsons' care for a while now, and, ordinarily, I'd offer you a chance to thank them and say goodbye. But, as you've seen, Mrs. Nelson's a little... under the weather at the moment. So... we'll try to arrange something later."

But of course, they won't, and every kid in line, from the oldest to youngest, knows it. The minute we get marched out those doors, we'll never see Uncle Nick or Aunt Kell again.

I feel sick to my stomach and scared — *really* scared. It's a different kind of scared than I feel when I'm around Rags, more familiar and, in an odd way, more terrible.

But then, from beside me, Darlene says, "No."

For a few seconds, the social workers look at her. Finally, Miss Lajola asks with what sounds like forced patience, "What's that, young lady?"

"I said no," the Top Girl repeats. Her face is all but expressionless, though her eyes blaze. Having been on the wrong end of those eyes a few times, especially lately, it's kind of nice to see them pointed at somebody else. "We're not going with you. Not any of us."

"I'm afraid you don't have a choice," Mrs. Lajola says, crossing her arms.

Surprisingly, it's Tyrone who replies. He's standing on the far side of the line, away from the older kids and next to the tods. For the first time, I get that his being there's no accident. He and Darlene have cooked this up. "Yeah, we do," he says, his tone even. "You ain't gonna pick me up and carry me, are you? And I ain't gonna let you pick up and carry any of the others."

"Please don't make us call the officers over."

"You haven't noticed," Darlene remarks with a grim smile. "They left with the paramedics."

The social workers whirl around and gasp, finding themselves alone in the lobby — well, except for all of *us*. They swap nervous looks.

This whole thing's gotten away from them. I don't know why Smirk and Neck Tattoo split with the ambulance dudes, but they did so without a word to anybody. Add to the fact that Jimmy's *still* not here and neither woman seems too bothered by the unchecked name on their clipboard, and I can't help wondering just how many palms got greased and how many corners got cut to make this "relocation" happen so fast. The System usually has its shit together better than this.

Turning back to us, Miss Reynolds says, "Well, stay right here. I'll call for more officers. I'm sure the Nelsons won't mind if I use their —"

Tyrone walks right past her, not menacing but with purpose. He crosses the lobby and, without a word, takes hold of the phone and rips its cord right out of the wall. Then he marches back and hands the useless contraption to Miss Reynolds, who stares at him with something close to real fear.

"Knock yourself out, lady," he tells her. "Thanks for helping my mom, by the way."

She stares at him, unable to speak.

Darlene says, "I guess you could go looking for a phone booth. There's some up on the boards."

"Yeah," Tyrone adds. "But, while you're doing that, we'll be headed to the hospital. Don't worry. Uncle Nick gave me a key. I'll lock up. Come on, homes."

And, with that, he scoops up one of the tods, takes another by the hand, and starts leading the line of kids through the revolving door, me included.

Reynolds and Lajola trail after us. Both of them go red-faced as they confront us on the sidewalk. "You can't do this! Young man!" Lajola declares. "This is a court-mandated —"

"We don't care," Darlene tells them, though I notice that she's not making eye contact. Nobody is, not even Tyrone at this point. We all get just how big a line we're crossing right now. These two white women may be just that, but they've got a whole lot of heavy-duty bureaucracy behind them. And, once they do get to a phone, that bureaucracy will hammer down on us like the fist of God.

Tyrone says, "We're going to the hospital to support our parents."

"You don't have any way of getting there!" Mrs. Lajola points out, actually sticking a finger in his face to do it.

"We'll walk. It ain't so far."

"No," Miss Reynolds says, her expression turning more thoughtful. "We'll drive you."

Lajola looks at her like she's lost her mind.

We all stop and kind of do the same thing.

She says, "You love the Nelsons. I think that's wonderful. I know it's not procedure, but these are special circumstances. I don't see any reason why we can't take you there and let you at least talk to your foster dad… find out how your foster mom's doing."

"You'll drive us there?" Darlene asks, motioning to the two white, unmarked vans parked directly in front of the hotel. I notice that the cop car Tish mentioned earlier is gone.

Reynolds looks at Lajola, who's making a face like she's just bitten into an onion. Like I said, she's one of the mean ones — a hard-ass who loathes disobedience and doesn't believe in rewarding it. Trust me, the System's full of them.

But Reynolds — maybe she's the other kind.

Maybe.

"Fine," Lajola says. "But after you… that is, once you know Mrs. Nelson is getting the best possible care, then we're going to proceed with the ordered relocation." She turns to Darlene and Tyrone, her hands on her hips. "Agreed?"

None of us say anything.

Reynolds remarks diplomatically, "Why don't we all revisit that a little later. One step at a time, okay?"

"Cool," Tyrone says.

Darlene nods.

And, just as easy as that, my sibs climb into the vans. Tyrone insists on riding with Mrs. Lajola, I think, because he doesn't trust her and is a little afraid she'll bolt with her half of the kids, given the chance. Darlene rides with Reynolds.

I'm about to get into Lajola's van, still thinking about Jimmy, who's being left behind, when I'm grabbed—hard.

Gasping, I try to struggle. But the two sets of hands on me are strong. They yank me from the van's open side door, spin me around, and drop me face-first onto the pavement hard enough to scrape my chin.

"What are you doing?" Lajola demands from behind the driver's seat.

Officer Smirk announces loudly, "Abigail Lowell, you're under arrest for conspiracy to commit murder. You have the right to remain silent. If you give up the right…"

While he's reciting the Miranda, he's twisting both my arms behind my back and fitting a cold pair of steel handcuffs onto my wrists. They hurt. It *all* hurts.

Craning my neck, I see Tyrone emerging from the van like a bear from a cave. "You get the hell away—"

That's as far as he gets before Neck Tattoo shoves the wrong end of a gun in his face. "Back off, kid," he growls. "Police business." Then he grins as if this is all somehow funny.

"Officer!" Reynolds says, exiting her own van and hurrying around to us. "This girl's in our charge!"

Smirk, having firmly shackled me, pulls me to my feet. I wince but don't cry out. Something tells me he *wants* me to cry out. To Reynolds, he says, "In the lobby a few minutes ago, this young woman admitted knowledge of a suspect sought for more than a dozen murders committed in the last forty-eight hours. I've contacted my sergeant and was instructed to arrest her and bring her in for questioning. You take care of the rest of the children. This one's ours."

"No!" This comes from Tish, her face awash with desperation. For his part, Tyrone's staring at me in helpless horror, Neck Tattoo's gun barrel all but pressed against his temple. Even Darlene looks dismayed.

"It's okay," I tell them, managing a smile. "Go make sure Aunt Kell's all right. I'll get this figured out and meet you there."

"Wouldn't count on that, little girl," Smirk says with—well—a smirk.

Seeing there's not much use in further protest, the social workers shut all of the van doors and start the engines. I half-expect Tyrone to make a final, stupid, heroic rescue attempt that'll probably land him in the hospital right beside Aunt Kell, or worse. But he doesn't. He just sits there, staring at me through the glass.

I offer him a nod that I hope shows more confidence than I feel.

He nods back, and I can tell at once that I haven't fooled anybody. I'm screwed, and we both know it.

As the vans pull away into Atlantic City traffic, the last thing I see is the younger kids, the middles. They look sadly back at me. Corinne's among them and, even from this distance, I can tell she's crying.

It's been an awful day for her, for all of them, and it's just getting started.

Thing is... when I think this, I don't even know how right I am.

CHAPTER 19

SOME COPS LIKE BEING ROUGH

— AND CARFANNO'S ONE OF THEM.

With Neck Tattoo following, watching the morning street for any unwelcome attention, Smirk drags me the length of the hotel and down the alley. Every step hurts since his iron grip on my arm is forcing me up onto my toes, making the cuffs dig into my wrists. Add to that the burning scrape on my chin and an aching hip that I got when he threw me to the ground, and I'm just a mess.

"You should learn to stay out of shit that ain't your business, little girl," the cop says as we approach his cruiser. It's parked about a third of the way down the alley, lights off and its nose pointed toward us, a dark bulk. It fills fully half the width between the hotel and the next building over, with maybe five feet clearance on either side—just enough space to open the doors.

I do my best to push past the pain and *think*. Smirk and Neck Tattoo moved the car. That's why they disappeared from the lobby. They wanted to get it off the street, both of them. But what for?

To limit how many folks saw me get arrested.

But that makes no sense. Unless—this isn't a lawful arrest.

Or a *real* one.

"I want… a lawyer," I gasp.

He doesn't answer.

"I got a right to a lawyer!"

"You might… if we were going anywhere to book you. But we're not."

"What?" I start struggling. A total waste of time, but something in his voice confirms for me that things are way worse than I ever thought they were.

Walking behind us, Neck Tattoo laughs.

So does Smirk. "Yeah… we're just going somewhere to have a chat. You're going to help make me a hero with my bosses, little girl.

My *real* bosses. And all that's going to take is you giving me your friend's name."

"I told you! I don't know it!"

"And I still don't believe you, especially after the way you mouthed off about him back in the lobby. Oh, you know him. I'll bet you two are *real* close. Not that it's going to matter where your foster dad's concerned. He's already dead. Ain't that right, Billy?"

"Right as rain," the big dude says cheerfully. "Man just don't know it yet."

"See? And Billy there knows what he's talking about."

I struggle harder as yet another wave of panic hits me. "You leave him alone! He's got nothing to do with this!"

Smirks stops us beside his cruiser. "Ain't my call. Is it, Billy?"

"Nope," Neck Tattoo says.

"Listen to me," I say. "Please—"

Instead of replying, Smirk opens the driver's side rear door and throws me across the seat. When I land badly and twist my arm, my cry of pain earns me more laughs from the pair of them.

Then a new voice says, "Get the hell away from her, pigs!"

Oh, no.

Both Smirk and Neck Tattoo look toward the car's trunk. It's an effort, but I manage to worm my legs into the well in front of me and crane my head back to look, too.

Jimmy's standing maybe a dozen feet further down the alley, right beside the hotel's open kitchen door. He's holding a baseball bat like he knows what he's doing with it. And, since he played ball after school last spring, maybe he does.

But these are cops, and cops got guns.

"Jesus," Smirk mutters. Then to Jimmy, he calls, "This is police business, kid. Drop the bat and get lost before you make a bad mistake."

In way of an answer, Jimmy points the bat directly at Neck Tattoo. "He ain't no cop!"

Neck Tattoo stiffens. Smirk looks mildly surprised. "No? And what makes you say that?"

"No badge. No cuffs. No stick. Just the shirt, pants, and shoes, shit you can get anywhere. Practically a Halloween costume!"

"I got a gun, you little punk," Neck Tattoo says. His hand goes to the pistol on his hip, which I now notice isn't the same as the one Smirk carries. Neck Tattoo's is bigger and has a pearl grip.

Not a cop's gun.

A thug's gun.

This is going from bad to worse. I don't know who exactly this big dude works for, but I can make a good guess.

"Well, how about *that*, Billy? The ladies back there didn't notice a thing. Neither did the Nelsons. But this kid pegged you right off from ten feet away!"

Neck Tattoo glowers, as motionless as a statue—but loads more dangerous.

"What's your name, kid?" Smirk asks Jimmy.

Jimmy, having a brain in his head, doesn't reply.

Again, the cop—the *real* cop—offers up a shrug. "Never mind. Billy, you think you can show this guy the error of his ways."

"Yeah," Neck Tattoo says.

"No shooting," Smirk tells him, serious now. "Shots get heard. Questions get asked."

"No problem."

And with that, Neck Tattoo starts walking toward Jimmy, not rushing but not strolling either. If the baseball bat gives him even a second's pause, he doesn't let on.

Meanwhile, Smirk slams the car door and says through the glass. "Just get comfortable, little girl. This won't take long. Why don't you relax and enjoy the show?"

I want to scream Jimmy's name again, but what would be the point? To yell a warning he doesn't need? At best, I'd distract him from the coming fight, a fight I already know with terrible certainty he's not going to win.

Frantically, I pull at the cuffs, but all that does is hurt. Outside the window, only inches from my head, Smirk leans against the car and crosses his arms. I can't see his face but can guess what expression he's wearing.

Jimmy braces himself and swings at Neck Tattoo, but the big dude moves in with surprising speed. He ducks, lets the bat whip a few inches above his head, then delivers a hard kidney jab that almost ends the fight right there. Jimmy twists in agony and drops the bat. He staggers a step or two, gasping and clutching his injured side. Then Neck Tattoo grabs his sweatshirt, whips him around, and hits him across the jaw. This time, the blow almost puts Jimmy down, but the fake cop won't have that. Instead, he grabs Jimmy's wobbling form and throws him against the alley wall.

That's when the real punishment starts.

And I think, *He's going to kill him!*

What happens next happens insanely fast.

The car door beside me gets pulled open. Check that—*ripped* open. It's so sudden and so hard that Smirk, taken completely by surprise, is knocked into the hotel's outer wall. I actually hear the *thunk* when his head meets the dusty bricks. Then he stumbles a few steps before toppling to the alley floor.

And standing over him is Rags.

As I watch, the alley's shadows seem to close around him, making him all but invisible. But I can still see the knife well enough, its blade a lethal black triangle in the gloom.

I stare at him, but he doesn't so much as glance in my direction. Instead, he hurtles deeper into the alley, toward the spot where Neck Tattoo seems to be breaking Jimmy, bone by bone.

Neck Tattoo, busy with his task, never sees it coming. He's got one arm under Jimmy's chin, holding him up against the wall, while his other fist is hard at work, cracking ribs. The big fake cop's grinning crazily, like this is all good fun.

Jimmy's stopped even trying to fight. He's just hanging there, moaning and as helpless as a fish on a meat hook.

Rags hits Neck Tattoo like a freight train, sending the dude flying. I can't begin to guess how he does this, being less than half the thug's size. Then again, this dude can move in hyperspeed and drop thirty feet without making a sound, so who am I to start quibbling now?

Jimmy, suddenly released, sucks in a huge lungful of air and collapses to the alley floor, his eyes blinking in confusion, trying to focus.

At least he's conscious.

Neck Tattoo hits the ground hard but manages to regain his feet almost immediately. This is a dude used to getting hit. Whirling around, he spies Rags still coming toward him, knife at the ready—and pulls his gun. Apparently, Smirk's warning is forgotten as he fires at the hooded figure with a kind of wild fury, the shots loud as mortar blasts in the alley.

The cop car's rear window cracks and then shatters. As one of its tires blows, I throw myself down across the bench seat, peering fearfully around a headrest. Any second now, I expect to get hit by another wild shot.

Luckily, that doesn't happen.

Meanwhile, about halfway between the car and the shooter, Rags *blurs*.

One second, he's in one spot. The next, he's somewhere else. Seeing this, Neck Tattoo tries to track him, still firing. Bullets bounce off the bricks on both sides of the alley, first left, then right. Rags blurs and blurs again, each time getting closer until, as the thug's hammer finally falls on an empty chamber, the *iwa acheté*, if that's what he really is, stands right in front of the big man.

"Who the hell are you?" Neck Tattoo demands. He's breathing hard, and there's a trapped-animal look on his face.

Rags glances over his shoulder at me. Then, turning back to Neck Tattoo, he says in a low, gravelly voice that's somehow clear as a bell, "*Mwen se yon gadyen.*"

The only part of that I get is *gadyen*.

Guardian.

Then, in one lightning-quick movement, Rags plants his knife in Neck Tattoo's chest.

This time, for a change, there's very little blood. The big thug simply wheezes and then topples, leaving Rags looming over him. Neck Tattoo twitches, his thick legs kicking spasmodically a few times.

Then he dies.

Rags reaches down and retrieves his blade.

Jesus…

I scramble out of the cop car, step over Smirk's unconscious body, and run to Jimmy. By the time I get there, Rags has vanished again, leaving Neck Tattoo's corpse in a heap further down the alley.

"You okay?" I ask Jimmy worriedly. He looks up at me, his eyes wide and cold sweat shining on his brow and cheeks. At first, I think it's pain I'm looking at. But then, when I try to touch him, to help him up, he flinches and yelps and tries to skitter along the wall away from me. That's when I get that what I'm seeing isn't pain, at least not most of it.

It's terror.

"Jimmy?" I ask, reaching for him a second time.

"Get away from me!" he screams, loud.

Then, a little to my surprise, he sort of rolls over and gets to his feet, using the wall for support. Doing this clearly hurts like hell, but he manages it anyway. That's how scared he is.

I want to follow him, maybe—I don't know—take his hand or something. But I hold my place, not wanting to spook him further.

"It's okay," I tell him. "It's over."

He stares at me like I've gone full-out crazy. "Over! *Over*? Abby, you killed that dude!"

I stare at him. "What?" I ask. It comes out as a kind of croak. Suddenly, I'm all cold inside, and I don't understand why.

Jimmy looks from the dead man to me and back again. "How?" he demands. "How... did you even *do* that?"

I shake my head, not because I disagree with him, though I do—but because I'm feeling lightheaded all of a sudden. It's weird. Kind of like pushing away a dream when you're waking up. "Do what? Jimmy, that was Rags! I didn't do anything!"

"*I saw you!*" he yells. He's got tears in his eyes. He's still wobbling on his feet, and I know I should be getting him out of this alley. After all, Smirk's down, but he might not be down for long. Except right now, in this moment, it's all I can do to process what he's telling me. I watch him wipe his mouth with a trembling hand. Blood from a split lip runs down his chin. "You ran by me. Fast. *So* freaking fast! But then, after you hit him and he went flying, you stopped. Just stopped. Still as stone. And, for a second, I could see your face under that big hood. It was *you!*"

"Look at me!" I tell him, not liking how high-pitched and desperate my own voice sounds. "I'm not wearing a hood! I'm not Rags!"

"You changed! I don't know how, but you changed! And you killed him!"

"Jimmy, listen!"

But he shakes his head, hard and quick. "No. No. No. I saw you! It's you! Last night... on the catwalk... when I climbed the ladder to find you, you weren't there! Sure, it was dark, but not that dark, not with all that light down on the stage. And you weren't there." He laughs, a nervous bubbly sound with nothing funny about it. "But then... all of a sudden... you *were*. You didn't step out of someplace, some corner or shadow. You just *appeared*, and you did it the moment that Rags dude disappeared."

"That's crazy!" I tell him. "Listen to yourself! Do you really think I could take down that many people, just me?"

"No! Yes! I don't know! But I saw you!"

"No!" I scream. I can't believe he's saying these things to me! And the way he's looking at me—it's like a knife to my heart.

Yeah, I get the irony.

"Abby," he says, and his tone is suddenly so calm, so reasonable, that I want to hit him. "Weren't you handcuffed?"

"What?"

"When I came out into the alley, that cop was shoving you in the back of his car. And your wrists were cuffed behind you. Weren't they?"

That stops me cold. Feeling a weird, detached kind of unreality, I raise both my hands.

The manacles are still there, fastened tight around my wrists, but the chain between them, two inches long and made of galvanized steel, is broken. Not cut, but pulled apart.

For a long moment, I stare at them, and once again, that coldness fills me. It's not fear, at least not the kind of fear you'd expect. Instead, it's more like dread, dread of something that I don't know.

Or maybe something I don't *want* to know.

Remember when I told you I didn't have a clue about what was really going on?

Well, right here is where that starts to change.

I look up at Jimmy. He looks back at me. There are a lot of things behind his eyes, though I'm relieved to see that one of them's concern—for me. "Abby," he whispers. "How'd you get out of the car? Those things don't got handles on the inside."

"Rags," I reply, my voice barely a whisper. I'm still holding up my wrists like an idiot. "He opened it for me."

"Uh uh," Jimmy says again. "I saw it. Right after that… dude you killed just now… started in on me, before you changed, I saw you kick open the door hard enough to flatten that cop."

"No…"

"Abby, I'm telling you, I *saw it!*"

Did he?

But, no. God, no. That would mean—

I cover my face with my hands, my cuffed hands, the cuffs I evidently broke with the incredible, impossible strength I don't have. All that was right before I knocked a two-hundred-pound thug a dozen feet and then harpooned him with the black blade I've never held in my life.

Except, none of that happened. None of that *could* have happened. Because, if it did —

If it did, then I'm Rags, and I've killed like a lot of people.

"No..." I hear myself say again.

Behind me, by the car, there comes a low, pained groan.

Carfanno.

"Abby, you gotta get out of here." Jimmy's voice sounds weirdly far away.

Blinking, I look at him again. God, he's a mess. Neck Tattoo knew what he was doing, a real pro. "We both do," I tell him. "You need a doctor."

"I'm okay. I been beat up plenty. I know how to do it."

"Maybe. Or maybe you got a broken rib or internal bleeding or something. Come on. Everybody else already went to the hospital to see Aunt Kell. Let's head that way. It ain't far."

"The hospital," Jimmy says, confused. "I thought they were relocating everybody."

"They are. But first —"

Then, again from behind me, I hear Smirk say, "What the holy hell hit me? Billy? Where are you?"

I run up and grab Jimmy's hand. He pulls away from me. "Go!" he says.

"Come with me!"

"No." And the look on his face nearly breaks my heart.

He's afraid of me.

"Hey, you two! What are you doing over there?" I look back to see Smirk coming toward us. He's not moving fast, and, at a glance, it's easy to see just how hard he hit his head when the door slammed him against the hotel wall. His hand fumbles for his gun, but he keeps missing, staggering and nearly falling with every step.

When I turn around again, Jimmy's gone. It's too far for him to have gone out the end of the alley. That leaves the hotel door.

I *could* follow him.

But there's the rest of my family to think about.

Uncle Nick.

Another head in a box.

"Abigail Lowell!" Smirk calls. "You stay right where you are!"

So, of course, I do the opposite, heading down the alley at a run. It's a mile or so to Atlantic City Hospital. If I move anything like fast, I can be there in maybe fifteen minutes.

Rags would be quicker. But I'm *not* Rags. Jimmy's wrong about that much. I don't know for sure what happened just now, but I definitely, positively *am not* Rags.

Right?

CHAPTER 20

ATLANTIC CITY HOSPITAL IS OLD

—LIKE A HUNDRED YEARS OLD, OR ALMOST. IT SITS ON SOUTH OHIO Avenue, just a few blocks off the boards and about a mile south of the Calm Sea Arms.

Now, I've never been much of a runner. I suck at track. But somehow, I cover that distance crazy fast, moving down Pacific Avenue at a dead run and weaving in and out through the folks on the sidewalk like I do this sort of thing every day. I turn a few heads, which figures. After all, I'm a city girl tearing along like I'm being chased, and on a school day to boot. Clearly no jogger. But nobody says a thing, much less tries to stop me.

And I get to the hospital in what's got to be record time.

It's a busy place, as city hospitals always are, even on weekday mornings.

I push through the revolving doors, which are electric and way more modern than the ones back at the hotel. Then I settle myself impatiently behind an old white couple who's talking with the receptionist, a big-bosomed lady with thick glasses on her nose and a smile that's so forced and so patient I wonder how her face doesn't crack. The old couple's here to visit his sister, who's up on the third floor. But neither of them seems to understand the directions to the elevator.

I wait my turn with something less than patience, hopping from one foot to the other, flooded with a kind of nervous energy. I'm scared for Aunt Kell, of course. And I'm worried about the whole relocation thing. And Jimmy. And, well, all of it.

But, right now, the only thing on my mind is warning Uncle Nick.

They're coming for you! Those crazy bastards are coming for you! I know you love Aunt Kell, but you need to run! Please. You're my father in every way that matters. Please, run!

Oh, and by the by, I think I might be a murderous Voodoo blood demon.

"Help you, miss?"

I snap back to the here-and-now. The old folks have moved on, and the receptionist points her tired, unsmiling smile at me.

"Yeah," I say. "I'm looking for my family. They came in not long ago. My… mom… had some kind of heart attack, I think. Her name's Kelley Nelson?"

The woman consults her computer, tapping away with lacquered fingers.

"Looks like she's still in Emergency. I'm so sorry to hear about her troubles. Since she hasn't been admitted to the hospital yet, I don't have any information on visitors. But you'll probably find them in the Emergency Room waiting area."

She takes a floorplan of the hospital from a handy stack on the counter and sketches me a quick map. All cool. But then she holds the sheet of paper out to me, and I take it—

—giving her a good look at the broken cuff around my wrist.

I see her see it, see her register it, and then watch her eyes crawl up to my face.

"Sweetie," she says, still smiling. "You've got some blood on your hand."

I do?

I look down at my fingers and, yeah, they're red. Not crazy red, not like last time, or the time before that, and it thankfully dried up during my run through the cold morning. Overall, I guess it's just about as much blood as you'd get on yourself if you stabbed a dude through the heart.

No…

"Oh," I hear myself say with a voice that's gone painfully dry. "Yeah. Sorry."

"Are you hurt?" she asks, though I can tell she's more nervous than concerned. If it were just the blood, she might buy a lie about an innocent cut. If it were just the broken shackle, she might swallow a line about trendy fashion statements.

But both together—well, that's a much harder sell.

I try desperately to think of what to say that will turn this something into nothing. What I come up with, what comes out of my mouth next, is the very definition of "the wrong thing."

"Uh… it's not my blood."

I see her stiffen and realize with a hard, cold certainty just how bad that sounds. Her eyes never leave my face. Her hand, the one holding up the hasty map, which I have the other end of, starts shaking a little bit.

I do my best to smile. "It's no big deal. Um… thanks."

She nods and lets go of the map. I take it and turn, my face flushing. I don't look at the damned thing. Instead, I spot a sign down near a set of double doors that says EMERGENCY and go for it. As I do, I hear her pick up the telephone. Might be nothing, I tell myself.

But it probably isn't.

Once I'm through the doors, I check the map. I'm going the right way. I follow the wide corridor for a bit and then turn right where indicated. It takes me to another corridor with a big waiting room at the end. I start that way, trying not to run, my mind racing.

Is the receptionist calling somebody? The cops? Security?

If so, then I've got no time. I need to find Uncle Nick, warn him, and make him believe me, before whoever-it-is shows up to drag me off.

Right now, nothing else matters.

"Abby?"

And there's the man himself. He's coming out of a room to my left with a sign reading PATIENT CARE #3. For a minute, I just stop and stare at him, my heart pounding in my chest. I can't believe my luck.

He looks quizzically at me. "What is it?" he asks.

I start to answer. But then my throat kind of closes.

And I run up and hug him, hard.

He hugs me right back, stroking my hair. In a gentle voice, he whispers, "It's going to be okay. She's okay. It was a heart attack but a mild one. She's conscious and resting. They're going to admit her, but she'll be fine." He says this in a rush like he's trying to convince himself as much as me.

Except that's not the comfort I'm looking for right now.

I hug him even tighter. I didn't realize until this moment just how bad I needed this.

Then, as if the morning's details are finally clicking, he pries me off and holds me at arm's length, looking me up and down. "How did you get here? Darlene told me you were arrested!"

I swallow. "I was. But I… got away."

"Got away? My God! How?" Then he looks down at my wrists and sees the broken handcuffs. For a moment, his brow wrinkles in thought. Then he meets my eyes again and asks, "Rags?"

I nod. "But listen, Uncle Nick. That's not important. You have to—"

"Tell me he didn't kill those cops!"

"One of 'em," I reply, almost choking on the words, on the memory. "But he wasn't a real cop. He was one of Bernard's thugs playing dress-up."

Uncle Nick processes this. "And Rags… killed him?"

"Yeah. But, please listen. I—"

"What about the other one, the white guy, the one from yesterday?"

"He got knocked on his ass, but he's all right."

"Where's Jimmy? Darlene told me he stayed behind."

My whole body starts trembling. This is turning out to be way harder than I thought, and I'm running out of time! "He's still at the hotel," I say. "Now shut up, will you! I need to tell you something important!"

His eyes flash at the whole "shut up" thing, but only for a second. Then they soften again, and he says, "All right, Abby. I'm sorry. All that'll wait. Say what you need to say."

A new voice announces, "You're too late, child."

With a shared gasp, we both look up the hallway, the same way I came only a minute ago. The corridor's empty right now, weirdly empty, considering this is a hospital in mid-morning.

Madame Adelaide's standing there, maybe fifteen feet off.

And beside her, dwarfing her, his huge body seeming to fill the hallway side-to-side, is Baptiste Bernard.

"Who are you?" Uncle Nick demands. Acting on what I sense is pure parental instinct, he straightens and puts himself between me and the Bernards.

I find myself loving him all the more for that.

Instead of replying, the old woman asks, "You're Nicholas Nelson, *oui*? The owner of that hotel?"

Uncle Nick's eyes narrow. He nods.

"Our good fortune then," Madame Adelaide continues. She smiles, and it's so cold that it turns my insides to ice. "My grandson and I have come here to take something of yours."

I watch Uncle Nick process this. "I told your lawyer. We're not selling."

The old woman chuckles. When she speaks again, her tone's relaxed, like she's describing her favorite gumbo recipe. "No. No, *bon gason*. That comes later. For now, all I need is your head."

Beside her, Dreads grins and opens the suit jacket he's wearing. Under it, in some kind of leather shoulder sheath, is a wicked-looking knife. Newer than Rags' and maybe not as big—but big enough.

"You're insane!" Uncle Nick exclaims, backing up a step and pushing me further behind him. Then, looking left and right, he screams, "Help! Help us!"

I've never heard him scream before. It scares the shit out of me. He calls up and down the hallway, so loud that somebody *has* to hear, *has* to come running. But no one does. And, somehow, the silence that answers him tells me that no one will, at least not in time to be of any use.

"Their minds are shut, *bon gason*," the old woman says. "I've shut them. They won't open again for a bit. Time enough to complete our business."

I suddenly grab my foster father, pulling him as hard as I can down the hall and away from—*them*. "Run! Get the hell out of here!"

"Abby... what...?"

"They're gonna kill you!"

Madame Adelaide says in a low, almost gleeful whisper, "Kill him, Baptiste. But save the girl for after. I think she may be the one we're looking for."

Dreads replies in a voice as deep as any ocean, "*Oui*, Grann."

And he charges.

Uncle Nick cries, "Abby, get out of the way!" He pulls his arm out of my grasp, once again putting himself between me and the dread-locked giant who's about to crash down on us like a wave. Instead, I dart around in front of him, screaming at him to run. Because, right now, I'm not worried about me. I'm worried about him. I'm worried about—

Baptiste knocks me aside like I weigh nothing. In an instant, I'm airborne, hurtling the width of the wide hospital corridor. When I hit the opposite wall, it's hard enough to crack the plaster and send shockwaves of pain racing through me from my toes to my head. The world swims as I crash to the tile floor, and suddenly it's all I can do to stay conscious.

With bleary, pain-wracked eyes, I watch Uncle Nick throw a punch that catches Dreads square in the jaw. The big man's head snaps but then snaps right back.

He grins, blood running down his chin. Uncle Nick stares at him, stunned. It was a good punch, a *solid* hit, and this walking tree took it without blinking an eye.

Then Baptiste Bernard scoops my foster father up in a bear hug, lifting him completely off the floor. Uncle Nick hits him again and again, giving it everything he's got. He bloodies the giant's nose, blackens his eye. But all Baptiste does is roar like a bear and squeeze his huge arms tighter and tighter.

"No!" I try to scream, but it comes out as a stunned and useless gurgle. Meanwhile, standing down the hall, Madame Adelaide is laughing, laughing and clapping her bony hands like she's watching a favorite child blow out his birthday candles.

I actually *hear* my father's back break.

He doesn't cry out. In fact, the only sound he makes is a kind of sickening wheeze as Baptiste crushes him to death. Then, when his body goes limp, the big dude drops him like a bag of garbage and stands there, bleeding and panting—

—and grinning.

"That was *good*, Grann," he says in his deep, deep voice. "That was so good."

His grandmother laughs all the harder.

I expect tears to well up, expect the grief and horror to freeze me like cold water. But, instead, what rises up inside me is more like fire than ice. I get my hands under me, climbing to my feet much more steadily than I have any right to expect. My eyes stay locked on my dead father's broken body and on the man—the *thing*—who did it, who did it and enjoyed it.

Dreads turns to face me, his smile disappearing. Behind us, down the hall, Madame Adelaide stops laughing.

"You have no power, child," she tells me. "You're nothing."

But in her words, I can hear the lie, plain as day. Because I *do* have power. I don't know how or why, not yet. But I have it. Sure, I've been running from it, running like hell. But I have it all the same.

"*Cher*," the old woman says to Baptiste, her tone careful now, even worried. "Come away from her."

But Baptiste doesn't move. His dark eyes spear me, clearly unafraid. And why not? I'm just a slip of a girl, less than half the size of the man he just crushed to death like it was nothing. Why would he ever retreat from the likes of me?

That's when I feel something fill my hand.

It's a weird sensation. Nothing there one second, and something the next. I feel old worn leather against my palm, strange and yet so familiar that my fingers close around it pretty much automatically.

What's more: I don't have to look down to know what it is I'm suddenly holding.

It's Rag's knife.

I've got no clue how it got there, and, as I bare my teeth at Dreads, I find that I don't much care. I have the knife — *my* knife — and that's all that matters.

"Baptiste!" Madame Adelaide cries. "*Pitit pitit*! Come here! Now!"

I take one more look at the murdered man on the floor. Nicholas Nelson was my father. He raised me, loved me, forgave me. He wrapped me in his arms and told me everything was okay, even when it wasn't.

"And you killed him," I hear myself whisper, my every muscle as taut as a loaded spring.

Dreads says nothing, though his dark eyes narrow with confusion and, maybe, a little wariness.

"Baptiste!" the old woman exclaims, and this time it's not a plea. It's a warning.

And it's too late.

I launch myself at him, clearing the six or seven feet between us in a single jump.

But Dreads is fast, incredibly fast for a dude so big. His huge hands shoot out and catch me under my arms as I leap at him, holding me up like I'm a toddler. Grinning, his grip tightens, his fingers crushing my lungs flat in an instant. Fresh pain tears through my body, bringing with it a hard certainty.

He's gonna do me like he did Uncle Nick.

This gets followed up by another hard certainty.

The hell he is.

I don't fight the hands. That's pointless. Instead, I use my knife to slash the big dude's face, running the edge of the blade across his forehead, down to the bone. For a second or two, he doesn't seem to notice. And why should he? You can't kill somebody by cutting their forehead, after all. There aren't enough big veins or arteries up there to do the job. Don't ask me how I know that — I just do, just like I know, while you won't bleed to death from a forehead cut, you will *bleed*.

Blood, a wide stream of it, hits his eyes in the next moment, blinding him.

With a cry, he throws me away.

I have just enough time to feel relieved that I can breathe again before the wall comes at me. Spinning in mid-air, I plant my feet against it, bend my knees to drain the momentum, and then launch myself again.

This time he *can't* see me coming!

I hear Madame Adelaide cry out in a language I shouldn't understand, *"Wete kò ou sou li, move lespri!"*

Except now, impossibly, I *do* understand it.

"Get away from him, dark spirit!"

Fat chance.

I land across Baptiste's shoulders. His hands, busy trying to wipe the blood that's still pouring into his eyes, reach for me. But where he was fast the first time, now he's slow. Very slow. Crazy slow. I'm not sure why that is, and, honestly, I don't give a shit. All that matters to me is that his defenses have dropped.

My knife goes to work.

Up and down. Up and down. Up and down.

Baptiste spins wildly, still trying to grab at me. But it's easy to stay out of his way, climbing the big dude like a maple tree, skirting around his thick head, and staying out of his slow, slow grasp.

Realizing he's in real trouble, Dreads fumbles for his own blade, pulling it out of the sheath under his now-bloody jacket. Clutching it in his huge fist, he tries to stab at me. As he does, I hit it with my knife, metal on metal, a single sharp *clang* that snaps the dude's pathetic weapon in half and knocks it from his grasp.

Baptiste starts screaming.

I'm on his back now, my legs over his shoulders and locked around his throat. And still, I'm using my knife — up and down, up and down, up and down — as, around me, the world turns red.

Deep red.

Adelaide screams, too, until the hallway fills with her cries. I take notice but pay them no mind. It's to be expected, after all, something I hear all the time as I do my business.

It's always been that way.

Finally, his screams over, the dying man beneath me collapses, dropping like a falling tree. As he does, I hop lightly off him and step away, regarding my handiwork with a critical eye.

My knife and me have done our work well.

Down the still-empty hallway, Madame Adelaide moans, her small body shaking. Her hands claw at the air as if to drag something down from Heaven. Then, realizing that I've finished, that my dance with her grandson's over, she goes quiet, her head lowered, the bones in her hair rattling.

Slowly, that head comes up, the eyes in her small skull almost glowing with black rage. "*Ou,*" she says. "*Ou tiye li.*"

It's Creole. I don't know how I know that, but I do. And, once again, I don't need Uncle Nick to tell me what it means. It's as clear to me as English, maybe more so, since it's the language that birthed me—the other me, the me that I am in this moment.

"*You killed him.*"

So, I reply in the same language, "*Yon lavi pou yon lavi.*"

"*A life for a life.*"

The old woman's eyes widen. They rake over first my father's broken body and then Baptiste's bloody form a few feet away. Finally, they return to mine. When she speaks again, it's in English, and the hatred that drips from her words makes me think of Hellfire. "You're strong. But you've not accepted. Not yet."

I almost ask, "Accepted what?" But I think I know.

"Tell me, child. Do you remember? Do you remember your theft?"

I don't reply. No, I don't remember. But standing there covered in blood and holding the bloody knife, I think I'm beginning to.

"You're taking the steps," Adelaide tells me, her voice low, her eyes burning. "You're done with the hiding, done the stepping out of yourself to watch from afar. Now, you're in it, working the power with your own hands, tasting the blood in your own mouth. But you've not finished, not yet. Which means I can yet kill you."

My grip on the knife tightens. My entire body *thrums* with energy, with potential action. You'd think what I did to Dreads would have emptied the tank, but it didn't. It's still there, as full as ever. "Then do it," I say. "Come get me."

The old woman doesn't move.

So, I take a step toward her. "What's the matter?" I ask. "Ain't you the all-powerful *bòkò*? Didn't you 'close all the minds' of the people in this place so your grandson could murder my father undisturbed? But you didn't help him, did you? While I was killing him…" I expect this word to catch in my throat, but it doesn't, and that terrifies me. "…you just stayed back, didn't you? Didn't lift a finger."

"Don't presume to know my power, Child of the Blood!" Adelaide exclaims. "I was doing my will before your great-grandmother took her first steps! That *ti gason*, whose life you took, was never my grandson, but many generations past that. Still, he *was* my blood, and that blood *will* be avenged. Do you hear me?"

"I'm standing right here, bitch," I say.

"Drunk on power. That's where you're at right now. Full of vinegar and thirsty for more death. *Oui*, I know that feeling. Indeed, so." She shakes her head, the bones in her hair rattling. "But no. Hot-blooded vengeance don't bring satisfaction, child. Satisfaction… *real* satisfaction, comes drenched in *cold* blood. You'll see. Oh, *oui*. You'll see what I mean, damned quick."

And, just like that, she's gone. I don't mean she walks off. I don't mean the hallway goes dark or anything like that. I mean, she just disappears, like she stepped right off the world, or maybe right out of the view of reality's camera—kind of the way Rags does, but different. Because, while Rags is always solid, on some level, I know that Adelaide wasn't.

Baptiste was here in the flesh. But she was a kind of ghost, no more real than the light coming out of a projector.

More black magic.

But what she did, what she had Dreads do, *that* was plenty real.

And now I find myself alone, alone with one dead man I loved and one I killed.

My righteous anger kind of melts away then, and what replaces it is an emptiness that tries to scoop out my soul and move in. Without even realizing I'm doing it, I sink to my knees in front of Uncle Nick. His eyes bulge wide open, seeing nothing, and his body is bent at an impossible angle. His face already looks gray and dead, without any of the energy and vitality that he walked around with every single day.

Even so, he's my father.

He is.

Sobbing, I pick up his head and place it on my lap, hugging it and rocking back and forth. Tears don't fill my eyes. They drown them, completely blinding me and spilling onto Uncle Nick's slack, open-mouthed face as if pouring from a faucet.

"I'm sorry," I tell him, though I know he can't hear me. "I'm so sorry... Daddy. This is all my fault..."

I don't know how long I sit there. Not too long, since it *is* a hospital, and I'm guessing whatever Adelaide did to people's "minds" to keep them from disturbing us while we fought is over.

So, I probably shouldn't be surprised when somebody starts screaming.

But surprised I am, so much so that I let go of my father and jump to my feet, my heart pounding. Whatever scary zen has been gripping me these past few minutes is apparently gone. Whirling around, I try to recapture that feeling of — readiness.

At the end of the corridor, filling the archway that leads into the Emergency Room waiting area, stands my family. Most of them anyhow. Tyrone's there. So are Darlene, Jeff, and Tish. It's Tish who screamed. I know that because she's still doing it.

Corinne's there, too. She's staring at me in utter horror. Well, they *all* are, but it's Corinne's face that burns the most. As I watch, she lets go with a wail of fear or grief and then turns and buries her face against Tyrone, who holds on tight to her, though his eyes — his accusing eyes — never leave mine.

And, suddenly, I understand what I must look like to them.

I'm once again drenched head to toe in blood, standing between the bodies of Baptiste Bernard — and our foster dad.

And I'm holding a knife.

"What did you do?" Darlene exclaims.

They're all maybe twenty-five feet away, too far for a conversation or even a complete explanation. But something tells me going toward them wouldn't be welcome. Not now. Maybe not ever again.

"He killed him!" I yell. It's the only thing I can think of.

None of them reply.

Tish, who's still screaming, lets Sarah pull her into a fierce hug. God, how I envy that hug.

Darlene points a shaking finger at Uncle Nick, or what's left of him. "What did you do?"

"It wasn't me!" I shout back, the words wrapped in sobs.

"Help!" Jeff starts yelling. "Help!"

Within seconds, almost all of them take up the same call.

And I know, with bitter, terrible certainty, that I've got to run.

So, I do.

CHAPTER 21

I MUST LOOK LIKE A MONSTER

— OR A PSYCHO OR SOMETHING AS I RUN THROUGH THE HOSPITAL HALLS. I pass folks, plenty of them. Some scream as I race by. Others call after me, asking what's wrong, only to see the bloody knife and retreat on the double. One big dude in a security guard's outfit tries to get in my way. But I duck around him like he's standing still.

As I leave him in my dust, I hear him cuss and start talking into his radio.

I keep running.

Reaching the lobby, I blow by the receptionist, the same one who drew me the map. I don't look at her, but out of the corner of my eye, I can *feel* her staring at me.

And she thought I had blood on me before!

Then I'm through the revolving doors — having left red handprints on the glass — and outside. The day's sunny, a bright cold morning. For a minute, I just stand there on Pacific Avenue, trying to figure out what to do next.

My heart pounds so hard that it almost hurts. The screams of my sibs still ring in my ears. And the sight of my father's back being broken is burned into my memory, both hot and cold at the same time.

I don't know which feels worse: Uncle Nick's horrible death, the fact that I then turned around and somehow butchered his killer — or the realization that I'm not sorry. Not even a little.

Folks are staring at me. Some of them actually stop, gawking like I'm a two-headed dog or something.

"She's got a knife!" one of them yells.

"Call the cops!" says somebody else.

That gets me moving. I push past them and cross the street. I don't have any clear idea of where I'm going. I just know that I need to be someplace else.

Anywhere except here.

I leave a trail of witnesses as I race down Pacific Avenue and turn onto Park Place. Yeah, *that* Park Place. This takes me right past the Claridge Hotel and Brighton Park, before steps appear at the end of the street to lead me up to the Boardwalk. I skip them, deciding instead to go *down* and slip through a spot I know beneath the stairs that lets you, if you're not afraid of spiders or rats, get *under* the boards.

Down here, everything stinks of garbage and urine. But it's not as dark as you'd think, what with daylight leaking in from the open ocean side and through small slits between most of the boards above me.

I keep moving, my breath now coming in heated gasps. It's harder to run down here, where sand has been mixed with broken bottles and other trash left behind by decades of tourists. Again, I'm not sure where I'm going — except, on some level, I am because I just got here.

Steel Pier.

Of course, there's no easy way to get inside from underneath, and no way am I risking the Boardwalk in broad daylight. So, instead, I find a spot somewhere in the checkerboard of steel pilings that hold the huge pier up. It's the same place, or close to it, where those bangers cornered Corinne and me. Was that really just two days ago?

Now Corinne thinks I'm a killer.

And she's right.

It's not until I finally stop, my chest heaving, and drop exhausted down onto the sand, that I have the time to think — really *think* — about what happened back there at the hospital.

Uncle Nick's dead.

The finality of it, the sheer no-take-backs of it, hits me like a kick in the gut. I start crying again. I guess "keening" is a better word, hugging my knees and rocking back and forth on the cold sand. I'm not worried about anybody hearing me. The tide's coming in, and the surf crashing against the pilings just fifty feet from where I'm at drowns out any sound little old me might make.

I cry for a long time, basically until I'm cried out until no more tears will come. Then I close my eyes, cross my arms over my knees and lower my head into them, blocking it all out. Everything. My arms smell coppery, the blood on my jacket sticky, and that's when I realize I'm still holding Rags' knife.

With a cry of disgust, I throw it at the water. It doesn't get that far but instead hits one of the steel pilings between here and there and somehow *skewers* it, burying itself halfway to the hilt in what looks like solid metal.

For an instant, I wonder how I did that. But then, in the next instant, I realize I don't give a shit.

Slowly, exhausted, I get up and go down to the water's edge. For most of a minute, I just stand there, with the surf all but touching my sneakers, and watch the roll of the sea. I like the Atlantic Ocean. It's big, and it looks so empty, when the truth is it's full of life.

Reaching my blood-caked hands down, I let the surf wash over them. The water's cold, but that doesn't bother me as much as it should. So, I rub my hands together and let the salty water flush away what's left of Baptiste Bernard. Then, cupping my now cleanish hands, I bend over and scoop the ocean onto my face, doing the same with the blood that's there, the blood I can still smell, still taste.

I briefly consider diving in and rinsing myself clean all in one go. But this isn't August, and the December Atlantic would freeze me to the bone. I've got enough to worry about without adding hypothermia to the list.

Besides, I'm still not all that sorry for what I did. Baptiste Bernard murdered my father—and I avenged him.

Aunt Kell would feel differently about it, of course. As much as her husband's death would kill her—and on top of what happened this morning with her heart, I'm afraid it just might—she's simply too Christian to buy the whole "eye for an eye" thing.

Thou shalt not kill. That's more her speed.

I wonder, in a vague sort of way, if I'm going to Hell now.

My stomach growls. Well, of course, it does. I haven't had a thing to eat since supper last night. But this seems a distant concern. So do the cops, though the front of my brain supposes it shouldn't. They'll be at the hospital by now, doing the detective thing: talking to my sibs, taking a statement from that receptionist, following my bloody footprints as I escaped out onto the street. Pretty soon, they'll be looking for me, a teenage murderess alone and on foot, covered in her victim's blood.

They probably won't look under here, at least not right away.

But it doesn't offer much hope for my future, does it? I mean, I won't be going back to school anytime soon.

Jesus...

But He doesn't appear.

Instead, someone else does.

Rags emerges from behind one of the pilings, the one with his knife sticking out of it. Coincidence? What do *you* think?

For a few seconds, he just stands there, with the ocean roiling behind him. His hands are empty. As I watch, he regards the jutting knife, tilting his hooded head thoughtfully. I expect him to grab it, take it back. After all, it's *his*. But he doesn't. Instead, he just faces me again.

I wait, expecting him to do something.

He just stands there, still as a statue.

Finally, I ask, "Well?"

No reply.

"I just killed somebody," I tell him. It's the first time I've said it out loud, and the four words seem to carve away a piece of my soul. "I did it 'cause he murdered my dad, right in front of me. And I ain't sorry. But…" I swallow back a sob. I do *not* want to cry in front of this dude. "…but every time I close my eyes, it ain't Uncle Nick dying that I see. It's *me*… sticking that knife, *your knife*, into that man, over and over."

Rags nods.

"What did you *do* to me?"

Again, no reply.

"What's happening to me?"

Still no reply.

"Am I… turning into… you?"

Rags takes a step toward me. Then another. He's moving deliberately slow like he's afraid of spooking me. But I'm not planning to run off. I mean, at this point, where would I run off *to*? The answers I need, if they exist at all, are right in front of me.

When he comes within three feet or so, the smell of him strong but, by now, familiar, he crouches down. I expect to be able to see—finally *see*—his face. But I can't. Too many shadows, maybe. Or maybe it's something else. For the first time, I begin to get that his disguise is older and deeper than simply darkness under a hood.

In a small whisper of a voice, I ask, "Who… *what*… are you?"

Honestly, I don't expect a reply. I mean, since I've met this dude, he's said like ten words to me.

Not exactly a chatterbox.

But this time, he *does* reply, his raspy voice like fingernails on a chalkboard. "*Iwa acheté.*"

"Broken angel," I say.

He nods once, slowly.

"Dark spirit."

He gives me another nod.

Then he does something that, crazy as it sounds, weirds me out worse than anything else. He reaches out and pokes my shoulder with one grime-covered finger. Then he says, "*Vanyan sòlda.*"

I blink. "Who? *Me?*"

He nods.

"I ain't no soldier!" I say, maybe louder than I should have. But if my outburst bothers him at all, it doesn't show. So, I keep right on going. "I'm just a girl from the streets, man! I ain't never hurt nobody in my life… before today. Before *you!*"

Again, he lifts his hand. This time, he offers it to me, palm up, the way he did in the boxing arena. At that time, I was too freaked out to take it. But a lot's happened since then, none of it good.

So now, I figure, *What have I got to lose?*

Hesitantly, a little shakily, I put my own hand into his. His skin feels cold, and the layer of dirt on it scrapes like sandpaper. But all that stuff goes away an instant later.

And suddenly, I'm dreaming.

Except I'm not. This isn't a dream. It's a memory. I know that not only because I recognize it, but because I'm awake and seeing it clearly for the first time.

It was three nights ago. I'd snuck out close to midnight and had made my way, as usual, to Steel Pier. Now I was inside, loving the cold silence, and in full creeper mode. I struck gold that night, or so I thought, having found an open door that's always been locked. Who'd left it that way and why, I couldn't guess and didn't much care. It was *new* territory to explore, something I thought I'd used up long ago.

So, I went in. I went in without a second thought. What I found was a flight of old stairs that took me down to a narrow corridor with a single door at the far end, painted a deep but peeling red. Getting more excited with each step, I approached this new find, pushing my way inside — and finding something weirder than I'd imagined.

The room was small, with what appeared like an altar against the far wall. At the time, I had no idea what I was looking at. But now, remembering it, I do. That room was no kind of chapel, not even one of those out-of-the-way *Vodou* churches that Uncle Nick described.

No. What I was looking at that night was nothing more or less than a *bòkò's* workshop, not too different from the basement at the Calm Sea Arms where Uncle Nick keeps — kept — his tools, his supplies, and the half-finished projects that Aunt Kell always bugged him about.

And not just any *bòkò*, either.

It was the workshop of Adelaide de la Fossa.

Reliving that memory is hard, almost painful. I want to scream at the girl I was back then, so recent and so, so long ago. I want to tell her to get out, to turn and run, and to never look back.

But I can't.

I can't because it's the past, my past, and it's already too late.

I remember stepping deeper into that terrible place, just a stupid, ignorant kid. I remember approaching the antique mirror standing atop the altar, propped up on its human skull.

"*Aksepte mwen.*"

When I dreamed of this place, that's where the dream always stopped. The memory, of course, doesn't.

I'll never fully understand what made me do what I did next. Call it a moth getting drawn to a flame, maybe. Call it idiotic, impulsive curiosity. Either way, I remember reaching out with my hand and touching the surface of that mirror. I expected it to be smooth, but it was rough, kind of like sandpaper, kind of like Rags' skin. I didn't say a word. If I had, maybe things would have happened differently. Just one more thing I'll never know.

But the touch was apparently enough to get the ball rolling.

"*Aksepte mwen.*"

I didn't know what it meant then any more than I did later when Rags said it again. But I know now. Whatever happened to me back in that hospital hallway, whatever's been happening to me these past couple of days, it's brought with it an understanding of a language that, a week ago, I barely knew existed.

"*Aksepte mwen.*" is Creole.

It means, "Accept me."

And, by touching that mirror the way I did, at the time I did, and being who I am, while it wasn't the same as saying "yes" (or "*oui*"), it opened the door just enough to let him in. Let *it* in.

The *iwa acheté*.

In this new memory — or maybe "reawakened" memory is more on the nose — something jolted through me when I touched that dark glass.

Standing there alone in that small cold workshop — with its altar to gods Aunt Kell would never approve of — I inadvertently finished Madame Adelaide's project. And something, something dark as night, cold as ice, and ancient as the universe, came pouring into me.

Terror, way past anything I'd ever known, seized me like a hand around my throat. I finally screamed and ran from that room, bouncing off the walls, blinded by tears, my heart threatening to rip right out of my chest. But even while I ran, I knew I couldn't run fast enough because whatever was back there wasn't, not anymore. Now it was inside me, wrapping itself around my soul!

I don't really remember finding my way out of the pier again, but obviously, I did. I *do* recall the cold night as I stood on the empty boards, my chest heaving. I'd been inside Steel Pier a hundred times, and never once had I been as scared as I was at that moment.

And then, on some level deep down inside, I thought, *Maybe I don't have to be that scared now.*

Maybe, just maybe, it didn't happen. Maybe I imagined it, dreamed it. Maybe, if I try real hard, I can walk away and forget.

Just — forget.

And that's exactly what I *did*.

Until now.

All that happened the night before Corinne asked me to sneak out of the hotel with her, go down to the beach, and look at the moon.

In the here-and-now, with the morning turning to afternoon and the sun making sharp shadows of the maze of pilings around us, Rags and I stare at each other. His eyes — because I can see them now — are brown like mine.

Because they *are* mine.

Because he's me.

Rags is me.

CHAPTER 22

PIECES FALL INTO PLACE

—ONE AFTER THE OTHER.

"Two nights ago, right here, when those bangers cornered Corinne and me…" I say, talking to Rags sure, but talking at least as much to myself, too. "Corinne said later that I left her. But I never did. I barely moved. In fact, I was standing over her the whole time. Except…" I look into the shadowed face under that huge hood. "…except I really wasn't, was I?"

Rags slowly shakes his head.

"I was… *you*. Or rather, *you* were *me*, and you *did* leave Corinne, but only to protect her. To… defend her."

Rags' scratchy-ass voice says one word. Just one. "*Gadyen*."

"Guardian," I translate.

He nods.

"Then where was I… *what* was I?" I ask. I don't expect some big, complicated answer. Rags isn't that much of a talker. In fact, I get the feeling that talking at all is hard for him—or it, or whatever. This is a creature of violence, not conversation. So, I do my best to answer my own question, feeling my way along, though we're so far off the map that I can't even see the edge of the paper anymore. "A part of me… my thoughts… my consciousness, the peaceful part, the *human* part I guess… got pushed aside. Nobody could see me. Nobody could hear me. And all I could do was… watch, while my body…" I feel a sudden flash of anger. "…*my* body trashed those dudes."

Rags nods again. No shame. No pride. Simply acknowledging a fact. *Oh, my God.*

I swallow. "Then, the next day, when the Bernards almost found us in the boxing arena, you grabbed me. And that's when we… switched? Is that the word?" When he doesn't respond, I keep going anyway. "You brought me into the mirror maze with you. But, by then, I wasn't really there either, was I? You'd already taken my body, and you brought my… my mind along to watch."

He nods.

"You *son of a bitch!*"

Rags doesn't reply.

"That dude who stumbled onto me didn't react 'cause he saw *me*, but because he saw *you* behind *me*. So, you killed him. And you made me watch!"

He still doesn't reply.

"And that night in the Golden Dome, on the catwalk, when my sibs got caught. We switched again. This time, my consciousness stayed up top, watching as always, while my body jumped down and..." My words trail off.

But Rags nods anyway.

"I chopped off Simon's hand and killed like a dozen of those Godfather types."

To my surprise, Rags shakes his head.

I feel myself scowl as I try to work through it. "Except, it wasn't *me*," I say. "My body, yeah. That's why I came out of it covered in blood — again. But not me. *I* was up on the catwalk."

He nods, quicker than normal, almost as if he's relieved.

"Same thing in the alley beside the hotel, with the big dude in the cop uniform."

Another nod.

"You took my body. That's how the handcuffs got broke. That's how the car door opened. You kicked it using my legs."

Yet another nod.

"But *how?*" I exclaim. "I ain't that strong! *Nobody's* that strong!"

It's a big question, complicated. So, I don't really expect an answer. Which is why I'm surprised when I get one.

"*Maji,*" he says.

Magic. He's strong, or rather *I'm* strong when he's "borrowing" me, for the same reason that Madame Adelaide can stop a mobster from talking with only a word.

Because of what he is. Because that's what having a bad-ass *iwa acheté* inside you does.

"But you don't kill everybody, do you?" I ask. My thoughts reel. "You only killed one of the bangers that first night and one of the bookends in the maze."

Rags nods.

"The rest you... hurt. Cut. Broke."

Another nod.

"Why?"

He looks at me for a long moment, and I get the feeling that he's *trying* to answer. Finally, with a frustrated shrug, he raises one hand, makes "gun" out of his fist, thumb, and forefinger, and kind of pantomimes shooting me.

I run through it in my head. All the killing. All the violence.

Then I say carefully, "You only killed the ones who shot at you… or tried to."

He nods, again looking relieved.

"Even Simon. You just chopped off his hand because he was going to shoot at Tyrone, and not you."

Yet another nod.

My head's getting light. All of this—awareness—is coming on too fast. I'm casually talking about stuff that was impossible just three days ago, stuff that should still *be* impossible. Yet here I am, not just discussing it but *believing* it. All of it.

I feel like vomiting. Maybe if there was something in my stomach, I would.

"What happened in the hospital?" I demand.

Rags pokes my shoulder again and repeats in his raspy voice, "*Vanyan sòlda.*"

And I understand, or think I do, though the understanding cuts me like a black-bladed knife. "That *was* me," I say.

He nods.

"I'd just seen Uncle Nick, my father, get crushed to death in front of me, and… somehow… this time *I* borrowed *you*."

He nods.

"Your speed. Your fancy moves. Your knife. But this time, my consciousness."

"*Vanyan sòlda,*" he repeats.

"There wasn't nothing 'valiant' about what I did to Dreads!" I tell him, almost shouting. "I hacked him to death!"

Rags says nothing.

More tears come. I didn't think I had any left, but it seems I do. I drop my head and cry for what seems a long time, sobbing like a baby. I know it won't do any good, but at the same time, it kind of does. There's just so much inside me that I'm scared I'll explode if I don't let it out somehow.

So, I cry.

Rags doesn't move, not a muscle. He just watches me the whole time. If I'd done this in the Calm Sea Arms, somebody — Uncle Nick, Aunt Kell, or maybe one of my sibs — would hug me, offer up a little comfort. But that isn't Rags, and good thing too. I think I'd lose my mind if this *thing* decided to dish out some kind of "warm embrace."

Finally, when the crying jag's over, I wipe impatiently at my cheeks. "Okay," I tell him, blowing out a sigh. "Now what do I do?"

Again, I'm speaking more to myself than to Rags, which makes it all the weirder when he answers me.

"Aksepte mwen."

I feel my heart, which has already had more than its share of aerobic activity today, try to jump into my throat. I scramble away from Rags, who watches me without moving. Then, when I figure I'm at a safe enough distance — *who am I kidding?* — I get to my feet on legs made stiff from the cold and just stare at him.

"Accept you? *Accept you?* Are you serious? You've already used my body to murder something like a dozen people! And you've turned me into a killer myself! How much more accepting can I possibly do?"

Rags, of course, doesn't reply. But he stands, moving slowly, as if once again afraid of spooking me.

This time, he should be. In fact, the only thing keeping me from running right now is the bitter fact that I've really got no place to go.

For most of a minute, we just stare at each other. We're both still under the pier. The only sound comes from the nearby surf. The pier itself, of course, is quiet. The Boardwalk, too, given how cold it is.

Finally, I break the silence. "It was Madame Adelaide who put you in that mirror."

He nods.

The old woman's words from the Golden Dome last night float up to the surface of my mind. *"I may have invited you, but someone else opened the door. Except, they ain't opened it all the way yet. No, you're here but only halfway."*

"She got you that far," I say. "And, when I touched it, out you popped. Yeah?"

Again, he nods.

Why do I still think of this thing as a 'he?'

Because, if I don't, I might start thinking 'she.'

Or 'me.'

No freaking way!

It takes some doing, but I manage to get my thoughts together. Slowly, real slowly, my heart slides back down my neck and settles where it belongs, giving me the room I need to work things out.

Some time ago, Madame Adelaide came to Atlantic City and, for some reason, set up her workshop in Steel Pier. Maybe she liked the quiet. Or maybe there was more to it than that. Either way, she did her *Vodou* stuff there and used that old mirror to conjure… or summon, or whatever… an *iwa acheté*. But that was as far as she went. Because then she left that place, that workshop. And, while she was out, I stumbled in and, like an idiot, touched the mirror and finished the spell, or almost finished it. I let the thing I call "Rags" into me, into my body, and, to a point, into my mind.

But not all the way.

I didn't "accept" him.

And I won't. Not a chance. Because I've got a sick feeling I know what "accepting" him will mean.

Still, all that raises another question. Why *did* the old *bòkò* split like that, leaving everything undone? There's only one reason I can think of. She never intended to accept Rags, herself. No, the *iwa acheté* was for someone else. Most likely a grandson. Baptiste or Simon.

And why not? One of those psychos with Rags inside of him would be—

—unstoppable.

"I'm the reason you didn't kill them all, ain't I?" I demand. "*All* the bangers. *All* the thugs. *All* the wiseguys. Adelaide said it herself. She didn't understand why you let any of them live. That ain't your nature."

He nods.

"But you only killed the dudes who shot at you, who threatened *my* body, *my* life with their bullets."

Again, he nods, watching me from the shadows.

"But if you'd gotten into one of the Bernards instead of me, they'd have had you butchering everyone you came across. Everyone. You'd like that, wouldn't you? I bet you'd rather be in one of them. Right now, you could be on a full-blown killing spree! What you've done with me's bad enough, mind. But it'd have been all the worse, maybe ten times worse, with Baldy or Dreads. Am I right?"

I expect a nod or at least no reaction.

What I get is a pretty hard shake of the head.

"No? It wouldn't be worse?"

No reply.

I try again. "No, you *wouldn't* rather be one of them?"

Rags nods.

"But why not? I'll bet either of them would've accepted you without a thought, all on Granny's say-so? With me, that ain't never gonna happen. So, what makes me a better… fit?"

He points at me. "*Vanyan sòlda.*"

That just pisses me off. "I keep telling you, I ain't no soldier!"

"*Gadyen.*"

"I ain't no guardian, neither!" I exclaim.

I'm tired, tired to my soul, what's left of it. Uncle Nick's dead, Aunt Kell's sick, Jimmy's afraid of me, and my other sibs are probably scattered by now, dropped off at different foster places with only a trash bag full of clothes and belongings — and memories of a home forever gone.

Oh, and I'm probably wanted for murder.

Suddenly, what this *iwa acheté* prefers or doesn't prefer means exactly jack to me. Suddenly, the only thing that matters is talking to someone I love, telling them what's going on, making them believe, and then maybe getting some — I don't know — guidance.

All this is so big, *too* big, and I feel helpless and utterly small.

An orphaned girl in Atlantic City.

Same old song.

Except now that song's got a body count.

"I'm outta here," I tell Rags, who hasn't moved an inch. Then I turn around and start marching toward the steps that'll take me up to the boards. As I do, I half expect him to dart in front of me, using some of that crazy speed of his. I half expect him to grab me, like he did in the arena, and drag me off somewhere.

But he doesn't. And I suppose I know why.

He can't. Because he's not there. He's *here*. Inside me.

Sweet Jesus, I need to talk to Aunt Kell.

The very idea seems to soothe my hurting soul. By now, my foster mother likely knows she's a widow. She also likely knows what I did to the dude who made her one. If so, will she want to see me at all? I mean, she just had a freaking heart attack!

For that matter, how the hell do I expect to get back into the hospital and to her room without setting alarms off every which way?

First, I gotta get clean.

So, I leave the beach without looking back. Where Rags goes, if he really "goes" anywhere, given what I now know about him, is his business.

I'm going home.

CHAPTER 23

HOME LOOKS THE SAME

— AS ALWAYS. IT'S WEIRDLY COMFORTING. THE CALM SEA ARMS IS RIGHT where it should be, steady as its name. But then, as I get closer, I see the lights of cop cars and ambulances, and suddenly my illusion of coming home turns out to be just that, an illusion.

I guess I shouldn't be surprised. After all, Rags slammed Officer Smirk and then iced Neck Tattoo, all in the alley beside the hotel. So, is it any wonder the place is now a crime scene?

Seems like a lot of the places I go lately get turned into crime scenes.

For half a minute or so, I stand on the sidewalk across the street. There aren't too many folks around on this cold afternoon — and those that are have mostly gathered across Virginia Avenue from me, at the mouth of the alley, checking out the commotion there.

I've ditched my coat, which has helped somewhat with the "blood all over me" problem. I *should* be freezing, but I'm not. That's the good news. The bad is that there's still plenty of blood in my hair and on my jeans and even still some on my face, despite the quick ocean rinse — all of which makes me look like a horror movie reject. It's only a matter of time before somebody notices, maybe somebody in a blue uniform.

I need to move.

Fortunately, we Nelson Kids know our home. We know it inside out and sideways. Yeah, there's the revolving door in the front. Yeah, there's the kitchen door and the fire escape in the alley. But there's *also* the stairs behind Kaplan's Drycleaning, which attaches to the hotel on the opposite side. Those steps lead up to the store's second floor, where an old iron ladder lets you onto the roof. And from there, you can cross to a third-floor window of the Calm Sea Arms.

Nothing to it, so long as nobody sees me.

This kind of thing's much easier after light's out, when the city's dark and quiet. I've never tried it in the middle of the afternoon, much less in the middle of the afternoon while covered in blood. Honest to

God, there are about a hundred ways I could get caught doing this. The only thing in my favor is that the drycleaners is closed, since its owner sold out to Simon Bernard after his brother got beaten to death in front of me and his head delivered to my foster parents in a box.

This is my life now.

But every once in a while, life throws you a little break. I don't get spotted, called out, or ratted on, and make it through the window and into one of the unused rooms on the Boy's Dorm without any problem.

Carefully, I poke my head out into the hallway. But there's nobody. It figures the cops would search the place, doesn't it? But, if so, they haven't done it yet, or maybe already did and found nobody.

That makes me wonder where Jimmy is.

I head down the main stairs to the second floor, treading as lightly as I can. Fortunately, the blood on me has dried, so I don't leave a trail of gory size six footprints on the carpet.

Yep. My life now.

My room's just as I left it, including my bunched-up panties and the trash bag that Tish handed me. Both are right there on the floor. I stare at them for a long moment, feeling all kinds of things, none of them good. Then I pull some fresh clothes out of my closet and head for the showers.

It's a rare thing for a Nelson Kid to be alone in the bathroom for any length of time. I wish I could say I enjoyed the opportunity, but right now it's hard to imagine enjoying anything again, ever.

The silence and the emptiness only remind me of how alone I really am.

I shower thoroughly. It takes a while. There's a lot of blood in my hair, my ears, and under my fingernails. And it's all caked and dried and takes a long time and a lot of hot water to clean off. If things were normal, I'd be catching hell for showering this long. The Calm Sea Arms' boiler isn't exactly generous.

I'm almost sorry when no one complains.

Finally, I dry off and pull on my clothes, listening the whole time. If anybody came in while I was showering, whether cops or killers, I might not have heard them. It was a calculated risk, like Kaplan's stairs.

But, once again, it looks like luck's on my side. I'll be gone in five minutes with no one the wiser.

At least, that's what I'm thinking as I step out of the bathroom—and walk straight into somebody's broad chest.

I scream.

Then I swing my fist wildly managing to connect with the somebody's chin.

Jimmy yells, "Ow! Jeez, Abbs! Are you *kidding* me?" He staggers back a step, rubbing his face and looking at me with irritation.

I stare at him. "What are you doing here?"

"I live here, remember?"

"There are… like… twenty cops outside."

"Yeah, I know. So far, they ain't come in." He crosses his arms. "Now what are *you* doing here?"

I look at him, trying to come up with an answer, trying to figure out what words would somehow put it all together. He's already afraid of me, and I don't blame him. *I'm* afraid of me. Maybe I should lie. But what kind of lie would work? What kind of lie am I even capable of, right now?

I like Jimmy. I might even more than like him. But none of that's going anywhere because I've got Rags inside me. And all this isn't done, not by a long shot.

But I'm also alone.

So, instead of answering, I kind of fall against him. I figure he'll push me away, like he did in the alley. But he doesn't. Instead, his arms close around me and, for a second, I'm afraid the waterworks will start up again. Thankfully, they don't.

But, damn, it feels good to be hugged.

Screw lies.

Finally, I pull back from him, look up into his eyes and say, "I got things to tell you." I shudder, fighting hard to keep from losing it again. "And ain't none of it good."

"Yeah," he replies, and there's something on his face that kind of looks like a smile but has about as much humor as a toothache. "I figured. So, tell me."

Which I do.

I tell him all of it, every bit. Everything I know. Everything you know.

When I'm done, he looks me up and down and doesn't say anything, not at first. A lot of things flash across his face. He takes a long, deep breath.

"Do you believe me?" I ask.

"Yeah."

"Are you afraid of me?"

"I dunno. Maybe, a little. But from what you say, it's *him* I gotta be afraid of. Rags."

"Rags won't hurt you."

Jimmy shakes his head. "I don't get how you can even say that! He's hurt a lot of people. He's made you kill somebody!"

"I know. But…" Except I've got no idea what comes next.

"Why you, Abbs?" he asks, taking my hand. I love the feeling of his warm fingers around mine. It reminds me of what we did, him and me, just this morning. It was the last time I felt even partway normal.

Jimmy says, "If all of this shit is somehow true, and this witch really did cook up a demon or something for one of her grandsons, then why did it go into you at all?"

Looking up into his eyes, I have to admit, "I don't know. I really don't. Just bad luck, maybe? Wrong place at the wrong time?"

He offers up another of those almost-smile smiles. "You and that damned pier."

And, despite myself, despite everything, I almost smile back. Because it's true. "Me and that damned pier," I reply.

Voices reach us from downstairs. They're faint, floating up the main staircase from the lobby. Jimmy looks alarmed. "They know we're here!" he whispers.

But I shake my head. "Uh uh. They're coming in to search, but they figure it's a waste of time since everybody got pulled out this morning."

"You can hear all that?"

I blink. "Yeah. Sure. Can't you?"

"Abby, it's all the way down in the lobby! This is like on the pier last night. Since when do you got super-hearing?"

I feel myself swallow. Thinking back, I realize he's right. I *am* able to hear stuff that's way too far away. I mean, right now, if I concentrate, I think I can hear the heartbeats of the cops downstairs. They're still talking, apparently in no hurry to search this "big old place," as they call it.

Then one of them says, *"Didn't Carfanno say they left one kid in the house? A teenage boy?"*

"Yeah, but I don't trust that bent jackass as far as I can throw him. He pulls more graft than anybody in the department."

"Why would he lie about a kid?"

"Who cares? Whatever happened to the naked guy in the alley, it wasn't no kid who did it. Even Carfanno said that. It was that homeless guy, the same one as under the pier. Guy's earning a rep on the street. You know all the call's we been getting, sightings around town."

"Sure. But they all turn out to be just ordinary street people, don't they?"

"So far."

"You figure the homeless guy is real?"

"Somebody *hit* those wise guys last night on Steel Pier."

"I thought that didn't 'officially' happen."

"Yeah, right."

"And you think it was the same guy as in the alley today?"

"That bastard, Carfanno, does."

"How is he? Carfanno, I mean. I heard he's got a concussion."

"How the hell should I know? I know he went straight out on medical leave, milking a bump on the head for all it's worth. Right now, he's probably locked away in that shitty little place he rents up on Presbyterian Avenue. You ever been there?"

"Naw."

"You ain't missing a thing. Place stinks of bug spray. He won't say, but I'll bet he's got a real roach problem."

"He's not married?"

"Left him years ago. Smart girl."

"But now he's the only cop who's seen the homeless guy."

"Yep. Detective Rauch had him work with a sketch artist, but from the way I hear it, what they got is just flat-out useless."

"Why do you figure the killer left that thug naked in the alley?"

"You really want to know?"

"Yeah. I asked, didn't I?"

"Carfanno called it in, right? He gets hit on the head beside his car and, when he comes to, he finds this guy in his underwear with a knife hole in his chest. At least, that's his story. Well, just between you and me, I'll bet you anything the vic was fully clothed and Carfanno stripped him before calling it in."

"Why would he do that?"

"Nobody'll work with him, anymore. Yet, the garage says two cops checked out his cruiser this morning. So, who was he with? And, if it wasn't a cop, then where'd that other guy get the uniform that the dispatcher says he had on?"

"You think Carfanno loaned somebody a police uniform? Seriously?"

"I wouldn't put anything past that guy."

"But why? Why the hell would anybody take a chance like that?"

"Damned if I know. But that's Carfanno. He's always running one scam or another. He'll be out on his ass in a month, mark my words. Bump on the head or no."

"Maybe. But none of that gets us closer to the homeless perp, or the girl from the hospital."

"Has anybody talked to the old lady?"

"Her name's Kelley Nelson and she's a good woman. I know her and I knew her husband. Show a little respect."

"Fine. Sorry."

"Forget it. Rauch says they got her drugged up pretty heavy on account of what happened to Nelson. They'll talk to her when the poor thing can talk."

"How about the other kids, then? The fosters?"

"They're getting relocated."

Jimmy says, "Abby, what are you—"

But I put a finger to his lips to shush him.

Downstairs, one of the cops says, "Family Services took them to the hospital, promising to let them say good-bye to Mrs. Nelson. But when everything went down, they were questioned and then given back to the social workers who, from what I heard, set out getting them all into different foster homes. It's a damned shame, if you ask me. The Nelsons have fostered something like two hundred kids in the last twenty years. This place was as good a home as anyone could want. And just like that—" He snaps his fingers. I hear it, clear as a bell. "He's dead, she's had a heart attack, and those poor kids are stuck in the System again."

"Beats Juvie."

"Way to empathize, asshole. Come on, let's get started. This place is going to take a while to go through."

And, with that, they divvy up the floors, and I stop listening.

"We gotta get out of here," I tell Jimmy.

"And go where?"

"The hospital. I… need to talk to Aunt Kell."

"She'll be guarded. And, from what you said, ain't they gonna… recognize you?"

I think. I think hard. Maybe I should skip Aunt Kell. If she's really as doped up as the cops said, she wouldn't be able to talk to me anyhow. Besides, what am I hoping to get from her? Advice? Forgiveness? Some kind of escape from the hell I've gotten myself into?

I don't know. I truly don't.

I just—really, really need to talk to my mom right now.

"I'm going," I tell Jimmy. "You wanna come?"

For a second, I think he'll refuse, decide instead to wait for the cops or maybe slip out on his own. But then his shoulders kind of square and he says, "I'm with you, Abbs."

The depth of my relief surprises me. "Okay. Cool. Get your coat. I've got an idea."

CHAPTER 24

THE HOSPITAL ALSO LOOKS THE SAME

— AS WHEN I RAN OUT OF IT A COUPLE OF HOURS AGO, EXCEPT FOR THE cop cars. There are three of them, two locals and a state cruiser parked on the street out front. Well, of course there are. That hallway where everything went down has *got* to be another crime scene after all.

The sun's getting low as Jimmy and I approach the place along Pacific Avenue, taking our time about it. I'm in all different clothes and different shoes. But my wardrobe's getting pretty thin. Showing up covered in blood every ten minutes can do that. So, instead of a coat, I'm wearing one of Jimmy's hoodies. It's way too big on me, but it covers my face, Rags-style.

Jimmy keeps fretting that I'll freeze to death without something warmer. But, for some reason, I don't feel the cold like I used to. Another change, like the super-hearing, maybe?

One more thing that scares me.

"You okay?" Jimmy asks.

"Not even close."

"Abbs, you can walk away from this. I'll give you bus fare. Get out of town. Change your name. Leave it all."

"They'll be watching the buses."

"Shit, girl. They're watching *here!*"

"I have to see her."

"It's crazy."

I stop and look hard into his face. "It's the last time I'm *ever* going to see her."

He swallows. "Yeah," he says after a moment. "Okay."

"I'll be waiting outside," I tell him. "Keeping my head down."

"I'll deliver. I promise."

"I know you will."

Then he does something I don't expect. He kisses me. It's not like before, short and sweet instead of long and deep and hot. This time it's not about passion, exactly. It's more about—something else.

But, afterward, when we finally separate, he doesn't say the words. You know — *those* words. He looks like he wants to, but he doesn't.

To be fair, I don't say them, either.

Looking back, I wish I did.

Then he crosses the street and heads in through the hospital's revolving doors.

I stick my hands in my pockets and watch him through the big glass windows as he walks up to the receptionist's desk, all casual. He's got to be thirty yards away from me, but I still see every detail of his every move, almost like I'm looking through binoculars.

Another superpower.

There are cops in the lobby. Two of them. I get the feeling they're just keeping an eye on things. After all, you can't shut down a hospital just because there was a murder in it. Or two. This is Atlantic City. Shit happens.

I can *hear* everything as well. True, there's a lot of traffic on the street, a lot of city noise. You'd think that would screw up reception, or whatever you call it. But I find that, with just a little bit of concentrating, I can block it all out and focus on the conversation going on at the reception desk.

"Can I help you?" the receptionist asks. She's not the same woman as before. This one's younger and her smile looks more real.

"I'm here to visit my aunt. Her name's Kelley Nelson."

Still smiling, the receptionist starts tapping on her computer. Jimmy watches her, fidgeting. I wish he wouldn't do that. But then I remember doing the same thing a few hours ago, and I cut him some slack.

After a few seconds, the receptionist's smile dips down. A little warily, she asks, *"Your aunt, you said?"*

Jimmy replies, *"Yeah."* Then, showing some serious acting creds, he adds, *"Is something wrong? She okay?"*

The two cops kind of saunter over to him. No surprise. Aunt Kell's name has become a trigger word.

The receptionist says quickly, *"Oh, yes! I'm sorry. Yes! It's just that her file is flagged. Um… are you local, young man?"*

"No," Jimmy lies smoothly. His eyes flick to the cops, looking bewildered and maybe wary, but not guilty. Honest to God, he deserves an Oscar. *"I'm from Philly. My uncle called this morning, said they were taking her to the hospital. Didn't say why. So, I grabbed the train."*

"I see," the woman replies.

"You got your folks with you, kid?" This comes from one of the cops.

Jimmy looks at him and shakes his head. *"Working. They'll come by a little later."*

"What's your name?" the other asks.

"Matt Nelson."

"Got any id?"

Jimmy looks worried. *"Like what?"*

"Driver's license?"

"Don't have one. Like I said, I took the train from Philly."

That seems to satisfy them. And why wouldn't it? The perp they're looking for is a girl, not a boy.

Even so, I breathe a little sigh of relief when they seem to lose interest and turn away.

The receptionist says, *"Unfortunately, your aunt's not cleared for visitors at this time."*

"What? Why not? What's going on?"

She bites her lip. Yeah, I really *can* see her biting her lip. *"It's… complicated, and I'm not in a position to give you more information than that. I'm sorry."*

Jimmy's shoulders sag. Well, we kind of figured on something like this, and so we came up with a Plan B. With a long sigh, he says, *"You got a gift shop?"*

"We do. It's right down the hall."

"Can I get her a card or something and have it sent up?"

The receptionist's smile returns. She likes the gesture. *"I don't see why not."*

So, Jimmy does just that, strolling right past the two cops like he's the most innocent dude on Planet Earth. He comes back five minutes later with a small vase of flowers and a card.

"It's lovely!" the receptionist assures him as he places the vase on the desktop and politely borrows one of her pens to fill out the card. Then, sliding it into its envelope, he writes Aunt Kell's name on the front and asks, sweet as you please, *"What room?"*

The receptionist, still admiring the flowers, replies without thinking. *"415."*

Jimmy adds the room number to the envelope and then sticks it in with the flowers. *"Thanks,"* he says. *"Um… is it cool if I wait in the lobby for my folks?"*

"Of course, sweetie. And, if you get hungry, there's a cafeteria downstairs and a nice coffee shop down the block."

Jimmy nods, leaves the gift, and strolls over to the window. Standing there, he looks across the street at me and scratches his nose. I scratch mine.

Then I give him as big a smile as I can manage under the circumstances.

After all, he delivered, as promised.

Making sure my hood's up, I cross the street and turn the corner, moving along the sidewalk past the hospital. There's a driveway up ahead for ambulances. I follow it to another entrance, this one with the word EMERGENCY in lit red letters above the doors. In a perfect world, or at least an *easier* one, I could maybe walk in there. It would still be tough getting to the fourth floor unchallenged, but sure as hell simpler than what I've got in mind right now.

Unfortunately, I can't risk it. After what happened—after what I did—a couple of hours ago in this very hospital, there's no telling how many cops are combing the place. If I'm going to pull this off, I need to get in there a different way, an unexpected way—

—a *Rags* way.

So, I skip the Emergency Room entrance and head instead to a shallow space beside it. It's not an alley exactly, but just a kind of nook, a place to tuck away a commercial dumpster.

I look around. There are a few folks in sight, but none of them are facing my way. So, looking as "yeah, it's perfectly cool for me to be doing this shit" as I possibly can, I saunter over and climb up onto the dumpster.

Okay, here comes the tricky part.

I take a deep breath and concentrate on my right hand. I told Jimmy this would work, and it will—I *think*. Because Rags isn't "out there" someplace. He's right here, inside me, and he's just waiting for me to ask for something like this—

—again, I *think*.

My hand's open, my fingers splayed.

Now, still concentrating, I close it, slowly making a fist.

And there it is.

As I hold up the black-bladed knife, I almost laugh. But I don't, partly because I'm worried about attracting attention, but mostly because I'm afraid of how it'll sound.

Instead, I lift my eyes, looking straight up the brick wall between me and the rows of upper floor windows. The fourth floor's maybe thirty-five feet above my head. Thirty-five feet. Not so bad. Except that I've never in my life managed to climb so much as a gym rope. Upper body strength isn't exactly my thing. So, what makes me imagine I can pull *this* off?

The fact that I can run like the wind, move like an Olympic gymnast, and speak Creole, that's what.

I take a deep breath. Then I jump as high as I can. This turns out to be quite a bit higher than I expected, taking me almost five feet up the wall. At the top of the jump, I swing my arm and drive the knife at the bricks. I half-expect it to bounce off, maybe even break, when it hits the hard, hundred-year-old mortar. But, instead, it just slides right in, like the wall's made of soft cheese. There isn't even any sound to speak of.

In the next instant, I'm hanging by one hand, six feet above the dumpster. This time I *do* laugh.

Step One done. On to Step Two.

I reach up with my other hand and take hold of the knife in a two-fisted grip. Then, and trust me, all this is more instinct than sense, I plant my sneakered feet against the wall and kind of kick off — and *up* — pulling the knife free at the same time.

I half-expect to blow the whole deal and go crashing down onto the dumpster. But, instead, I clear another five feet of wall and, right at the top, manage to plant the knife again.

Damn! No upper body strength my ass!

I'm right beside the second-floor windows now, so I risk a peek. I'm hoping to see a hospital bedroom, preferably an empty one. But no such luck. It's a hallway, and I count at least a half-dozen folks, mostly in white coats, moving around in there.

Next stop, third floor.

The view through *that* window looks more or less the same as the one below it, making my heart sink a little further. But, since I've come too far to give up now, I keep going, "knife-jumping" up the wall to the fourth floor. Aunt Kell's floor.

The hallway's the same, maybe slightly less busy — but busy enough that no way am I going to be able to get in there without somebody seeing me.

Who knew sneaking into a crowded hospital in the middle of the day would be so hard?

At least no one's spotted me doing my weird drunk Spiderman thing up the side of the building—yet. But it's only a matter of time.

With my feet propped up for support and gripping the knife in my right hand, I use my left to explore the window. It's not like the more modern ones I've seen, something that I was counting on. This here's an older model, with panes that slide left and right and a heavy aluminum screen for letting in fresh air. Apparently, nobody's gotten around to putting the storm windows in, if they even have them.

That's good for me.

My fingers find the top corner of the screen and pull it free. It's easy, *way* easier than it should be. But, since I'm thirty feet up with only a little shoe traction and a knife keeping me from falling, I don't sweat my good fortune. Instead, as the screen tumbles down, bouncing loudly—too loudly—against the dumpster, I reach for the edge of the window and push.

I'm worried it'll be latched; in which case I'll have to break the glass. But it's not. I mean, why would it be? We're four stories up.

Sound floods out through the now-open window, beeps and buzzes and the low hum of conversation. Hospital white noise.

Step Three.

Hanging onto the knife, I swing one leg over and up, hooking my knee around the windowpane. Then, shifting my body weight, I push off with my other foot and pull the knife free.

For a split second, I think I've blown it. For a split second, the world opens up below me and I know—*know*—I'm about to drop like a stone. After that, I can get into the hospital the old-fashioned away, assuming the fall doesn't kill me.

But then I'm through the window and lying on the hallway floor, gulping for air.

An instant later, two things happen. The first is a loud voice, a dude's voice, coming from the hospital grounds outside. "Hey, what are you— Dan, did you see that! I think somebody just went in that window!"

Shit.

At the same time, a woman in scrubs comes through a door not five feet from where I'm lying. She takes one look at me, the open window, and the knife—

—and then she starts screaming.

Double shit.

I jump to my feet, motioning for her to calm down. But all she sees is me waving a black-bladed machete around and screams all the harder. Suddenly, three more people, two women and a man, approach us, looking concerned.

With a groan, I start running. There's a sign on the wall pointing me toward the numbered patient rooms. 415 is straight down on the left. I push past two more scrubs, almost knocking them over as I race in that direction. Behind me, someone calls for security. Someone else calls for 911. And the nurse keeps screaming.

Triple shit.

I expect there to be a guard or something outside Aunt Kell's room, but there isn't. There *is*, however, a folding chair and a half-drunk cup of coffee on the floor beside it, making me think the cop, or guard, or whatever is off taking a leak.

Small favors.

With lots of folks gasping and yelling and pointing at me, I push open the door to Room 415 and step inside.

There are two beds, separated by an open curtain. The bed nearest the door is empty. The one by the window isn't. The room's dimly lit; its drapes drawn. The first thing I do is check the door for a lock. Big surprise, it doesn't have one. So, instead, I grab a heavy visitor's chair and jam it under the handle. This actually works pretty well, or seems to, so that I feel safe enough to look around.

Aunt Kell's asleep on her back. There's an IV in her arm and wires running from under her hospital gown to a machine that's beeping off her heartbeats. A blanket's been draped over her and tucked in around her legs.

At the sight of her, I feel heartsick. For a long moment, all I can do is stand there, watching her, my mouth dry. She became a widow today, a reality that can't have truly hit her yet.

Slowly, I go to her side and take her hand. Her skin feels cold.

"Aunt Kell?"

She stirs. A moment later, someone pounds on the door. I expect it, but the sound still makes me jump. What can I say? I'm a little fried right now.

"Aunt Kell?" I say again.

Her eyes flutter open, but don't immediately focus. Seconds tick by. Then, in a hopeful whisper that almost kills me, she asks, "Nicky?"

I try to answer, swallow, and try again. "It's Abigail, Aunt Kell."

Her head turns toward me. She looks small, so small, so different from the powerful, generous, loving woman who raised me. "Abby?"

"Yeah."

"What are you doing here?"

There's more pounding outside. Voices. Someone insists I'm armed and that they should wait for the cop to get back.

I don't have much time.

"Um… visiting you," I tell Aunt Kell.

I expect her to start asking me questions. I don't know how much she knows about what's been happening. But, instead, her face crumples and she says in a broken whisper, "He's dead."

I have to choke back a sob. "I know."

"They won't tell me what happened."

I don't—can't—reply to that.

She says, "It's all falling apart, Abby."

"I know," I tell her again.

"My children are gone. My husband. I don't…" Her eyes close for a second, but then open again. "The nurse gave me something. She said it would calm me. But it's not really working."

I suddenly feel like dirt. No, worse than that, I feel like a little kid. I've come here, taking this awful risk, to ask a drugged, grieving woman for advice about me being halfway possessed by a Haitian blood spirit. I mean, *seriously*?

At least, the pounding on the door has stopped.

"Aunt Kell," I say, trying to keep the tremor out of my voice. "There's some stuff I gotta tell you."

When she looks at me, I can see she's trying to listen. But her eyes keep sliding in and out of focus. Before I even start talking, they slip to half-mast and she whispers, "My poor Nicky."

Oh, God.

"Why are you bothering, child?"

Fighting down a scream, I twist my head around.

Madame Adelaide is standing in the corner by the window.

When she sees me seeing her, she sort of smiles. It's the kind of smile that you'd expect to see on a wolf that's about to chow down on some rabbit. In a soft voice that's anything but soft, she says, "This poor madame has lost so much today. Why burden her with your problems, especially since there's not a thing she can do for you?"

Instinctively, I put myself between the two women and raise my knife — I mean Rag's knife.

I half-expect to be shaking. Let's face it: I'm nobody's hero.

But my hand's steady as a rock.

The only response I get from the old lady, however, is a laugh. "So brave. So foolish," she says, and I'm gripped by a sudden, terrifying desire to slice the condescending smile right off her face.

Except, like before, I don't think she's really here. This is another ghost, another black-magic projection.

I say through clenched teeth. "You leave her be!"

Adelaide makes a dismissive gesture. "Child, I got no interest in that there woman. She's nothing to me. Besides, her faith is around her. I can feel it from here. It's *strong*, stronger than most, and I don't got the time or the need to try to get past it. But you," She points a long bony finger at me and says in a voice that's lost all trace of amusement. "With *you*, I got a quarrel. And now, I have me the way to settle the score."

"What's… that mean?"

"You stole from me. Have you remembered yet? Why yes, I do think you have. You took from me a power that it cost me months to summon, and you took it away without even knowing you did it. But you know now, am I right?"

I don't say anything.

The old woman keeps talking anyhow. "So much *maji*, wasted on the likes of you. So much beautiful darkness. That *iwa acheté* you got inside you is as old as the world, a thing of blood, a thing of power. To imagine it tied to your little, useless soul… it *sickens* me!"

"He picked me," I say. It comes out sounding more whiney than defiant. I'm not even sure if it's true.

At that, the old woman laughs uproariously. "Picked you? *You?* I was going to give it a real vessel! I was going to give it my Baptiste, a warrior! A man to be feared. A man worthy of such a *manyifik lespri nwa*!"

"*Magnificent dark spirit.*"

Of all the words I might pick to describe Rags, "magnificent" wouldn't be one of them.

Adelaide blows out a sigh. "Well, what's done is done. There's no undoing it now."

"Then why are you here?" I ask.

Her grin is wide and terrifying. Just seeing it makes my knees go weak. "Why, child, only to tell you how you'll pay for my *cher*, Baptiste. Didn't I say vengeance is cold?"

Those last words send a chill down my spine. I try to speak, but nothing comes out.

"I've made myself a little collection today," the old woman whispers. "Ten sweet innocent lambs. They're not enough of course. For what I've in mind, two more are needed. One I collected along with them, and the other I'll have soon. And, when I do, they'll serve both my vengeance and my purpose. Their blood will help me make my other *cher*, my Simon, the man to be truly feared in this city. He will be *nepe mwen, vanjeur mwen an.*"

"My sword, my avenger."

In a small voice, a squeak of a voice, I ask her, "Who do you have?"

Again, she waves dismissively. "Oh, I don't know their names. One is a grown woman. Older than I'd like but she has a good heart. The rest…" She laughs, the sound inhuman. "…the rest I think you call *family*."

"No!" Aunt Kell screams. I wasn't even sure she was still conscious. When she sits bolt upright, the machine she's wired to starts beeping like crazy. In her hand is a small silver cross, taken from the nightstand. It's the one she always wears around her neck. "You will *not* hurt my babies!"

To my surprise, Madame Adelaide recoils and covers her eyes, the way a vampire might. "You can't stop it! Not you and not your God! I'll have my revenge!" Then, her face a twisted snarl, she waves a hand at me and exclaims, "A parting gift before I go, child! Get used to it!"

An instant later, she's gone, like before in the hallway — just *gone*.

"Abagail… was that *her*?" Aunt Kell asks me, sounding more alert than before. The *bòkò*?"

I'm shaking like a leaf. It's all I can do to answer, "Yeah."

Without warning, the door bursts open, knocking the chair aside. Standing there is a cop. With him are two security guards. A trifecta of trouble. The cop has his gun drawn. "Drop the knife!" he exclaims.

An instant later, one of the security guards hits the light switch.

Overhead fluorescent lamps come on, illuminating everything. Aunt Kell's still sitting up, the silver cross in her hand. The corner, where Madame Adelaide had been only seconds ago, is now empty.

And me? Well, I'm suddenly covered in blood, head to toe, just like I was before.

"A parting gift before I go, child."

"Get used to it."

Oh, come on…

CHAPTER 25

I DROP THE KNIFE

—AND RAISE MY HANDS, SHOWING THE COP THAT THEY'RE NOW EMPTY. The black blade hits the floor point first and buries itself a few inches into the tile, kind of the way it did in that piling earlier.

Both the cop and I look down at it.

Then I take a step back, putting a little space between the weapon and me.

And, from the look on the cop's face, it was probably the smart move.

"Get on the floor!" The cop and the two security dudes behind him all yell this at exactly the same time. Perfect unison. It might be funny, except for the fact that nothing's ever going to be funny again.

I look back at Aunt Kell, who's staring at me, wide-eyed. I expect her to start screaming. But she doesn't. Instead, she fixes me with her eyes and says, "You save them, Abigail Lowell! You save my children! Do you hear me?"

And I suddenly understand why I really came here this afternoon.

I just got all the advice I need.

"I hear you, Mamma," I say.

Then I face the three dudes. They're coming at me slowly, looking around, maybe searching for the source of the blood that covers me. But, of course, there's nothing. This time, the blood came from nowhere.

From *maji*.

"Get down on the floor!" the cop yells again. Then, to the nearest security dude, he says, "Step back. I got this."

"It's our job, man!"

"Step the hell back!" the cop repeats, yelling this time. For a second, a split second, the three of them all glare at each other. It seems a crazy time to be measuring manhoods, but hey, guys are guys—and it gives me the opening I need.

I throw myself at the cop first, seizing his gun and ripping it away before he can react. Then, with my other hand, I grab the front of his shirt and kind of throw him. He's twice my size, but he goes flying anyway, clearing the empty bed before crashing to the floor.

He looks almost as surprised as I am.

One of the security dudes comes next. He's got no gun, but his nightstick is out and swinging. Except, he's slow, *so* slow. I duck under it, slip past him as he moves by me, turn and shove my foot into his ass, hard. With a cry that's weirdly also in slow motion, he stumbles forward, arms pinwheeling, and hits the corner where Madame Adelaide was standing—face first.

As the third dude reaches for me, I hit him in the gut with my shoulder. His breath leaves him in a long wheeze as he crashes back through the door.

And, just like that, I'm in the hallway.

There have got to be twenty people out here, doctors, nurses, orderlies, and even a few curious patients. All of them are staring at me the way a herd of gazelles eyes a lioness.

So, I say the stupidest possible thing, under the circumstances. "Um… pardon me." Then I lower my head and barrel forward, praying they all get out of the way.

They do. Some of them scream and fall while they're at it, but they do.

About fifty feet ahead is the end of the hallway and the fourth-floor window I came in through. It's closed now, most likely against the chill. But, at this point, I don't think that's a problem.

You best still be with me, Rags…

I clear the distance, running full tilt, and dive at the window, closing my eyes and keeping my head low. At worst, I'll hit the heavy glass and crack either it or my skull. At best—I'll go right through it.

I go right through it.

As the glass explodes around me, I half-expect to be cut to ribbons. But that doesn't happen. Oh sure, a few shards stick me here and there, but the pain is nothing, less than nothing.

It's yet another marvel that I simply don't have time to marvel at.

Suddenly, I'm in open air, a foot clear of the hospital's outside wall. Then two feet. Then I'm falling. But, weirdly, it's a controlled fall. I know exactly how to turn my body, how to shift my weight, and how to bend my knees, so that I hit the ground in front of the dumpster just right—and roll with my momentum.

A second later, I'm up on my feet and running full-tilt back toward Pacific Avenue. By now, Jimmy should already be there, having made his excuses to the receptionist and crossed the street to meet me at the same corner where we said good-bye.

And there he is!

As I get close, I can see him. But my relief doesn't last, because he's not alone. Two dudes are with him, *on* him, both big and scary-looking. They've got him by the arms and are dragging him somewhere. He's yelling, cussing like crazy, but this is Atlantic City — and no way is anybody going to help him. A few folks have stopped to watch, like the people in the hospital corridor. But the rest are either crossing the street or walking around the fight, giving the whole thing a wide berth.

Jimmy spots me.

"Abby!" he screams.

Then, as I run toward him, the two thugs toss him into the back of a sedan. They climb in right after, yelling for the driver to "Go! Go! Go!" As the car peels away, I cut across Pacific Avenue, trying to catch it, wondering if I can — I don't know — rip the door off its hinges or something. But, at the last second, the driver guns it and the car screeches out into late-day traffic, drawing curses and angry honks.

Jimmy!

Shit!

Number twelve.

I don't know that for sure, but it makes sense. Terrible sense.

My entire family. All except poor dead Uncle Nick and poor heartbroken Aunt Kell. My sibs. Every one of them.

And it's my fault. It's Adelaide's revenge on me.

"You save them, Abigail Lowell! You save my children!"

Except, I *can't*. I don't know where they are.

But — maybe Rags does.

As shouts sound from somewhere in or around the hospital at my back, I make for the beach. Folks clear out of my way as I charge through them, running faster than I've ever run in my life. To them, I must be like a bloody blur moving through the late afternoon.

The wind's really kicking up by the time I reach the Boardwalk. I don't bother going under the boards this time. Sure, I'm still a wanted fugitive, but right now, I don't care. There aren't any people around in this cold, anyhow.

I've got the beach to myself.

Steel Pier's north of me, way up the beach, just a long blocky shape in the deepening gloom. But I don't bother going there, either. No need. I just run down to the edge of the water, until the cold Atlantic surf, roiled by the wind, just misses my shoes. Then I call out at the top of my voice, "Rags!"

It's the first time I've ever called him that, at least when I was addressing *him* and not talking to others *about* him. But something tells me he'll know who I mean, just like something tells me he'll come when I call.

And he does.

I sense him before I see him, just that squirmy feeling of being watched. With a gasp, I whirl around and there he is, standing six feet away, his booted feet planted in the sand.

"She's got my family," I tell him. Just saying the words out loud brings tears to my eyes. But I force them down. I've got a promise to keep.

He nods.

Does that mean he already knows or that he's just acknowledging what I told him?

Who cares?

I swallow and say, "What happens if I accept you?"

At first, I worry he won't, or can't, answer. Like I said before, talking's hard for him. Finally, in his sandpaper voice, he manages to reply, "*Nou vin yon sèl.*"

"*We become one.*"

"Jesus," I mutter. My heart starts hammering. "Forever?"

He nods.

Now my stomach twists and I begin to tremble. I don't know exactly what "we become one" means, but I can make some solid guesses. It means no more high school. No prom. No college. No normal life at all.

It means no Jimmy.

But if I don't do it, there won't be a Jimmy either, because that bitch'll kill him. She'll kill them all.

"Why me?" I ask. "I mean, did you *have* to come out of that mirror when I touched it like a fool? Or did you... choose to?"

Again, it takes him a while to reply. This exchange is as hard for him as it is for me.

At last, he says, "*Vle vin yon sòlda vanyan.*"

"I want to be a valiant soldier."

I stare at him, finally understanding.

Baptiste Bernard, with Rags inside him, would have become a monster. Fueled by the *iwa acheté*, he'd have taken over the city, killing everyone and anyone in his path. Nothing could have stopped the wave of blood. And Simon would have been no different. With either of the Bernard Bros, we'd all have drowned in the carnage and death, which of course is exactly what their *bòkò* grandmother wanted.

But with *me* —

"I'm not valiant," I tell him. "I'm no kind of soldier. I'm just... a girl."

He shakes his head and raises one hand to point at me. *"Bonjan. Brav. Gadyen,"* he rasps.

"Strong. Brave. Guardian."

Strong? Brave? None of that's true! Hell, lately, all I've *been* is scared. And a guardian? I've managed to lose my father, and I'm on the verge of losing everyone else. Some guardian!

But to Rags, all that must seem like shining virtue beside what he is and what he was summoned here to do. Since linking up with me, Rags has taken lives, plenty of them, way more than I care to count. But he hasn't taken as many as he could have. Not even close. And the lives he took weren't in any way innocent. Not one. All of them were killers, like him.

Like *me*, now.

I'm looking at a demon, a demon who wants to be — better.

"If I accept you," I say. It's a chore to get out every single word. "Can you save them?"

This time, his answer is almost immediate, *"Nou ka sove yo, Abby."*

"We can save them, Abby."

How weird it is to hear my name come out of whatever passes for a mouth under that hood. It chills me way more than the cold wind or the sea spray. For a second or two, no longer, I think about running again. Just running. I think about getting away from here, from him, from all the blood and all the misery. And all the grief.

But I can't. Because I promised. Because they're my family. And because —

— because maybe I *am* a *gadyen*.

"Abby," he says again, stepping forward and offering me his grubby, dirt-crusted hand. The next word is in English. And, from the way he kind of spits it out, I can tell that it's hard for him. Crazy hard.

"P—lease."

I think of Jimmy, Tish, and Corinne. I think of Darlene and Tyrone. I think of Jeff and Sarah. I think of Lita and Gabe. And I think of the tods, Keisha and Joline. Yeah, I know it's the first time I've told you the little ones' names. Well, it wasn't important before. It *is* now. All of them are important now.

I draw a breath. Then another. They're the last breaths I'll ever take just being me.

Then I reach out, take his hand, and say in Creole, "*Mwen aksepte ou.*"

"*I accept you.*"

Rags makes another sound, not words this time, but a kind of sigh.

Then, before my eyes, he just sort of blows away. It's not the same as his vanishing act. That feels more like somebody leaving a room. This seems—permanent. He's gone. Rags, as I knew him, is forever gone.

So are his clothes, those filthy, foul-smelling garments that earned him his nickname. Because, like him, they weren't really *real*. The Rags I've been seeing was just a kind of placeholder, an outline for something shapeless while it waited for a form of its own. And now that I've accepted him, they're no longer needed.

The broken *iwa* has moved.

Moved into me.

I'm his shape.

I always have been.

Only now he ain't "borrowing" me no more.

I feel him—it, since there isn't a "him" anymore—pour into me completely, unseen but as tangible, as *real* as I am. It floods me, but weirdly not in a scary way. It's more like *completion*, not of me, exactly, but of the bargain we made, the obligation I unknowingly took on when I touched that mirror.

I don't move, can't move, as the *iwa acheté* reaches every part of me. It's electric and yet somehow soothing, frightening, and yet oddly natural. My mind *opens*, and I suddenly see everything around me with a clarity I never knew existed, never imagined could exist. I know every inch of the beach around me, every grain of sand, every particle of wind. I can even predict, with perfect awareness, how that wind will affect each of those grains of sand, how that sand will move as the waves continue rolling, and how the creatures in that ocean will be swept about by the outgoing tide.

So clear. So absolute.

So beautiful.

And it isn't over.

I look around and find, to my surprise, that time's passing fast, incredibly fast. Stars are popping out overhead, not individually either, but by the dozen. The wind gets crazy strong, and the sand under my feet shifts weirdly as the tide visibly recedes, sliding away from my sneakers like somebody's pulled the plug on the ocean.

Twilight becomes dark. Dark becomes full dark.

Hours become seconds.

That's how long it takes for *me* to become Rags.

When full awareness finally comes back and I manage to do something as normal and mundane as checking my watch, I see with astonishment and no small bit of horror that it's now past midnight.

I've been on this beach for something like seven hours.

Good thing the tide was going out instead of coming in. Otherwise, I might have been swept out to sea before I even realized it.

I could have drowned. A stupid death.

I wonder if I even can *drown now…*

Then my breath catches. What has all this transformation stuff cost me? Rags promised we could save my family. But what if, while I was standing here "accepting" him, Bernard and his Granny murdered them all?

No.

I stop, listening.

It wasn't a word, exactly. Rags isn't talking to me. Rags doesn't exist anymore. He's gone. *I'm* gone. And what's left is a kind of mix of the two of us, a — conglomeration. Everything I am and everything he is. And it's an ancient power I'm keyed into right now.

If they were dead, I'd know.

It's weird to be so certain of something like that, something outside the senses. But I *am* certain, and that certainty brings relief with it, as well as a hard resolve.

I look down at the sweatshirt and jeans I'm wearing, still covered in the blood that Adelaide conjured up. I'm not cold. I'm not tired. I'm not hungry. All that shit's behind me now. But, from the outside, I'm still Abby Lowell, a harmless-looking teenage girl.

That won't do.

Now I'm Rags. A new Rags, sure. But still Rags. And I need to look the part.

Bernard's thugs, the gangbangers, even the cops have gotten to know the "homeless guy" who's been racking up a body count these past few days. They've all seen what he — me — we — can do, and they're learning to fear it.

I can use that.

So, with the wind blowing in my face and the ocean at my back, I spread my arms.

And Rags' clothes come to me. Now get this: I don't "put them on." I'll never again have to do anything so ordinary as pull up a pair of pants. That kind of thing is for mortals, not the likes of me. Instead, the trousers and coat just kind of *transfer* onto me, the boots over my feet, shoes and all, followed by the threadbare, woolen coat with its over-long sleeves and dark buttons.

And, finally, last but never least, the hood, Rag's mystery, drapes itself over my head.

I expect the smell to offend me, but it doesn't. Like all of this, whatever *this* is, it feels — normal.

Rag's knife, of course, isn't here. I left it back in Aunt Kell's hospital room, sticking out of the tile like Excalibur. By now, the cops have probably locked it up somewhere, bagged and tagged as evidence.

Not that it matters.

All I have to do is reach out for it with my mind — and then close my right hand.

So, I do it now.

And there it is. It fills my fist with its familiar weight, its black blade sharper than any razor.

Rags' knife.

My knife.

I was wrong when I said there was no Rags anymore.

I am Rags.

We are Rags.

And we have work to do.

I start running back up the beach toward the boards. Overhead, the sky is awash with stars. The night is my ally, my comfort, my protection. The shadows are my home. And I have a mission.

My family's missing, in trouble.

The first thing to do is find out where Simon Bernard and the *bòkò* have taken them.

And I know just who to ask.

CHAPTER 26

THE CITY CALLS TO ME

—EVERY CORNER, EVERY STREET, EVERY BUILDING. AS I MOVE THROUGH IT, shadow by shadow, with the wind whipping around me, I stick to the rooftops. It's simpler that way. The folks on the street would only slow me down. Besides, I'd scare them, and a part of me, the Abby Lowell part, doesn't want that.

The other part of me, however, would feast on their fear.

So, for both our sakes, I keep away from the sidewalks.

Presbyterian Avenue is an easy street to search. It's only a block long and sits tucked away in North Atlantic City, between Baltic and Arctic. It consists mostly of garages belonging to a bunch of adjacent two-story twins, a few stand-alone homes that have been split into multi-family dwellings, and a tiny cluster of apartments above a storefront at the end of the block. Now, I don't know which house or apartment's the right one. But, then again, I don't have to.

All I've got to do is listen.

When I arrive, I settle myself on top of the first house, having vaulted over the empty street from the roof across the way as easily as you might use stepping stones to cross a creek.

Once there, I pause and open my ears. Within seconds, I can tell how many people are in each apartment by counting the heartbeats. The problem is it's late, going on one in the morning, and almost everyone's asleep. Still, I know the dude I'm looking for lives alone, which means I can skip the places with more than one occupant. As for the rest, well, sometimes I need to get closer. So, I move along the outside of the house, quiet as quiet can be, until I find a window close enough to let my nose do the work.

The dude I'm looking for has a smell. I noticed it before but didn't know how to name it. I do now.

It's greed.

When I don't find him, I move on.

That's how it goes as I travel along the block. House to house. Heartbeat to heartbeat.

Until—

To be honest, I almost skip the place. Two heartbeats. But something makes me pause. Pause and sniff the air. Sniff the air and listen harder.

Bingo.

It turns out Carfanno, aka Officer Smirk, isn't alone in his third-floor walk-up after all, and whoever his guest is, the two of them are doing plenty of talking.

Also, that cop back in the hotel was right. Even from up here, on the gable above one of his windows, I can smell the bug spray.

" *— head hurts like a mother! I'm lucky I'm alive. If that psycho hadn't been more interested in Billy than me, I'd have been the one with his heart practically cut out!"*

The other dude talks. I know the voice, though it takes me a couple of seconds to place it.

The Lawyer Man. Shanks.

"I'm sure it was awful, Joe. I can assure you that Mr. Bernard is grateful for everything you've suffered on his behalf. That's why I'm here."

"A check for two grand? A lousy two grand? I had to strip your man down to his skivvies, Shanks! Couldn't have anybody in the department asking about the uniform. And believe you me, that wasn't easy! Billy must've weighed 220, and I had a freaking concussion! I'm lucky I didn't pass out again before I dumped it, shoes and all, down the sewer."

"It showed considerable ingenuity, Joe. I think — "

"Damn right, it did! And that kind of thinking's worth way more than what you showed up with!"

"Take it easy. Believe me, Mr. Bernard has every intention of— "

"Save it, Shanks. Here's what you can tell that Haitian bastard. I've had it. The entire department knows I'm on the take. Hell, nobody'll even partner with me anymore. I'm a freaking pariah, all because your boss doesn't know how to keep a low profile. Jesus, a dozen wise guys died last night… and that animal brother of his got killed this morning, right after he murdered Nick Nelson in broad daylight! Damn it, do these people have any subtlety at all?"

"Mistakes were made. And, let's be honest, some of them you made yourself. Nobody told you to 'arrest' the Lowell girl."

"I was going to take her someplace and make her talk. Billy was onboard. In fact, he was pretty gung-ho about it!"

"But, instead, she got away, and another of Mr. Bernard's people is dead."

"I told you! That wasn't my fault. It was that homeless guy!"

"All right, Joe. Calm down. What is it you want?"

"Twenty grand. Enough to get me out of the city and settle me someplace else with a new name."

"That's rather a lot of money."

"Yeah? Well, now that I think about it, let's make it thirty. Otherwise, I march into the DA's office tomorrow and turn state's evidence. How's that sound, Mr. Lawyer?"

"Joe, you really want to reconsider your position. Mr. Bernard rewards loyalty handsomely but takes a dim view of its opposite."

"Call him. Tell him what I said. Tell him I don't give a rat's ass how dim his view is."

"For your sake, I won't do that. Besides, right now, I'm afraid he's not somewhere that has access to a phone."

"Why not? Where is he?"

"I'd rather not say."

And I figure, *enough.*

Leaning over the gable, I drive my knife into the wood between its peak and the window. Then I just kind of flip myself over, holding onto the knife handle. At the last second, I twist my body and crash, feet first, through the window glass like it isn't there. Shards cut me, but, as before, while leaving the hospital, they're nothing.

Blood is my friend.

The room's small, with only a tiny kitchenette, a two-person Formica table, a sofa-bed, a couple of chairs, and a TV, all of it second-hand shit. Smirk's got all the style of a penniless frat boy.

The two dudes are at the table. Carfanno's got a half-drunk beer in front of him. Shanks, dressed to the nines, has nothing but an open briefcase. Both of them stare at me, first in confusion and then mounting alarm.

Smirk cusses and pulls a thirty-eight revolver from a shoulder rig he's wearing. He levels it at me, throwing out words that would make a truck driver blush.

My first thought is a "Rags thought." I should lop his hand right off at the wrist like I did—*he* did—to Simon back in the Golden Dome. In fact, I'm all ready to do just that, acting more on instinct than conscious thought. Then I stop myself.

Vanyan sòlda.

Doing such a thing'll likely kill him. He doesn't have a handy witch-doctor grandmother to save his life. And this visit isn't about killing.

That'll come later.

So, instead, just as he readies to fire, I move on him, fast as a blink, grab his wrist and twist it. The bones crack and pop like logs on a fire as he screams and drops the gun. Then with a casual toss, I introduce him to the refrigerator. It rattles as it says hello. Smirk slumps to the floor.

I turn to Lawyer Man.

Shanks is staring at me, wide-eyed. He's clutching his suitcase to his chest, as if either trying to shield himself with it or somehow protect it.

"You stay the hell away from me!" he screams, shrieks really.

My hood's still up, making me wonder what, if anything, he can see of my face. "Or you'll what?" I ask. I half-expect my voice to come out all raspy, the way Rags' did. But it doesn't. I just sound like, well, me. It's weirdly disappointing.

The lawyer seems confused, too. He blinks, lowers his briefcase, and looks me up and down. "Who are you?"

Behind me, Smirk groans a little.

I take a step toward Shanks, who backs up. But, like I said, the place is small, and that one step puts his shoulders against a cupboard.

"Where are they?" I ask.

He's still looking me over, trying to figure me out. He thinks maybe he can talk his way out of this, that maybe it's not as bad as it seems. Desperate hope. I can smell it on him. "Who? I don't know who you mean."

"My family. The kids from the Nelsons' house. Where'd she take them?"

"You're… that *girl*! That Lowell girl!" The two sentences practically vomit out of him, and the amount of relief I hear in his voice annoys the shit out of me. He figures he's safe now. I'm not Rags, however I'm dressed. I'm just a kid.

I take another step toward him. He looks worried, but not worried enough.

"See here, miss," he says, straightening up. "This is breaking and entering. How would you like to spend the night in jail? One phone call, and I can make that happen. Now—"

I pounce on him.

He tries to scream, but I've got my hand on his throat before he can. With it, I scoop him up, flip him over, and slam him down on his back atop the small table. The whole room shakes.

Then I touch my knife to his cheek and run it along the skin below his eye. The cut's not deep, but it bleeds.

He tries to scream again, but I'm not giving him the air to do it. Not yet.

"Listen up," I say to him. "Tell me where they are, or I'll take your eyes."

His face went pale, his expression a mask of naked terror.

I relax my grip on his throat, and he heaves and coughs. Then he says, "What… what *are* you?"

"That's a stupid question, Lawyer Man. Last chance."

"Steel Pier. They're at Steel Pier."

Of course, they are.

I should have guessed. To be honest, a part of me expected it. I'll bet you did, too. But I didn't have time to take chances and follow hunches. That's why I came here first.

"Where on the pier?" I ask.

"I… don't know."

He's lying. The stench of it stings my nose. I smile, though I still don't know if he can see my face. Then I run my knife along the skin under his other eye. If he doesn't get them stitched up, these slices will leave some interesting scars. In any case, the blood smells good, much better than his lying.

"Try again," I whisper.

He squeezes his eyes shut. "He'll kill me." It comes out as a terrified whimper. "Simon and that old bitch. She's completely crazy! She swears that damned pier is the source of her 'power.'" He actually gives me the air quotes. "Everything I do for Simon, I have to do it on the pier. They don't even want to buy it, just *use* it! So, there I am, paying off the right people at Resorts so that—"

"Look at me," I tell him.

He doesn't respond. He's crying now, tears mixing with blood. His bottom lip quivers. I know I should feel sorry for him. I guess I should also feel guilty about what I'm doing to him.

But I don't feel either one.

"Look at me!" I yell.

With a cry of fear, his eyes snap open.

"Listen good," I say through clenched teeth. "All this babbling shit is over. You're gonna tell me everything... and I mean *everything*... about how my family got taken. Then I want to know what happened to the social workers who were with them. Then I want to know exactly how many dudes Bernard has as guards. And *then* I want to know what Adelaide's got planned. Last of all, I want to know *exactly* where they all are. You tell me all that and nothing else, or I'm gonna start cutting pieces off and feeding them to you. Beginning with right *here*."

I move my knife and show him where I mean.

I think I'll leave that to your imagination.

Shanks sobs. Then he starts talking.

But, before he gets more than a sentence out, I see a flash of hope in his eyes. Then I hear a gun hammer click back behind me.

Forgot all about Smirk.

"You crazy little—" Carfanno exclaims, his voice high pitched with rage.

I turn and throw.

My knife plants itself to the hilt in the bent cop's chest before he can fire. For an instant, he looks at it in utter bewilderment. In the next instant, the revolver falls from his hand, and he topples over backward, hitting the stove with his skull hard enough to kill him if he weren't already dead.

I stare down at the crooked cop, not sure what I feel. It isn't like with Baptiste. That was vengeance, white-hot and personal. This had just been—just been—

—*like swatting a fly.*

I take a deep breath. Then another. I wish I could say my heart's pounding, but it really isn't. My whole body's totally, frighteningly calm.

"*Iwa acheté*," I say to nobody in particular.

Then I look back at Shanks.

And the lawyer starts talking again.

CHAPTER 27

IT'S MY LAST TRIP TO STEEL PIER

—ONLY I DON'T KNOW IT. NOT YET.

According to Shanks, the women from Family Services, Reynolds and Lajola, stayed at the hospital with my sibs until after Uncle Nick died and everything else went down. Then, once I went on the run, they half-marched, half-dragged them back to the vans. Shanks told me he got the story from one of Bernard's thugs, who got it from Lajola.

Apparently, that particular social worker had been bribed to "alter my family's destinations."

See? One of the mean ones.

"I wasn't there," Shanks explains, stammering and stuttering his way through the story. "I only heard it from one of the other… employees who was. Mrs. Lajola led the vans into a pre-determined alley somewhere in the city's south end, where Mr. Bernard's people waited. Once there, everyone in both vans, including Ms. Reynolds, was transferred to an unmarked delivery van."

"'Transferred,' I say, the edge of my knife pressed up under his nose. "What's that mean? Were they tied up?"

"I… wasn't there."

I flick my wrist, lopping off the very tip of his nose. He squeals as blood trickles down onto his lips. "Try again," I suggest.

"Yes. That is… I think so."

"Were they hurt?"

"No!" he exclaims, so emphatically that I think I believe him. "She didn't want them harmed in any way!"

"She? Adelaide?"

"Yes."

"What happened to Lajola? Did she get taken, too? Or was she paid off and left there?"

Shanks visibly swallows. "She… um…"

"They killed her, didn't they?"

He tries to nod, but my blade is back under his nose, and he thinks better of it. Instead, he replies simply, "Yes."

"Where are they in the pier?" I ask.

"There's a big open space on the first floor. Mr. Bernard has chairs set up there. Twelve of them."

I do the math in my head. "With Reynolds, that only makes eleven."

"They brought in another boy later on."

Jimmy.

Adelaide now has her twelve "innocent lambs."

"What's she want them for?" I demand, fresh anger rising up inside me. The thing is — this anger feels somehow good. Powerful.

"I don't know! That bitch is crazy! She said something about a spell, whatever that means. All I can tell you is that some of the brats were cursing like truckers, so much so that Mr. Bernard finally ordered everyone to be gagged. When he did that, though, his grandmother looked disappointed. She said that she *liked* their fear. It fueled her!"

And, you know what? In that moment, looking into this dude's wide, terrified eyes, I kind of *got* the old witch's point.

His fear was fueling *me.*

"One last thing," I tell him. "My sibs. You said she wants them for a spell. Did she *do* the spell yet?"

"I... don't think so. She said it needed to wait."

"Wait for what?" I ask.

His eyes, which had glassed over, now fix on me. "For *you.*"

I leave Shanks alive, passed out but breathing. Not Rags' usual MO, but I figure it's safe enough. Even if he wakes up in time to warn anyone, he won't. For one thing, he's too scared. For another, there are no phones on the pier, which means the only way he can tell anybody anything is by going there in person.

And he knows *I'll* be there.

So, like I said, I left him alive.

Time to go to the Boardwalk.

I'm coming, you bitch. Put out all the dogs you want. They won't stop me. Neither will your pig of a grandson. Me and my knife are going to make you pay.

I get there as fast as I can, which is pretty fast, especially considering I'm on foot. By the time I arrive, it's pushing two a.m. and a starlit sky shines over the ocean. I settle myself on a rooftop within sight of the pier's main entrance. No limo this time. Just two dudes in suits and topcoats, standing more or less at attention, illuminated by the glow coming from Resorts Casino.

Both have a musky, male odor, the one on the left with added aftershave. They're not saying anything. Good little watchdogs.

I drop to the boards, landing without a sound, and cross in a blur to the pier's facing corner. There I crouch, hugged by shadows, and watch them a moment longer before I move.

I don't want to kill them. A part of me, the Rags part, thinks that's a mistake. But I ignore it. I've already taken two lives today, and I'll be taking others before I'm done. I don't need more blood on my conscience than that, do I?

So, instead, I slip in close behind them, just darkness sliding easily and silently through more darkness. As I creep up, one of them says, "Do you hear something, man?"

"Just the wind," the other replies. "Cold as a witch's—"

I straighten up and hit that guy on the top of his head with the handle of my knife. I hear his skull crack, and he drops like a sack of sand. The other dude, to both his credit and stupidity, moves fast, pulling a gun on me and opening his mouth to yell a warning.

Instinctively, I lash out with my knife.

It's way too easy for me to cut his throat before either he or his pistol can make a sound.

Damn it!

With a sigh, I drag both men, one alive and one not, deeper into the shadows. They've got to be two hundred pounds apiece, but I have no trouble moving them. It's easy, in fact.

Very easy, in fact.

Afterward, I let myself into the pier.

There aren't any thugs in the Lobby or anywhere else that I can immediately see or smell. But up ahead, around the far side of the big staircase, I hear voices. And crying.

Muffled crying.

"Christ, it's cold in here!"

"Be glad you're not outside with Ramos and Joe."

"How long do we gotta stay here? It's been hours and... nothing."

"You heard Mr. Bernard. We stay until the homeless guy shows up. Payback."

"I don't get it."

"You ain't paid to get it."

As I draw closer, I pick up their scent. Two guards. But not the only two. Two more are stationed close to the rear of the Theater, near where the old indoor merry-go-round used to stand. And another two have put themselves off to the right, where Alfie the Sea Lion once gave his shows. Six heartbeats. Counting the two outside, that makes eight thugs in total. Just like Shanks said.

It's amazing how honest folks get when you hold a knife under their nose.

Of course, there are other heartbeats, too. Twelve of them, all in a row. The hostages. And two more. The witch and her grandson.

It's almost like I can *see* them.

I move forward, keeping out of sight. No reason to show myself. Not yet. My plan is to get close, use the shadows to hide me, and then take them down, two at a time. After that, I'll get my sibs clear and come back in for Simon and Adelaide.

A good plan. So good, in fact, that all of five seconds go by before it gets blown.

A familiar voice says, "She's here."

I freeze.

Everyone goes quiet.

The heartbeats all start racing. Folks are scared up ahead.

They should be.

"Come on out, child," Madame Adelaide says.

My every instinct tells me to do no such thing. So, I let her eat silence.

"Are you sure, Grann?" It's Simon's voice. He sounds nervous.

"Sure as the moon will rise, *cher*. It's me who brought that *iwa* to this world. I'd know the stink of it anywhere."

I hear the sound of metal on metal, a knife being drawn from its sheath.

"Hear me, Abigail Lowell," Adelaide says, speaking loudly. "Step out where I can see you now, or I'll make one of these lambs bleed more than I already have."

She won't kill them. Vengeance on me aside, doing so would spoil whatever spell she's cast.

Don't ask me how I know that. It's a Rags thing.

"Maybe I'll take an eye outta one of them little ones," the *bòkò* declares. "Don't worry, though, I'll still leave 'em one… so's to see what comes next!"

Shit.

My instincts scream at me not to do as she says. The part of me that's Rags is talking about strategy and tactics. But then Rags never had a family, I'll bet.

"Okay!" I call. "I'm coming out."

And I do, letting myself kind of slide into view from amidst the shadows and into the open.

Twelve chairs have been lined up against the wall behind the big staircase, flanked by two of Bernard's bookends. In those chairs, held down by tightly knotted ropes, sit my sibs—well, my sibs and one social worker. Reynolds might be the only adult in the bunch, but she looks just as scared as the rest. Some of the kids have soiled themselves. Not a surprise since they've been trussed up like this for hours, and Bernard doesn't seem like the kind to allow bathroom breaks, even if the pier still *had* a working bathroom.

It doesn't. Trust me, I know.

They all look my way as I appear. Tish and Darlene both scream behind their gags. The sound of it's a little hoarse, making me think they've been doing a lot of that today. On each kid, from the oldest to the youngest, a trail of blood runs from a small neck puncture.

Adelaide did that to them. She needed their blood for whatever spell's she's been working.

Fresh anger flares up.

Every thug draws down on me. They all have pistols, though I notice their hands shake a bit as they point them in my direction. Trained killers or not, they know full well who I am and what I've been doing to their homeboys over the last couple of days.

"There she is, and all fully cooked!" This comes from Adelaide, who's standing over by one of the shuttered concessions. Her grandson stands beside her, much taller yet somehow much smaller than she is. He's got a gun of his own, a nickel-plated revolver.

I notice that the old woman holds a cup in her hands. It looks like it's made of hammered pewter or some such thing, dull gray in color.

"Let's kill her, Grann," Baldy says. His words are hard, but I can smell what's coming off of him. Not fear exactly. I'm not sure this dude's ego would ever let him be really afraid. But he's wary as hell and pissed, too. *Major* pissed. He's looking at the girl who killed his brother, and we both know he knows it.

"We will, *cher*. Make no mistake. But first things first. You, there!" She points a bony finger at one of the thugs guarding my sibs. "If this one so much as takes a step, why don't you just go ahead and shoot one of them lambs. In the knee, mind you. Not the chest or head. You hear me, boy?"

"Yes, ma'am," the thug replies. And he dutifully points his pistol at Tyrone's right knee cap. Tyrone squirms, but his bonds are way too tight. He's sweating, despite the cold, and the gag in his mouth looks like it's half-choking him.

"Good. Very good." Adelaide turns to Simon and nods. "Now then, *cher*. She's here. It's time. Drink up." She offers him the pewter cup.

He grimaces. "Grann, do I have to? It's—"

To my surprise, to *everyone's* surprise, she slaps his face. She must be stronger than she looks because Simon actually staggers a step, cussing and rubbing his cheek. For a moment, just a moment, his eyes flash when he looks back at her, but then he recoils when she shoves a finger into his face. "Everything I done, boy, has been for you 'n your brother! It should be Baptiste over there—" She points right at me. "—wielding that knife! It took me years to find this place and months to cast that spell, and if either of you fools had been where you were supposed to be three nights back, all would now be well. But, no! You were *scared*, just like you're scared now!"

"We don't need your *Vodou*!" Simon shoots back. "We all but got the hotel! We can just kill the little bitch and be done with it!"

Adelaide fumes, looking like she wants to slap him again. "You don't need my *maji*? Without it, you wouldn't have a hand right now, boy!"

Simon looks uncomfortably at his gun hand. I can't see any sign of scarring on his wrist, not even a seam. "Yeah. Yeah, I know that, Grann. But now—"

His grandmother talks right over him. "With the *iwa acheté*, we coulda had this whole city! Ugh. The pair of you. Your brother had strength and heart but no brains. You got strength and brains but no heart. But you're all that's left, all that remains of my line. And you *will* prosper in this country! Do you hear me? You will prosper and thrive because I'm Adelaide de la Fosse, and that is what I want! Now... drink!" She shoves the cup at him a second time.

I glance around the room. The thugs are all watching Simon's dressing down. One or two even smirk a little. Their boss is losing major cred right now. But then I glance over at the one beside Tyrone, the one with the business end of his gun against my brother's kneecap. *His* eyes are on me, watchful as a hawk.

He'll be first.

Simon retreats another step. "It stinks to hell, Grann! What's it going to do to me, anyhow?"

"I told you! It'll make you strong! Not the same strong… not *iwa acheté* strong, but strong enough to do what needs doing!"

Simon's jaw stiffens. "I already *am* strong! And I'll prove it. Just watch! My guys'll put twenty bullets in her."

Adelaide looks utterly disgusted. Under her breath, she mutters, "*Lach*!" as she turns her back on him.

Simon looks stricken. And I guess I don't blame him.

She just called him a coward in Creole.

"Do it, then," the old woman says. "If you can. But hear me, all of you… not one of them lambs dies before *I* say so. If one does, if one bullet goes astray and takes a single wrong life, then I'll make you wish you ain't never been born. That's a promise!"

Baldy looks relieved. "Sure. Sure, *Grann*." He points at the two thugs standing closest to him, over where the merry-go-round used to be—it's just a round patch on the floor now, less discolored than the rest. "Stewie. Giff. Waste the little bitch. But shoot straight, you hear me? The rest of you, just hang tight until I say different."

Both dudes nod and open fire.

I guess I'm supposed to be scared. But I'm not. In fact, in the split second before the first shot rings out, the only thing I really think is: *Now.*

I do my blur thing, crossing the ten feet between me and the dude on Tyrone in less than a heartbeat. As I move, I sense more than feel four bullets burn past my head and drill into the rear of the staircase. Then, I've got my hand on the thug's gun wrist and my knife at his throat.

He tries to follow orders. I've got to give him that. But I jerk the gun away so that the shot slams into the concrete floor.

An instant later, my blade's at his throat, and he's dead.

An instant after that, I throw his body at the dudes currently shooting at me.

It's easy, *so* easy, almost like lobbing a stuffed bear at the tods. Looks much the same, too—with the thug's limbs flopping back and forth as he sails at least fifteen feet through the air. Simon and Adelaide, standing as they are off to the side, have time to get clear. But the dudes firing on me don't.

The dead man hits them like a two-hundred-pound cannonball. Instead of just knocking them down, the force drives them against the wall, crushing them there. I can actually hear ribs breaking and skulls cracking.

Then all of them hit the floor.

And I think, *Three-for-one sale.*

My stomach twists.

So… what? I'm quipping now?

"Kill her, damn it!" Simon exclaims, waving at his remaining employees.

Then Madame Adelaide adds, her voice like the edge of a knife, "Do *not* hit the lambs!"

My sibs, who were mostly crying a moment ago behind their gags, are now screaming.

And I wonder who it is they're most afraid of.

Then I move.

There are three more thugs in the room. One stands beside Miss Reynolds. The other two are over by the old sea lion show. All of them are doing the same thing—shooting at me.

The dude next to the social worker is closest, and his shots are buzzing right over my sibs' heads. So, I take him first.

Jumping up to the ceiling, I drive my knife into the hard, salt-soaked joists, just as his latest shot drills the air below me and punches a hole in the pier's southern wall. Then, I brace my feet, kick off the ceiling, and kind of ride the knife under and over, pulling it free at the same time and using the momentum to slam me into the thug before he can adjust his aim.

My blade finds him, quick and silent. He doesn't even get a chance to cry out.

As he falls, I go with him, and we hit the floor together. I roll free at the last instant, just as six bullets drill into the corpse I've left behind.

Blood pools, red and steaming in the cold.

The last two thugs panic now. They've abandoned their posts and are shooting crazily, and only some of the shots are really aimed at me. One parts Jeff's hair, leaving behind a thin line of blood that I smell but immediately dismiss. Another misses Miss Reynolds by like a half-inch.

The social worker screams into her gag, tears running down her cheeks. Worse, trussed up beside her, little Keisha, all of five years old, lets out a muffled shriek that I know, with sick certainty, she'll be working through in therapy for the rest of her life.

The thought pisses me off even more, and I throw myself at the last two shooters.

Apparently, it pisses off somebody else, too.

"Fools!" the *bòkò* cries. "*Kochon maladwa!* What did I tell you?"

She called them "clumsy pigs," like it matters.

Then, just as I'm about to hit the righthand thug like a rhino, the dude bursts into flames. Where those flames come from is a total mystery. There's certainly no open fire in here, just some battery-powered arc lights that Simon's set up. Nevertheless, those flames consume the dude in seconds, burning so hot that I have to turn away or lose my eyebrows.

You know the old saying, "went up like a Christmas tree?"

Well, he does.

Screaming and still shooting, he spins around. One of his shots manages to hit his partner, if that's what they were, full in the face. The other guy dies instantly, with first his gun and then his body dropping to the floor. Meanwhile, Burning Man, still dancing in a kind of wild, desperate agony that might have made me feel sorry for him if he hadn't just shot at my family, stumbles and falls into a stack of boxes.

"You see?" Madame Adelaide yells, slapping Simon repeatedly. For his part, Baldy is looking at the carnage, at me, as if he can't quite believe what's just happened. "She'll come for us next, *ti gason*! For *me*! Drink! *Drink now!*"

I have time to think, *I really don't want him drinking that.*

But then Simon Bernard, terrified way past the point of worrying about whatever's in that cup, throws it back like a drunk doing shots.

He gags and stumbles, the goblet falling from his hands.

His fingers claw at his throat.

Meanwhile, Adelaide turns to me, beaming with victory. "Behold, *iwa acheté*! See what *my* power brings!"

And, deep inside me, an alarm of some kind goes off.

The blood of a dozen innocents, mixed with a bòkò's urine and a vermin's beating heart.

A potion?

An honest-to-God potion?

You've got to be freaking kidding me!

An instant later, Simon Bernard stops gagging and raises his head. When he smiles, I can see the blood coating his teeth, teeth that suddenly look really, really long.

"Cher," the old woman says in a voice as sweet as sugar. "Do me a kindness… and kill this little, thieving whelp."

I think, *Great*.

And then it starts.

CHAPTER 28

My First Thought Is "Zombie"

—but I can already see this is something else. Uncle Nick told me that real zombies aren't like the ones in the movies. They're passive things, unable to defend themselves, much less attack.

Whatever Madame Adelaide's potion made of her grandson, "zombie" isn't the word for it.

"Two-legged gorilla demon" might be better.

He crosses the space between us in a single leap. I try to dodge, but he grabs me, just kind of scoops me up under one arm, and throws me. It reminds me of the way Baptiste tossed me back in the hospital, except this is *way* harder and *way* faster. For a split second, the floor and ceiling do this crazy dance, and then I hit the wall hard enough to ring my head like a bell.

Pain drills its way up my back as I crash down.

Nearby, Adelaide laughs while Simon roars in triumph.

That's when I smell the smoke.

The dude Adelaide torched is cooked now, and he's managed to set fire to a pile of boxes stacked against the opposite wall. I don't know what's in them, something Resorts tucked away for a rainy day, apparently. But whatever it is *burns* easy, and already yellow flames lick their way up the old, dried wood boards toward the ceiling.

I climb to my feet, dazed, trying to shake off the hit.

In the meantime, Simon's coming again. He's grinning crazily, his teeth huge and his mouth impossibly wide. Red veins, thick as spaghetti, run along his cheeks and down his neck, disappearing into the collar of a fancy coat that suddenly looks too small for him.

Is this dude getting… bigger?

As if to answer my question, both his fancy leather shoes split and fall apart with his every churning step, leaving behind stocking feet that have got to be half the size of snow shovels.

Yep. Definitely bigger.

Meanwhile, the old woman keeps laughing.

I look from the demon to my sibs and then down at my knife. Options flash through my mind. I reject one after another. Then, just as Baldy's arms—which are now a lot longer and thicker than they were pre-potion—reach for me, I make the call.

The arms snap shut like a bear trap. But I duck just in time to miss getting crushed to paste between them. Then, crouched down, I drive my knife into his gut up to its hilt. The flesh is thick and weirdly hard. It's like stabbing a slab of leather. But Simon roars in pain, momentarily distracted.

Pulling out the knife, hoping real damage has been done but, on some level, knowing better, I run to where Jimmy's tied up. He's staring at me in wide-eyed horror. All of them are. But I ignore that as I slash with my blade and cut the bonds at his right wrist.

He doesn't move.

Then I plunge the knife into the wood chair seat, right between his knees.

He jumps and lets out a little muffled yelp. But at least it snaps him back to the Now.

"Cut yourself free and get them out!" I tell him.

With his hand loose, the first thing he does is pull out the gag. "A—Abby?" he gasps. "What—"

I seize his head in both my hands and scream, *"Just do it!"*

That's when Simon grabs me from behind.

He lifts me over his head, slamming me into the ceiling hard enough that the world goes momentarily black. His hands are at my waist, his fingers so long now that they reach all the way around me. I pry at them, but I've only got two small hands, and he's got ten fingers. As he squeezes my ribs to the point of breaking, I realize the math's not on my side here.

So, instead, I drive both my thumbs into his eyes.

He roars, the sound deafening, and throws me again.

This time, though, I'm ready—or, at least, *more* ready. He's hurtled me toward where the merry-go-round used to be. It's close to his grandmother, closer probably than he intended, assuming whatever the potion's doing to him has left him with such things as "intentions," other than, you know, killing me. Adelaide's laughter dies as she jumps clear of me, moving quicker than I'd have thought.

I twist as I come down and manage to land on my feet, my boots sliding across the concrete floor as I eat the momentum. Simon, blinking with eyes that are bloodied but apparently still working, whirls toward me, his face a snarling rictus. Behind him, and to my immense relief, Jimmy's cut himself loose and is busily freeing Sarah, who's in the chair beside him. The problem is that he's got a lot of people to free, and the fire's spreading. Fortunately, my blade is crazy sharp and cuts through the stiff ropes like they're butter.

So, I guess it's a race.

But, damn, I miss that knife!

Simon charges yet again.

"He'll kill you, child," Adelaide tells me. "You just see if he don't!"

I turn and clock her.

My fist catches her in the jaw. I'm not gentle about it, either. She's lifted right off the floor, only to then drop like a ragdoll. She lands hard. Very hard.

I don't have the time to wonder if I've killed her, and, things being what they are, I don't much care, so long as she's out of commission for a while. Part of this is anger. Part is spite. But the rest is practicality. My family's trying to escape, and this woman can apparently set people on fire with her freaking mind!

Simon's on top of me a second later, his head down and charging like a bull. I manage to sidestep—almost, but he catches me with his shoulder and throws me back. I crash right through a window in the rear of the Theater and tumble out into the December air. Overhead, the stars look like cold jewels. Around and below me, the ocean rumbles like distant, rhythmic thunder.

I land on my back, the wind knocked out of me.

Jesus, that dude's strong!

It makes me wonder why Adelaide bothered with the mirror and Rags at all. I mean, if she could whip up a potion able to do *that* to somebody, why would she need to summon an *iwa* in the first place?

There's something to that, something important. I'm sure of it.

I just don't have the time to work it out.

My vision, which has been swimming since my head hit the cement, clears. I crane my neck in time to see Simon emerge through the shattered Theater window. There's so much of him now that he has to duck and twist to squeeze through the jagged frame. His coat's torn to rags, and his suit pants are now ripped floods that have totally lost their crease.

I almost laugh at that.

Oh, who am I kidding? I don't laugh at all.

As he spots me and thunders forward, I jump to my feet, looking for a weapon. But there's not exactly a lot of loose stuff just lying around on Steel Pier anymore. I'm standing in that big parking area I described earlier, the one with all the old buses and trolley cars. It offers a good amount of cover, but not much in the weapon department.

I mean, I'm strong, but I'm not "pick-up-a-bus-and-throw-it" strong.

On the other hand, maybe *he* is.

So, I run.

He chases me, snapping and howling like a rabid dog.

I throw myself into the rows of buses, keeping low and moving fast. Once I break his line of sight, I duck under one bus, rolling quickly and quietly until I reach the other side, and then jump up onto the roof of the next. One aisle over, I can see the top of his head — *Jeez, this guy is tall now!* — as he searches for me. Roaring, he shoves aside first one bus, then another. I move around him, trying to stay clear of his view, using the time to *think*.

This dude's pretty much an animal now. My rabid dog comparison's right on the money. But a rabid dog is only of so much use. Adelaide wants *power*. She wants to run this city and maybe later an even bigger slice of the pie. It's an old song. The only thing new is the way she's going about it.

Vodou.

But also not. A *bòkò* believes in *Vodou* the way a Satanist believes in God.

Nevertheless, black magic aside, the old woman's really no different than that Spagliano dude in the Golden Dome. A gangster. Somebody who wants control over others. Except Adelaide knows she'll never be accepted as a "boss" on the Atlantic City streets. She's too old, too small, too — female.

So, instead, she set out to give power to her kin. Baptiste or Simon. She planned it out, where and how to make it all happen. She picked Steel Pier because — well, I'm not entirely sure. But there's energy here, the energy born of thousands upon thousands of people moving through this place every summer, *millions* over the course of the century. All those beating hearts, all those excited breaths.

I jump from one bus to another, making no noise. Baldy hasn't spotted me yet, but he's looking. He's looking hard.

In the meantime, I keep flipping through my "Rags file," the part of me that knows about this stuff. And there's a lot there, way more than I've got time for right now.

But this much becomes clear: Over time, Steel Pier became a kind of battery, a storage dump for energy that Madame Adelaide could tap — *has* been tapping. There are other places like it, of course. Plenty of them. But few that used to be *so* busy and are now *so* empty, so utterly and completely forgotten.

So, here was where she set up shop and did her business. And she almost pulled it off, too. Except for this dumb girl who wandered in while she was out fetching one of her grandsons to help complete the spell. If I hadn't done that, if Rags hadn't sensed me and called to me from inside that mirror, then the power in me would now be in one of them.

Bad news for this town. This state. Hell, the whole world, maybe.

But it didn't happen.

I happened instead.

A nearby trolley car topples over, the crash loud enough to momentarily drown out the surf. Simon roars in frustration.

Instead, Adelaide used my sibs' blood to whip up a potion to turn Simon into *this*.

But a rabid dog can't "boss" anything.

That means Adelaide didn't get her only remaining grandson to drink that potion to make him a "gangster czar." She did it for revenge. Maybe she didn't tell him that. In fact, the more I think about it, the likelier it is she *didn't* tell him. Sure, he loved his brother, the brother I killed. But something tells me Simon Bernard never loved anybody *this* much.

So, what's all that mean? Even if I'm right, what good does it do me?

Then, just as I'm about to have it figured, Baldy finds me.

Whether by instinct, or more brains than I gave him credit for, it finally occurs to him to climb a bus himself. Now, standing about fifty feet away, His red eyes bore into me, marking me the way a lion marks a zebra.

Then he comes at me.

I drop off the bus and make for the nearest shadows. They're at the edge of the pier, where a squat, weatherworn building is all that remains of Tabier's Tarzan Jungle. To my left is a big, heavy steel trash-can, rusted with age and chained to the railing. It looks like something I could heft, assuming I manage to break the chain. But Baldy would probably just swat it aside. Ahead of me, the Golden Dome gleams in the starlight. It might be possible to hide in there.

But then I hear him coming and know I'll never make it in time.

I turn to face him just as a huge hand slashes at my head. I dodge it and use my momentum to literally roll right under his legs. Missing me, he staggers forward, almost losing his balance. So, whirling around, I kick him in the ass, half-hoping to knock him through the rails and down into the surf.

No such luck. He staggers a step or two more, catches himself, and begins turning again.

As he does, I leap up and give him a hit to his face that honestly would've killed a normal dude. He flinches, but only for a moment, and then he backhands me hard enough to send me tumbling halfway back to the buses.

For the second time that night, everything *almost* goes black.

Then I hear him coming and — somehow — find my feet, just in time to dodge a stomp that would have turned my spine into string cheese.

He's too big, I think desperately. *Too strong. He's…*

Then I see him turn toward me again, and I notice how his chest heaves.

… he's getting tired.

Behind him, the Theater's ablaze. I can only hope Jimmy got every-body out of there and safely onto the boards. A plume of smoke rises high into the air, obscuring half the night sky. This whole place is falling apart around me. But right now, the only thing I can see is Simon Bernard looking just a little bit — smaller.

And suddenly, I realize why Adelaide needed Rags, why she didn't just cook up this concoction for Baptiste or Simon from the beginning.

It don't last.

He takes a step toward me, then another, building up a head of steam. The potion might have a time limit on it, but that time's not up. Not quite yet. And between now and then, this thing could still tear me limb from limb.

Unless I make it so he can't.

Turning away from him, I run for the trashcan I spotted earlier. He follows. Of course, he does.

As single-minded as a dog chasing a cat.

And, right now, I'm counting on it.

I grab the trashcan and rip it free. As I hoped, its chain snaps easy. Then I toss it aside. It isn't the can I'm after.

As Simon's footfalls get closer, slapping hard against the concrete, I scoop up the chain in both hands. It's about eight feet long and pretty heavy, thick as a garden hose. I *think* it'll be enough.

He lunges, his mouth open like he means to grab me and bite me in half. I wait for the last possible second, then I pivot out of the way and, sweet as you please, loop the chain around his neck. As he tries to track me, I yank it hard, making him gag, and, for a half-second, no more, he overbalances again, feet scrambling for purchase.

So, I throw myself at him with everything I've got, slamming my shoulder in under his chin and driving him back toward the railing. He roars and makes a grab for me but misses as we both hit the old aluminum rails, which bend and begin to give way.

Baldy, bigger and heavier, does the rest of the work for me, kicking with his feet and clawing at the chain around his neck. By the time the railing collapses completely, he's way too far over to stop himself, and, together, we both start falling down into the cold black water twenty feet below.

Now, I'm not kidding myself here. The fall won't kill him. He's way too strong for that.

But I've got something else in mind.

As we go over, I throw one end of the chain around the nearest vertical railing post. While the rail gave way, the post that held it is still anchored in the concrete of the pier and won't be going anywhere anytime soon.

At the last second, I scramble up Baldy's big body, kick him hard in the face to launch myself and make it back up to the pier. Once there, I hit the concrete, roll over, plant my feet against the post, and grip both ends of the chain with all I'm worth. I've got no way to knot it, so all I can hope is that I'm strong enough to *be* the knot, myself.

Below the lip, Baldy struggles wildly against the steel links digging into his neck. His feet kick. His arms flail. But the edge of the pier's out of reach, and there's just nothing else for him to grab. Within a minute, his struggles grow weaker. And weaker.

I hang on desperately, the chain cutting into the skin of my palms. I think I'm screaming, but with the monster making so much noise, it's hard to be certain.

Then, finally, his struggles stop.

Gasping, I lean forward enough to peer over the edge.

The old Simon Bernard is back, now just a normal-sized hairless dude with normal-sized hands and no black magic veins showing in his purple face.

I won.

But that's not enough. Not quite.

So, I take a page from Uncle Nick's book. Gathering up as much of the chain as I can, I give it several hard, twisty yanks.

I know I'm done—I know *he's* done—when I feel his body fall into the ocean. Without a head, I mean.

The only way to be sure.

CHAPTER 29

WHAT'S LEFT OF ME

—STRUGGLES TO MY FEET AND HEADS FOR THE FRONT OF THE PIER.

The Theater's a mass of flames and smoke now, so I cross the parking lot to the railing on the north side and jump over it, landing in the sand and then running up to the nearest stairs that'll take me to the Boardwalk.

By now, at least a hundred people have gathered to watch the flames, which light things up for blocks around. No sirens, though. The Fire Department either hasn't arrived yet or hasn't even been called.

But I don't give a shit about any of that. I'm just scanning the boards for my sibs.

Finally, I spot them. They're all huddled together against a closed storefront on the opposite side of the pier, away from everyone. Slowly, I move toward them, still using the shadows, unnoticed by everybody in the crowd.

Then, when I'm within a dozen feet or so, I let them see me.

Tyrone spots me first. Then he nudges Darlene and Jimmy and points. I stop where I am, not knowing if I should come closer, not knowing what to expect from them. After all, I'm not Abby anymore, at least not the Abby they all know.

I'm a monster in rags.

They talk amongst themselves. I can hear it. Reynolds, the social worker, is trying to assume charge, but my sibs ignore her, instead taking their cues from the Top Boy and Top Girl. Finally, they decide that Jeff and Sarah will take the middles and tods home to the hotel. Tyrone gives Jeff the key and, with a final, nervous glance tossed in my direction, they leave.

Except Corrine, who stamps her foot and refuses to go.

And Reynolds? She takes one look at me and all but runs off. I don't blame her. She's one of the good ones, sure. But she's no saint.

Once the others have split, Tyrone, Darlene, Jimmy, Tish, and Corinne approach me. They do this slow like I'm a growling dog or something.

I get it.

Tyrone licks his lips and asks, "You... okay?"

I nod. The irony of doing that in my hood isn't lost on me.

"What happened?" Darlene asks.

"It's over," I reply.

"Did you... kill him?" Jimmy asks.

"Yeah."

"Jesus," Tish breathes.

"You're Rags," Corinne says.

"Yeah."

Darlene swallows nervously, her eyes raking me from head to toe. She looks *awful*. Her hair's a rat's nest, and her face, usually so perfectly made-up, has been turned ragged from stress and fear. There's a small cut above her left eye, already scabbing over. I wonder where she got it.

The old me might have quietly celebrated, if only a little. A stuck-up Top Girl gets her comeuppance. But, right now, the only thing I feel for my foster sister is love. Well, that and maybe a kind of pity.

Next to what I am now, she seems so — *small*.

In fact, if I'm honest, they all do.

Finally, Darlene says, "Well, it's over, so you can stop now, right?"

Standing beside her, Jimmy and Tyrone both nod.

"Yeah," Tish adds. God bless her, she actually tries to smile. "So, let's go home!"

Only Corinne looks unsurprised when I shake my head.

"Why the hell not?" Jimmy demands.

By way of a reply, I reach out my hand. He looks at it, blinking. Then he looks down at the knife he's still holding.

"Oh," he says.

He starts to offer me the black blade, handling it gingerly, like it's a ticking time bomb or something. But I do him one better by *calling* the knife, kind of the way I called it at the hospital and again on the beach. Like so much else about being Rags, it comes easy to me. Scary easy. That weapon is a part of me, almost like an extension of my arm. We belong to each other on a level that goes way deeper than the physical.

Jimmy gasps as the knife vanishes from his grip and settles into mine.

They all jump back. Tyrone's arm closes protectively around Darlene. Tish puts her hand to her mouth. She looks like she's trembling, and not from the cold.

"That's why the hell not," I tell them.

"Just let it go, Abby!" Jimmy exclaims. "Chuck all that shit you've got on in the ocean and come back with us. Please!"

"I can't. I made a deal."

"What deal?" Corinne asks.

Before I can answer her, Tyrone does it for me. "You became this to save us. And now you can't…" His words trail off.

"It's okay," I tell him. I try to smile but don't quite manage it. They can't see my face under the big hood anyway.

"No, it's not!" Tish exclaims. "Come on, Abbs!"

"Go home," I tell them.

"It's not our home, not anymore," Darlene says. "Oh, that Reynolds chick told us we can stay there tonight. But she's going to be by in the morning to… what'd she say? 'Collect us and resume relocation.'"

No, she won't.

But I don't say that out loud. "Go home and get some rest, all of you. I'll see you soon."

Tyrone nods. So does Tish, though maybe a bit more tearfully. They wave, but none of them take a single step closer.

Again, except Corinne. Darlene actually utters a frightened cry when the girl runs up and hugs me, wrapping her thin arms around my waist.

"I love you," she whispers.

It takes me a few ticks, but I manage to return the hug, just a little. The old Abby was just getting into hugs. But now, as Rags', well—

But this is Corinne. So, I say, meaning it, "I love you too, pumpkin." Then I look up at the rest and add, "I love y'all. Remember that."

Gently but firmly, I push Corinne away, turn her around, and nudge her back toward the others. Darlene grabs the girl like she's pulling her from the jaws of death itself.

And maybe that's exactly what she did.

"Abby—" Jimmy says, a plea in his voice.

"Abby's not here," I tell him.

Then I call to the shadows, letting them envelop and conceal me. And the night cooperates, accepting me into its darkness like a prodigal daughter.

Looking back, I can tell from my sibs' reaction that I did it right.

Rags has vanished before their eyes.

For a few more minutes, I watch them — watch over them — unseen. They linger a bit longer, mostly, I think, because Jimmy doesn't want to move. He keeps shaking off first Tish's and then Tyrone's gentle hand on his shoulder, calling my name, over and over while Corinne cries, pressed against Darlene.

But, finally, resignedly, they all turn and leave the Boardwalk.

A short time later, the fire department shows up. To be fair to them, it's not that easy getting hook and ladder trucks close enough to a pier to do any good. Besides, anyone can see it's a lost cause.

Steel Pier's gone, cleansed by fire.

That saddens me, but it kind of relieves me, too. Because the place *was* a battery, one that lured Madame Adelaide and might have eventually lured others.

Better it be ashes. Better for everybody.

Madame Adelaide.

It isn't hard to find her. Push comes to shove, she's an old woman and can't move all that fast. Besides, she's got a *smell* to her, an odor of dark power that mortals — God, I'm already thinking of them as 'mortals!' — can't detect, but which hits my nose almost like skunk spray.

All I have to do is follow it.

I find her about a block off the Boardwalk, in a grubby, urine-soaked alley behind Resorts. She's sitting cross-legged in the shadow of a big commercial dumpster. She's got burns on her arm and part of her face. A lot of her hair's gone, and what's left is singed. Getting out of that burning Theater cost her.

As I come up to her, her eyes are closed. At first, I don't know if she's asleep or meditating. But then those eyes snap open and fix on me.

"*Jwenn mwen*," she remarks. It's Creole for "*Found me.*"

"*Oui,*" I reply.

She grins. It's a wicked grin — there's just no other word for it. "You won't kill me, child."

"You tried to murder my family," I say. There should probably be more anger there, but right now, there just isn't. I'm simply stating a fact.

"*Oui.* But you *did* murder mine."

I nod.

For a moment, just a moment, her face crumples into something resembling real grief. "My poor Bap and Simon. They were good boys."

"They were monsters, and so are you."

She eyes me. "You're one to say. How many lives have you taken, *lespri Bondye fè nwa*?"

I feel a twinge of guilt. But it's small and far away, a little bit of the old Abby whispering hello from the darkness. "I took what needed taking."

"Well enough said," she replies with a grudging nod. "You'll make a fine vessel. I was right about you. That day you passed by me on the street. I *smelled* the blood in you."

"What blood?"

"Haitian blood. *Royal* blood. Who were your parents, child?"

"I don't know."

She seems to consider this. "One day, you will, I expect. With blood like yours, Fate will find you sooner or later."

I have no idea what to say to that, so I say nothing.

She grins again. "But you won't kill me."

"Why not? You think you can stop me? We both know you got your power from the pier. With it gone, I don't figure there's much left in your tank."

She offers a dismissive wave with a withered hand turned sickly red from burns. "Not much, no. Now, I'm just an old woman, alone in the world and without magic. So why bother taking my life?"

"Yeah," I tell her. "But what will you be tomorrow?"

Adelaide looks hard at me, her eyes flashing the way they did before. "*Ki diferans sa fè*?" she asks bitterly. *What difference does it make?* "Even if I say that I'll come back someday. Even if I say that I'll be strong again by then, strong enough to hunt you down, hunt your *fanmi* down, and kill them all in front of you. Even if I say I'll see all you love torn down around you, you still won't kill me."

My anger rises. The knife, *my* knife, suddenly feels very good in my hands. "Why not?"

Her grin comes a third time, weirdly triumphant, given her situation. "Because, like I said, I'm just an old woman, burned and broken. And Abby Lowell don't have it in her to murder a helpless, grieving grann in cold blood."

For most of a minute, I stand over her, my blade ready. I listen to her heartbeat, and mine, and the heartbeats of hundreds of people in the big hotel and the surrounding block. If Adelaide de la Fosse had her way, all of those people would either die or be bound to her, bow before her and call her "boss."

But, right now, she's — nothing. And she knows I know it.

When I turn away, I hear her utter a quiet little laugh. It's soft, barely there at all, but it stops me in my tracks.

And she knows me, *too.*

Or thinks she does.

"You're right," I say with my back to her. "Abby Lowell can't kill you."

Her laughter stops cold when I turn to face her again. And something she sees makes her eyes go wide with terror.

Then I whisper, "But Rags can."

CHAPTER 30

NOW I WATCH AND LISTEN

—FROM THE DARKNESS. THE NIGHT NOURISHES ME, COMFORTS ME, EASES my loneliness. Around me, Atlantic City thrums with the energy of life, success and failure, happiness and heartbreak.

I know about all of those.

So does my family.

"Is he another one?" Sarah asks. *"This man downstairs with Aunt Kell."* She and the rest, except the tods, are up on the fourth floor having a hearing. But this hearing isn't like the others. This time, nobody's in trouble. This time, they *all* are, or might be. It's their new reality since the Calm Sea Arms reopened, and since they lost Uncle Nick—

—and me.

"Yeah," Tyrone replies. *"Says he wants to buy us out. I only heard some of it before Aunt Kell chased me away, but enough to know the dude's a snake, just like all the others."*

"What's this make it? The fifth one since that night on the pier?" This comes from Jeff. He sounds worried.

"Sixth," Jimmy corrects. *He* doesn't sound worried, not exactly. But I can tell he's—I guess "subdued" is probably the best word. He always is these days.

Corrine says, *"It's okay. Abby will protect us."*

"How many times do I have to tell you not to talk about that!" Darlene snaps.

"She will!" my little sister insists. I can almost see her crossing her arms and scowling prettily in that way she has. It makes me smile under my hood. That's nice. I don't smile much these days.

"She's taken care of the rest," Tish points out. *"Especially the two of them that wouldn't take 'no' for an answer."*

"Right, by murdering them!" Darlene exclaims. She makes an accusation of it, though I have to wonder *who* exactly she's accusing. Me, I suppose, except I'm not there. I'm listening from the roof. I listen

from the roof quite a lot these days. It's the closest I can get to them.

It's the closest I *should* get to them.

"She only killed one," Tish says, sounding defensive. *"The other she just — "*

"Blinded," Tyrone finishes for her. But, unlike Darlene, he doesn't sound angry about it. *"Dude had it coming if you ask me. Besides, Abby's been doing other shit, hasn't she? They said in the paper she caught up with that asshole who's been going around attacking women on the boards."*

"So what?" Darlene demands. *"She gets a pass for killing people so long as she only kills the 'right' people?"* I can almost hear the air quotes. She sounds mad, but then she kind of idles on sounding mad. As it happens, I know she and Tyrone recently hooked up, popping each other's cherries while everybody else in the hotel slept.

Well, everybody except *me.*

It's been three months, and things are happening in town, always happening. New casinos have opened, with more already being announced. They're reshaping the city, bringing in more money and tourists than we've seen in a long time.

But they're bringing trouble, too.

"I don't know why you're always so pissed," Sarah says to Darlene. *"After all, Abby got us back in the hotel, didn't she?"*

"We don't know that for sure!" Darlene replies sharply.

Jimmy says, his voice barely a whisper, *"Of course, we do."*

Jeff picks up the thread, still talking to Darlene, *"You saw Reynolds' face when she came by that day. We all did. She said she'd let us stay at the Calm Sea Arms, all nice and official, just so long as we called off our 'friend with the knife.' Who else do you think she meant?"*

Darlene doesn't reply, which is as close to an admission of defeat as she ever gives anybody.

Because, of course, Jimmy and Jeff are right. Sarah too.

They're all here because of me.

Since I paid my midnight visit to the social worker, things have settled down, more or less. Kids still go to school. Kids still come home. Since Aunt Kell came home from the hospital, Tyrone has started helping out with the running of the place, managing the books and doing routine handyman stuff. He says, after graduation, he's going to apply to nearby Stockton College part-time and stay on at the Calm Sea Arms. Darlene, on the other hand, got accepted to Howard on some grant or other and will be checking herself out of the System, for good and all, when she turns eighteen in a few weeks. She says she'll be back, but I don't think Tyrone and the others really believe her.

I know I don't.

But, whatever. She's my sister, and I wish her well.

Corrine is the only one who ever really talks about me. She says she misses me. She says she wishes I'd come home. I think Jimmy feels the same way, which is why he's been moping around like he has. I guess I miss them too, though that part of me is harder to find each day.

I leave them to their hearing, which is really more like a therapy session. They're working through their grief and their uncertainty. I wish I could tell them it's okay, that I'm making it okay, that I will *always* make it okay.

And, in that spirit, I turn my attention to another conversation that's going on down in the lobby. This one is between Aunt Kell and the dude Tyrone was describing. It's an old song, familiar now, but I listen anyway. I listen because this dude is edgier than most. He reminds me of Shanks—who, by the way, left town a while ago.

"It's a kind offer, Mr. Berkowitz," my foster mother tells him, her tone respectful in an impatient sort of way. *"But, as I explained on the phone yesterday, the hotel's not for sale."*

"So, you said, Mrs. Nelson. And so I've heard from every realtor and city official I've spoken with. But my client's determined. This property is too valuable to be wasted as an orphanage."

This time, my mom's voice turns down the respect and cranks up the impatience. Her "cardiac event" and the subsequent loss of her husband have affected her; no doubt about that. But she's still Kelley Nelson, and she doesn't take anybody's shit. *"It's neither 'wasted' nor an 'orphanage.' It's our home."*

"A poor choice of words," Berkowitz says, backpedaling. *"But, with the money we're offering, you could find another… home. A better one."*

"Upend my family, you mean? Force my children to leave their friends, their neighborhood, their schools? All so someone like you can build yet another gawdy gambling den?"

"I didn't come here to upset you."

"And yet here I am, upset. Mr. Berkowitz, the answer is no. It's firm, and it's final."

I can smell the change come over the man and I think, *Here we go.*

Jekyll's about to turn into Hyde.

"Mrs. Nelson, what's say we put our cards on the table, shall we? This is our last offer. We're going to have this property. My client has already invested too much time and money into acquiring the entire block and has no intention of letting this old dinosaur of a hotel get in the way of progress. So, while we'd prefer to pay you handsomely and help you resettle… if necessary, I'm sure we could find less gentle means of convincing you."

I can almost picture Aunt Kell crossing her arms over her ample bosom. *"I'm sorry. I don't quite take your meaning?"*

When he speaks again, his voice is low, as if he doesn't want to be overheard. *"Fires happen, Mrs. Nelson,"* Berkowitz says. *"And, sadly, children are occasionally run down in the street."*

For a moment, there's silence. But just for a moment. Then my mom responds to him, her tone carefully even, *"I think you should apologize, Mr. Berkowitz. Then you should leave. It's not wise to threaten me or my family."*

"Why's that? What are you going to do about it?"

"Me? Nothing."

He smells confused for a moment. Then he laughs. *"You're talking about her, aren't you? What do the papers call her?"*

"Rags," Aunt Kell replies.

"A runaway," he says. *"A teenage girl dressed like a hobo. The news says she's some kind of vigilante."*

"That's a word for it, I suppose."

"Does she live here? I know the cops are looking for her…"

"I don't know where she lives. But she's close. She's always close. And she doesn't like it when people like you come in, waving money and threats. You'd do well to forget about us, Mr. Berkowitz. Just apologize to me, right here and now, and tell your clients to walk away while they still can."

He laughs harshly. Why do they always have such harsh laughs?

"Are you saying I should be scared, Mrs. Nelson? Are you saying I should be afraid of this… girl?"

"No," my mom says with an edge to her voice that's as sharp as any blade. *"I'm saying you should be terrified."*

At that moment, I hear a shout from the sidewalk below. I glance down to see Corinne, little Corinne, pointing up at me and calling to the others.

Apparently, in my eagerness to hear everything going on in the lobby, I dropped my guard and let the shadows recede. Now, I'm crouching atop the hotel sign on the roof, partially lit by the neon.

And the moon. Corinne's moon.

Oops.

Below me, I hear footsteps. Corinne's alert has been heard through the open windows on the Girls and Boys Dorms, and my sibs are responding, all of them. They're rumbling down the main staircase, a minor stampede, rushing past Aunt Kell and her visitor without a glance. I can see them pouring through the revolving doors and gathering into a group around Corinne, who's still pointing up at me.

Faces. Eleven of them, aged from five to seventeen. My brothers and sisters. The only family I've ever known.

After a few moments, Aunt Kell and Berkowitz come out as well. Maybe the lawyer, if that's what he really is, got curious when he saw the parade of kids. Or maybe coming out here was my mom's idea.

In the commotion, I missed that part of their conversation.

But, either way, there's no reason not to take the opportunity to drive Aunt Kell's point home.

So, I stand, straightening up atop the sign, and let the shadows fall away completely. The night is cloudless, and the moon's full, giving everyone a very clear view as I raise my black knife high above my head.

Then, once I'm sure Berkowitz is staring up at me, open-mouthed, I lower my arm and point the knife straight at him.

"Oh… my… God…" I hear him say, more or less under his breath.

And then he's *gone*, all but running up the street toward where his Beamer's parked.

Some of my sibs laugh. Most don't.

Then, as all their eyes turn again to me, their faces shining in the moonlight, I do something I rarely do. I pull back my hood, exposing my face. To be honest, I don't really know what I look like now. Me, I suppose, but a grubbier me, since showering isn't exactly doable these days. Also, I imagine they see a harder me, no longer afraid, but no longer exactly kind, either — the *me* that I needed to become to be what I am.

Aunt Kell, her eyes focused on me, lifts the silver cross from her bosom and kisses it.

Corinne and some of the other younger kids are crying.

Tish, as always, has her hand to her mouth. I wonder if she's stifling a scream.

Jimmy, with Jeff and Sarah beside him, looks stricken. He calls my name, a sob in his voice.

Darlene falls against Tyrone, who has his arm around her.

Then, he looks up — and nods.

Tyrone gets it.

Aunt Kell does too. So, do the rest. To one degree or another, my family understands what I am now and what I have to do.

Slowly, deliberately I replace my hood and then call the night around me again. In this way, I disappear from their sight, lost in the shadows. Shortly, I'll be heading off to pay a visit to Mr. Berkowitz. The knife-pointing bit was good. But, with dudes like him, it's sometimes necessary to drive the point home.

Pun intended, or maybe not.

We'll see.

In reality, though, I won't be going far. I *never* go far. My place is here, watching over them.

Their silent *gadyen*.

Their *vanyan sòlda*.

I don't think about this new existence too much. I don't bother wondering how long it might or might not last. I've got enough "today" on my plate. No need to fret too much about "tomorrow."

Because change *is* happening in Atlantic City. Big change. Now, change can be good. It can bring opportunity and hope. But it can also be bad, and the wrong kind of change could run roughshod over my home and the people who live here. My family knows that, even if, these days, they rarely speak of it, or me.

Just like they also know that Abby Lowell, a sixteen-year-old girl from the streets, can't protect the people she loves.

But Rags can.

ABOUT THE AUTHOR

TY DRAGO IS A FULL-TIME WRITER AND THE AUTHOR OF TEN PUBLISHED novels, including his five-book *Undertakers* series, the first of which has been optioned for a feature film. *Torq*, a dystopian YA superhero adventure, was released by Swallow's End Publishing in 2018, and *Dragons*, a YA science fiction genre-bender, through eSpec Books in 2021. Add to these one novelette, myriad short stories and articles, and appearances in two anthologies. He's also the founder, publisher, and managing editor of ALLEGORY (www.allegoryezine.com), a highly successful online magazine that, for more than twenty years, has featured speculative fiction by new and established authors worldwide.

Ty's currently just completed *The New Americans,* a work of historical fiction and a collaborative effort with his father, who passed away in 1992. If that last sentence leaves you with questions, check out his podcast, "Legacy: The Novel Writing Experience," to get the whole story.

He lives in New Jersey with his wife Helene, plus one cat and one dog.

FAMILY BY CHOICE

ABD
Agnomaly
Amy Grech
Angela Yuriko Smith
Anna Taborska
Annelise Pichardo
Anonymous Reader
April Grey
Arthur Kinsman
Aven Lumi
Avis Crane
Becky Wood
Bill Ginger
Brian W. Matthews
Carl W Bishop
Carlos Valcarcel
Carol Mammano
Caroline Cooney
Chandler Klang Smith
Charles E. Wood
Cheri Kannarr
Chris Ryan
Christopher J. Burke
Cori Paige
Craig Hackl
curtis steinhour
Dale A. Russell
Damon Griffin
Dan Dalal
Danielle Ackley-McPhail
David Swisher
Diane Raimonde

Drew Biehl
Drew Cucuzza
Dusk Zer0
Ef Deal
Fiona A. Elder
Frieda Schultz
Gail Trotter
Gary Phillips
Giusy Rippa
Hank Blumenthal
Howard Blakeslee
Isaac 'Will It Work' Dansicker
J.R. Murdock
Janet Lees
Janito V. F. Filho
Jeff LaSorsa
Jenn Whitworth
Jennifer L. Pierce
Jessica Sarchet
John L. French
Jonathan Lees
Jp
Karen M
Karl Markovich
Kierin Fox
Kirk Larson
KJSP
L. E. Daniels
L.E. Custodio
Lakota Lara
Lara Frater
Lark Cunningham

Laurel Anne Hill
Laurie Jones
Lisa Kruse
Lisa Morton
Liz
Lorraine J. Anderson
Lou Rera
Lynne Hansen
Mallory N Pate
Mandi
Marc "mad" W.
Marc L Abbott
Maria T
Martha Huggins
Maya G Goldstein
Meghan Arcuri
Michele Clemente
Michele Kutner
Nathan Toby
Nicholas Diak
Nicholas Stephenson
Rachel & Jim Larson

Rachel Brune
Randee Dawn
Rebecca E. Hoffman
Reckless Pantalones
Robert Claney
Robert P. Ottone
Sarah
Sasquatch N
Scott Schaper
Scout McLoud
Sherry
Steph Parker
Stephen Ballentine
Steven Van Patten
Tasha Turner
The Creative Fund by BackerKit
Thomas Alan Horne
Timothy DuBois
Venessa Giunta
Victoria Navarra
WD Stancil